"HER MOST SEDUCTIVE AND TEMPESTUOUS
WORK TO DATE." —*Tulsa World*

"[NORA ROBERTS] IS

P9-EMN-794

From the *New York Times* bestselling author of *Tears of the Moon* and *River's End* comes a seductive and suspenseful novel of dangerous liaisons and family betrayals . . .

$\mathcal{S}$ANCTUARY

Photographer Jo Ellen Hathaway thought she'd escaped the house called Sanctuary long ago. She'd spent her loneliest years there, after the sudden, unexplained disappearance of her mother. Yet the sprawling resort off the Georgia coast continues to haunt her dreams. And now, even more haunting are the pictures someone is sending her: strange close-ups and candids, culminating in the most shocking portrait of all—a photo of her mother . . . naked, beautiful, and dead. Now Jo must return to the island, and to her bitterly estranged family—and, with the help of one man, learn the truth about the tragic past. But Sanctuary may be the most dangerous place of all . . .

"Sometimes the atmosphere of a novel is so powerfully rendered that the setting assumes the importance of another character. Anne Rivers Siddons has this knack, and so does Nora Roberts."
—*Chicago Tribune*

"[Roberts] delivers believable characters and keeps the story moving."
—*Minneapolis Star Tribune*

"Roberts has a talent for vivid description: The sounds and smells of this verdant island waft from the page."
—*Publishers Weekly*

continued on next page . . .

More praise for

SANCTUARY . . .

"WHAT A GREAT ESCAPIST READ! . . . Fresh and fast-paced . . . Be sure to turn the stove off and the answering machine on, because you may find the fifteen minutes you planned to sit down with this book will mysteriously expand to an hour or two."
—*The Free Lance-Star*

"A BRILLIANT WORK that will enhance even further the reputation of romantic suspense's top gun."
—*Under the Covers*

"VERY SATISFYING . . . Emotionally complex, laden with dynamic characters and highly charged love scenes, this is a story to savor long after you've finished it."
—*BookPage*

"LUSH SCENERY, LOTS OF ROMANCE."   —*People*

"A STRONG STORY LINE."
—*The Cedar Rapids Gazette*

"VIVID DESCRIPTIONS, finely crafted characterizations and razor-edged plot."
—*Tulsa World*

. . . And for Nora Roberts's previous novels

MONTANA SKY

They are sisters—and strangers. Now they must learn to live as a family—in order to gain an inheritance worth twenty million dollars . . .

"EXCITING, ROMANTIC, GREAT FUN."
—*Cosmopolitan*

"ROBERTS PAINTS A VIVID PICTURE of the raw beauty of Big Sky country." —*Chicago Tribune*

"SEXUAL TENSION AND SEXY DIALOGUE . . . surprise . . . humor . . . a good read." —*Kirkus Reviews*

"A RICH NARRATIVE . . . Roberts balances the tension . . . with three romances, crackling dialogue, and a snappy infusion of humor." —*Publishers Weekly*

"PASSION, SUSPENSE, AND EMOTIONAL POWER."
—*Tulsa World*

TRUE BETRAYALS

A thrilling story of family secrets and unexpected passions, set against the high-stakes world of championship Thoroughbred racing . . .

"AN ABSOLUTELY TERRIFIC SUMMER READ."
—*The Orlando Sentinel*

HIDDEN RICHES

In the intriguing world of antique dealing, Dora Conroy discovers the price of breathless desire—and the schemes of an obsessed killer . . .

"A HEROINE WHO WILL CHARM READERS."
—*USA Today*

continued on next page . . .

PRIVATE SCANDALS

Behind the scenes of a television talk show, young and ambitious Deanna Reynolds is about to learn the price of her success . . .

"TOP-NOTCH . . . First-rate reading."   —*Rendezvous*

HONEST ILLUSIONS

Nothing is as it seems at a carnival—as Roxy Nouvelle discovers when a charming con man steps into her life . . .

"ROXY AND LUKE WILL STEAL YOUR HEART."
—Catherine Coulter

And don't miss Nora Roberts's bestselling trilogies . . .

BORN IN FIRE
BORN IN ICE
BORN IN SHAME

Three novels featuring the Concannon sisters of Ireland—women of ambition and talent, bound by the timeless spirit and restless beauty of their land.

DARING TO DREAM
HOLDING THE DREAM
FINDING THE DREAM

The saga of three women who shared a home and a childhood—but grew to fulfill their own unique destinies . . .

RIVER'S END

Her most seductively suspenseful tale yet—a story of one woman's shattered innocence, the terrifying search for truth, and a heart's journey toward healing . . .

"A PAGE-TURNER."
—The Washington Post Book World

"Roberts keeps the suspense building . . . Her fans will love this book."
—Chicago Sun-Times

THE REEF

On a search for treasure in the depths of the Caribbean, marine archaeologist Tate Beaumont is forced into an uneasy alliance with salvager Matthew Lassiter, a man who stirs up danger—and desire . . .

"SUSPENSEFUL."
—People

"PAGE-TURNING."
—USA Today

"A PERFECT BOOK TO CURL UP WITH."
—The Denver Post

And don't miss the first two books in Nora Roberts's enchanting new Irish trilogy . . .

JEWELS OF THE SUN
TEARS OF THE MOON

Titles by Nora Roberts

RIVER'S END
THE REEF
INNER HARBOR
RISING TIDES
SEA SWEPT
HOMEPORT
SANCTUARY
FINDING THE DREAM
HOLDING THE DREAM
DARING TO DREAM
MONTANA SKY
BORN IN SHAME
BORN IN ICE
BORN IN FIRE
TRUE BETRAYALS
HIDDEN RICHES
PRIVATE SCANDALS
HONEST ILLUSIONS
DIVINE EVIL
CARNAL INNOCENCE
GENUINE LIES
PUBLIC SECRETS
SWEET REVENGE
BRAZEN VIRTUE
SACRED SINS
HOT ICE
JEWELS OF THE SUN
TEARS OF THE MOON

CAROLINA MOON
in hardcover from G. P. Putnam's Sons

Titles written as J. D. Robb

NAKED IN DEATH
GLORY IN DEATH
IMMORTAL IN DEATH
RAPTURE IN DEATH
CEREMONY IN DEATH
VENGEANCE IN DEATH
HOLIDAY IN DEATH
CONSPIRACY IN DEATH
WITNESS IN DEATH

SANCTUARY

NORA ROBERTS

JOVE BOOKS, NEW YORK

If you purchased this book without a cover, you should be aware that this book is stolen property. It was reported as "unsold and destroyed" to the publisher, and neither the author nor the publisher has received any payment for this "stripped book."

This is a work of fiction. Names, characters, places, and incidents are either the product of the author's imagination or are used fictitiously, and any resemblance to actual persons, living or dead, business establishments, events, or locales is entirely coincidental.

This Jove Book contains the complete text of the hardcover edition. It has been completely reset in a typeface designed for easy reading and was printed from new film.

SANCTUARY

A Jove Book / published by arrangement with
the author

PRINTING HISTORY
G. P. Putnam's Sons edition / March 1997
Jove edition / May 1998

All rights reserved.
Copyright © 1997 by Nora Roberts.
Cover illustration copyright © 1997 by Wendell Minor.
Author photograph by John Earle.
This book, or parts thereof, may not be reproduced in
any form without permission.
For information address: The Berkley Publishing Group,
a division of Penguin Putnam Inc.,
375 Hudson Street, New York, New York 10014.

The Penguin Putnam Inc. World Wide Web site address is
http://www.penguinputnam.com

ISBN: 0-515-12273-4

A JOVE BOOK®
Jove Books are published by The Berkley Publishing Group,
a division of Penguin Putnam Inc.,
375 Hudson Street, New York, New York 10014.
JOVE and the "J" design are trademarks
belonging to Penguin Putnam Inc.

PRINTED IN THE UNITED STATES OF AMERICA

20   19   18   17   16   15   14   13   12   11

To the Ladies of the Lounge

SANCTUARY

PART ONE

When weather-beaten I come back...
My body a sack of bones, broken within...

—JOHN DONNE

ONE

SHE DREAMED OF SANC-
tuary. The great house gleamed bride-white in the moonlight, as majestic a force breasting the slope that reigned
over eastern dunes and western marsh as a queen upon
her throne. The house stood as it had for more than a
century, a grand tribute to man's vanity and brilliance,
near the dark shadows of the forest of live oaks, where
the river flowed in murky silence.

Within the shelter of trees, fireflies blinked gold, and
night creatures stirred, braced to hunt or be hunted. Wild
things bred there in shadows, in secret.

There were no lights to brighten the tall, narrow windows of Sanctuary. No lights to spread welcome over its
graceful porches, its grand doors. Night was deep, and the
breath of it moist from the sea. The only sound to disturb
it was of wind rustling through the leaves of the great
oaks and the dry clicking—like bony fingers—of the palm
fronds. The white columns stood like soldiers guarding
the wide veranda, but no one opened the enormous front
door to greet her.

As she walked closer, she could hear the crunch of sand

and shells on the road under her feet. Wind chimes tinkled, little notes of song. The porch swing creaked on its
chain, but no one lazed upon it to enjoy the moon and
the night.

The smell of jasmine and musk roses played on the air,
underscored by the salty scent of the sea. She began to
hear that too, the low and steady thunder of water spilling
over sand and sucking back into its own heart.

The beat of it, that steady and patient pulse, reminded
all who inhabited the island of Lost Desire that the sea
could reclaim the land and all on it at its whim.

Still, her mood lifted at the sound of it, the music of
home and childhood. Once she had run as free and wild
through that forest as a deer, had scouted its marshes,
raced along its sandy beaches with the careless privilege
of youth.

Now, no longer a child, she was home again.

She walked quickly, hurrying up the steps, across the
veranda, closing her hand over the big brass handle that
glinted like a lost treasure.

The door was locked.

She twisted it right, then left, shoved against the thick
mahogany panel. *Let me in*, she thought as her heart began
to thud in her chest. *I've come home. I've come back.*

But the door remained shut and locked. When she
pressed her face against the glass of the tall windows
flanking it, she could see nothing but darkness within.

And was afraid.

She ran now, around the side of the house, over the
terrace, where flowers streamed out of pots and lilies
danced in chorus lines of bright color. The music of the
wind chimes became harsh and discordant, the fluttering
of fronds was a hiss of warning. She struggled with the
next door, weeping as she beat her fists against it.

Please, please, don't shut me out. I want to come home.

She sobbed as she stumbled down the garden path. She
would go to the back, in through the screened porch. It

was never locked—Mama said a kitchen should always be open to company.

But she couldn't find it. The trees sprang up, thick and close, the branches and draping moss barred her way.

She was lost, tripping over roots in her confusion, fighting to see through the dark as the canopy of trees closed out the moon. The wind rose up and howled and slapped at her in flat-handed, punishing blows. Spears of saw palms struck out like swords. She turned, but where the path had been was now the river, cutting her off from Sanctuary. The high grass along its slippery banks waved madly.

It was then she saw herself, standing alone and weeping on the other bank.

It was then she knew she was dead.

Jo fought her way out of the dream, all but felt the sharp edges of it scraping her skin as she dragged herself to the surface of the tunnel of sleep. Her lungs burned, and her face was wet with sweat and tears. With a trembling hand, she fumbled for the bedside lamp, knocking both a book and an overfilled ashtray to the floor in her hurry to break out of the dark.

When the light shot on, she drew her knees up close to her chest, wrapped her arms around them, and rocked herself calm.

It was just a dream, she told herself. Just a bad dream.

She was home, in her own bed, in her apartment and miles from the island where Sanctuary stood. A grown woman of twenty-seven had no business being spooked by a silly dream.

But she was still shaking when she reached for a cigarette. It took her three tries to manage to light a match.

Three-fifteen, she noted by the clock on the nightstand. That was becoming typical. There was nothing worse than the three A.M. jitters. She swung her legs over the side of the bed and bent down to pick up the overturned ashtray.

She told herself she'd clean up the mess in the morning. She sat there, her oversized T-shirt bunched over her thighs, and ordered herself to get a grip.

She didn't know why her dreams were taking her back to the island of Lost Desire and the home she'd escaped from at eighteen. But Jo figured any first-year psych student could translate the rest of the symbolism. The house was locked because she doubted anyone would welcome her if she did return home. Just lately, she'd given some thought to it but had wondered if she'd lost the way back.

And she was nearing the age her mother had been when she had left the island. Disappeared, abandoning her husband and three children without a second glance.

Had Annabelle ever dreamed of coming home, Jo wondered, and dreamed the door was locked to her?

She didn't want to think about that, didn't want to remember the woman who had broken her heart twenty years before. Jo reminded herself that she should be long over such things by now. She'd lived without her mother, and without Sanctuary and her family. She had even thrived—at least professionally.

Tapping her cigarette absently, Jo glanced around the bedroom. She kept it simple, practical. Though she'd traveled widely, there were few mementos. Except the photographs. She'd matted and framed the black-and-white prints, choosing the ones among her work that she found the most restful to decorate the walls of the room where she slept.

There, an empty park bench, the black wrought iron all fluid curves. And there, a single willow, its lacy leaves dipping low over a small, glassy pool. A moonlit garden was a study in shadow and texture and contrasting shapes. The lonely beach with the sun just breaking the horizon tempted the viewer to step inside the photo and feel the sand rough underfoot.

She'd hung that seascape only the week before, after returning from an assignment on the Outer Banks of North

Carolina. Perhaps that was one reason she'd begun to think about home, Jo decided. She'd been very close. She could have traveled a bit south down to Georgia and ferried from the mainland to the island.

There were no roads to Desire, no bridges spanning its sound.

But she hadn't gone south. She'd completed her assignment and come back to Charlotte to bury herself in her work.

And her nightmares.

She crushed out the cigarette and stood. There would be no more sleep, she knew, so she pulled on a pair of sweatpants. She would do some darkroom work, take her mind off things.

It was probably the book deal that was making her nervous, she decided, as she padded out of the bedroom. It was a huge step in her career. Though she knew her work was good, the offer from a major publishing house to create an art book from a collection of her photographs had been unexpected and thrilling.

Natural Studies, by Jo Ellen Hathaway, she thought as she turned into the small galley kitchen to make coffee. No, that sounded like a science project. *Glimpses of Life?* Pompous.

She smiled a little, pushing back her smoky red hair and yawning. She should just take the pictures and leave the title selection to the experts.

She knew when to step back and when to take a stand, after all. She'd been doing one or the other most of her life. Maybe she would send a copy of the book home. What would her family think of it? Would it end up gracing one of the coffee tables where an overnight guest could page through it and wonder if Jo Ellen Hathaway was related to the Hathaways who ran the Inn at Sanctuary?

Would her father even open it at all and see what she had learned to do? Or would he simply shrug, leave it untouched, and go out to walk his island? Annabelle's island.

It was doubtful he would take an interest in his oldest daughter now. And it was foolish for that daughter to care.

Jo shrugged the thought away, took a plain blue mug from a hook. While she waited for the coffee to brew, she leaned on the counter and looked out her tiny window.

There were some advantages to being up and awake at three in the morning, she decided. The phone wouldn't ring. No one would call or fax or expect anything of her. For a few hours she didn't have to be anyone, or do anything. If her stomach was jittery and her head ached, no one knew the weakness but herself.

Below her kitchen window, the streets were dark and empty, slicked by late-winter rain. A streetlamp spread a small pool of light—lonely light, Jo thought. There was no one to bask in it. Aloneness had such mystery, she mused. Such endless possibilities.

It pulled at her, as such scenes often did, and she found herself leaving the scent of coffee, grabbing her Nikon, and rushing out barefoot into the chilly night to photograph the deserted street.

It soothed her as nothing else could. With a camera in her hand and an image in her mind, she could forget everything else. Her long feet splashed through chilly puddles as she experimented with angles. With absent annoyance she flicked at her hair. It wouldn't be falling in her face if she'd had it trimmed. But she'd had no time, so it swung heavily forward in a tousled wave and made her wish for an elastic band.

She took nearly a dozen shots before she was satisfied. When she turned, her gaze was drawn upward. She'd left the lights on, she mused. She hadn't even been aware she'd turned on so many on the trip from bedroom to kitchen.

Lips pursed, she crossed the street and focused her camera again. Calculating, she crouched, shot at an upward angle, and captured those lighted windows in the dark building. *Den of the Insomniac*, she decided. Then with a half laugh that echoed eerily enough to make her shudder, she lowered the camera again.

God, maybe she was losing her mind. Would a sane woman be out at three in the morning, half dressed and shivering, while she took pictures of her own windows?

She pressed her fingers against her eyes and wished more than anything else for the single thing that had always seemed to elude her. Normality.

You needed sleep to be normal, she thought. She hadn't had a full night's sleep in more than a month. You needed regular meals. She'd lost ten pounds in the last few weeks and had watched her long, rangy frame go bony. You needed peace of mind. She couldn't remember if she had ever laid claim to that. Friends? Certainly she had friends, but no one close enough to call in the middle of the night to console her.

Family. Well, she had family, of sorts. A brother and sister whose lives no longer marched with hers. A father who was almost a stranger. A mother she hadn't seen or heard from in twenty years.

Not my fault, Jo reminded herself as she started back across the street. It was Annabelle's fault. Everything had changed when Annabelle had run from Sanctuary and left her baffled family crushed and heartbroken. The trouble, as Jo saw it, was that the rest of them hadn't gotten over it. She had.

She hadn't stayed on the island guarding every grain of sand like her father did. She hadn't dedicated her life to running and caring for Sanctuary like her brother, Brian. And she hadn't escaped into foolish fantasies or the next thrill the way her sister, Lexy, had.

Instead she had studied, and she had worked, and she had made a life for herself. If she was a little shaky just now, it was only because she'd overextended, was letting the pressure get to her. She was a little run-down, that was all. She'd just add some vitamins to her regimen and get back in shape.

She might even take a vacation, Jo mused as she dug her keys out of her pocket. It had been three years—no, four—since she had last taken a trip without a specific assignment. Maybe Mexico, the West Indies. Someplace where the pace was slow and the sun hot. Slowing down and clearing her mind. That was the way to get past this little blip in her life.

As she stepped back into the apartment, she kicked a small, square manila envelope that lay on the floor. For a moment she simply stood, one hand on the door, the other holding her camera, and stared at it.

Had it been there when she left? Why was it there in the first place? The first one had come a month before, had been waiting in her stack of mail, with only her name carefully printed across it.

Her hands began to shake again as she ordered herself to close the door, to lock it. Her breath hitched, but she leaned over, picked it up. Carefully, she set the camera aside, then unsealed the flap.

When she tapped out the contents, the sound she made was a long, low moan. The photograph was very professionally done, perfectly cropped. Just as the other three had been. A woman's eyes, heavy-lidded, almond-shaped, with thick lashes and delicately arched brows. Jo knew their color would be blue, deep blue, because the eyes were her own. In them was stark terror.

When was it taken? How and why? She pressed a hand to her mouth, staring down at the photo, knowing her eyes mirrored the shot perfectly. Terror swept through her, had her rushing through the apartment into the small second bedroom she'd converted to a darkroom. Frantically she yanked open a drawer, pawed through the contents, and found the envelopes she'd buried there. In each was another black-and-white photo, cropped to two by six inches.

Her heartbeat was thundering in her ears as she lined them up. In the first the eyes were closed, as if she'd been photographed while sleeping. The others followed the waking process. Lashes barely lifted, showing only a hint of iris. In the third the eyes were open but unfocused and clouded with confusion.

They had disturbed her, yes, unsettled her, certainly, when she found them tucked in her mail. But they hadn't frightened her.

Now the last shot, centered on her eyes, fully awake and bright with fear.

Stepping back, shivering, Jo struggled to be calm. Why only the eyes? she asked herself. How had someone gotten close enough to take these pictures without her being aware of it? Now, whoever it was had been as close as the other side of her front door.

Propelled by fresh panic, she ran into the living room, and frantically checked the locks. Her heart was battering against her ribs when she fell back against the door. Then the anger kicked in.

Bastard, she thought. He wanted her to be terrorized. He wanted her to hide inside those rooms, jumping at shadows, afraid to step outside for fear he'd be there watching. She who had always been fearless was playing right into his hands.

She had wandered alone through foreign cities, walked mean streets and empty ones, she'd climbed mountains and hacked through jungles. With the camera as her shield, she'd never given a thought to fear. And now, because of a handful of photos, her legs were jellied with it.

The fear had been building, she admitted now. Growing and spiking over the weeks, level by level. It made her feel helpless, so exposed, so brutally alone.

Jo pushed herself away from the door. She couldn't and wouldn't live this way. She would ignore it, put it aside. Bury it deep. God knew she was an expert at burying traumas, small and large. This was just one more.

She was going to drink her coffee and go to work.

By eight she had come full circle—sliding through fatigue, arcing through nervous energy, creative calm, then back to fatigue.

She couldn't work mechanically, not even on the most basic aspect of darkroom chores. She insisted on giving every step her full attention. To do so, she'd had to calm down, ditch both the anger and the fear. Over her first cup of coffee, she'd convinced herself she had figured out the reasoning behind the photos she'd been receiving. Someone admired her work and was trying to get her attention, engage her influence for their own.

That made sense.

Occasionally she lectured or gave workshops. In addition, she'd had three major shows in the last three years. It wasn't that difficult or that extraordinary for someone to have taken her picture—several pictures, for that matter.

That was certainly reasonable.

Whoever it was had gotten creative, that was all. They'd enlarged the eye area, cropped it, and were sending the photos to her in a kind of series. Though the photos appeared to have been printed recently, there was no telling when or where they'd been taken. The negatives might be a year old. Or two. Or five.

They had certainly gotten her attention, but she'd overreacted, taken it too personally.

Over the last couple of years, she had received samples of work from admirers of hers. Usually there was a letter attached, praising her own photographs before the sender went into a pitch about wanting her advice or her help, or in a few cases, suggesting that they collaborate on a project.

The success she was enjoying professionally was still relatively new. She wasn't yet used to the pressures that went along with commercial success, or the expectations, which could become burdensome.

And, Jo admitted as she ignored her unsteady stomach and sipped coffee that had gone stone cold, she wasn't handling that success as well as she might.

She would handle it better, she thought, rolling her aching head on her aching shoulders, if everyone would just leave her alone to do what she did best.

Completed prints hung drying on the wet side of her darkroom. Her last batch of negatives had been developed and, sitting on a stool at her work counter, she slid a contact sheet onto her light board, then studied it, frame by frame, through her loupe.

For a moment she felt a flash of panic and despair. Every print she looked at was out of focus, blurry. Goddamn it, goddamn it, how could that be? Was it the whole roll? She shifted, blinked, and watched the magnified image of rising dunes and oat grass pop clear.

With a sound somewhere between a grunt and a laugh she sat back, rolled her tensed shoulders. "It's not the prints that are blurry and out of focus, you idiot," she muttered aloud. "It's you."

She set the loupe aside and closed her eyes to rest them. She lacked the energy to get up and make more coffee. She knew she should go eat, get something solid into her system. And she knew she should sleep. Stretch out on the bed, close everything off and crash.

But she was afraid to. In sleep she would lose even this shaky control.

She was beginning to think she should see a doctor, get something for her nerves before they frayed beyond repair. But that idea made her think of psychiatrists. Undoubtedly they would want to poke and pry inside her brain and dig up matters she was determined to forget.

She would handle it. She was good at handling herself. Or, as Brian had always said, she was good at elbowing everyone out of her way so she could handle everything herself.

What choice had she had—had any of them had when they'd been left alone to flounder on that damned spit of land miles from nowhere?

The rage that erupted inside her jolted her, it was so sudden, so powerful. She trembled with it, clenched her fists in her lap, and had to bite back the hot words she wanted to spit out at the brother who wasn't even there.

Tired, she told herself. She was just tired, that was all. She needed to put work aside, take one of those over-the-counter sleeping aids she'd bought and had yet to try, turn off the phone and get some sleep. She would be steadier then, stronger.

When a hand fell on her shoulder, she ripped off a scream and sent her coffee mug flying.

"Jesus! Jesus, Jo!" Bobby Banes scrambled back, scattering the mail he carried on the floor.

"What are you doing? What the hell are you doing?" She bolted off the stool and sent it crashing, as he gaped at her.

"I—you said you wanted to get started at eight. I'm only a few minutes late."

Jo fought for breath, gripped the edge of her worktable to keep herself upright. "Eight?"

Her student assistant nodded cautiously. He swallowed hard and kept his distance. To his eye she still looked wild and ready to attack. It was his second semester working with her, and he thought he'd learned how to anticipate her orders, gauge her moods, and avoid her temper. But he didn't have a clue how to handle that hot fear in her eyes.

"Why the hell didn't you knock?" she snapped at him.

"I did. When you didn't answer, I figured you must be in here, so I used the key you gave me when you went on the last assignment."

"Give it back. Now."

"Sure. Okay, Jo." Keeping his eyes on hers, he dug into the front pocket of his fashionably faded jeans. "I didn't mean to spook you."

Jo bit down on control and took the key he held out. There was as much embarrassment now, she realized, as fear. To give herself a moment, she bent down and righted her stool. "Sorry, Bobby. You did spook me. I didn't hear you knock."

"It's okay. Want me to get you another cup of coffee?"

She shook her head and gave in to her knocking knees. As she slid onto the stool, she worked up a smile for him. He was a good student, she thought—a little pompous about his work yet, but he was only twenty-one.

She thought he was going for the artist-as-college-student look, with his dark blond hair in a shoulder-length ponytail, the single gold hoop earring accenting his long, narrow face. His teeth were perfect. His parents had believed in braces, she thought, running her tongue over her own slight overbite.

He had a good eye, she mused. And a great deal of potential. That was why he was here, after all. Jo was always willing to pay back what had been given to her.

Because his big brown eyes were still watching her warily, she put more effort into the smile. "I had a rough night."

"You look like it." He tried a smile of his own when she lifted a brow. "The art is in seeing what's really there, right? And you look whipped. Couldn't sleep, huh?"

Vain was one thing Jo wasn't. She shrugged her shoulders and rubbed her tired eyes. "Not much."

"You ought to try that melatonin. My mother swears by it." He crouched to pick up the broken shards of the mug. "And maybe you could cut back on the coffee."

He glanced up but saw she wasn't listening. She'd gone on a side trip again, Bobby thought. A new habit of hers. He'd just about given up on getting his mentor into a healthier lifestyle. But he decided to give it one more shot.

"You've been living on coffee and cigarettes again."

"Yeah." She was drifting, half asleep where she sat.

"That stuff'll kill you. And you need an exercise program. You've dropped about ten pounds in the last few weeks. With your height you need to carry more weight. And you've got small bones—you're courting osteoporosis. Gotta build up those bones and muscles."

"Uh-huh."

"You ought to see a doctor. You ask me, you're anemic. You got no color, and you could pack half your equipment in the bags under your eyes."

"So nice of you to notice."

He scooped up the biggest shards, dumped them in her waste can. Of course he'd noticed. She had a face that drew attention. It didn't matter that she seemed to work overtime to fade into the background. He'd never seen her wear makeup, and she kept her hair pulled back, but anyone with an eye could see it should be framing that oval face with its delicate bones and exotic eyes and sexy mouth.

Bobby caught himself, felt heat rise to his cheeks. She would laugh at him if she knew he'd had a little crush on her when she first took him on. That, he figured, had been as much professional admiration as physical attraction. And he'd gotten over the attraction part. Mostly.

But there was no doubt that if she would do the minimum to enhance that magnolia skin, dab some color on that top-heavy mouth and smudge up those long-lidded eyes, she'd be a knockout.

"I could fix you breakfast," he began. "If you've got something besides candy bars and moldy bread."

Taking a long breath, Jo tuned in. "No, that's okay. Maybe we'll stop somewhere and grab something. I'm already running behind."

She slid off the stool and crouched to pick up the mail. "You know, it wouldn't hurt you to take a few days off, focus on yourself. My mom goes to this spa down in Miami.''

His words were only a buzzing in her ear now. She picked up the manila envelope with her name printed neatly on it in block letters. She had to wipe a film of sweat from her brow. In the pit of her stomach was a sick ball that went beyond dread into fear.

The envelope was thicker than the others had been, weightier. *Throw it away*, her mind screamed out. *Don't open it. Don't look inside.*

But her fingers were already scraping along the flap. Low whimpering sounds escaped her as she tore at the little metal clasp. This time an avalanche of photos spilled out onto the floor. She snatched one up. It was a well-produced five-by-seven black-and-white.

Not just her eyes this time, but all of her. She recognized the background—a park near her building where she often walked. Another was of her in downtown Charlotte, standing on a curb with her camera bag over her shoulder.

''Hey, that's a pretty good shot of you.''

As Bobby leaned down to select one of the prints, she slapped at his hand and snarled at him, ''Keep away. Keep back. Don't touch me.''

''Jo, I . . .''

''Stay the hell away from me.'' Panting, she dropped on all fours to paw frantically through the prints. There was picture after picture of her doing ordinary, everyday things. Coming out of the market with a bag of groceries, getting in or out of her car.

He's everywhere, he's watching me. Wherever I go, whatever I do. He's hunting me, she thought, as her teeth began to chatter. He's hunting me and there's nothing I can do. Nothing, until . . .

Then everything inside her clicked off. The photograph in her hand shook as if a brisk breeze had kicked up inside the room. She couldn't scream. There seemed to be no air inside her.

She simply couldn't feel her body any longer.

The photograph was brilliantly produced, the lighting and use of shadows and textures masterful. She was naked, her skin glowing eerily. Her body was arranged in a restful pose, the fragile chin dipped down, the head gently angled. One arm draped across her midriff, the other was flung up over her head in a position of dreaming sleep.

But the eyes were open and staring. A doll's eyes. Dead eyes.

For a moment, she was thrown helplessly back into her nightmare, staring at herself and unable to fight her way out of the dark.

But even through terror she could see the differences. The woman in the photo had a waving mass of hair that fanned out from her face. And the face was softer, the body riper than her own.

"Mama?" she whispered and gripped the picture with both hands. "Mama?"

"What is it, Jo?" Shaken, Bobby listened to his own voice hitch and dip as he stared into Jo's glazed eyes. "What the hell is it?"

"Where are her clothes?" Jo tilted her head, began to rock herself. Her head was full of sounds, rushing, thundering sounds. "Where is she?"

"Take it easy." Bobby took a step forward, started to reach down to take the photo from her.

Her head snapped up. "Stay away." The color flashed back into her cheeks, riding high. Something not quite sane danced in her eyes. "Don't touch me. Don't touch her."

Frightened, baffled, he straightened again, held both hands palms out. "Okay. Okay, Jo."

"I don't want you to touch her." She was cold, so cold. She looked down at the photo again. It was Annabelle. Young, eerily beautiful, and cold as death. "She shouldn't have left us. She shouldn't have gone away. Why did she go?"

"Maybe she had to," Bobby said quietly.

"No, she belonged with us. We needed her, but she didn't want us. She's so pretty." Tears rolled down Jo's cheeks, and the picture trembled in her hand. "She's so beautiful. Like a fairy princess. I used to think she was a princess. She left us. She left us and went away. Now she's dead."

Her vision wavered, her skin went hot. Pressing the photo against her breasts, Jo curled into a ball and wept.

"Come on, Jo." Gently, Bobby reached down. "Come on with me now. We'll get some help."

"I'm so tired," she murmured, letting him pick her up as if she were a child. "I want to go home."

"Okay. Just close your eyes now."

The photo fluttered silently to the floor, facedown atop all the other faces. She saw writing on the back. Large bold letters.

DEATH OF AN ANGEL

Her last thought, as the dark closed in, was Sanctuary.

TWO

AT FIRST LIGHT THE AIR was misty, like a dream just about to vanish. Beams of light stabbed through the canopy of live oaks and glittered on the dew. The warblers and buntings that nested in the sprays of moss were waking, chirping out a morning song. A cock cardinal, a red bullet of color, shot through the trees without a sound.

It was his favorite time of day. At dawn, when the demands on his time and energy were still to come, he could be alone, he could think his thoughts. Or simply be.

Brian Hathaway had never lived anywhere but Desire. He'd never wanted to. He'd seen the mainland and visited big cities. He'd even taken an impulsive vacation to Mexico once, so it could be said he'd visited a foreign land.

But Desire, with all its virtues and flaws, was his. He'd been born there on a gale-tossed night in September thirty years before. Born in the big oak tester bed he now slept in, delivered by his own father and an old black woman who had smoked a corncob pipe and whose parents had been house slaves, owned by his ancestors.

The old woman's name was Miss Effie, and when he

was very young she often told him the story of his birth. How the wind had howled and the seas had tossed, and inside the great house, in that grand bed, his mother had borne down like a warrior and shot him out of her womb and into his father's waiting arms with a laugh.

It was a good story. Brian had once been able to imagine his mother laughing and his father waiting, wanting to catch him.

Now his mother was long gone and old Miss Effie long dead. It had been a long, long time since his father had wanted to catch him.

Brian walked through the thinning mists, through huge trees with lichen vivid in pinks and red on their trunks, through the cool, shady light that fostered the ferns and shrubby palmettos. He was a tall, lanky man, very much his father's son in build. His hair was dark and shaggy, his skin tawny, and his eyes cool blue. He had a long face that women found melancholy and appealing. His mouth was firm and tended to brood more than smile.

That was something else women found appealing—the challenge of making those lips curve.

The slight change of light signaled him that it was time to start back to Sanctuary. He had to prepare the morning meal for the guests.

Brian was as contented in the kitchen as he was in the forest. That was something else his father found odd about him. And Brian knew—with some amusement—that Sam Hathaway wondered if his son might be gay. After all, if a man liked to cook for a living, there must be something wrong with him.

If they'd been the type to discuss such matters openly, Brian would have told him that he could enjoy creating a perfect meringue and still prefer women for sex. He simply wasn't inclined toward intimacy.

And wasn't that tendency toward distance from others a Hathaway family trait?

Brian moved through the forest, as quietly as the deer

that walked there. Suiting himself, he took the long way around, detouring by Half Moon Creek, where the mists were rising up from the water like white smoke and a trio of does sipped contentedly in the shimmering and utter silence.

There was time yet, Brian thought. There was always time on Desire. He indulged himself by taking a seat on a fallen log to watch the morning bloom.

The island was only two miles across at its widest, less than thirteen from point to point. Brian knew every inch of it, the sun-bleached sand of the beaches, the cool, shady marshes with their ancient and patient alligators. He loved the dune swales, the wonderful wet, undulating grassy meadows banked by young pines and majestic live oaks.

But most of all, he loved the forest, with its dark pockets and its mysteries.

He knew the history of his home, that once cotton and indigo had been grown there, worked by slaves. Fortunes had been reaped by his ancestors. The rich had come to play in this isolated little paradise, hunting the deer and the feral hogs, gathering shells, fishing both river and surf.

They'd held lively dances in the ballroom under the candle glow of crystal chandeliers, gambled carelessly at cards in the game room while drinking good southern bourbon and smoking fat Cuban cigars. They had lazed on the veranda on hot summer afternoons while slaves brought them cold glasses of lemonade.

Sanctuary had been an enclave for privilege, and a testament to a way of life that was doomed to failure.

More fortunes still had gone in and out of the hands of the steel and shipping magnate who had turned Sanctuary into his private retreat.

Though the money wasn't what it had been, Sanctuary still stood. And the island was still in the hands of the descendants of those cotton kings and emperors of steel. The cottages that were scattered over it, rising up behind the dunes, tucked into the shade of the trees, facing the wide swath of Pelican Sound, passed from generation to generation, ensuring that only a handful of families could claim Desire as home.

So it would remain.

His father fought developers and environmentalists with equal fervor. There would be no resorts on Desire, and no well-meaning government would convince Sam Hathaway to make his island a national preserve.

It was, Brian thought, his father's monument to a faithless wife. His blessing and his curse.

Visitors came now, despite the solitude, or perhaps because of it. To keep the house, the island, the trust, the Hathaways had turned part of their home into an inn.

Brian knew Sam detested it, resented every footfall on the island from an outsider. It was the only thing he could remember his parents arguing over. Annabelle had wanted to open the island to more tourists, to draw people to it, to establish the kind of social whirl her ancestors had once enjoyed. Sam had insisted on keeping it unchanged, untouched, monitoring the number of visitors and overnight guests like a miser doling out pennies. It was, in the end, what Brian believed had driven his mother away—that need for people, for faces, for voices.

But however much his father tried, he couldn't hold off change any more than the island could hold back the sea.

Adjustments, Brian thought as the deer turned as a unit and bounded into the concealing trees. He didn't care for adjustments himself, but in the case of the inn they had been necessary. And the fact was, he enjoyed the running of it, the planning, the implementing, the routine. He liked the visitors, the voices of strangers, observing their varying habits and expectations, listening to the occasional stories of their worlds.

He didn't mind people in his life—as long as they didn't intend to stay. In any case, he didn't believe people stayed in the long run.

Annabelle hadn't.

Brian rose, vaguely irritated that a twenty-year-old scar had unexpectedly throbbed. Ignoring it, he turned away and took the winding upward path toward Sanctuary.

When he came out of the trees, the light was dazzling. It struck the spray of a fountain and turned each individual drop into a rainbow. He looked at the back end of the garden. The tulips were rioting dependably. The sea pinks looked a little shaggy, and the . . . what the hell was that purple thing anyway? he asked himself. He was a medi-ocre gardener at best, struggling constantly to keep up the grounds. Paying guests expected tended gardens as much as they expected gleaming antiques and fine meals.

Sanctuary had to be kept in tiptop shape to lure them, and that meant endless hours of work. Without paying guests, there would be no means for upkeep on Sanctuary at all. So, Brian thought, scowling down at the flowers, it was an endless cycle, a snake swallowing its own tail. A trap without a key.

"Ageratum."

Brian's head came up. He had to squint against the sunlight to bring the woman into focus. But he recognized the voice. It irritated him that she'd been able to walk up behind him that way. Then again, he always viewed Dr. Kirby Fitzsimmons as a minor irritation.

"Ageratum," she repeated, and smiled. She knew she annoyed him, and considered it progress. It had taken nearly a year before she'd been able to get even that much of a reaction from him. "The flower you're glaring at. Your gardens need some work, Brian."

"I'll get to it," he said and fell back on his best weapon. Silence.

He never felt completely easy around Kirby. It wasn't just her looks, though she was attractive enough if you went for the delicate blond type. Brian figured it was her manner, which was the direct opposite of delicate. She was efficient, competent, and seemed to know a little about every damn thing.

Her voice carried what he thought of as high-society New England. Or, when he was feeling less charitable, damn Yankee. She had those Yankee cheekbones, too. They set off sea-green eyes and a slightly turned-up nose. Her mouth was full—not too wide, not too small. It was just one more irritatingly perfect thing about her.

He kept expecting to hear that she'd gone back to the mainland, closed up the little cottage she'd inherited from her granny and given up on the notion of running a clinic on the island. But month after month she stayed, slowly weaving herself into the fabric of the place.

And getting under his skin.

She kept smiling at him, with that mocking look in her eyes, as she pushed back a soft wave of the wheat-colored hair that fell smoothly to her shoulders. "Beautiful morning."

"It's early." He stuck his hands in his pockets. He never knew quite what to do with them around her.

"Not too early for you." She angled her head. Lord, he was fun to look at. She'd been hoping to do more than look for months, but Brian Hathaway was one of the natives of this little spit of land that she was having trouble winning over. "I guess breakfast isn't ready yet."

"We don't serve till eight." He figured she knew that as well as he did. She came around often enough.

"I suppose I can wait. What's the special this morning?"

"Haven't decided." Since there was no shaking her off, he resigned himself when she fell into step beside him.

"My vote's for your cinnamon waffles. I could eat a dozen." She stretched, linking her fingers as she lifted her arms overhead.

He did his best not to notice the way her cotton shirt strained over small, firm breasts. Not noticing Kirby Fitzsimmons had become a full-time job. He wound around the side of the house, through the spring blooms that lined the path of crushed shells. "You can wait in the guest parlor, or the dining room."

"I'd rather sit in the kitchen. I like watching you cook." Before he could think of a way around it, she'd stepped up into the rear screened porch and through the kitchen door.

As usual, it was neat as a pin. Kirby appreciated tidiness in a man, the same way she appreciated good muscle tone and a well-exercised brain. Brian had all three qualities, which was why she was interested in what kind of lover he'd make.

She figured she would find out eventually. Kirby always worked her way toward a goal. All she had to do was keep chipping away at that armor of his.

It wasn't disinterest. She'd seen the way he watched her on the rare occasions when his guard was down. It was sheer stubbornness. She appreciated that as well. And the contrasts of him were such fun.

She knew as she settled on a stool at the breakfast bar that he would have little to say unless she prodded. That was the distance he kept between himself and others. And she knew he would pour her a cup of his really remarkable coffee, and remember that she drank it light. That was his innate hospitality.

Kirby let him have his quiet for a moment as she sipped the coffee from the steaming mug he'd set before her. She hadn't been teasing when she'd said she liked to watch him cook.

A kitchen might have been a traditionally female domain, but this kitchen was all male. Just like its overseer, Kirby thought, with his big hands, shaggy hair, and tough face.

She knew—because there was little that one person on the island didn't know about the others—that Brian had had the kitchen redone about eight years before. And he'd created the design, chosen the colors and materials. Had made it a working man's room, with long granite-colored counters and glittering stainless steel.

There were three wide windows, framed only by curved and carved wood trim. A banquette in smoky gray was tucked under them for family meals, though, as far as she knew, the Hathaways rarely ate as a family. The floor was creamy white tile, the walls white and unadorned. No fancy work for Brian.

Yet there were homey touches in the gleam of copper pots that hung from hooks, the hanks of dried peppers and garlic, the shelf holding antique kitchen tools. She imagined he thought of them as practical rather than homey, but they warmed the room.

He'd left the old brick hearth alone, and it brought back reminders of a time when the kitchen had been the core of this house, a place for gathering, for lingering. She liked it in the winter when he lighted a fire there and the scent of wood burning mixed pleasurably with that of spicy stews or soups bubbling.

To her, the huge commercial range looked like something that required an engineering degree to operate. Then again, her idea of cooking was taking a package from the freezer and nuking it in the microwave.

"I love this room," she said. He was whipping something in a large blue bowl and only grunted. Taking that as a response, Kirby slid off the stool to help herself to a second cup of coffee. She leaned in, just brushing his arm, and grinned at the batter in the bowl. "Waffles?"

He shifted slightly. Her scent was in his way. "That was what you wanted, wasn't it?"

"Yeah." Lifting her cup, she smiled at him over the rim. "It's nice to get what you want. Don't you think?"

She had the damnedest eyes, he thought. He'd believed in mermaids as a child. All of them had had eyes like Kirby's. "It's easy enough to get it if all you want is waffles."

He stepped back, around her, and took a waffle iron

out of a lower cabinet. After he'd plugged it in, he turned, and bumped into her. Automatically he lifted a hand to her arm to steady her. And left it there.

"You're underfoot."

She eased forward, just a little, pleased by the quick flutter in her stomach. "I thought I could help."

"With what?"

She smiled, let her gaze wander down to his mouth, then back. "With whatever." What the hell, she thought, and laid her free hand on his chest. "Need anything?"

His blood began to pump faster. His fingers tightened on her arm before he could prevent it. He thought about it, oh, he thought about it. What would it be like to push her back against the counter and take what she kept insisting on putting under his nose?

That would wipe the smirk off her face.

"You're in my way, Kirby."

He had yet to let her go. That, she thought, was definite progress. Beneath her hand his heartbeat was accelerated. "I've been in your way the best part of a year, Brian. When are you going to do something about it?"

She saw his eyes flicker before they narrowed. Her breathing took on an anticipatory hitch. *Finally*, she thought and leaned toward him.

He dropped her arm and stepped back, the move so unexpected and abrupt that this time she did nearly stumble. "Drink your coffee," he said. "I've got work to do here."

He had the satisfaction of seeing that he'd pushed one of her buttons for a change. The smirk was gone, all right. Her delicate brows were knit, and under them her eyes had gone dark and hot.

"Damn it, Brian. What's the problem?"

Deftly, he ladled batter onto the heated waffle iron. "I don't have a problem." He slanted a look at her as he closed the lid. Her color was up and her mouth was thinned. Spitting mad, he thought. Good.

"What do I have to do?" She slammed her coffee cup down, sloshing the hot liquid onto his spotless counter. "Do I have to stroll in here naked?"

His lips twitched. "Well, now, that's a thought, isn't it? I could raise the rates around here after that." He cocked his head. "That is, if you look good naked."

"I look *great* naked, and I've given you numerous opportunities to find that out for yourself."

"I guess I like to make my own opportunities." He opened the refrigerator. "You want eggs with those waffles?"

Kirby clenched her fists, reminded herself that she'd taken a vow to heal, not harm, then spun on her heel. "Oh, stuff your waffles," she muttered and stalked out the back door.

Brian waited until he heard the door slam before he grinned. He figured he had come out on top of that little tussle of wills and decided to treat himself to her waffles. He was just flipping them onto a plate when the door swung open.

Lexy posed for a moment, which both she and Brian knew was out of habit rather than an attempt to impress her brother. Her hair was a tousled mass of spiraling curls that flowed over her shoulders in her current favorite shade, Renaissance Red.

She liked the Titian influence and considered it an improvement over the Bombshell Blonde she'd worn the last few years. That was, she'd discovered, a bitch to maintain.

The color was only a few shades lighter and brighter than what God had given her, and it suited her skin tones, which were milky with a hint of rose beneath. She'd inherited her father's changeable hazel eyes. This morning they were heavy, the color of cloudy seas, and already carefully accented with mascara and liner.

"Waffles," she said. Her voice was a feline purr she'd practiced religiously and made her own. "Yum."

Unimpressed, Brian cut the first bite as he stood, and shoveled it into his mouth. "Mine."

Lexy tossed back her gypsy mane of hair, strolled over to the breakfast bar and pouted prettily. She fluttered her lashes and smiled when Brian set the plate in front of her. "Thanks, sweetie." She laid a hand on his cheek and kissed the other.

Lexy had the very un-Hathaway-like habit of touching, kissing, hugging. Brian remembered that after their mother had left, Lexy had been like a puppy, always leaping into someone's arms, looking for a snuggle. Hell, he thought, she'd only been four. He gave her hair a tug and handed her the syrup.

"Anyone else up?"

"Mmm. The couple in the blue room are stirring. Cousin Kate was in the shower."

"I thought you were handling the breakfast shift this morning."

"I am," she told him with her mouth full.

He lifted a brow, skimmed his gaze over her short, thin, wildly patterned robe. "Is that your new waitress uniform?"

She crossed long legs and slipped another bite of waffle between her lips. "Like it?"

"You'll be able to retire on the tips."

"Yeah." She gave a half laugh and pushed at the waffles on her plate. "That's been my lifelong dream—serving food to strangers and clearing away their dirty plates, saving the pocket change they give me so I can retire in splendor."

"We all have our little fantasies," Brian said lightly and set a cup of coffee, loaded with cream and sugar, beside her. He understood her bitterness and disappointment, even if he didn't agree with it. Because he loved her, he cocked his head and said, "Want to hear mine?"

"Probably has something to do with winning the Betty Crocker recipe contest."

"Hey, it could happen."

"I was going to be somebody, Bri."

"You are somebody. Alexa Hathaway, Island Princess."

She rolled her eyes before she picked up her coffee. "I didn't last a year in New York. Not a damn year."

"Who wants to?" The very idea gave him the creeps. Crowded streets, crowded smells, crowded air.

"It's a little tough to be an actress on Desire."

"Honey, you ask me, you're doing a hell of a job of it. And if you're going to sulk, take the waffles up to your room. You're spoiling my mood."

"It's easy for you." She shoved the waffles away. Brian nabbed the plate before it slid off the counter. "You've got what you want. Living in nowhere day after day, year after year. Doing the same thing over and over again. Daddy's practically given the house over to you so he can tromp around the island all day to make sure nobody moves so much as one grain of his precious sand."

She pushed herself up from the stool, flung out her arms. "And Jo's got what she wants. Big-fucking-deal photographer, traveling all over the world to snap her pictures. But what do I have? Just what do I have? A pathetic résumé with a couple of commercials, a handful of walk-ons, and a lead in a three-act play that closed in Pittsburgh on opening night. Now I'm stuck here again, waiting tables, changing other people's sheets. And I hate it."

He waited a moment, then applauded. "Hell of a speech, Lex. And you know just what words to punch. You might want to work on the staging, though. The gestures lean toward grandiose."

Her lips trembled, then firmed. "Damn you, Bri." She jerked her chin up before stalking out.

Brian picked up her fork. Looked like he was two for two that morning, he thought, and decided to finish off her breakfast as well.

• • •

Within an hour Lexy was all smiles and southern sugared charm. She was a skilled waitress—which had saved her from total poverty during her stint in New York—and served her tables with every appearance of pleasure and unhurried grace.

She wore a trim skirt just short enough to irritate Brian, which had been her intention, and a cap-sleeved sweater that she thought showed off her figure to best advantage. She had a good one and worked hard to keep it that way.

It was a tool of the trade whether waitressing or acting. As was her quick, sunny smile.

"Why don't I warm that coffee up for you, Mr. Benson? How's your omelette? Brian's an absolute wonder in the kitchen, isn't he?"

Since Mr. Benson seemed so appreciative of her breasts, she leaned over a bit further to give him full bang for his buck before moving to the next table.

"You're leaving us today, aren't you?" She beamed at the newlyweds cuddling at a corner table. "I hope y'all come back and see us again."

She sailed through the room, gauging when a customer wanted to chat, when another wanted to be left alone. As usual on a weekday morning, business was light and she had plenty of opportunity to play the room.

What she wanted to play was packed houses, those grand theaters of New York. Instead, she thought, keeping that summer-sun smile firmly in place, she was cast in the role of waitress in a house that never changed, on an island that never changed.

It had all been the same for hundreds of years, she thought. Lexy wasn't a woman who appreciated history. As far as she was concerned, the past was boring and as tediously carved in stone as Desire and its scattering of families.

Pendletons married Fitzsimmonses or Brodies or Verdons. The island's Main Four. Occasionally one of the sons or daughters took a detour and married a mainlander.

Some even moved away, but almost invariably they remained, living in the same cottages generation after generation, sprinkling a few more names among the permanent residents.

It was all so . . . predictable, she thought, as she flipped her order pad brightly and beamed down at her next table.

Her mother had married a mainlander, and now the Hathaways reigned over Sanctuary. It was the Hathaways who had lived there, worked there, sweated time and blood over the keeping of the house and the protection of the island for more than thirty years now.

But Sanctuary still was, and always would be, the Pendleton house, high on the hill.

And there seemed to be no escaping from it.

She stuffed tips into her pocket and carried dirty plates away. The minute she stepped into the kitchen, her eyes went frigid. She shed her charm like a snake sheds its skin. It only infuriated her more that Brian was impervious to the cold shoulder she jammed in his face.

She dumped the dishes, snagged the fresh pot of coffee, then swung back into the dining room.

For two hours she served and cleared and replaced setups—and dreamed of where she wanted to be.

Broadway. She'd been so sure she could make it. Everyone had told her she had a natural talent. Of course, that was before she went to New York and found herself up against hundreds of other young women who'd been told the same thing.

She wanted to be a serious actress, not some airheaded bimbo who posed for lingerie ads and billed herself as an actress-model. She'd fully expected to start at the top. After all, she had brains and looks and talent.

Her first sight of Manhattan had filled her with a sense of purpose and energy. It was as if it had been waiting for her, she thought, as she calculated the tab for table six. All those people, and that noise and vitality. And, oh, the stores with those gorgeous clothes, the sophisticated restaurants, and the overwhelming sense that everyone had something to do, somewhere to go in a hurry.

She had something to do and somewhere to go too.

Of course, she'd rented an apartment that had cost far too much. But she hadn't been willing to settle for some cramped little room. She treated herself to new clothes at Bendel's, and a full day at Elizabeth Arden. That ate a large chunk out of her budget, but she considered it an investment. She wanted to look her best when she answered casting calls.

Her first month was one rude awakening after another. She'd never expected so much competition, or such desperation on the faces of those who lined up with her to audition for part after part.

And she did get a few offers—but most of them involved her auditioning on her back. She had too much pride and too much self-confidence for that.

Now that pride and self-confidence and, she was forced to admit, her own naïveté, had brought her full circle.

But it was only temporary, Lexy reminded herself. In a little less than a year she would turn twenty-five and then she'd come into her inheritance. What there was of it. She was going to take it back to New York, and this time she'd be smarter, more cautious, and more clever.

She wasn't beaten, she decided. She was taking a sabbatical. One day she would stand onstage and feel all that love and admiration from the audience roll over her. Then she would be someone.

Someone other than Annabelle's younger daughter.

She carried the last of the plates into the kitchen. Brian was already putting the place back into shape. No dirty pots and pans cluttered his sink, no spills and smears spoiled his counter. Knowing it was nasty, Lexy turned her wrist so that the cup stacked on top of the plates tipped, spilling the dregs of coffee before it shattered on the tile.

"Oops," she said and grinned wickedly when Brian turned his head.

"You must enjoy being a fool, Lex," he said coolly. "You're so good at it."

"Really?" Before she could stop herself, she let the rest of the dishes drop. They hit with a crash, scattering food and fragments of stoneware all over. "How's that?"

"Goddamn it, what are you trying to prove? That you're as destructive as ever? That somebody will always come behind you to clean up your mess?" He stomped to a closet, pulled out a broom. "Do it yourself." He shoved the broom at her.

"I won't." Though she already regretted the impulsive act, she shoved the broom back at him. The colorful Fiestaware was like a ruined carnival at their feet. "They're your precious dishes. You clean them up."

"You're going to clean it up, or I swear I'll use this broom on your backside."

"Just try it, Bri." She went toe-to-toe with him. Knowing she'd been wrong was only a catalyst for standing her ground. "Just try it and I'll scratch your damn eyes out. I'm sick to death of you telling me what to do. This is my house as much as it is yours."

"Well, I see nothing's changed around here."

Their faces still dark with temper, both Brian and Lexy turned—and stared. Jo stood at the back door, her two suitcases at her feet and exhaustion in her eyes.

"I knew I was home when I heard the crash followed by the happy voices."

In an abrupt and deliberate shift of mood, Lexy slid her arm through Brian's, uniting them. "Look here, Brian, another prodigal's returned. I hope we have some of that fatted calf left."

"I'll settle for coffee," Jo said, and closed the door behind her.

THREE

JO STOOD AT THE WINDOW
in the bedroom of her childhood. The view was the same.
Pretty gardens patiently waiting to be weeded and fed.
Mounds of alyssum were already golden and bluebells
were waving. Violas were sunning their sassy little faces,
guarded by the tall spears of purple iris and cheerful yellow tulips. Impatiens and dianthus bloomed reliably.

There were the palms, cabbage and saw, and beyond
them the shady oaks where lacy ferns and indifferent
wildflowers thrived.

The light was so lovely, gilded and pearly as the clouds
drifted, casting soft shadows. The image was one of
peace, solitude, and storybook perfection. If she'd had the
energy, she'd have gone out now, captured it on film and
made it her own.

She'd missed it. How odd, she thought, to realize only
now that she'd missed the view from the window of the
room where she'd spent nearly every night of the first
eighteen years of her life.

She'd whiled away many hours gardening with her
mother, learning the names of the flowers, their needs and

37

habits, enjoying the feel of soil under her fingers and the sun on her back. Birds and butterflies, the tinkle of wind chimes, the drift of puffy clouds overhead in a soft blue sky were treasured memories from her early childhood.

Apparently she'd forgotten to hold on to them, Jo decided, as she turned wearily from the window. Any pictures she'd taken of the scene, with her mind or with her camera, had been tucked away for a very long time.

Her room had changed little as well. The family wing in Sanctuary still glowed with Annabelle's style and taste. For her older daughter she'd chosen a gleaming brass half-tester bed with a lacy canopy and a complex and fluid design of cornices and knobs. The spread was antique Irish lace, a Pendleton heirloom that Jo had always loved because of its pattern and texture. And because it seemed so sturdy and ageless.

On the wallpaper, bluebells bloomed in cheerful riot over the ivory background, and the trim was honey-toned and warm.

Annabelle had selected the antiques—the globe lamps and maple tables, the dainty chairs and vases that had always held fresh flowers. She'd wanted her children to learn early to live with the precious and care for it. On the mantel over the little marble fireplace were candles and seashells. On the shelves on the opposite wall were books rather than dolls.

Even as a child, Jo had had little use for dolls.

Annabelle was dead. No matter how much of her stubbornly remained in this room, in this house, on this island, she was dead. Sometime in the last twenty years she had died, made her desertion complete and irrevocable.

Dear God, why had someone immortalized that death on film? Jo wondered, as she buried her face in her hands. And why had they sent that immortalization to Annabelle's daughter?

DEATH OF AN ANGEL

Those words had been printed on the back of the photograph. Jo remembered them vividly. Now she rubbed the heel of her hand hard between her breasts to try to calm her heart. What kind of sickness was that? she asked herself. What kind of threat? And how much of it was aimed at herself?

It had been there, it had been real. It didn't matter that when she got out of the hospital and returned to her apartment, the print was gone. She couldn't let it matter. If she admitted she'd imagined it, that she'd been hallucinating, she would have to admit that she'd lost her mind.

How could she face that?

But the print hadn't been there when she returned. All the others were, all those everyday images of herself, still scattered on the darkroom floor where she'd dropped them in shock and panic.

But though she searched, spent hours going over every inch of the apartment, she didn't find the print that had broken her.

If it had never been there . . . Closing her eyes, she rested her forehead on the window glass. If she'd fabricated it, if she'd somehow wanted that terrible image to be fact, for her mother to be exposed that way, and dead—what did that make her?

Which could she accept? Her own mental instability, or her mother's death?

Don't think about it now. She pressed a hand to her mouth as her breath began to catch in her throat. Put it away, just like you put the photographs away. Lock it up until you're stronger. Don't break down again, Jo Ellen, she ordered herself. You'll end up back in the hospital, with doctors poking into both body and mind.

Handle it. She drew a deep, steadying breath. Handle it until you can ask whatever questions have to be asked, find whatever answers there are to be found.

She would do something practical, she decided, something ordinary, attempt the pretense, at least, of a normal visit home.

She'd already lowered the front of the slant-top desk and set one of her cameras on it. But as she stared at it she realized that was as much unpacking as she could handle. Jo looked at the suitcases lying on the lovely bedspread. The thought of opening them, of taking clothes out and hanging them in the armoire, folding them into drawers was simply overwhelming. Instead she sat down in a chair and closed her eyes.

What she needed to do was think and plan. She worked best with a list of goals and tasks, recorded in the order that would be the most practical and efficient. Coming home had been the only solution, so it was practical and efficient. It was, she promised herself, the first step. She just had to clear her mind, somehow—clear it and latch on to the next step.

But she drifted, nearly dreaming.

It seemed like only seconds had passed when someone knocked, but Jo found herself jerked awake and disoriented. She sprang to her feet, feeling ridiculously embarrassed to have nearly been caught napping in the middle of the day. Before she could reach the door, it opened and Cousin Kate poked her head in.

"Well, there you are. Goodness, Jo, you look like three days of death. Sit down and drink this tea and tell me what's going on with you."

It was so Kate, Jo thought, that frank, no-nonsense, bossy attitude. She found herself smiling as she watched Kate march in with the tea tray. "You look wonderful."

"I take care of myself." Kate set the tray on the low table in the sitting area and waved one hand at a chair. "Which, from the looks of you, you haven't been doing. You're too thin, too pale, and your hair's a disaster of major proportions. But we'll fix that."

Briskly she poured tea from a porcelain teapot decked with sprigs of ivy into two matching cups. "Now, then."

She sat back, sipped, then angled her head.

"I'm taking some time off," Jo told her. She'd driven down from Charlotte for the express purpose of giving herself time to rehearse her reasons and excuses for coming home. "A few weeks."

"Jo Ellen, you can't snow me."

They'd never been able to, Jo thought, not any of them, not from the moment Kate had set foot in Sanctuary. She'd come days after Annabelle's desertion to spend a week and was still there twenty years later.

They'd needed her, God knew, Jo thought, as she tried to calculate just how little she could get away with telling Katherine Pendleton. She sipped her tea, stalling.

Kate was Annabelle's cousin, and the family resemblance was marked in the eyes, the coloring, the physical build. But where Annabelle, in Jo's memory, had always seemed soft and innately feminine, Kate was sharp-angled and precise.

Yes, Kate did take care of herself, Jo agreed. She wore her hair boyishly short, a russet cap that suited her fox-at-alert face and practical style. Her wardrobe leaned toward the casual but never the sloppy. Jeans were always pressed, cotton shirts crisp. Her nails were neat and short and never without three coats of clear polish. Though she was fifty, she kept herself trim and from the back could have been mistaken for a teenage boy.

She had come into their lives at their lowest ebb and had never faltered. Had simply been there, managing details, pushing each of them to do whatever needed to be done next, and, in her no-nonsense way, bullying and loving them into at least an illusion of normality.

"I've missed you, Kate," Jo murmured. "I really have."

Kate stared at her a moment, and something flickered over her face. "You won't soften me up, Jo Ellen. You're in trouble, and you can choose to tell me or you can make me pry it out of you. Either way, I'll have it."

"I needed some time off."

That, Kate mused, was undoubtedly true; she could tell just from the looks of the girl. Knowing Jo, she doubted very much if it was a man who'd put that wounded look in her eyes. So that left work. Work that took Jo to strange and faraway places, Kate thought. Often dangerous places of war and disaster. Work that she knew her young cousin had deliberately put ahead of a life and a family.

Little girl, Kate thought, *my poor, sweet little girl. What have you done to yourself?*

Kate tightened her fingers on the handle of her cup to keep them from trembling. "Were you hurt?"

"No. No," Jo repeated and set her tea down to press her fingers to her aching eyes. "Just overwork, stress. I guess I overextended myself in the last couple of months. The pressure, that's all."

The photographs. Mama.

Kate drew her brows together. The line that formed between them was known, not so affectionately, as the Pendleton Fault Line. "What kind of pressure eats the weight off of you, Jo Ellen, and makes your hands shake?"

Defensively, Jo clasped those unsteady hands together in her lap. "I guess you could say I haven't been taking care of myself." Jo smiled a little. "I'm going to do better."

Tapping her fingers on the arm of the chair, Kate studied Jo's face. The trouble there went too deep to be only professional concerns. "Have you been sick?"

"No." The lie slid off her tongue nearly as smoothly as planned. Very deliberately she blocked out the thought of a hospital room, almost certain that Kate would be able to see it in her mind. "Just a little run-down. I haven't been sleeping well lately." Edgy under Kate's steady gaze, Jo rose to dig cigarettes out of the pocket of the jacket she'd tossed over a chair. "I've got that book deal—I wrote you about it. I guess it's got me stressed out.'' She flicked on her lighter. "It's new territory for me.''

"You should be proud of yourself, not making yourself sick over it.''

"You're right. Absolutely.'' Jo blew out smoke and fought back the image of Annabelle, the photographs. "I'm taking some time off.''

It wasn't all, Kate calculated, but it was enough for now. "It's good you've come home. A couple of weeks of Brian's cooking will put some meat on you again. And God knows we could use some help around here. Most of the rooms, and the cottages, are booked straight through the summer.''

"So business is good?'' Jo asked without much interest.

"People need to get away from their own routines and pick up someone else's. Most that come here are looking for quiet and solitude or they'd be in Hilton Head or on Jekyll. Still, they want clean linen and fresh towels.''

Kate tapped her fingers, thinking briefly of the work stretched out before her that afternoon. "Lexy's been lending a hand,'' she continued, "but she's no more dependable than she ever was. Just as likely to run off for the day as to do what chores need doing. She's dealing with some disappointments herself, and some growing-up pains.''

"Lex is twenty-four, Kate. She should be grown up by now.''

"Some take longer than others. It's not a fault, it's a fact.'' Kate rose, always ready to defend one of her chicks, even if it was against the pecks of another.

"And some never learn to face reality,'' Jo put in. "And spend their lives blaming everyone else for their failures and disappointments.''

"Alexa is not a failure. You were never patient enough with her—any more than she was with you. That's a fact as well.''

"I never asked her to be patient with me." Old resentments surfaced like hot grease on tainted water. "I never asked her, or any of them, for anything."

"No, you never asked, Jo," Kate said evenly. "You might have to give something back if you ask. You might have to admit you need them if you let them need you. Well, it's time you all faced up to a few things. It's been two years since the three of you have been in this house together."

"I know how long it's been," Jo said bitterly. "And I didn't get any more of a welcome from Brian and Lexy than I'd expected."

"Maybe you'd have gotten more if you'd expected more." Kate set her jaw. "You haven't even asked about your father."

Annoyed, Jo stabbed out her cigarette. "What would you like me to ask?"

"Don't take that snippy tone with me, young lady. If you're going to be under this roof, you'll show some respect for those who provide it. And you'll do your part while you're here. Your brother's had too much of the running of this place on his shoulders these last few years. It's time the family pitched in. It's time you were a family."

"I'm not an innkeeper, Kate, and I can't imagine that Brian wants me poking my fingers into his business."

"You don't have to be an innkeeper to do laundry or polish furniture or sweep the sand off the veranda."

At the ice in her tone, Jo responded in defense and defiance. "I didn't say I wouldn't do my part, I just meant—"

"I know exactly what you meant, and I'm telling you, young lady, I'm sick to death of that kind of attitude. Every one of you children would rather sink over your heads in the marsh than ask one of your siblings for a helping hand. And you'd strangle on your tongue before you asked your daddy. I don't know whether you're competing or just being ornery, but I want you to put it aside while you're here. This is home. By God, it's time it felt like one.''

"Kate," Jo began as Kate headed for the door.

"No, I'm too mad to talk to you now."

"I only meant . . ." When the door shut smartly, Jo let the air out of her lungs on a long sigh.

Her head was achy, her stomach knotted, and guilt was smothering her like a soaked blanket.

Kate was wrong, she decided. It felt exactly like home.

From the fringes of the marsh, Sam Hathaway watched a hawk soar over its hunting ground. Sam had hiked over to the landward side of the island that morning, leaving the house just before dawn. He knew Brian had gone out at nearly the same hour, but they hadn't spoken. Each had his own way, and his own route.

Sometimes Sam took a Jeep, but more often he walked. Some days he would head to the dunes and watch the sun rise over the water, turning it bloody red, then golden, then blue. When the beach was all space and light and brilliance, he might walk for miles, his eyes keenly judging erosion, looking for any fresh buildup of sand.

He left shells where the water had tossed them.

He rarely ventured onto the interdune meadows. They were fragile, and every footfall caused damage and change. Sam fought bitterly against change.

There were days he preferred to wander to the edge of the forest, behind the dunes, where the lakes and sloughs were full of life and music. There were mornings he needed the stillness and dim light there rather than the thunder of waves and the rising sun. He could, like the patient heron waiting for a careless fish, stand motionless as minutes ticked by.

There were times among the ponds and stands of willow and thick film of duckweed that he could forget that any world existed beyond this, his own. Here, the alligator hidden in the reeds while it digested its last meal and the turtle sunning on the log, likely to become gator bait itself, were more real to him than people.

But it was a rare, rare thing for Sam to go beyond the ponds and into the shadows of the forest. Annabelle had loved the forest best.

Other days he was drawn here, to the marsh and its mysteries. Here was a cycle he could understand—growth and decay, life and death. This was nature and could be accepted. No man caused this or—as long as Sam was in control—would interfere with it.

At the edges he could watch the fiddler crabs scurrying, so busy in the mud that they made quiet popping sounds, like soapsuds. Sam knew that when he left, raccoons and other predators would creep along the mud, scrape out those busy crabs, and feast.

That was all part of the cycle.

Now, as spring came brilliantly into its own, the waving cordgrass was turning from tawny gold to green and the turf was beginning to bloom with the colors of sea lavender and oxeye. He had seen more than thirty springs come to Desire, and he never tired of it.

The land had been his wife's, passed through her family from generation to generation. But it had become his the moment he'd set foot on it. Just as Annabelle had become his the moment he'd set eyes on her.

He hadn't kept the woman, but through her desertion he had kept the land.

Sam was a fatalist—or had become one. There was no avoiding destiny.

The land had come to him from Annabelle, and he tended it carefully, protected it fiercely, and left it never.

Though it had been years since he'd turned in the night reaching out for the ghost of his wife, he could find her anywhere and everywhere he looked on Desire.

It was both his pain and his comfort.

Sam could see the exposed roots of trees where the

river was eating away at the fringe of the marsh. Some said it was best to take steps to protect those fringes. But Sam believed that nature found its way. If man, whether with good intent or ill, set his own hand to changing that river's course, what repercussions would it have in other areas?

No, he would leave it be and let the land and the sea, the wind and the rain fight it out.

From a few feet away, Kate studied him. He was a tall, wiry man with skin tanned and ruddy and dark hair silvering. His firm mouth was slow to smile, and slower yet were those changeable hazel eyes. Lines fanned out from those eyes, deeply scored and, in that oddity of masculinity, only enhancing his face.

He had large hands and feet, both of which he'd passed on to his son. Yet Kate knew Sam could move with an uncanny and soundless grace that no city dweller could ever master.

In twenty years he had never welcomed her nor expected her to leave. She had simply come and stayed and fulfilled a purpose. In weak moments, Kate allowed herself to wonder what he would think or do or say if she simply packed up and left.

But she didn't leave, doubted she ever would.

She'd been in love with Sam Hathaway nearly every moment of those twenty years.

Kate squared her shoulders, set her chin. Though she suspected he already knew she was there, she knew he wouldn't speak to her unless she spoke first.

"Jo Ellen came in on the morning ferry."

Sam continued to watch the hawk circle. Yes, he'd known Kate was there, just as he'd known she had some reason she thought important that would have brought her to the marsh. Kate wasn't one for mud and gators.

"Why?" was all he said, and extracted an impatient sigh from Kate.

"It's her home, isn't it?"

His voice was slow, as if the words were formed reluctantly. "Don't figure she thinks of it that way. Hasn't for a long time."

"Whatever she thinks, it *is* her home. You're her father and you'll want to welcome her back."

He got a picture of his older daughter in his mind. And saw his wife with a clarity that brought both despair and outrage. But only disinterest showed in his voice. "I'll be up to the house later on."

"It's been nearly two years since she's been home, Sam. For Lord's sake, go see your daughter."

He shifted, annoyed and uncomfortable. Kate had a way of drawing out those reactions in him. "There's time, unless she's planning on taking the ferry back to the mainland this afternoon. Never could stay in one place for long, as I recall. And she couldn't wait to get shed of Desire."

"Going off to college and making a career and a life for herself isn't desertion."

Though he didn't move or make a sound, Kate knew the shaft had hit home, and was sorry she'd felt it necessary to hurl it. "She's back now, Sam. I don't think she's up to going anywhere for a while, and that's not the point."

Kate marched up, took a firm hold on his arm, and turned him to face her. There were times you had to shove an obvious point in Sam's face to make him see it, she thought. And that was just what she intended to do now.

"She's hurting. She doesn't look well, Sam. She's lost weight and she's pale as a sheet. She says she hasn't been ill, but she's lying. She looks like you could knock her down with a hard thought."

For the first time a shadow of worry moved into his eyes. "Did she get hurt on her job?"

There, finally, Kate thought, but was careful not to show the satisfaction. "It's not that kind of hurt," she said more gently. "It's an inside hurt. I can't put my finger on it, but it's there. She needs her home, her family. She needs her father.''

"If Jo's got a problem, she'll deal with it. She always has.''

"You mean she's always had to,'' Kate tossed back. She wanted to shake him until she'd loosened the lock he had snapped on his heart. "Damn it, Sam, be there for her.''

He looked beyond Kate, to the marshes. "She's past the point where she needs me to bandage up her bumps and scratches.''

"No, she's not.'' Kate dropped her hand from his arm. "She's still your daughter. She always will be. Belle wasn't the only one who went away, Sam.'' She watched his face close in as she said it and shook her head fiercely. "Brian and Jo and Lexy lost her, too. But they shouldn't have had to lose you.''

His chest had tightened, and he turned away to stare out over the marsh, knowing that the pressure inside him would ease again if he was left alone. "I said I'd be up to the house later on. Jo Ellen has something to say to me, she can say it then.''

"One of these days you're going to realize you've got something to say to her, to all of them.''

She left him alone, hoping he would realize it soon.

FOUR

BRIAN STOOD IN THE
doorway of the west terrace and studied his sister. She
looked frail, he noted, skittish. Lost somehow, he thought,
amid the sunlight and flowers. She still wore the baggy
trousers and oversized lightweight sweater that she'd arrived in, and had added a pair of round wire-framed sunglasses. Brian imagined that Jo wore just such a uniform
when she hunted her photographs, but at the moment it
served only to add to the overall impression of an invalid.

Yet she'd always been the tough one, he remembered.
Even as a child she'd insisted on doing everything herself,
on finding the answers, solving the puzzles, fighting the
fights.

She'd been fearless, climbing higher in any tree, swimming farther beyond the waves, running faster through the
forest. Just to prove she could, Brian mused. It seemed to
him Jo Ellen had always had something to prove.

And after their mother had gone, Jo had seemed hell-
bent on proving she needed no one and nothing but herself.

Well, Brian decided, she needed something now. He

51

stepped out, saying nothing as she turned her head and looked at him from behind the tinted lenses. Then he sat down on the glider beside her and put the plate he'd brought out in her lap.

"Eat," was all he said.

Jo looked down at the fried chicken, the fresh slaw, the golden biscuit. "Is this the lunch special?"

"Most of the guests went for the box lunch today. Too nice to eat inside."

"Cousin Kate said you've been busy."

"Busy enough." Out of habit, he pushed off with his foot and set the glider in motion. "What are you doing here, Jo?"

"Seemed like the thing to do at the time." She lifted a drumstick, bit in. Her stomach did a quick pitch and roll as if debating whether to accept food. Jo persisted and swallowed. "I'll do my share, and I won't get in your way."

Brian listened to the squeak of the glider for a moment, thought about oiling the hinges. "I haven't said you were in my way, as I recollect," he said mildly.

"In Lexy's way, then." Jo took another bite of chicken, scowled at the soft-pink ivy geraniums spilling over the edges of a concrete jardiniere carved with chubby cherubs. "You can tell her I'm not here to cramp her style."

"Tell her yourself." Brian opened the thermos he'd brought along and poured freshly squeezed lemonade into the lid. "I'm not stepping between the two of you so I can get my ass kicked from both sides."

"Fine, stay out of it, then." Her head was beginning to ache, but she took the cup and sipped. "I don't know why the hell she resents me so much."

"Can't imagine." Brian drawled it before he lifted the thermos and drank straight from the lip. "You're successful, famous, financially independent, a rising star in your field. All the things she wants for herself." He picked up the biscuit and broke it in half, handing a portion to Jo as the steam burst out. "I can't think why that'd put her nose out of joint."

"I did it by myself for myself. I didn't work my butt off to get to this point to show her up." Without thinking, she stuffed a bite of biscuit in her mouth. "It's not my fault she's got some childish fantasy about seeing her name in lights and having people throw roses at her feet."

"Your seeing it as childish doesn't make the desire any less real for her." He held up a hand before Jo could speak. "And I'm not getting in the middle. The two of you are welcome to rip the hide off each other in your own good time. But I'd say right now she could take you without breaking a sweat."

"I don't want to fight with her," Jo said wearily. She could smell the wisteria that rioted over the nearby arched iron trellis—another vivid memory of childhood. "I didn't come here to fight with anyone."

"That'll be a change."

That lured a ghost of a smile to her lips. "Maybe I've mellowed."

"Miracles happen. Eat your slaw."

"I don't remember you being so bossy."

"I've cut back on mellow."

With what passed as a chuckle, Jo picked up her fork and poked at the slaw. "Tell me what's new around here, Bri, and what's the same." Bring me home, she thought, but couldn't say it. Bring me back.

"Let's see, Giff Verdon built on another room to the Verdon cottage."

"Stop the presses." Then Jo's brow furrowed. "Young Giff, the scrawny kid with the cowlick. The one who was always mooning over Lex?"

"That's the one. Filled out some, Giff has, and he's right handy with a hammer and saw. Does all our repair work now. Still moons over Lexy, but I'd say he knows what he wants to do about it now."

Jo snorted and, without thinking, shoveled in more slaw. "She'll eat him alive."

Brian shrugged. "Maybe, but I think she'll find him tougher to chew up than she might expect. The Sanders girl, Rachel, she got herself engaged to some college boy in Atlanta. Going to move there come September."

"Rachel Sanders." Jo tried to conjure up a mental image. "Was she the one with the lisp or the one with the giggle?"

"The giggle—sharp enough to make the ears bleed." Satisfied that Jo was eating, Brian stretched an arm over the back of the glider and relaxed. "Old Mrs. Fitzsimmons passed on more than a year back."

"Old Mrs. Fitzsimmons," Jo murmured. "She used to shuck oysters on her porch, with that lazy hound of hers sleeping at her feet beside the rocker."

"The hound passed, too, right after. Guess he didn't see much point in living without her."

"She let me take pictures of her," Jo remembered. "When I was a kid, just learning. I still have them. A couple weren't bad. Mr. David helped me develop them. I must have been such a pest, but she just sat there in her rocker and let me practice on her."

Sitting back, Jo fell into the rhythm of the glider, as slow and monotonous as the rhythm of the island. "I hope it was quick and painless."

"She died in her sleep at the ripe old age of ninety-six. Can't do much better than that."

"No." Jo closed her eyes, the food forgotten. "What was done with her cottage?"

"Passed down. The Pendletons bought most of the Fitzsimmons land back in 1923, but she owned her house and the little spit of land it sits on. Went to her granddaughter." Brian lifted the thermos again, drank deeply this time. "A doctor. She's set up a practice here on the island."

"We have a doctor on Desire?" Jo opened her eyes,

lifted her brows. "Well, well. How civilized. Are people actually going to her?"

"Seems they are, little by little, anyway. She's dug her toes in."

"She must be the first new permanent resident here in what, ten years?"

"Thereabouts."

"I can't imagine why . . ." Jo trailed off as it struck her. "It's not Kirby, is it? Kirby Fitzsimmons? She spent summers here a couple of years running when we were kids."

"I guess she liked it well enough to come back."

"I'll be damned. Kirby Fitzsimmons, and a doctor, of all things." Pleasure bloomed, a surprising sensation she nearly didn't recognize. "We used to pal around together some. I remember the summer Mr. David came to take photographs of the island and brought his family."

It cheered her to think of it, the young friend with the quick northern voice, the adventures they'd shared or imagined together. "You would run off with his boys and wouldn't give me the time of day," Jo continued. "When I wasn't pestering Mr. David to let me take pictures with his camera, I'd go off with Kirby and look for trouble. Christ, that was twenty years ago if it was a day. It was the summer that . . ."

Brian nodded, then finished the thought. "The summer that Mama left."

"It's all out of focus," Jo murmured, and the pleasure died out of her voice. "Hot sun, long days, steamy nights so full of sound. All the faces." She slipped her fingers under her glasses to rub at her eyes. "Getting up at sunrise so I could follow Mr. David around. Bolting down cold ham sandwiches and cooling off in the river. Mama dug out that old camera for me—that ancient box Brownie— and I would run over to the Fitzsimmons cottage and take pictures until Mrs. Fitzsimmons told Kirby and me to scoot. There were hours and hours, so many hours, until the sun went down and Mama called us home for supper.''

She closed her eyes tight. "So much, so many images, yet I can't bring any one of them really clear. Then she was gone. One morning I woke up ready to do all the things a long summer day called for, and she was just gone. And there was nothing to do at all.''

"Summer was over," Brian said quietly. "For all of us.''

"Yeah.'' Her hands had gone trembly again. Jo reached in her pockets for cigarettes. "Do you ever think about her?''

"Why would I?''

"Don't you ever wonder where she went? What she did?'' Jo took a jerky drag. In her mind she saw long-lidded eyes empty of life. "Or why?''

"It doesn't have anything to do with me." Brian rose, took the plate. "Or you. Or any of us anymore. It's twenty years past that summer, Jo Ellen, and a little late to worry about it now.''

She opened her mouth, then shut it again when Brian turned and walked back into the house. But she was worried about it, she thought. And she was terrified.

Lexy was still steaming as she climbed over the dunes toward the beach. Jo had come back, she was sure, to flaunt her success and her snazzy life. And the fact that she'd arrived at Sanctuary hard on the heels of Lexy's own failure didn't strike Lexy as coincidence.

Jo would flap her wings and crow in triumph, while Lexy would have to settle for eating crow. The thought of it made her blood boil as she raced along the tramped-down sand through the dunes, sending sand flying from her sandals.

Not this time, she promised herself. This time she would hold her head up, refuse to be cast as inferior in the face of Jo's latest triumph, latest trip, latest wonder.

She wasn't going to play the hotshot's baby sister any longer. She'd outgrown that role, Lexy assured herself. And it was high time everyone realized it.

There was a scattering of people on the wide crescent of beach. They had staked their claims with their blankets and colorful umbrellas. She noted several with the brightly striped box lunches from Sanctuary.

The scents of sea and lotions and fried chicken assaulted her nostrils. A toddler shoveled sand into a red bucket while his mother read a paperback novel in the shade of a portable awning. A man was slowly turning into a lobster under the merciless sun. Two couples she had served that morning were sharing a picnic and laughing together over the clever voice of Annie Lennox on their portable stereo.

She didn't want them—any of them—to be there. On her beach, in her personal crisis. To dismiss them, she turned and walked away from the temporary development, down the curve of beach.

She saw the figure out in the water, the gleam of tanned, wet shoulders, the glint of sun-bleached hair. Giff was a reliable creature of habit, she thought, and he was just exactly what the doctor called for. He invariably took a quick swim during his afternoon break. And, Lexy knew, he had his eye on her.

He hadn't made a secret of it, she mused, and she wasn't one to resent the attentions of an attractive man. Particularly when she needed her ego soothed. She thought a little flirtation, and the possibility of mindless sex, might put the day back on track.

People said her mother had been a flirt. Lexy hadn't been old enough to remember anything more than vague images and soft scents when it came to Annabelle, but she believed she'd come by her skill at flirtation naturally. Her mother had enjoyed looking her best, smiling at men. And if the theory of a secret lover was fact, Annabelle had done more than smile at at least one man.

In any case, that's what the police had concluded after months of investigation.

Lexy thought she was good at sex; she had been told so often enough to consider it a fine personal skill. As far as she was concerned, there was little else that compared to it for shouldering away tension and being the focus of someone's complete attention.

And she liked it, all the hot, slick sensations that went with it. It hardly mattered that most men didn't have a clue whether a woman was thinking about them or the latest Hollywood pretty boy while it was going on. As long as she performed well and remembered the right lines.

Lexy considered herself born to perform.

And she decided it was time to open that velvet curtain for Giff Verdon.

She dropped the towel she'd brought with her onto the packed sand. She didn't have a doubt that he was watching her. Men did. As if onstage, Lexy put her heart into the performance. Standing near the edge of the water, she slipped off her sunglasses, let them fall heedlessly onto the towel. Slowly, she stepped out of her sandals, then, taking the hem of the short-skirted sundress she wore, she lifted it, making the movements a lazy striptease. The bikini underneath covered little more than a stripper's G-string and pasties would have.

Dropping the thin cotton, she shook her head, skimmed her hair back with both hands, then walked with a siren's swagger of hips into the sea.

Giff let the next wave roll over him. He knew that every movement, every gesture Lexy made was deliberate. It didn't seem to make any difference. He couldn't take his eyes off her, couldn't prevent his body from going tight and hard and needy as she stood there, all luscious curves and pale gold skin, with her hair spiraling down like sun-kissed flames.

As she walked into the water, and it moved up her

body, he imagined what it would be like to rock himself inside her to the rhythm of the waves. She was watching him too, he noted, her eyes picking up the green of the sea, and laughing.

She dipped down, rose up again with her hair shiny and wet, water sliding off her skin. And she laughed out loud.

"Water's cold today," she called out. "And a little rough."

"You don't usually come in till June."

"Maybe I wanted it cold today." She let the wave carry her closer. "And rough."

"It'll be colder and rougher tomorrow," he told her. "Rain's coming."

"Mmm." She floated on her back a moment, studying the pale blue sky. "Maybe I'll come back." Letting her feet sink, she began to tread water as she watched him.

She'd grown accustomed to his dark brown eyes watching her like a puppy when they were teenagers. They were the same age, had grown up all but shoulder to shoulder, but she noticed there had been a few changes in him during her year in New York.

His face had fined down, and his mouth seemed firmer and more confident. The long lashes that had caused the boys to tease him mercilessly in his youth no longer seemed feminine. His light brown hair was needle-straight and streaked from the sun. When he smiled at her, dimples—another curse of his youth—dented his cheeks.

"See something interesting?" he asked her.

"I might." His voice matched his face, she decided. All grown-up and male. The flutter in her stomach was satisfying, and unexpectedly strong. "I just might."

"I figure you had a reason for swimming out here mostly naked. Not that I didn't enjoy the view, but you want to tell me what it is? Or do you want me to guess?"

She laughed, kicking against the current to keep a teasing distance between them. "Maybe I just wanted to cool off."

"I imagine so." He smiled back, satisfied that he understood her better than she could ever imagine. "I heard Jo came in on the morning ferry."

The smile slid away from her face and left her eyes cold. "So what?"

"So, you want to blow off some steam? Want to use me to do it?" When she hissed at him and started to kick out to swim back to shore, he merely nipped her by the waist. "I'll oblige you," he said as she tried to wiggle free. "I've been wanting to anyway."

"Get your hands—" The end of her demand was lost in a surprised grunt against his mouth. She'd never expected reliable Giff Verdon to move so quickly, or so decisively.

She hadn't realized his hands were so big, or so hard, or that his mouth would be so . . . sexy as it crushed down on hers with the cool tang of the sea clinging to it. For form's sake she shoved against him, but ruined it with a throaty little moan as her lips parted and invited more.

She tasted exactly as he'd imagined—hot and ready, the sex kitten mouth slippery and wet. The fantasies he'd woven for over ten years simply fell apart and reformed in fresh, wild colors threaded with helpless love and desperate need.

When she wrapped her legs around his waist, rocked her body against his, he was lost.

"I want you." He tore his mouth from hers to race it along her throat while the waves tossed them about and into a tangle of limbs. "Damn you, Lex, you know I've always wanted you."

Water flowed over her head, filled it with roaring. The sea sucked her down, made her giddy. Then she was in the dazzling sunlight again with his mouth fused to hers.

"Now, then. Right now." She panted it out, amazed at how real the need was, that tight, hot little ball of it. "Right here."

He'd wanted her like this as long as he could remember. Ready and willing and eager. His body pulsed toward pain with the need to be in her, and of her. And he knew if he let that need rule, he would take her and lose her in one flash.

Instead he slid his hands down from her waist to cup and knead her bottom, used his thumbs to torment her until her eyes went dark and blind. "I've waited, Lex." And let her go. "So can you."

She struggled to stay above the waves, sputtered out water as she gaped at him. "What the hell are you talking about?"

"I'm not interested in scratching your itch and then watching you walk off purring." He lifted a hand to push back his dripping hair. "When you're ready for more than that, you know where to find me."

"You son of a bitch."

"You go work off your mad, honey. We'll talk when you've had time to think it through calm." His hand shot out, grabbed her arm. "When I make love with you, that's going to be it for both of us. You'll want to think about that too."

She shoved his hand away. "Don't you touch me again, Giff Verdon."

"I'm going to do more than touch you," he told her as she dove under to swim toward shore. "I'm going to marry you," he said, only loud enough for his own ears. He let out a long breath as he watched her stride out of the water. "Unless I kill myself first."

To ease the throbbing in his system, he sank under the water. But as the taste of her continued to cling to his mouth, he decided he was either the smartest man on Desire or the stupidest.

Jo had just drummed up the energy to take a walk and had reached the edges of the garden when Lexy stormed up the path. She hadn't bothered to towel off, so the little sundress was plastered against her like skin. Jo straightened her shoulders, lifted an eyebrow.

"Well, how's the water?"

"Go to hell." Breath heaving, humiliation still stinging, Lexy planted her feet. "Just go straight to hell."

"I'm beginning to think I've already arrived. And so far my welcome's been pretty much as expected."

"Why should you expect anything? This place means nothing to you and neither do we."

"How do you know what means anything to me, Lexy?"

"I don't see you changing sheets, clearing tables. When's the last time you scrubbed a toilet or mopped a damn floor?"

"Is that what you've been doing this afternoon?" Jo skimmed her gaze up Lexy's damp and sandy legs to her dripping hair. "Must have been some toilet."

"I don't have to explain myself to you."

"Same goes, Lex." When Jo started to move past, Lexy grabbed her arm and jerked.

"Why did you come back here?"

Weariness swamped her suddenly, made her want to weep. "I don't know. But it wasn't to hurt you. It wasn't to hurt anybody. And I'm too tired to fight with you now."

Baffled, Lexy stared at her. The sister she knew would have waded in with words, scraped flesh with sarcasm. She'd never known Jo to tremble and back off. "What happened to you?"

"I'll let you know when I figure it out." Jo shook off the hand blocking her. "Leave me alone, and I'll do the same for you."

She walked quickly down the path, took its curve toward the sea. She barely glanced at the dune swale with its glistening grasses, never looked up to follow the flight of the gull that called stridently. She needed to think, she told herself. Just an hour or two of quiet thought. She would figure out what to do, how to tell them. If she should tell them at all.

Could she tell them about her breakdown? Could she tell anyone that she'd spent two weeks in the hospital because her nerves had snapped and something in her mind had tilted? Would they be sympathetic, ambivalent, or hostile?

And what did it matter?

How could she tell them about the photograph? No matter how often she was at sword's point with them, they were her family. How could she put them through that, dredging up the pain and the past? And if any of them demanded to see it, she would have to tell them it was gone.

Just like Annabelle.

Or it had never existed.

They would think her mad. Poor Jo Ellen, mad as a hatter.

Could she tell them she'd spent days trembling inside her apartment, doors locked, after she'd left the hospital? That she would catch herself searching mindlessly, frantically, for the print that would prove she wasn't really ill?

And that she had come home, because she'd finally had to accept that she was ill. That if she had stayed locked in that apartment alone for another day, she would never have found the courage to leave it again.

Still, the print was so clear in her mind. The texture, the tones, the composition. Her mother had been young in the photograph. And wasn't that the way Jo remembered her—young? The long waving hair, the smooth skin? If she was going to hallucinate about her mother, wouldn't she have snapped to just that age?

Nearly the same age she herself was now, Jo thought. That was probably another reason for all the dreams, the fears, the nerves. Had Annabelle been as restless and as edgy as her daughter was? Had there been a lover after all? There had been whispers of that, even a child had been able to hear them. There'd been no hint of one, no suspicion of infidelity before the desertion. But afterward the rumors had been rife, and tongues had clucked and wagged.

But then, Annabelle would have been discreet, and clever. She had given no hint of her plans to leave, yet she had left.

Wouldn't Daddy have known? Jo wondered. Surely a man knew if his wife was restless and dissatisfied and unhappy. She knew they had argued over the island. Had that been enough to do it, to make Annabelle so unhappy that she would turn her back on her home, her husband, her children? Hadn't he seen it, or had he even then been oblivious to the feelings of the people around him?

It was so hard to remember if it had ever been different. But surely there had once been laughter in that house. Echoes of it still lingered in her mind. Quick snapshots of her parents embracing in the kitchen, of her mother laughing, of walking on the beach with her father's hand holding hers.

They were dim pictures, faded with time as if improperly fixed, but they were there. And they were real. If she had managed to block so many memories of her mother out of her mind, then she could also bring them back. And maybe she would begin to understand.

Then she would decide what to do.

The crunch of a footstep made her look up quickly. The sun was behind him, casting him in shadow. A cap shielded his eyes. His stride was loose and leggy.

Another long-forgotten picture snapped into her mind. She saw herself as a little girl with flyaway hair racing down the path, giggling, calling, then leaping high. And his arms had reached out to catch her, to toss her high, then hug her close.

Jo blinked the picture away and the tears that wanted to come with it. He didn't smile, and she knew that no matter how she worked to negate it, he saw Annabelle in her.

She lifted her chin and met his eyes. "Hello, Daddy."

"Jo Ellen." He stopped a foot away and took her measure. He saw that Kate had been right. The girl looked ill, pale, and strained. Because he didn't know how to touch her, didn't believe she would welcome the touch in any case, he dipped his hands into his pockets. "Kate told me you were here."

"I came in on the morning ferry," she said, knowing the information was unnecessary.

For a difficult moment they stood there, more awkward than strangers. Sam shifted his feet. "You in trouble?"

"I'm just taking some time off."

"You look peaked."

"I've been working too hard."

Frowning, he looked deliberately at the camera hanging from a strap around her neck. "Doesn't look like you're taking time off to me."

In an absent gesture, she cupped a hand under the camera. "Old habits are hard to break."

"They are that." He huffed out a breath. "There's a pretty light on the water today, and the waves are up. Guess it'd make a nice picture."

"I'll check it out. Thanks."

"Take a hat next time. You'll likely burn."

"Yes, you're right. I'll remember."

He could think of nothing else, so he nodded and started up the path, moving past her. "Mind the sun."

"I will." She turned away quickly, walking blindly now because she had smelled the island on him, the rich, dark scent of it, and it broke her heart.

Miles away in the hot red glow of the darkroom light, he slipped paper, emulsion side up, into a tray of developing fluid. It pleased him to re-create the moment from so many years before, to watch it form on the paper, shadow by shadow and line by line.

He was nearly done with this phase and wanted to linger, to draw out all the pleasure before he moved on.

He had driven her back to Sanctuary. The idea made him chuckle and preen. Nothing could have been more perfect. It was there that he wanted her. Otherwise he would have taken her before, half a dozen times before.

But it had to be perfect. He knew the beauty of perfection and the satisfaction of working carefully toward creating it.

Not Annabelle, but Annabelle's daughter. A perfect circle closing. She would be his triumph, his masterpiece.

Claiming her, taking her, killing her.

And every stage of it would be captured on film. Oh, how Jo would appreciate that. He could barely wait to explain it all to her, the one person he was certain would understand his ambition and his art.

Her work drew him, and his understanding of it made him feel intimate with her already. And they would become more intimate yet.

Smiling, he shifted the print from the developing tray to the stop bath, swishing it through before lifting it into the fixer. Carefully, he checked the temperature of the wash, waiting patiently until the timer rang and he could switch on the white light and examine the print.

Beautiful, just beautiful. Lovely composition. Dramatic lighting—such a perfect halo over the hair, such lovely shadows to outline the body and highlight skin tones. And the subject, he thought. Perfection.

When the print was fully fixed, he lifted it out of the tray and into the running water of the wash. Now he could allow himself to dream of what was to come.

He was closer to her than ever, linked to her through the photographs that reflected each of their lives. He could barely wait to send her the next. But he knew he must choose the time with great care.

On the worktable beside him a battered journal lay open, its precisely written words faded from time.

The decisive moment is the ultimate goal in my work. Capturing that short, passing event where all the elements, all the dynamics of a subject reach a peak. What more decisive moment can there be than death? And how much more control can the photographer have over this moment, over the capturing of it on film, than to plan and stage and cause that death? That single act joins subject and artist, makes him part of the art, and the image created.

Since I will kill only one woman, manipulate only one decisive moment, I have chosen her with great care.

Her name is Annabelle.

With a quiet sigh, he hung the print to dry and turned on the white light to better study it.

"Annabelle," he murmured. "So beautiful. And your daughter is the image of you."

He left Annabelle there, staring, staring, and went out to complete his plans for his stay on Desire.

FIVE

❦

THE FERRY STEAMED ACROSS
Pelican Sound, heading east to Lost Desire. Nathan Delaney stood at the starboard rail as he had once before as
a ten-year-old boy. It wasn't the same ferry, and he was
no longer a boy, but he wanted to re-create the moment
as closely as possible.

It was cool with the breeze off the water, and the scent
of it was raw and mysterious. It had been warmer before,
but then it had been late May rather than mid-April.

Close enough, he thought, remembering how he and his
parents and his young brother had all crowded together at
the starboard rail of another ferry, eager for their first
glimpse of Desire and the start of their island summer.

He could see little difference. Spearing up from the land
were the majestic live oaks with their lacy moss, cabbage
palms, and glossy-leaved magnolias not yet in bloom.

Had they been blooming then? A young boy eager for
adventure paid little attention to flowers.

He lifted the binoculars that hung around his neck. His
father had helped him aim and focus on that long-ago
morning so that he could catch the quick dart of a wood-

69

pecker. The expected tussle had followed because Kyle had demanded the binoculars and Nathan hadn't wanted to give them up.

He remembered his mother laughing at them, and his father bending down to tickle Kyle to distract him. In his mind, Nathan could see the picture they had made. The pretty woman with her hair blowing, her dark eyes sparkling with amusement and excitement. The two young boys, sturdy and scrubbed, squabbling. And the man, tall and dark, long of leg and rangy of build.

Now, Nathan thought, he was the only one left. Somehow he had grown up into his father's body, had gone from sturdy boy to a man with long legs and narrow hips. He could look in a mirror and see reflections of his father's face in the hollow cheeks and dark gray eyes. But he had his mother's mouth, firmly ridged, and her deep brown hair with hints of gold and red. His father had said it was like aged mahogany.

Nathan wondered if children were really just montages of their parents. And he shuddered.

Without the binoculars he watched the island take shape. He could see the wash of color from wildflowers— pinks and violets from lupine and wood sorrel. A scatter of houses was visible, a few straight or winding roads, the flash of a creek that disappeared into the trees. Mystery was added by the dark shadows of the forest where feral pigs and horses had once lived, the gleam of the marshes and the blades of waving grasses gold and green in the streaming morning sunlight.

It was all hazed with distance, like a dream.

Then he saw the gleam of white on a rise, the quick wink that was sun shooting off glass. Sanctuary, he thought, and kept it in his sights until the ferry turned toward the dock and the house was lost from view.

Nathan turned from the rail and walked back to his Jeep. When he was settled inside with only the hum of the ferry's engines for company, he wondered if he was crazy coming back here, exploring the past, in some ways repeating it.

He'd left New York, packed everything that mattered into the Jeep. It was surprisingly little. Then again, he'd never had a deep-seated need for things. That had made his life simpler through the divorce two years before. Maureen had been the collector, and it saved them both a great deal of time and temper when he offered to let her strip the West Side apartment.

Christ knew she'd taken him up on it and had left him with little more than his own clothes and a mattress.

That chapter of his life was over, and for nearly two years now he'd devoted himself to his work. Designing buildings was as much a passion as a career for him, and with New York as no more than a home base, he had traveled, studying sites, working wherever he could set up his drawing board and computer. He'd given himself the gift of time to study other buildings, explore the art of them, from the great cathedrals in Italy and France to the streamlined desert homes in the American Southwest.

He'd been free, his work the only demand on his time and on his heart.

Then he had lost his parents, suddenly, irrevocably. And had lost himself. He wondered why he felt he could find the pieces on Desire.

But he was committed to staying at least six months. Nathan took it as a good sign that he'd been able to book the same cottage his family had lived in during that summer. He knew he would listen for the echo of their voices and would hear them with a man's ear. He would see their ghosts with a man's eyes.

And he would return to Sanctuary with a man's purpose.

Would they remember him? The children of Annabelle?

He would soon find out, he decided, when the ferry bumped up to the dock.

He waited his turn, watching as the blocks were removed from the tires of the pickup ahead of him. A family of five, he noted, and from the gear he could see that they would be camping at the facility the island provided. Nathan shook his head, wondering why anyone would choose to sleep in a tent on the ground and consider it a vacation.

The light dimmed as clouds rolled over the sun. Frowning, he noted that they were coming in fast, flying in from the east. Rain could come quickly to barrier islands, he knew. He remembered it falling in torrents for three endless days when he'd been there before. By day two he and Kyle had been at each other's throats like young wolves.

It made him smile now and wonder how in God's name his mother had tolerated it.

He drove slowly off the ferry, then up the bumpy, pitted road leading away from the dock. With his windows open he could hear the cheerfully blaring rock and roll screaming out of the truck's radio. Camper Family, he thought, was already having a great time, impending rain or not. He was determined to follow their example and enjoy the morning.

He would have to face Sanctuary, of course, but he would approach it as an architect. He remembered that its heart was a glorious example of the Colonial style—wide verandas, stately columns, tall, narrow windows. Even as a child he'd been interested enough to note some of the details.

Gargoyle rainspouts, he recalled, that personalized rather than detracted from the grand style. He'd scared the piss out of Kyle by telling him they came alive at night and prowled.

There was a turret, with a widow's walk circling it. Balconies jutting out with ornate railings of stone or iron. The chimneys were soft-hued stones mined from the mainland, the house itself fashioned of local cypress and oak.

There was a smokehouse that had still been in use, and slave quarters that had been falling to ruin, where he and Brian and Kyle had found a rattler curled in a dark corner.

There were deer in the forest and alligators in the marshes. Whispers of pirates and ghosts filled the air. It was a fine place for young boys and grand adventures. And for dark and dangerous secrets.

He passed the western marshlands with their busy mud and thin islands of trees. The wind had picked up, sending the cordgrass rippling. Along the edge two egrets were on patrol, their long legs like stilts in the shallow water.

Then the forest took over, lush and exotic. Nathan slowed, letting the truck ahead of him rattle out of sight. Here was stillness, and those dark secrets. His heart began to pound uncomfortably, and his hands tightened on the wheel. This was something he'd come to face, to dissect, and eventually to understand.

The shadows were thick, and the moss dripped from the trees like webs of monstrous spiders. To test himself he turned off the engine. He could hear nothing but his own heartbeat and the voice of the wind.

Ghosts, he thought. He would have to look for them there. And when he found them, what then? Would he leave them where they drifted, night after night, or would they continue to haunt him, muttering to him in his sleep?

Would he see his mother's face, or Annabelle's? And which one would cry out the loudest?

He let out a long breath, caught himself reaching for the cigarettes he'd given up over a year before. Annoyed, he turned the ignition key but got only a straining rumble in return. He pumped the gas, tried it again with the same results.

"Well, shit," he muttered. "That's perfect."

Sitting back, he tapped his fingers restlessly on the wheel. The thing to do, of course, was to get out and look under the hood. He knew what he would see. An engine. Wires and tubes and belts. Nathan figured he knew as much about engines and wires and tubes as he did about brain surgery. And being broken down on a deserted road was exactly what he deserved for letting himself be talked into buying a friend's secondhand Jeep.

Resigned, he climbed out and popped the hood. Yep, he thought, just as he'd suspected. An engine. He leaned in, poked at it, and felt the first fat drop of rain hit his back.

"Now it's even more perfect." He shoved his hands in the front pockets of his jeans and scowled, continued to scowl while the rain pattered on his head.

He should have known something was up when his friend had cheerfully tossed in a box of tools along with the Jeep. Nathan considered hauling them out and beating on the engine with a wrench. It was unlikely to work, but it would at least be satisfying.

He stepped back, then froze as the ghost stepped out of the forest shadows and watched him.

Annabelle.

The name swam through his mind, and his gut clenched in defense. She stood in the rain, still as a doe, her smoky red hair damp and tangled, those big blue eyes quiet and sad. His knees threatened to give way, and he braced a hand on the fender.

Then she moved, pushed back her wet hair. And started toward him. He saw then that it was no ghost, but a woman. It was not Annabelle, but, he was sure, it was Annabelle's daughter.

He let out the breath he'd been holding until his heart settled again.

"Car trouble?" Jo tried to keep her voice light. The way he was staring at her made her wish she'd stayed in the trees and let him fend for himself. "I take it you're not standing here in the rain taking in the sights."

"No." It pleased him that his voice was normal. If there was an edge to it, the situation was cause enough to explain it. "It won't start."

"Well, that's a problem." He looked vaguely familiar, she thought. A good face, strong and bony and male. Interesting eyes as well, she mused, pure gray and very direct. If she were inclined to portrait photography, he'd have been a fine subject. "Did you find the trouble?"

Her voice was honey over cream, gorgeously southern. It helped him relax. "I found the engine," he said and smiled. "Just where I suspected it would be."

"Uh-huh. And now?"

"I'm deciding how long I should look at it and pretend I know what I'm looking at before I get back in out of the rain."

"You don't know how to fix your car?" she asked, with such obvious surprise that he bristled.

"No, I don't. I also own shoes and don't have a clue how to tan leather." He started to yank down the hood, but she raised a hand to hold it open.

"I'll take a look."

"What are you, a mechanic?"

"No, but I know the basics." Elbowing him aside, she checked the battery connections first. "These look all right, but you're going to want to keep an eye on them for corrosion if you're spending any time on Desire."

"Six months or so." He leaned in with her. "What am I keeping my eye on?"

"These. Moisture can play hell with engines around here. You're crowding me."

"Sorry." He shifted his position. Obviously she didn't remember him, and he decided to pretend he didn't remember her. "You live on the island?"

"Not anymore." To keep from bumping it on the Jeep, Jo moved the camera slung around her neck to her back.

Nate stared at it, felt the low jolt. It was a high-end Nikon. Compact, quieter and more rugged than other designs, it was often a professional's choice. His father had had one. He had one himself.

"Been out taking pictures in the rain?"

"Wasn't raining when I left," she said absently. "Your fan belt's going to need replacing before long, but that's not your problem now." She straightened, and though the skies had opened wide, seemed oblivious to the downpour. "Get in and try it so I can hear what she sounds like."

"You're the boss."

Her lips twitched as he turned and climbed back into the Jeep. No doubt his male ego was dented, she decided. She cocked her head as the engine groaned. Lips pursed, she leaned back under the hood. "Again!" she called out to him, muttering to herself. "Carburetor."

"What?"

"Carburetor," she repeated and opened the little metal door with her thumb. "Turn her over again."

This time the engine roared to life. With a satisfied nod, she shut the hood and walked around to the driver's side window. "It's sticking closed, that's all. You're going to want to have it looked at. From the sound of it, you need a tune-up anyway. When's the last time you had it in?"

"I just bought it a couple of weeks ago. From a former friend."

"Ah. Always a mistake. Well, it should get you where you're going now."

When she started to step back, he reached through the window for her hand. It was narrow, he noted, long, both elegant and competent. "Listen, let me give you a lift. It's pouring, and it's the least I can do."

"It's not necessary. I can—"

"I could break down again." He shot her a smile, charming, easy, persuasive. "Who'll fix my carburetor?"

It was foolish to refuse, she knew. More foolish to feel trapped just because he had her hand. She shrugged. "All right, then." She gave her hand a little tug, was relieved when he immediately released it. She jogged around the Jeep and climbed dripping into the passenger seat.

"Well, the interior's in good shape."

"My former friend knows me too well." Nathan turned on the wipers and looked at Jo. "Where to?"

"Up this road, then bear right at the first fork. Sanctuary isn't far—but then nothing is on Desire."

"That's handy. I'm heading to Sanctuary myself."

"Oh?" The air in the cab was thick and heavy. The driving rain seemed to cut them off from everything, misting out the trees, muffling all the sound. Reason enough to be uncomfortable, she told herself, but she was sufficiently annoyed with her reaction to angle her head and meet his eyes directly. "Are you staying at the big house?"

"No, just picking up keys for the cottage I'm renting."

"For six months, you said?" It relieved her when he began to drive, turned those intense gray eyes away from her face and focused on the road. "That's a long vacation."

"I brought work with me. I wanted a change of scene for a while."

"Desire's a long way from home," she said, then smiled a little when he glanced at her. "Anyone from Georgia can spot a Yankee. Even if you keep your mouth shut, you move differently." She pushed her wet hair back. If she'd walked, Jo thought, she'd have been spared making conversation. But talk was better than the heavy, rain-drenched silence. "You've got Little Desire Cottage, by the river."

"How do you know?"

"Oh, everybody knows everything around here. But my family rents the cottages, runs them and the inn, the restaurant. As it happens I was assigned Little Desire, stocked the linens and so forth just yesterday for the Yankee who's coming to stay for six months."

"So you're my mechanic, landlord, and housekeeper. I'm a lucky man. Who exactly do I call if my sink backs up?"

"You open the closet and take out the plunger. If you

need instructions for use, I'll write them down for you. Here's the fork.''

Nathan bore right and climbed. "Let's try that again. If I wanted to grill a couple of steaks, chill a bottle of wine, and invite you to dinner, who would I call?''

Jo turned her head and gave him a cool look. "You'd have better luck with my sister. Her name is Alexa.''

"Does she fix carburetors?''

With a half laugh, Jo shook her head. "No, but she's very decorative and enjoys invitations from men.''

"And you don't?''

"Let's just say I'm more selective than Lexy.''

"Ouch.'' Whistling, Nathan rubbed a hand over his heart. "Direct hit.''

"Just saving us both some time. There's Sanctuary,'' she murmured.

He watched it appear through the curtain of rain, swim out of the thin mists that curled at its base. It was old and grand, as elegant as a Southern Belle dressed for company. Definitely feminine, Nate thought, with those fluid lines all in virginal white. Tall windows were softened by arched trim, and pretty ironwork adorned balconies where flowers bloomed out of clay pots of soft red.

Her gardens glowed, the blooms heavy-headed with rain, like bowing fairies at her feet.

"Stunning,'' Nathan said, half to himself. "The more recent additions blend perfectly with the original structure. Accent rather than modernize. It's a masterful harmony of styles, classically southern without being typical. It couldn't be more perfect if the island had been designed for it rather than it being designed for the island.''

Nathan stopped at the end of the drive before he noticed that Jo was staring at him. For the first time there was curiosity in her eyes.

"I'm an architect,'' he explained. "Buildings like this grab me right by the throat.''

"Well, then, you'll probably want a tour of the inside.''

"I'd love one, and I'd owe you at least one steak dinner for that."

"You'll want my cousin Kate to show you around. She's a Pendleton," Jo added as she opened her door. "Sanctuary came down through the Pendletons. She knows it best. Come inside. You can dry off some and pick up the keys."

She hurried up the steps, paused on the veranda to shake her head and scatter rain from her hair. She waited until he stepped up beside her.

"Jesus, look at this door." Reverently, Nathan ran his fingertips over the rich, carved wood. Odd that he'd forgotten it, he thought. But then, he had usually raced in through the screened porch and through the kitchen.

"Honduran mahogany," Jo told him. "Imported in the early eighteen-hundreds, long before anyone worried about depleting the rain forests. But it is beautiful." She turned the heavy brass handle and stepped with him into Sanctuary.

"The floors are heart of pine," she began and blocked out an unbidden image of her mother patiently paste-waxing them. "As are the main stairs, and the banister is oak carved and constructed here on Desire when it was a plantation, dealing mostly in Sea Island cotton. The chandelier is more recent, an addition purchased in France by the wife of Stewart Pendleton, the shipping tycoon who rebuilt the main house and added the wings. A great deal of the furniture was lost during the War Between the States, but Stewart and his wife traveled extensively and selected antiques that suited them and Sanctuary."

"He had a good eye," Nathan commented, scanning the wide, high-ceilinged foyer with its fluid sweep of glossy stairs, its glittering fountain of crystal light.

"And a deep pocket," Jo put in. Telling herself to be patient, she stood where she was and let him wander.

The walls were a soft, pale yellow that would give the illusion of cool during those viciously hot summer after-

noons. They were trimmed in dark wood that added rich-
ness with carved moldings framing the high plaster
ceiling.

The furnishings here were heavy and large in scale, as
befitted a grand entranceway. A pair of George II arm-
chairs with shell-shaped backs flanked a hexagonal cre-
dence table that held a towering brass urn filled with
sweetly scented lilies and wild grasses.

Though he didn't collect antiques himself—or anything
else, for that matter—he was a man who studied all as-
pects of buildings, including what went inside them. He
recognized the Flemish cabinet-on-stand in carved oak,
the giltwood pier mirror over a marquetry candle stand,
the delicacy of Queen Anne and the flash of Louis XIV.
And he found the mix of periods and styles inspired.

"Incredible." His hands tucked in his back pockets, he
turned back to Jo. "Hell of a place to live, I'd say."

"In more ways than one." Her voice was dry, and just
a little bitter. It had him lifting a brow in question, but
she added nothing more. "We do registration in the front
parlor."

She turned down the hallway, stepped into the first
room on the right. Someone had started a fire, she observed, probably in anticipation of the Yankee, and to
keep the guests at the inn cheerful on a rainy day if they
wandered through.

She went to the huge old Chippendale writing desk and
opened the top side drawer, flipped through the paperwork
for the rental cottages. Upstairs in the family wing was
an office with a workaday file cabinet and a computer
Kate was still struggling to learn about. But guests were
never subjected to such drearily ordinary details.

"Little Desire Cottage," Jo announced, sliding the contract free. She noted it had already been stamped to in-
dicate receipt of the deposit and signed by both Kate and
one Nathan Delaney.

Jo laid the paperwork aside and opened another drawer

to take out the keys jingling from a metal clip that held the cottage name. "This one is for both the front and the rear doors, and the smaller one is for the storage room under the cottage. I wouldn't store anything important in there if I were you. Flooding is a hazard that near the river."

"I'll remember that."

"I took care of setting up the telephone yesterday. All calls will be billed directly to the cottage and added to your bill monthly." She opened another drawer and took out a slim folder. "You'll find the usual information and answers in this packet. The ferry schedule, tide information, how to rent fishing or boating gear if you want it. There's a pamphlet that describes the island—history, flora and fauna—Why are you staring at me like that?" she demanded.

"You've got gorgeous eyes. It's hard not to look at them."

She shoved the folder into his hands. "You'd be better off looking at what's in here."

"All right." Nathan opened it, began to page through. "Are you always this jittery, or do I bring that out in you?"

"I'm not jittery, I'm impatient. Not all of us are on vacation. Do you have any questions—that pertain to the cottage or the island?"

"I'll let you know."

"Directions to your cottage are in the folder. If you'd just initial the contract here, to confirm receipt of the keys and information, you can be on your way."

He smiled again, intrigued at how rapidly her southern hospitality was thinning. "I wouldn't want to wear out my welcome," he said, taking the pen she offered him. "Since I intend to come back."

"Breakfast, lunch, and dinner are served in the inn's dining room. The service hours are also listed in your folder. Box lunches are available for picnics."

The more she talked, the more he enjoyed hearing her voice. She smelled of rain and nothing else and looked—when you looked into those lovely blue eyes—as sad as a bird with a broken wing.

"Do you like picnics?" he asked her.

She let out a long sigh, snatched the pen back from him, and scrawled her initials under his. "You're wasting your time flirting with me, Mr. Delaney. I'm just not interested."

"Any sensible woman knows that a statement like that only presents a challenge." He bent down to read her initials, "J.E.H."

"Jo Ellen Hathaway," she told him in hopes of hurrying him along.

"It's been a pleasure being rescued by you, Jo Ellen." He offered a hand, amused when she hesitated before clasping it with hers.

"Try Zeke Fitzsimmons about that tune-up. He'll get the Jeep running smoothly for you. Enjoy your stay on Desire."

"It's already started on a higher note than I'd expected."

"Then your expectations must have been very low." She slid her hand free and led the way back to the front door. "The rain's let up," she commented, as she opened the door to moist air and mist. "You shouldn't have any trouble finding the cottage."

"No." He remembered the way perfectly. "I'm sure I won't. I'll see you again, Jo Ellen." Will have to, he thought, for a number of reasons.

She inclined her head, shut the door quietly, and left him standing on the veranda wondering what to do next.

SIX

On HIS THIRD DAY ON DE-
sire, Nathan woke in a panic. His heart was booming, his
breath short and strangled, his skin iced with sweat. He
shot up in bed with fists clenched, his eyes searching the
murky shadows of the room.

Weak sunlight filtered through the slats of the blinds
and built a cage on the thin gray carpet.

His mind stayed blank for an agonizing moment,
trapped behind the images that crowded it. Moonlit trees,
fingers of fog, a woman's naked body, her fanning dark
hair, wide, glassy eyes.

Ghosts, he told himself as he rubbed his face hard with
his hands. He'd expected them, and they hadn't disappointed him. They clung to Desire like the moss clung to
the live oaks.

He swung out of bed and deliberately—like a child
daring sidewalk cracks—walked through the sun bars. In
the narrow bathroom he stepped into the white tub,
yanked the cheerfully striped curtain closed, and ran the
shower hot. He washed the sweat away, imagined the

panic as a dark red haze that circled and slid down the drain.

The room was thick with steam when he dried off. But his mind was clear again.

He dressed in a tattered short-sleeved sweatshirt and ancient gym shorts, then with his face unshaven and his hair dripping headed into the kitchen to heat water for instant coffee. He looked around, scowled again at the carafe and drip cone the owners had provided. Even if he could have figured out the proper measuring formula, he hadn't thought to bring coffee filters.

At that moment he would have paid a thousand dollars for a coffeemaker. He set the kettle on the front burner of a stove that was older than he was, then walked over to the living room section of the large multipurpose room to flip on the early news. The reception was miserable, and the pickings slim.

No coffeemaker, no pay-per-view, Nathan mused as he tuned in the sunrise news on one of the three available channels. He remembered how he and Kyle had whined over the lack of televised entertainment.

How are we supposed to watch The Six Million Dollar Man *on this stupid thing? It's a gyp.*

You're not here to keep your noses glued to the TV screen.

Aw, Mom.

It seemed to him the color scheme was different now. He had a vague recollection of soft pastels on the wide, deep chairs and straight-backed sofa. Now they were covered in bold geometric prints, deep greens and blues, sunny yellows.

The fan that dropped from the center pitch of the ceiling had squeaked. He knew, because he'd been compelled to tug on the cord, that it ran now with only a quiet hiss of blades.

But it was the same long yellow-pine dining table separating the rooms—the table he and his family had gathered around to eat, to play board games, to put together eye-crossingly complex jigsaw puzzles during that summer.

The same table he and Kyle had been assigned to clear after dinner. The table where his father had lingered some mornings over coffee.

He remembered when their father had shown him and Kyle how to punch holes in the lid of a jar and catch lightning bugs. The evening had been warm and soft, the hunt and chase giddy. Nathan remembered watching the jar he'd put beside his bed wink and glow, wink and glow, lulling him to sleep.

But in the morning all the lightning bugs in his jar had been dead, smothered, as the book atop the lid had plugged all the holes. He still couldn't remember putting it there, that battered copy of *Johnny Tremaine*. The dark corpses in the bottom of the jar had left him feeling sick and guilty. He'd snuck out of the house and dumped them in the river.

He chased no more lightning bugs that summer.

Irritated at the memory, Nathan turned away from the TV, went back to the stove to pour the steaming water over a spoonful of coffee. He carried the mug out onto the screened porch to look at the river.

Memories were bound to surface now that he was here, he reminded himself. That was why he'd come. To remember that summer, step by step, day by day. And to figure out what to do about the Hathaways.

He sipped coffee, winced a little at its false and bitter taste. He'd discovered that a great deal of life was false and bitter, so he drank again.

Jo Ellen Hathaway. He remembered her as a skinny, sharp-elbowed girl with a sloppy ponytail and a lightning temper. He hadn't had much use for girls at ten, so he'd paid her little attention. She'd simply been one of Brian's little sisters.

Still was, Nathan thought. And she was still skinny.

Apparently her temper was still in place as well. The
streaming ponytail was gone. The shorter, choppy cut
suited her personality if not her face, he decided. The
carelessness of it, the nod to fashion. The color of it was
like the pelt of a wild deer.

He wondered why she looked so pale and tired. She
didn't seem the type to pine away over a shattered affair
or relationship, but something was hurting. Her eyes were
full of sorrow and secrets.

And that was the problem, Nathan thought with a half
laugh. He had a weakness for sad-eyed women.

Better to resist it, he told himself. Wondering what was
going on behind those big, sad, bluebell eyes was bound
to interfere with his purpose. What he needed was time
and objectivity before he took the next step.

He sipped more coffee, told himself he'd get dressed
shortly and walk to Sanctuary for a decent cup and some
breakfast. It was time to go back, to observe and to plan.
Time to stir more ghosts.

But for now he just wanted to stand here, look through
the thin mesh of screen, feel the damp air, watch the sun
slowly burn away the pearly mists that clung to the
ground and skimmed like fairy wings over the river.

He could hear the ocean if he listened for it, a low,
constant rumble off to the east. Closer he could identify
the chirp of birds, the monotonous drumming of a woodpecker hunting insects somewhere in the shadows of the
forest. Dew glistened like shards of glass on the leaves of
cabbage palms and palmettos, and there was no wind to
stir them and make them rattle.

Whoever chose this spot for the cottage chose well, he
thought. It sang of solitude, offered view and privacy. The
structure itself was simple and functional. A weathered
cedar box on stilts with a generous screened porch on the
west end, a narrow open deck on the east. Inside, the main
room had a pitched ceiling to add space and an open feel.
On each end were two bedrooms and a bath.

He and Kyle had each had a room in one half. As the elder, he laid claim to the larger room. The double bed made him feel very grown-up and superior. He made a sign for the door: Please Knock Before Entering.

He liked to stay up late, reading his books, thinking his thoughts, listening to the murmur of his parents' voices or the drone of the TV. He liked to hear them laugh at something they were watching.

His mother's quick chuckle, his father's deep belly laugh. He'd heard those sounds often throughout his childhood. It grieved him that he would never hear them again.

A movement caught his eye. Nathan turned his head, and where he'd expected a deer he saw a man, slipping along the river bank like the mist. He was tall and lanky, his hair dark as soot.

Because his throat had gone dry, Nathan forced himself to lift his mug and drink again. He continued to watch as the man walked closer, as the strengthening sun slanted over his face.

Not Sam Hathaway, Nathan realized as the beginnings of a smile tugged at his lips. Brian. Twenty years had made them both men.

Brian glanced up, squinted, focused on the figure behind the screen. He'd forgotten the cottage was occupied now and made a note to himself to remember to take his walks on the opposite side of the river. Now, he supposed, he would have to make some attempt at conversation.

He lifted a hand. "Morning. Didn't mean to disturb you."

"You didn't. I was just drinking bad coffee and watching the river."

The Yankee, Brian remembered, a six-month rental. He could all but hear Kate telling him to be polite, to be sociable. "It's a nice spot." Brian stuck his hands in his pockets, annoyed that he'd inadvertently sabotaged his own solitude. "You settling in all right?"

"Yeah, I'm settled." Nathan hesitated, then took the next step. "Are you still hunting the Ghost Stallion?"

Brian blinked, cocked his head. The Ghost Stallion was a legend that stretched back to the days when wild horses had roamed the island. It was said that the greatest of these, a huge black stallion of unparalleled speed, ran the woods. Whoever caught him, leaped onto his back, and rode would have all his wishes granted.

Throughout childhood it had been Brian's deepest ambition to be the one to catch and ride the Ghost Stallion.

"I keep an eye out for him," Brian murmured and stepped closer. "Do I know you?"

"We camped out one night, across the river, in a patched pup tent. We had a rope halter, a couple of flashlights, and a bag of Fritos. Once we thought we heard hooves pounding, and a high, wild whinny." Nathan smiled. "Maybe we did."

Brian's eyes widened and the shadows in them cleared away. "Nate? Nate Delaney? Son of a bitch!"

The screen door squeaked in welcome when Nathan pushed it open. "Come on up, Bri. I'll fix you a cup of lousy coffee."

Grinning, Brian climbed up the stairs. "You should have let me know you were coming, that you were here." Brian shot out a hand, gripped Nathan's. "My cousin Kate handles the cottages. Jesus, Nate, you look like a derelict."

With a rueful smile, Nathan rubbed a hand over the stubble on his chin. "I'm on vacation."

"Well, ain't this a kick in the ass. Nate Delaney." Brian shook his head. "What the hell have you been doing all these years? How's Kyle, your parents?"

The smile faltered. "I'll tell you about it." Pieces of it, Nathan thought. "Let me make that lousy coffee first."

"Hell, no. Come on up to the house. I'll fix you a decent cup. Some breakfast."

"All right. Let me get some pants and shoes on."

"I can't believe you're our Yankee," Brian commented as Nathan started inside. "Goddamn, this takes me back."

Nathan turned back briefly. "Yeah, me too."

A short time later Nathan was sitting at the kitchen counter of Sanctuary, breathing in the heavenly scents of coffee brewing and bacon frying. He watched Brian deftly chopping mushrooms and peppers for an omelette.

"Looks like you know what you're doing."

"Didn't you read your pamphlet? My kitchen has a five-star rating." Brian slid a mug of coffee under Nathan's nose. "Drink, then grovel."

Nathan sipped, closed his eyes in grateful pleasure. "I've been drinking sand for the last two days and that may be influencing me, but I'd say this is the best cup of coffee ever brewed in the civilized world."

"Damn right it is. Why haven't you come up before this?"

"I've been getting my bearings, being lazy." Getting acquainted with ghosts, Nathan thought. "Now that I've sampled this, I'll be a regular."

Brian tossed his chopped vegetables into a skillet to sauté, then began grating cheese. "Wait till you get a load of my omelette. So what are you, independently wealthy that you can take six months off to sit on the beach?"

"I brought work with me. I'm an architect. As long as I have my computer and my drawing board, I can work anywhere."

"An architect." Whisking eggs, Brian leaned against the counter. "You any good?"

"I'd put my buildings against your coffee any day."

"Well, then." Chuckling, Brian turned back to the stove. With the ease of experience he poured the egg mixture, set bacon to drain, checked the biscuits he had browning in the oven. "So what's Kyle up to? He ever get rich and famous like he wanted?"

It was a stab, hard and fast in the center of the heart.

Nathan put the mug down and waited for his hands and voice to steady. "He was working on it. He's dead, Brian. He died a couple of months ago."

"Jesus, Nathan." Shocked, Brian swung around. "Jesus, I'm sorry."

"He was in Europe. He'd been more or less living there the last couple of years. He was on a yacht, some party. Kyle liked to party," Nathan murmured, rubbing his temple. "They were tooling around the Med. The verdict was he must have had too much to drink and fallen overboard. Maybe he hit his head. But he was gone."

"That's rough. I'm sorry." Brian turned back to his skillet. "Losing family takes a chunk out of you."

"Yeah, it does." Nathan drew a deep breath, braced himself. "It happened just a few weeks after my parents were killed. Train wreck in South America. Dad was on assignment, and ever since Kyle and I hit college age, Mom traveled with him. She used to say it made them feel like newlyweds all the time."

"Christ, Nate, I don't know what to say."

"Nothing." Nathan lifted his shoulders. "You get through. I figure Mom would have been lost without Dad, and I don't know how either one of them would have handled losing Kyle. You've got to figure everything happens for a reason, and you get through."

"Sometimes the reason stinks," Brian said quietly.

"A whole hell of a lot of the time the reason stinks. Doesn't change anything. It's good to be back here. It's good to see you."

"We had some fine times that summer."

"Some of the best of my life." Nathan worked up a smile. "Are you going to give me that omelette, or are you going to make me beg for it?"

"No begging necessary." Brian arranged the food on a plate. "Genuflecting afterward is encouraged."

Nathan picked up a fork and dug in. "So, fill me in on

the last two decades of the adventures of Brian Hathaway.''

''Not much of an adventure. Running the inn takes a lot of time. We get guests year-round now. Seems the more crowded and busy life in the outside world gets, the more people want to get the hell away from it. For weekends, anyhow. And when they do, we house them, feed them, entertain them.''

''It sounds like a twenty-four/seven proposition.''

''Would be, on the outside. Life still moves slower around here.''

''Wife, kids?''

''Nope. You?''

''I had a wife,'' Nathan said dryly. ''We gave each other up. No kids. You know, your sister checked me in. Jo Ellen.''

''Did she?'' Brian brought the pot over to top off Nathan's cup. ''She just got here herself about a week ago. Lex is here, too. We're one big happy family.''

As Brian turned away, Nathan lifted his eyebrows at the tone. ''Your dad?''

''You couldn't dynamite him off Desire. He doesn't even go over to the mainland for supplies anymore. You'll see him wandering around.'' He glanced over as Lexy swung through the door.

''We've got a couple of early birds panting for coffee,'' she began. Then, spotting Nathan, she paused. Automatically she flipped back her hair, angled her head, and aimed a flirtatious smile. ''Well, kitchen company.'' She strolled closer to pose against the counter and give him a whiff of the Eternity she'd rubbed on her throat from a magazine sample that morning. ''You must be special if Brian's let you into his domain.''

Nathan's hormones did the quick, instinctive dance that made him want to laugh at both of them. A gorgeous piece of fluff was his first impression, but he revised it when he took a good look into her eyes. They were sharp and very self-aware. "He took pity on an old friend," Nathan told her.

"Really." She liked the rough-edged look of him, and pleased herself by basking in the easy male approval on his face. "Well, then, Brian, introduce me to your old friend. I didn't know you had any."

"Nathan Delaney," Brian said shortly, going over to fetch the second pot of freshly brewed coffee. "My kid sister, Lexy."

"Nathan." Lexy offered a hand she'd manicured in Flame Red. "Brian still sees me in pigtails."

"Big brother's privilege." It surprised Nathan to find the siren's hand firm and capable. "Actually, I remember you in pigtails myself."

"Do you?" Mildly disappointed that he hadn't lingered over her hand, Lexy folded her elbows on the bar and leaned toward him. "I can't believe I've forgotten you. I make it a policy to remember all the attractive men who've come into my life. However briefly."

"You were barely out of diapers," Brian put in, his voice dripping sarcasm, "and hadn't polished your femme-fatale routine yet. Cheese and mushroom omelettes are the breakfast special," he told her, ignoring the vicious look she shot in his direction.

She caught herself before she snarled, made her lips curve up. "Thanks, sugar." She purred it as she took the coffeepot he thrust at her, then she fluttered her lashes at Nathan. "Don't be a stranger. We get so few interesting men on Desire."

Because it seemed foolish to resist the treat, and she seemed so obviously to expect it, Nathan watched her sashay out, then turned back to Brian with a slow grin. "That's some baby sister you've got there, Bri."

"She needs a good walloping. Coming on to strange men that way."

"It was a nice side dish with my omelette." But Nathan held up a hand as Brian's eyes went hot. "Don't worry

about me, pal. That kind of heartthrob means major headaches. I've got enough problems. You can bet your ass
I'll look, but I don't plan to touch."

"None of my business," Brian muttered. "She's bound
and determined not just to look for trouble but to find it."

"Women who look like that usually slide their way out
of it too." He swiveled when the door opened again. This
time it was Jo who walked through it.

And women who look like that, Nathan thought, don't
slide out of trouble. They punch their way out.

He wondered why he preferred that kind of woman,
and that kind of method.

Jo stopped when she saw him. Her brows drew together
before she deliberately smoothed her forehead. "You look
right at home, Mr. Delaney."

"Feeling that way, Miss Hathaway."

"Well, that's pretty formal," Brian commented as he
reached for a clean mug, "for a guy who pushed her into
the river, then got a bloody lip for his trouble when he
tried to fish her out again."

"I didn't push her in." Nathan smiled slowly as he
watched Jo's brows knit again. "She slipped. But she did
bloody my lip and call me a Yankee pig bastard, as I
recall."

The memory circled around her mind, nearly skipped
away, then popped clear. Hot summer afternoon, the
shock of cool water, head going under. And coming up
swinging. "You're Mr. David's boy." The warmth spread
in her stomach and up to her heart. For a moment her
eyes reflected it and made his pulse trip. "Which one?"

"Nathan, the older."

"Of course." She skimmed her hair back, not with the
studied seductiveness of her sister but with absentminded
impatience. "And you did push me. I never fell in the
river unless I wanted to or was helped along."

"You slipped," Nathan corrected, "then I helped you
along."

She laughed, a quick, rich chuckle, then took the mug Brian offered. "I suppose I can let bygones be, since I gave you a fat lip—and your father gave me the world."

Nathan's head began to throb, fast and vicious. "My father?"

"I dogged him like a shadow, pestered him mercilessly about how he took pictures, why he took the ones he did, how the camera worked. He was so patient with me. I must have been driving him crazy, interrupting his work that way, but he never shooed me away. He taught me so much, not just the basics but how to look and how to see. I suppose I owe him for every photograph I've ever taken."

The breakfast he'd just eaten churned greasily in his stomach. "You're a professional photographer?"

"Jo's a big-deal photographer," Lexy said with a bite in her voice as she came back in. "The globe-trotting J. E. Hathaway, snapping her pictures of other people's lives as she goes. Two omelettes, Brian, two sides of hash browns, one bacon, one sausage. Room 201's having breakfast, Miss World Traveler. You've got beds to strip."

"Exit, stage left," Jo murmured when Lexy strode out again. "Yes," she said, turning back to Nathan. "Thanks in large part to David Delaney, I'm a photographer. If it hadn't been for Mr. David, I might be as frustrated and pissed off at the world as Lexy. How is your father?"

"He's dead," Nathan said shortly and pushed himself up from the stool. "I've got to get back. Thanks for breakfast, Brian."

He went out fast, letting the screen door slam behind him.

"Dead? Bri?"

"An accident," Brian told her. "About three months ago. Both his parents. And he lost his brother about a month later."

"Oh, God." Jo ran a hand over her face. "I put my foot in that. I'll be back in a minute."

She set the mug down and raced out the door to chase Nathan down. "Nathan! Nathan, wait a minute." She caught him on the shell path that wound through the garden toward the trees. "I'm sorry." She put a hand on his arm to stop him. "I'm so sorry I went on that way."

He pulled himself in, fought to think clearly over the pounding in his temples. "It's all right. I'm still a little raw there."

"If I'd known—" She broke off, shrugged her shoulders helplessly. She'd likely have put her foot in it anyway, she decided. She'd always been socially clumsy.

"You didn't." Nathan clamped down on his own nerves and gave the hand still on his arm a light squeeze. She looked so distressed, he thought. And she'd done nothing more than accidentally scrape an open wound. "Don't worry about it."

"I wish I'd managed to keep in touch with him." Her voice went wistful now. "I wish I'd made more of an effort so I could have thanked him for everything he did for me."

"Don't." He bit the word off, swung around to her with his eyes fierce and cold. "Thanking someone for where your life ended up is the same as blaming them for it. We're all responsible for ourselves."

Uneasy, she backed off a step. "True enough, but some people influence what roads we take."

"Funny, then, that we're both back here, isn't it?" He stared beyond her to Sanctuary, where the windows glinted in the sun. "Why are you back here, Jo?"

"It's my home."

He looked back at her, pale cheeks, bruised eyes. "And that's where you come when you feel beat up and lost and unhappy?"

She folded her arms across her chest as if chilled. She,

usually the observer, didn't care to be observed quite so clear-sightedly. "It's just where you go."

"It seems we decided to come here at almost the same time. Fate? I wonder—or luck." He smiled a little because he was going to go with the latter.

"Coincidence." She preferred it. "Why are you back here?"

"Damned if I know." He exhaled between his teeth, then looked at her again. He wanted to soothe that sorrow and worry from her eyes, hear that laugh again. He was suddenly very certain it would ease his soul as much as hers. "But since I am, why don't you walk me back to the cottage?"

"You know the way."

"It'd be a nicer walk with company. With you."

"I told you I'm not interested."

"I'm telling you I am." His smile deepened as he reached up to tuck a stray lock of hair behind her ear. "It'll be fun seeing who nudges who to the other side."

Men didn't flirt with her. Ever. Or not that she had ever noticed. The fact that he was doing just that, and she noticed, only irritated her. The inherent Pendleton Fault Line dug between her brows. "I've got work to do."

"Right. Bed stripping in 201. See you around, Jo Ellen."

Because he turned away first, she had the opportunity to watch him walk into the trees. Deliberately she shook her hair so that it fell over her ears again. Then she rolled her shoulders as if shrugging off an unwelcome touch.

But she was forced to admit she was already more interested than she wanted to be.

SEVEN

NATHAN TOOK A CAMERA
with him. He felt compelled to retrace some of his father's
footsteps on Desire—or perhaps to eradicate them. He
chose the heavy old medium-range Pentax, one of his father's favorites and surely, he thought, one that David
Delaney had brought to the island with him that summer.

He would have brought the bulky Hasselblad view
camera as well, and the clever Nikon, along with a collection of lenses and filters and a mountain of film. Nathan
had brought them all, and they were neatly stored, as his
father had taught him, back at the cottage.

But when his father hiked out to hunt a shot, he would
most usually take the Pentax.

Nathan chose the beach, with its foaming waves and
diamond sand. He slipped on dark glasses against the
fierce brilliance of the sun and climbed onto the marked
path between the shifting dunes, with their garden of sea
oats and tangle of railroad vines. The wind kicked in from
the sea and sent his hair flying. He stood at the crest of
the path, listening to the beat of the water, the smug
squeal of gulls that wheeled and dipped above it.

Shells the tide had left behind were scattered like pretty toys along the sand. Tiny dunes whisked up by the wind were already forming behind them. The busy sanderlings were rushing back and forth in the spume, like businessmen hustling to the next meeting. And there, just behind the first roll of water, a trio of pelicans flew in military formation, climbing and wheeling as a unit. One would abruptly drop, a dizzying headfirst dive into the sea, and the others would follow. A trio of splashes, then they were up again, breakfast in their beaks.

With the ease of experience, Nathan lifted his camera, widened the aperture, increased the shutter speed to catch the motion, then homed in on the pelicans, following, following as they skimmed the wave crests, rose into their climb. And capturing them on the next bombing dive.

He lowered the camera, smiled a little. Over the years he'd gone long stretches of time without indulging in his hobby. He planned to make up for it now, spending at least an hour a day reacquainting himself with the pleasure and improving his eye.

He couldn't have asked for a more perfect beginning. The beach was inhabited only by birds and shells. His footprints were the only ones to mar the sand. That was a miracle in itself, he thought. Where else could a man be so entirely alone, borrow for a while this kind of beauty, along with peace and solitude?

He needed those things now. Miracles, beauty, peace. Cupping a hand over the camera, Nathan walked down the incline to the soft, moist sand of the beach. He crouched now and then to examine a shell, to trace the shape of a starfish with a fingertip.

But he left them where he found them, collecting them only on film.

The air and the exercise helped settle the nerves that had jangled before he'd left Sanctuary. She was a photographer, Nathan thought, as he studied a pretty, weather-silvered cottage peeking out from behind the dunes. Had his father known that the little girl he'd played mentor to one summer had gone on to follow in his footsteps? Would he have cared? Been proud, amused?

He could remember when his father had first shown him the workings of a camera. The big hands had covered his small ones, gently, patiently guiding. The smell of aftershave on his father's cheeks, a sharp tang. Brut. Yes, Brut. Mom had liked that best. His father's cheek had been smoothly shaven, pressed against his. His dark hair would have been neatly combed, smooth bumps of waves back from the forehead, his clear gray eyes soft and serious.

Always respect your equipment, Nate. You may want to make a living from the camera one day. Travel the world on it and see everything there is to see. Learn how to look and you'll see more than anyone else. Or you'll be something else, do something else, and just use it to take moments away with you. Vacations, family. They'll be your moments, so they'll be important. Respect your equipment, learn to use it right, and you'll never lose those moments.

"How many did we lose, anyway?" Nathan wondered aloud. "And how many do we have tucked away that we'd be better off losing?"

"Excuse me?"

Nathan jerked when the voice cut through the memory, when a hand touched his arm. "What?" He took a quick step in retreat, half expecting one of his own ghosts. But he saw a pretty, delicately built blonde staring up at him through amber-tinted lenses.

"Sorry. I startled you." She tilted her head, and her eyes stayed focused, unblinking, on his face. "Are you all right?"

"Yeah." Nathan dragged a hand through his hair, ignored the uncomfortably loose sensation in his knees. Less easily ignored was the acute embarrassment as the woman continued to study him as if he were some alien smear on a microscope slide. "I didn't know anyone else was around."

"Just finishing up my morning run," she told him, and he noted for the first time that she wore a sweat-dampened gray T-shirt over snug red bike shorts. "That's my cottage you were staring at. Or through."

"Oh." Nathan ordered himself to focus on it again, the silvered cedar shakes, the sloping brown roof with its jut of open deck for sunning. "You've got a hell of a view."

"The sunrises are the best. You're sure you're all right?" she asked again. "I'm sorry to poke, but when I see a guy standing alone on the beach looking as if he'd just been slapped with a two-by-four and talking to himself, I've got to wonder. It's my job," she added.

"Beach police?" he said dryly.

"No." She smiled, held out a friendly hand. "Doctor. Doctor Fitzsimmons. Kirby. I run a clinic out of the cottage."

"Nathan Delaney. Medically sound. Didn't an old woman used to live there? A tiny woman with white hair up in a bun."

"My grandmother. Did you know her? You're not a native."

"No, no, I remember, or have this impression of her. I spent a summer here as a kid. Memories keep popping out at me. You just walked into one."

"Oh." The eyes behind the amber lenses lost their clinical shrewdness and warmed. "That explains it. I know just what you mean. I spent several summers here growing up, and memories wing up at me all the time. That's why I decided to relocate here when Granny died. I always loved it here."

Absently, she grabbed her toe, bending her leg back, heel to butt, to stretch out. "You'd be the Yankee who's taken Little Desire Cottage for half a year."

"Word travels."

"Doesn't it just? Especially when it doesn't have far

to go. We don't get many single men renting for six months. A number of the ladies are intrigued.'' Kirby repeated the process on the other leg. ''You know, I think I might remember you. Wasn't it you and your brother who palled around with Brian Hathaway? I remember Granny saying how those Delaney boys and young Brian stuck together like a dirt clod.''

''Good memory. You were here that summer?''

''Yes, it was my first summer on Desire. I suppose that's why I remember it best. Have you seen Brian yet?'' she asked casually.

''He just fixed me breakfast.''

''Magic in an egg.'' It was Kirby's turn to look past the cottage, beyond it. ''I heard Jo's back. I'm going to try to get up to the house after the clinic closes today.'' She glanced at her watch. ''And since it opens in twenty minutes, I'd better go get cleaned up. It was nice seeing you again, Nathan.''

''Nice seeing you. Doc,'' he added as she began to jog toward the dunes.

With a laugh, she turned, jogged backward. ''General practice,'' she called out. ''Everything from birth to earth. Come in for what ails you.''

''I'll keep it in mind.'' He smiled and watched her ponytail swing sassily as she ran through the valley between the dunes.

Nineteen minutes later, Kirby put on a white lab coat over her Levi's. She considered the coat a kind of costume, designed to reassure the reluctant patient that she was indeed a doctor. That and the stethoscope tucked in its pocket gave the islanders the visual nudge many of them needed to let Granny Fitzsimmons's little girl poke into their orifices.

She stepped into her office, formerly her grandmother's well-stocked pantry off the kitchen. Kirby had left one wall of shelves intact, to hold books and papers and the clever little combo fax and copy machine that kept her linked with the mainland. She'd removed the other shelves, since she had no plans to follow her grandmother's example and put by everything from stewed tomatoes to watermelon pickles.

She'd muscled the small, lovingly polished cherrywood desk into the room herself. It had traveled with her from Connecticut, one of the few pieces she'd brought south. It was outfitted with a leather-framed blotter and appointment book that had been a parting gift from her baffled parents.

Her father had grown up on Desire and considered himself fortunate to have escaped.

She knew both of her parents had been thrilled when she'd decided to follow in her father's footsteps and go into medicine. And they had assumed she would continue to follow, into his cardiac surgery specialty, into his thriving practice, and right along to the platinum-edged lifestyle both of them so enjoyed.

Instead she'd chosen family practice, her grandmother's weather-beaten cottage, and the simplicity of island life.

She couldn't have been happier.

Tidily arranged with the appointment book that bore her initials in gold leaf were a snazzy phone system with intercom—in the unlikely event that she should ever need an assistant—and a Lucite container of well-sharpened Ticonderoga pencils.

Kirby had spent her first few weeks of practice doing little more than sharpening pencils and wearing them down again by doodling on the blotter.

But she'd stuck, and gradually she'd begun to use those pencils to note down appointments. A baby with the croup, an old woman with arthritis, a child spiking a fever with roseola.

It had been the very young or the very old who'd trusted her first. Then others had come to have their stitches sewn, the aches tended, their stomachs soothed.

Now she was Doc Kirby, and the clinic was holding its own.

Kirby scanned her appointment book. An annual gyn, a follow-up on a nasty sinus infection, the Matthews boy had another earache, and the Simmons baby was due in for his next immunizations. Well, her waiting room wasn't going to be crowded, but at least she'd keep busy through the morning. And who knew, she thought with a chuckle, there could be a couple of emergencies to liven up the day.

Since Ginny Pendleton was her gyn at ten o'clock, Kirby calculated she had at least another ten minutes. Ginny was invariably late for everything. Pulling the necessary chart, she stepped back into the kitchen, poured the last of the coffee from the pot she'd made early that morning, and took it with her to the examining room.

The room where she'd once dreamed away summer nights was now crisp and clean. She had posters of wildflowers on the white walls rather than the pictures of nervous systems and ear canals that some doctors decorated with. Kirby thought they made patients jumpy.

After sliding the chart into the holder inside the door, she took out one of the backless cotton gowns—she thought paper gowns humiliating—and laid it out on the foot of the examining table. She hummed along with the quiet Mozart sonata from the stereo she'd switched on. Even those who eschewed classical would invariably relax to it, she'd found.

She'd arranged everything she'd need for the basic yearly exam and had finished off her coffee when she heard the little chime that meant the door at the clinic entrance had opened.

"Sorry, sorry," Ginny came in on the run as Kirby stepped into the living room that served as the waiting area. "The phone rang just as I was leaving."

She was in her middle twenties, and Kirby was continually telling her that her fondness for the sun was going to haunt her in another ten years. Her hair was white-blond, shoulder-length, frizzed mercilessly, and crying out for a root job.

Ginny came from a family of fishermen, and though she could pilot a boat like a grinning pirate, clean a fish like a surgeon, and shuck oysters with dizzying speed and precision, she preferred working at the Heron Campground, helping the novice pitch a tent, assigning sites, keeping the books.

For her doctor's appointment, she'd spruced herself up with one of her favored western shirts in wild-plum purple with white fringe. Kirby wondered with idle curiosity how many internal organs were gasping for oxygen beneath the girdle-tight jeans.

"I'm always late." Ginny sent her a sunny, baffled smile that made Kirby laugh.

"And everyone knows it. Go ahead in and pee in the bottle first. You know the routine. Then go into the exam room. Take everything off, put the gown on opening to the front. Just give a holler when you're ready."

"Okay. It was Lexy on the phone," she called out as she scurried down the hall in her cowboy boots and shut the door. "She's feeling restless."

"Usually is," Kirby replied.

Ginny continued chatting as she left the bathroom and turned into the exam room.

"Anyway, Lexy's going to come down to the campground tonight about nine o'clock." There was a thud as the first boot hit the floor. "Number twelve is free. It's one of my favorites. We thought we'd build us a nice fire, knock off a couple of six-packs. Wanna come?"

"I appreciate the offer." There was another thud. "I'll think about it. If I decide to come by, I'll bring another six-pack."

"I wanted her to ask Jo, but you know how huffy Lex gets. Hope she will, though." Ginny's voice was breathless, leading Kirby to imagine she was peeling herself out of the jeans. "You seen her yet? Jo?"

"No. I'm going to try to catch her sometime today."

"Do them good to sit down and tie one on together. Don't know why Lexy's so pissed off at Jo. Seems to be pissed off at everybody, though. She went on about Giff too. If I had a man who looked like Giff eyeing me up one side and down the other the way he does her, I wouldn't be pissed off at anything. And I'm not saying that because we're cousins. Fact is, if we weren't blood-related, I'd jump his bones in a New York minute. All set in here."

"I'd give odds Giff will wear her down," Kirby commented, taking out the chart as she came in. "He's got a stubborn streak as wide as hers. Let's check your weight. Any problems, Ginny?"

"Nope, been feeling fine." Ginny stepped on the scale and firmly shut her eyes. "Don't tell me what it is."

Chuckling, Kirby tapped the weight up the line. One thirty. One thirty-five. Whoops, she thought. One forty-two.

"Have you been exercising regularly, Ginny?"

Eyes still tightly shut, Ginny shifted from side to side. "Sort of."

"Aerobics, twenty minutes, three times a week. And cut back on the candy bars." Because she was female as well as a doctor, Kirby obligingly zeroed out the scale before Ginny opened her eyes. "Hop up on the table, we'll check your blood pressure."

"I keep meaning to watch that Jane Fonda tape. What do you think about lipo?"

Kirby snugged on the BP cuff. "I think you should take a brisk walk on the beach a few times a week and imagine carrot sticks are Hershey bars for a while. You'll lose that extra five pounds without the Hoover routine. BP's good. When was your last period?"

"Two weeks ago. It was almost a week late, though. Scared the shit out of me."

"You're using your diaphragm, right?"

Ginny folded her arms over her middle, tapped her fingers. "Well, most of the time. It's not always convenient, you know."

"Neither is pregnancy."

"I always make the guy condomize. No exceptions. There's a couple of really cute ones camped at number six right now."

Sighing, Kirby snapped on her gloves. "Casual sex equals dangerous complications."

"Yeah, but it's so damn much fun." Ginny smiled up at the dreamy Monet poster Kirby had tacked to the ceiling. "And I always fall in love with them a little. Sooner or later, I'm going to come across the big one. The right one. Meantime, I might as well sample the field."

"Minefield," Kirby muttered. "You're selling yourself short."

"I don't know." Trying to imagine herself walking through those misty flowers in the poster, Ginny tapped her many-ringed fingers on her midriff. "Haven't you ever seen a guy and just wanted him so bad everything inside you curled up and shivered?"

Kirby thought of Brian, caught herself before she sighed again. "Yeah."

"I just love when that happens, don't you? I mean it's so . . . primal, right?"

"I suppose. But primal and inconvenience aside, I want you using that diaphragm."

Ginny rolled her eyes. "Yes, doctor. Oh, hey, speaking of men and sex, Lexy says she got a load of the Yankee and he is prime beef."

"I got a load of him myself," Kirby replied.

"Was she right?"

"He's very attractive." Gently, Kirby lifted one of Ginny's arms over her head and began the breast exam.

"Turns out he's an old friend of Bri's—spent a summer here with his parents. His father was that photographer who did the picture book on the Sea Islands way back. My mother's still got a copy."

"The photographer. Of course. I'd forgotten that. He took pictures of Granny. He made a print and matted it, sent it to her after he left. I still have it in my bedroom."

"Ma got the book out this morning when I told her. It's really nice," Ginny added as Kirby helped her sit up. "There's one of Annabelle Hathaway and Jo gardening at Sanctuary. Ma remembered he took the pictures the summer Annabelle ran off. So I said maybe she ran off with the photographer, but Ma said he and his wife and kids were still on the island after she left."

"It was twenty years ago. You'd think people would forget and leave it alone."

"The Pendletons are Desire," Ginny pointed out. "Annabelle was a Pendleton. And nobody ever forgets anything on the island. She was really beautiful," she added, scooting off the table. "I don't remember her very well, but seeing the picture brought it back some. Jo would look like that if she put some effort into it."

"I imagine Jo prefers to look like Jo. You're healthy, Ginny, go ahead and get dressed. I'll meet you outside when you're done."

"Thanks. Oh, and Kirby, try to make it by the campground. We'll make it a real girls' night out. Number twelve."

"We'll see."

At four, Kirby closed the clinic. Her only emergency walk-in had been a nasty case of sunburn on a vacationer who'd fallen asleep on the beach. She'd spent fifteen minutes after her last patient sprucing up her makeup, brushing her hair, dabbing on fresh perfume.

She told herself it was for her own personal pleasure, but as she was heading over to Sanctuary, she knew that was a lie. She was hoping she looked fresh enough, smelled good enough, to make Brian Hathaway suffer.

She took the beach door. Kirby loved that quick, shocking thrill of seeing the ocean so near her own home. She watched a family of four playing in the shallows and caught the high music of the children's laughter over the hum of the sea.

She slipped on her sunglasses and trotted down the steps. The narrow boardwalk she'd had Giff build led her around the house, away from the dunes. Rising out of the sand was a stand of cypress, bent and crippled by the wind that even now blew sand around her ankles. Bushes of bayberry and beach elder grew in the trough. She added her own tracks to those that crisscrossed the sand.

She circled the edges of the dune swale, islander enough to know and respect its fragility. In moments, she had left the hot brilliance of sand and sea for the cool, dim cave of the forest.

She walked quickly, not hurrying, but simply with her mind set on her destination. She was used to the rustles and clicks of the woods, the shifts of sound and light. So she was baffled when she found herself stopping, straining her ears and hearing her own heart beating fast and high in her throat.

Slowly, she turned in a circle, searching the shadows. She'd heard something, she thought. Felt something. She could feel it now, that crawling sensation of being watched.

"Hello?" She hated herself for trembling at the empty echo of her own voice. "Is someone there?"

The rattle of fronds, the rustle that could be deer or rabbit, and the heavy silence of thickly shaded air. Idiot, she told herself. Of course there was no one there. And if there were, what would it matter? She turned back, continued down the well-known path and ordered herself to walk at a reasonable pace.

Sweat snaked cold down the center of her back, and

her breath began to hitch. She clamped down on the rising fear and swung around again, certain she would catch a flash of movement behind her. There was nothing but twining branches and dripping moss.

Damn it, she thought and rubbed a hand over her speeding heart. Someone was there. Crouched behind a tree, snugged into a shadow. Watching her. Just kids, she assured herself. Just a couple of sneaky kids playing tricks.

She walked backward, her eyes darting side to side. She heard it again, just a faint, stealthy sound. She tried to call out again, make some pithy comment on rude children, but the terror that had leaped into her throat snapped it closed. Moving on instinct, she turned and increased her pace.

When the sound came closer, she abandoned all pride and broke into a run.

And the one who watched her snickered helplessly into his hands, then blew a kiss at her retreating back.

Her breath heaving, Kirby pounded through the trees, sneakers slapping the path in a wild tattoo. She gulped in a sob as she saw the light change, brighten, then flash as she burst out of the trees. She looked back over her shoulder, prepared to see some monster leaping out behind her.

And screamed when she ran into a solid wall of chest and arms banded tight around her.

"What's wrong? What happened?" Brian nearly picked her up in his arms, but she clamped hers around him and burrowed. "Are you hurt? Let me see."

"No, no, I'm not hurt. A minute. I need a minute."

"Okay. All right." He gentled his hold and stroked her hair. He'd been yanking at weeds on the outer edge of the garden when he'd heard the sounds of her panicked race through the forest. He'd just taken the first steps forward to investigate when she shot out of the trees and dead into him.

Now her heart was thudding against his, and his own was nearly matching its rhythm. She'd scared the life out of him—that wild-animal look in her eyes when she jerked her head around as if expecting to be attacked from behind.

"I got spooked," she managed and clung like a burr. "It was just kids. I'm sure it was just kids. It felt like I was being stalked, hunted. It was just kids. It spooked me."

"It's all right now. Catch your breath." She was so small, he thought. Delicate back, tiny waist, silky hair. Hardly aware of it, he gathered her closer. It was odd that she should fit against him so well and at the same time seem fragile enough for him to pick up and tuck safely in his pocket.

Christ, she smelled good. He lowered his cheek to the top of her head for a moment, indulged in the scent and texture of her hair as he slowly stroked the tension out of her neck.

"I don't know why I panicked that way. I never panic." And because the sensation was subsiding, she became gradually aware that he was holding her. Very close. That his hands were moving over her. Very smoothly. His lips were in her hair. Very softly.

Her slowing heart rate kicked up again, but this time it had nothing to do with panic.

"Brian." She murmured it, ran her hands up his back as she lifted her head.

"You're all right now. You're okay." And before he knew what he was doing, his mouth was on hers.

It was like a fist in the gut, a breath-stealing blow that sent his brain reeling and buckled his knees. Then her lips were parting under his, so warm and smooth, with sexy little purrs slipping between them and into his mouth.

He went deeper, nipping her tongue, then soothing it while his hands slid down over snug denim to mold her bottom and angle heat against heat.

She stopped thinking the instant his mouth took over hers. The novelty of that experience was a separate, giddy thrill. Always she'd been able to separate her intellect, to somehow step outside herself in a way, to direct and control the event. But now she was swirled into it, lapped by sensation after sensation.

His mouth was hot and hungry, his body hard, his hands big and demanding. For the first time in her life, she truly felt delicate, as though she could be snapped in two at his whim.

For reasons she couldn't understand, the sensation was unbearably arousing. Murmuring his name against his busy mouth, she hooked her hands over the back of his shoulders. Her head tipped back limply. For the first time with a man she teetered on the brink of absolute and unquestioning surrender.

It was the change, the sudden pliancy, the helpless little moan, that snapped him back. He'd dragged her up to her toes, his fingers were digging into her flesh, and the single image that had lodged in his mind was that of taking her on the ground.

In his mother's garden, for Christ's sake. In the daylight. In the shadow of his own home. Disgusted with both of them, Brian jerked her out to arm's length.

"That's what you wanted, wasn't it?" he said furiously. "You went to a lot of trouble to prove I'm as weak as the next guy."

Colors were still swimming in her head. "What?" She blinked to clear her vision. "What?"

"The damsel-in-distress routine worked. Score one for your side."

She came back to earth with a thud. His eyes were as hard and hot as his mouth had been, but with passion of a different sort. When his words and the meaning behind them registered, her own widened with shocked indignation.

"Do you honestly believe I staged this, made a fool of myself just so you'd kiss me? You arrogant, conceited, self-important son of a bitch!" Insulted to the core, she shoved him away. "I don't have routines, and I'm not now nor will I ever be a damsel of any sort. And furthermore, kissing you is not a major goal in my life."

She pushed her tousled hair back, squared her shoulders. "I came here to see Jo, not you. You just happened to be in the way."

"I suppose that's why you jumped into my arms and wrapped yourself around me like a snake."

She drew a breath, determined to cloak herself in calm and dignity. "The problem here, Brian, is that you wanted to kiss me, and you enjoyed it. Now you have to blame me, accuse me of perpetrating some ridiculous female ruse, because you want to kiss me again. You want to get your hands on me the way you just had them on me, and for some reason that really ticks you off. But that's your problem. I came here to see Jo."

"She's not here," Brian said between his teeth. "She's out with her cameras somewhere."

"Well, then, you just give her a message for me. Heron Campground, nine o'clock, site twelve. Girls' night out. Think you can remember that, or do you want to write it down?"

"I'll tell her. Anything else?"

"No, not a thing." She turned, then hesitated. Pride or no, she simply couldn't face going back into the trees alone just yet. She shifted directions and headed down the shell path. It would more than double the distance home, she thought, but a good sweaty walk would help her work off her temper.

Brian frowned at her back, then into the woods. He had a sudden and certain feeling that none of what had just happened had been a pretense. And that, he decided, made him not only a fool but a nasty one.

"Hold on, Kirby, I'll give you a ride back."

"No, thanks."

"Damn it, I said hold on." He caught up with her, took

her arm, and was stunned by the ripe fury on her face when she whirled around.

"I'll let you know when I want you to touch me, Brian, and I'll let you know when I want anything from you. In the meantime . . ." She jerked free. "I'll take care of myself."

"I'm sorry." He cursed himself even as he said it. He hadn't meant to. And the raised-eyebrow, wide-eyed look she sent him made him wish he'd sawed off his tongue first.

"I beg your pardon, did you say something?"

Too late to back out, he thought, and swallowed the bitter pill. "I said I'm sorry. I was out of line. Let me drive you home."

She inclined her head, regally, he thought, and her smile was smug. "Thank you. I'd appreciate it."

EIGHT

"YOU WERE SUPPOSED TO bring a six-pack, not fancy wine, big shot." Already disposed to complain, Lexy loaded her sleeping bag and gear into Jo's Land Rover.

"I like wine." Jo kept her voice mild and her sentences short.

"I don't know why you want to spend the night dishing in the woods anyway." Lexy scowled at Jo's tidily rolled and top-grade sleeping bag. Always the best for Jo Ellen, she thought sourly, then shoved her two six-packs of Coors into the cargo area. "No piano bar, no room service, no fawning maître d'."

Jo thought of the nights she'd spent in a tent, in second-rate motels, shivering in the cab of her four-wheeler. Anything to get the shot. She muscled in the bag of groceries she'd begged off of Brian, shoved her hair back. "I'll survive somehow."

"I set this up, you know. I set it up because I wanted to get the hell away from here for one night. I wanted to relax with friends. My friends."

Jo slammed the rear door, clenched her teeth as the

115

sound echoed like a gunshot. It would be easier to walk
away, she thought. Just turn around and go back into the
house and leave Lexy to find her own way to the campground.

Damned if she was going to take the easy way.

"Ginny's my friend too, and I haven't seen Kirby in
years." Leaving it at that, she circled around to the
driver's side, climbed behind the wheel, and waited.

The pleasant anticipation she'd felt when Brian had re-
layed Kirby's invitation had disappeared, leaving a churning pit in her stomach. But she was determined to follow
through, not to be chased away by her sister's bitchiness.

She was bound to have a miserable time now, but by
God she was going. And so, she thought when her sister
slammed in beside her, was Lexy.

"Seat belt," Jo ordered, and Lexy let out an exasperated huff of breath as she strapped in. "Listen, why don't
we just get drunk and pretend we can tolerate each other
for one night? An actress of your astonishing range
shouldn't have any trouble with that."

Lexy cocked her head, aimed a brilliant smile. "Fuck
you, sister dear."

"There you go." Jo started the engine, reaching for a
cigarette out of habit the minute it turned over.

"Would you not smoke in the car?"

Jo punched in the lighter. "My car."

She headed north, her tires singing musically on the
shell road. The air rushing in the windows was a beautiful
balm. She used it to soothe her raw nerves and made no
complaint when Lexy turned the stereo up full blast. Loud
music meant no conversation, and no conversation meant
no arguments. At least for the drive to camp.

She drove fast, the memory of every curve in the road
coming back to her. That too, soothed. So little had
changed. Dark still fell quickly here, and the night brought
the sounds of wind and sea that made the island seem a

huge place to her. A world where the tides ruled depend-ably.

She remembered driving fast along this road with the wind rushing through her hair and the radio screaming. Lexy had been beside her then too.

The spring before Jo had left the island, a soft, fragrant spring. She would have been eighteen then, she remem-bered, and Lexy just fifteen. They'd been giggling, and there'd been the best part of a quart of Ernest and Julio between them to help the mood along. Cousin Kate had been visiting her sister in Atlanta, so there'd been no one to wonder where two teenage girls had gone off to.

There had been freedom and foolishness, and a con-nection, Jo thought, that they'd lost somewhere along the way. The island remained as it was, always. But those two young girls were gone.

"How's Giff?" Jo heard herself ask.

"How should I know?"

Jo shrugged. Even all those years back, Giff had had his eye on Lexy. And even all those years back, Lexy had known it. Jo simply wondered if that had stayed constant. "I haven't seen him since I've been back. I heard he was doing carpentry and whatnot."

"He's a jerk. I don't pay any attention to what he's doing." Lexy scowled out the window as she remembered the way he'd kissed her brainless. "I'm not interested in island boys. I like men." She turned back, shot a chal-lenging look. "Men with style and money."

"Know any?"

"Quite a few, actually." Lexy hooked an arm out the window, easing into a pose of casual sophistication. "New York's bursting with them. I like a man who knows his way around. Our Yankee, for example."

Jo felt her spine stiffen, deliberately relaxed it. "Our Yankee?"

"Nathan Delaney. He has the look of a man who knows

his way around . . . women. I'd say he's exactly my type. Rich.''

"Why do you think he's rich?"

"He can afford a six-month vacation. An architect with his own company has to have financial substance. He's traveled. Men who've traveled know how to show a woman interesting pieces of the world. He's divorced. Divorced men appreciate an amiable woman."

"Done your research, haven't you, Lex."

"Sure." She stretched luxuriously. "Yes, indeedy, I'd say Nathan Delaney is just my type. He should keep me from being bored brainless for the next little while."

"Until you can get back to New York," Jo put in. "Shift hunting grounds."

"Exactly."

"Interesting." Jo's headlights splashed the discreet sign for Heron Campground. She cut her speed and took the turn off Shell Road into a land of sloughs and marsh grass. "I always figured you thought more of yourself than that."

"You have no idea what I think about anything, including myself."

"Apparently not."

They fell into a humming silence disturbed only by the shrill peeping of frogs. At a sharp cracking sound, Jo shuddered involuntarily. It was the unmistakable sound of a gator crunching a turtle between its jaws. She thought she understood exactly what that turtle felt in those last seconds of life. The sensation of being helplessly trapped by something large and feral and hungry.

Because her fingers trembled, she gripped the wheel tighter. She hadn't been consumed, she reminded herself. She'd escaped, she'd bought some time. She was still in control.

But the anxiety attack was pinching away at her with insistent little fingers. She made herself breathe in, breathe out, slow, normal. God, just be normal. She turned the radio off.

She passed the little check-in booth, empty now as the sun had set, and concentrated on winding her way through the chain of small lakes. Lights flickered here and there from campfires. Ghost music floated out of radios, then vanished. Where the hillocks of grass parted, she could see the delicate white glow of lily pads in the moonlight.

She would walk back, she told herself, take pictures, focus on the silence and the emptiness. On being alone. On being safe.

"There's Kirby's car."

Too much roaring in the ears, Jo thought, and forced out another breath. "What?"

"The snazzy little convertible there. That's Kirby's. Just park behind it."

"Right." Jo maneuvered the Land Rover into position and found when she cut the engine that the air was full of sound. The humming and peeping and rustling of the little world hidden behind the dunes and beyond the edge of the forest. It was ripe with scent as well, water and fish and damp vegetation.

She climbed out of the car, relieved to step into so much life.

"Jo Ellen!"

Kirby dashed out of the dark and grabbed Jo in a hard hug. Quick, spontaneous embraces always caught Jo off guard. Before she could steady herself, Kirby was pulling back, her hands still firm on Jo's arms, her smile huge and delighted.

"I'm so glad you came! I'm so glad to see you! Oh, we have a million years to catch up on. Hey, Lexy. Let's get your gear and pop a couple of tops."

"She brought wine," Lexy said, pulling open the cargo door.

"Great, we'll pop some corks too, then. We've got a mountain of junk food to go with it. We'll be sick as dogs by midnight.'' Chattering all the way, Kirby dragged Jo to the back of the Land Rover. "Good thing I'm a doctor. What's this?" She dived into the grocery bag. "Pâté. You got pâté?"

"I nagged Brian," Jo managed to say.

"Good thinking." Kirby hefted the food bag, then hooked Lexy's six-pack. "I've got these. Ginny's getting the fire going. Need a hand with the rest?"

"We can get it." Jo shouldered her camera bag, tucked her bedroll under one arm, and clinked the bottles of wine together. "I'm sorry about your grandmother, Kirby."

"Thanks. She lived a long life, exactly as she wanted to. We should all be that smart. Here, Lexy, I can get that bag." Kirby beamed at both of them, deciding she'd just about cut the edge off the tension that had been snarling in the air when they'd arrived. "Christ, I'm starving. I missed dinner."

Lexy slammed the rear door shut. "Let's go, then. I want a beer."

"Shit, my flashlight's in my back pocket." Kirby turned, angled a hip. "Can you get it?" she asked Jo.

With a little shifting and some flexible use of fingers, Jo pried it out and managed to switch it on. They headed down the narrow path single file.

Site twelve was already set up and organized, a cheerful fire burning bright in a circle of raked sand. Ginny had her Coleman lantern on low and an ice chest filled. She sat on it, eating from a bag of chips and drinking a beer.

"There she is." Ginny lifted the beer can in toast. "Hey, Jo Ellen Hathaway. Welcome home."

Jo dumped her bedroll and grinned. For the first time, she felt home. And felt welcome. "Thanks."

"A doctor." Jo sat cross-legged by the campfire, sipping Chardonnay from a plastic glass. One bottle was already nose down in the sand. "I can't imagine it. When we were kids, you always talked about being an archaeologist or something, a female Indiana Jones, exploring the world."

"I decided to explore anatomy instead." Comfortably drunk, Kirby spread more of Brian's excellent duck pâté on a Ritz cracker. "And I like it."

"We all know about your work, Jo, but is there someone special in your life?" Kirby asked, trying to steer the conversation in Jo's direction.

"No. You?"

"I've been working on your brother, but he isn't co-operating."

"Brian." Jo choked on her wine, sucked in air. "Brian?" she repeated.

"He's single, attractive, intelligent." Kirby licked her thumb. "He makes great pâté. Why not Brian?"

"I don't know. He's . . ." Jo gestured widely. "Brian."

"He pretends to ignore her." Lexy sat up and reached for the pâté herself. "But he doesn't."

"He doesn't?" Kirby looked over, eyes narrowed. "How do you know?"

"An actor has to observe people, their role playing." Lexy waved a hand airily. "You make him nervous, which irritates him. Which means you irritate him because he notices you."

"Really?" Though her head was spinning, Kirby finished off her wine and poured another glass. "Has he said anything about me? Does he—Wait." She held up a hand and rolled her eyes. "This is so high school. Forget I asked."

"The less Brian says about anything, the more it's on his mind," Lexy told her. "He hardly ever mentions your name."

"Really?" Kirby said again and began to perk up. "Is that so? Well, well. Maybe I'll give him another chance after all."

She blinked as a light flashed in her eyes. "What's that for?" she demanded as Jo lowered her camera.

"You looked so damn smug. Shift over closer to Lex, Ginny. Let me get the three of you."

"Here she goes," Lexy muttered, but she flipped her hair back and posed nevertheless.

It was rare for her to take portraits, even candid ones. Jo indulged herself, letting them mug or preen for the camera, framing them in, adjusting the angle, letting the burst of light from her strobe flash illuminate them.

They were beautiful, she realized, each in her own unique fashion. Ginny, with her bottle-blonde frizz and wide-open smile; Lexy, so self-aware and sulky; Kirby, carelessly confident and classy.

They were hers, Jo thought. Each one of them, for different reasons, was part of her. She'd forgotten that for too long.

Her vision blurred before she knew her eyes had flooded with tears. "I've missed you all. I've missed you so much." She set the camera aside hastily, then rose from her crouch. "I've got to pee."

"I'll go with her," Kirby murmured as Jo rushed out of the clearing. She snagged a flashlight and hurried after. "Jo. Hey." She had to double her pace to catch up, grab Jo's arm. "Are you going to tell me what's wrong?"

"My bladder's full. As a doctor, you should recognize the symptom."

When Jo started to turn, Kirby simply tightened her grip. "Honey, I'm asking as your friend, and as a doctor. Granny would have said you look peaked. I can tell from this brief session that you're run-down and stressed out. Won't you tell me what's wrong?"

"I don't know." Jo pressed a hand to her eyes because they wanted to fill up again. "I can't talk about it. I just need some space."

"Okay." Trust always had to be gained by degrees, Kirby thought. "Will you come and see me? Let me give you a physical?"

"I don't know. Maybe. I'll think about it." Jo steadied

herself and managed a smile. "There is one thing I can tell you."

"What?"

"I've got to pee."

"Well, why didn't you say so?" Chuckling, Kirby aimed the light on the path. "You go running out of camp without a light, you could end up gator bait." Cautious, Kirby scanned the thick vegetation fringing the near pond.

"I think I could walk this island blind. It stays with you. I missed it more than I realized, Kirby, but I still feel like a stranger here. It's a shaky line to walk."

"You haven't been home two weeks. Give yourself that time you said you need."

"I'm trying. Me first," Jo said and ducked into the little outhouse.

Kirby started to laugh, then found herself shuddering. The minute Jo closed the door she felt completely alone, completely exposed. The sounds of the slough seemed to rush toward her, over her. Rustles and calls and plops. Clouds drifted slyly over the moon and had her gripping her flashlight in both hands.

Ridiculous, she told herself. It was just a leftover re-action to her experience in the woods that afternoon. She was hardly alone. There were campsites pocketed all through the area. She could even see the flicker of lights from lanterns and fires. And Jo was only a single wooden door away.

There was nothing to be frightened of, she reminded herself. There was nothing and no one on the island that meant her any harm.

And she nearly whimpered with relief when Jo stepped out again.

"You're up," Jo told her, still buttoning her jeans. "Take the flash. I nearly fell in. It's black as death in there, and nearly as atmospheric."

"We could have walked over to the main toilets."

"I wouldn't have needed them by the time I got there."

"Good point. Wait for me, okay?"

Jo hummed assent and leaned back against the door. Then almost immediately straightened when she heard footsteps padding softly to her right. She tensed, told herself that the reaction was a by-product of city living, and watched a light bob closer.

"Hello, there." The male voice was low and pleasant.

She ordered herself to relax. "Hello. We'll be out of your way in a minute."

"No problem. I was just taking a little moonlight walk before I turned in. I'm over at site ten." He took a few steps closer but stayed in the shadows. "Beautiful night. Beautiful spot. I never expected to see a beautiful woman."

"You never know what you'll see on the island." Jo squinted as the light from his lantern reflected into her eyes. "That's part of its charm."

"It certainly is. And I'm enjoying every bit of it. An adventure in every step, don't you think? The anticipation of what's to come. I'm a fan of . . . anticipation."

No, she realized, his voice wasn't pleasant. It was like syrup—too sweet, too thick, and it carried that exaggerated drawl that Yankees insultingly believed mimicked the South.

"Then I'm sure you won't be disappointed in what Desire has to offer."

"From where I'm standing, the offerings are perfect."

If she'd had the flashlight, she would have abandoned manners and shined it in his face. It was the voice coming out of the dark, she told herself, that made it seem so eerie and dangerous. When the door creaked beside her, she turned quickly and reached for Kirby's hand before Kirby had stepped all the way out.

"We've got company," Jo said, annoyed that her voice was too high and too bright. "This is a popular spot tonight. Number ten was just passing through."

But when she looked back, raising Kirby's hand that

held the flash, there was no one there. With a panicked sound in her throat, Jo grabbed the flashlight and waved it frantically over the dark grass and trees.

"He was here. There was someone here. I didn't imagine it. I didn't."

"All right." Gently, Kirby laid a hand on Jo's shoulder, concerned by the trembling. "It's all right. Who was he?"

"I don't know. He was just there. He talked to me. Didn't you hear?"

"No, I didn't hear anything."

"He was almost whispering. That's why. He didn't want you to hear him. But he was there." Her fingers gripped Kirby's like a vise, the panic beating like bat wings in her stomach. "I swear he was right over there."

"I believe you, honey, why wouldn't I?"

"Because he's gone, and . . ." She trailed off, rocked herself for a moment to regain her balance. "I don't know. Christ, I'm a mess. It was dark, he startled me. I couldn't see his face." She blew out a breath, dragged her hair back with both hands. "He creeped me out, I guess."

"It's no big deal. I got spooked in the woods today walking to Sanctuary. Ran like a rabbit."

Jo let out a little laugh, scrubbed her clammy palms dry on the thighs of her jeans. "Really?"

"Jumped gibbering into Brian's arms. Made him feel big and male enough to kiss me, though, so it wasn't a complete loss."

Jo sniffled, grateful that she could feel her legs solidly under her again. "So, how was it?"

"Terrific. I believe I'll definitely give him another chance." She gave Jo's hand a squeeze. "Okay now?"

"Yeah. Sorry."

"No problem. Spooky place." Her grin flashed. "Let's sneak back and scare the hell out of Lex and Ginny."

• • • •

As they started off, hands linked, he watched them from the shadows. He smiled to himself, enjoying the music of quiet female voices drifting away. It was best, he realized, that she had come with the other one. He might have felt compelled to move to the next stage if Jo Ellen had wandered so neatly into him alone.

And he wasn't ready, not nearly ready, to move from anticipation to reality. There was still so much to prepare, so much to enjoy.

But, oh, how he wanted her. To taste that sexy, top-heavy mouth, to spread those long thighs, to close his hands around that pretty white throat.

He closed his eyes and let the image of it roll through his brain. The frozen image of Annabelle, so still and so perfect, shifted into hot life and became his. Became Jo.

A portion of the journal he carried with him played through his head.

Murder fascinates us all. Some would deny it, but they are liars. Man is helplessly drawn to the mirror of his own mortality. Animals kill to survive—for food, for territory, for sex. Nature kills without emotion.

But man also kills for pleasure. It has always been so. We alone among the animals know that the taking of a life is the essence of control and power.

Soon I'll experience the perfection of that. And capture it. My own immortality.

He shuddered in pleasure.

Anticipation, he mused as he turned on his light again to guide his way. Yes, he was a huge fan of anticipation.

NINE

⮌⮎

THE CHEERFUL WHISTLING woke Nathan. As he drifted in that netherworld just under full consciousness, he dreamed of a bird chirping happily on the near branch of the maple tree outside his window. There had been one in his youth, a mockingbird that sang its morning song every day for a full summer, greeting him so reliably that he had named it Bud.

Hazy, hot days filled with the important business of bike riding and ball playing and Popsicle licking.

The insistent wake-up call caused Nathan to greet every morning with a grin and a quick salute to Bud. He'd been devastated when Bud deserted him in late August, but Nathan's mother said that Bud had probably gone off early for his winter vacation.

Nathan rolled over and thought how odd it was that Bud should know how to whistle "Ring of Fire." In the half dream the bird hopped onto the windowsill, a cartoon bird now, a Disney character with sleek black feathers and Johnny Cash's weathered, been-there-done-that face.

When the bird began executing some sharp choreography that included high kicks and fancy spins, Nathan jerked himself awake. He stared at the window, half expecting to see a richly animated cartoon extravaganza.

"Jesus." He ran his hands over his face. "No more canned chili at midnight, Delaney."

He rolled over facedown on the pillow. Then he realized that while the bird wasn't there, the whistling was.

Grunting, he crawled out of bed and stepped into the cutoffs he'd stepped out of the night before. Brain bleary, he blinked at the clock, winced, then stumbled out of the room to find out who the hell was so cheerful at six-fifteen.

He followed the whistling—it was "San Antonio Rose" now—out the screened porch, down the steps. A shiny red pickup was parked behind his Jeep in the short drive. Its owner was under the house, standing on a step-ladder and doing something to the ductwork while whistling his heart out. The ropy muscles rippling outside and under the thin blue T-shirt had Nathan readjusting his thoughts of quick murder.

Maybe he could take Whistling Boy, he considered. They looked to be close to the same height. He couldn't see the face, but the gimme cap, the snug jeans, and scruffy work boots said youth to Nathan.

He'd think about killing him after coffee, he decided.

"What the hell are you doing?"

Whistling Boy turned his head, shot a quick, cheerful grin from under the bill of his cap. "Morning. You got some leaks here. Gotta get it up and running right before AC weather hits."

"You're air-conditioning repair?"

"Hell, I'm everything repair." He stepped off the ladder, swiping a hand clean on the seat of his jeans before holding it out to Nathan. "I'm Giff Verdon. I fix anything."

Nathan studied the friendly brown eyes, the crooked incisor, dimples, the shaggy mess of sun-streaked hair spilling out of the cap, and gave up. "You fix coffee? Decent coffee?"

"You got the makings, I can fix it."

"They got some sort of cone thing with a . . ." Nathan illustrated vaguely with his hands. "Pot."

"Drip coffee. That's the best. You look like you could use some, Mr. Delaney."

"Nathan. I'll give you a hundred dollars for a real pot of coffee."

Giff gave a chuckling laugh, slapped Nathan smartly on the back. "You need it that bad, it's free. Let's go fix you up."

"You always start work at dawn?" Nathan asked as he shuffled up the steps behind Giff.

"Get an early start, you enjoy more of the day." He headed directly to the stove, filled the kettle at the sink. "Got any filters?"

"No."

"Well, we'll jury-rig her, then." Giff tore off some paper towels, folded them cleverly, and slipped them into the plastic cone. "You're an architect, right?"

"Yeah."

Nathan ran his tongue over his teeth, thought fleetingly about brushing them. After coffee. Worlds could be conquered, oceans could be crossed, women could be seduced. After coffee. Life would be worth living again. After coffee.

"I used to think I'd be one."

"Used to think you'd be one what?" Nathan prompted as Giff dug into the cabinet over the stove for coffee.

"An architect. I could always see these places in my head, houses mostly, windows, rooflines, shades of brick and siding. Right down to the fancy work." Giff scooped coffee out of the can and into the cone with the careless precision of habit. "I could even walk myself inside, go through the layout. Sometimes I'd shift things around.

That stairway doesn't belong over there, it's better over here.''

"I know what you mean."

"Well, I could never afford the schooling or the time to go off and study, so I build instead."

In anticipation, Nate got out two mugs. "You're a builder?"

"Well, now, I don't know if I'd say that. Nothing that fancy, really. I do add-ons, fix things up." He patted the tool belt cocked with gunslinger swagger on his hip. "Swing a hammer. Always something needs to be done around here, so I keep busy. Maybe one of these days I'll take one of the houses in my head and build it from the ground up."

Nathan leaned back against the counter and tried not to drool as Giff poured boiling water into the cone. "Have you done any work at Sanctuary?"

"Sure. This and that. I worked on the crew that re-modeled the kitchen for Brian over there. Miz Pendleton's got in her mind to add on a little bathhouse. A solarium, like. Something where she can put a Jacuzzi tub and maybe an exercise room. People look for that kind of thing now when they're on vacation. I'm putting together a design for her."

"The south side," Nathan said to himself. "The light would be right, and it could be worked right into the gardens."

"Yep, just what I was figuring." Giff's smile widened. "I guess I'm on the right track there if you thought the same."

"I'd like to see your drawings for it."

"Yeah?" Surprise and pleasure zipped through him. "Great. I'll bring them by sometime when I got them a little more complete. Better payment than a hundred bucks for the coffee. Drip takes time," he added, noting the way Nathan was eyeing the slowly filling pot. "The best things do."

When Nathan was in the shower, sipping his second cup while hot water pounded the back of his neck, he had to agree that Giff was right. Some things were worth the wait. His mind was clear again, his system all but singing with caffeine. By the time he was dressed and had downed cup number three, he was primed for the hike to Sanctuary and set for an enormous breakfast.

Both the pickup and Giff were gone when Nathan walked down the steps again. Off to fix up something else, Nathan decided. He knew Giff had been amused when he'd asked him to write down the instructions for brewing drip coffee, step by step. But Nathan dealt better with a clear outline.

He caught himself whistling "I Walk the Line." Back to Johnny Cash, he thought, with a shake of his head. And he didn't even like country music.

When he stepped into the forest, dim and green, he deliberately slowed his steps and followed the gentle bend of the river under the arching sway of limbs and moss. Because it always struck him as entering a church, he stopped whistling.

A flutter of color caught his eye, and he stopped to watch a sunny yellow butterfly flit along the path. To the left, the lances of palmettos, tangled vines, and twisted trunks formed a wall that reached up and up, giving him glimpses of scarlet from the flowering vine, snatches of vivid blue sky through the forks of branches.

Though it was a detour, he kept to the river path a bit longer, knowing that the water would widen and lead him deeper into the cool stillness.

Then he saw her, crouched beside a fallen log. Her baggy jacket was pushed up past her elbows, her hair was pulled back into a stubby tail. She had one knee on the damp ground, the other foot planted for balance.

He couldn't have said why he found that so attractive. Why he found her so . . . interesting.

But he stayed where he was, and remained silent, watching Jo set up her shot.

He thought he knew what she was after. The play of light on the water, the shadows of trees on the dark surface, the faint breath of mist just fading. A small, intimate miracle. And the way the river curved, just beyond, Nathan thought. The way it disappeared around that bend where the grass was high and wet and the trees thick made one wonder what could be seen, if you only walked on.

When he saw the doe step out to the left, he stepped forward quietly and crouched behind her. She jolted when he laid a hand on her shoulder, so he squeezed.

"Ssh. To the left," he murmured near her ear. "Ten o'clock."

Though her heart had leaped and pounded, Jo shifted the camera. When she focused on the doe, she took a steadying breath and waited.

She caught the doe, head lifted, scenting the air. Then again her shutter clicked as the deer scanned the river and looked across directly at the two humans, crouched and still. Her arms began to ache as seconds passed into minutes. But she didn't move, unwilling to risk losing a shot. The reward came when the doe picked her way gracefully through the grass and the yearling slipped out of the trees and joined her at the verge to drink.

Light slanted down in dreamy white shafts that slid like liquid through the faint, swimming mist, and the deers' tongues sent ripples spreading soft and slow over the dark water.

She would underexpose, just a bit, she thought, to accent that otherworldly aura rather than go for the crisp clarity of reality. The prints should look enchanted, with the faintest of fairy-tale blurs.

She didn't lower her camera until she'd run out of film, and even then she remained silent, watching while the deer meandered downriver and around the bend.

"Thanks. I might have missed them."

"No, I don't think so."

She turned her head, had to will herself not to jerk back. She hadn't realized he was quite that close, or that his hand still made warm connection with her shoulder. "You move quietly, Nathan. I never heard you."

"You were pretty absorbed. Did you get the shot you were working on before the deer?"

"We'll see."

"I've been taking some shots myself. Old hobby."

"Natural that it would be. It'd be in your blood."

He didn't care for the sound of that and shook his head. "No, I don't have a passion for it. Just an amateur's interest. And a lot of equipment."

She never knew whether it was easier to speak of such losses, or say nothing. So she said nothing.

"In any case," he continued, "I've got all the professional equipment now, and a very minor skill." He smiled at her. "Not like yours."

"How do you know I have any skill when you haven't seen my work?"

"Excellent question. I could say the opinion comes from watching you work just now. You have the patience, the silent grace, the stillness. Stillness is an attractive quality."

"Maybe, but I've been still long enough." She started to rise, but he shifted his hand from her shoulder to her elbow and drew her up with him. "I don't want to keep you from your walk."

"Jo Ellen, you keep brushing me off, I'm going to get a complex." She looked more rested, he thought. There was a little color in her cheeks—but that could have been brought on by annoyance. He smiled and lifted the single-lens reflex camera that hung around her neck. "I've got this model."

"Do you?" Remembering his upbringing, she stopped herself from tugging the camera away from him. "As I said, it would be hard for you not to have some interest in photography. Was your father disappointed that you didn't follow in his f-steps?''

"No." Nathan continued to study the Nikon, remembering his father patiently instructing him on aperture, field of vision. "My parents never wanted me to be anything but what I wanted to be. Anyway, Kyle made his living with a camera.''

"Oh, I didn't realize." Kyle was dead too, she remembered abruptly and, without thinking, touched a hand to Nathan's. "Look, if it's a tender spot, there's no need to poke at it.''

"You can't ignore it either." Nathan shrugged his shoulders. "Kyle based himself in Europe—Milan, Paris, London. He did a lot of fashion photography.''

"It's an art of its own.''

"Sure. And you take pictures of rivers.''

"Among other things.''

"I'd like to see.''

"Why?''

"We've just established that it's an interest of mine.'' He released her camera. "I'm going to spend more time on it while I'm here. And I'd like to see your work. Like you said, it's . . . connected to my father.''

It was the right tack to take. He could almost see her mind change from automatic refusal to agreement. "I brought some with me. You could take a look sometime, I suppose.''

"Good. How about now? I was heading over to Sanctuary anyway.''

"All right, but I don't have a lot of time. I'm still on housekeeping duty.'' She started to bend to pick up her camera bag, but he beat her to it.

"I've got it.''

Jo walked with him, dug her cigarettes out of her jacket pocket. "This isn't another come-on, is it?''

"It would be if I'd thought of it. I've still got that steak waiting.''

"It's going to get freezer burn." She exhaled, studied him through narrowed eyes. "Why did your wife leave you?"

"What makes you think she left me?"

"Okay—why did you leave her?"

"We left each other." He brushed some low-hanging moss out of their way. "Marriage canceled through lack of interest. Are you trying to gauge what kind of husband I was before you let me grill you a piece of meat?"

"No." But the annoyance in his tone made her lips twitch. "But I would have if I'd thought of it. Why don't we leave that topic, and I'll ask you how you've enjoyed your first week on Desire."

He stopped, turned, looked at her. "Isn't this just about where you fell into the water that summer?"

She lifted a brow. "No, actually, it was quite a bit farther downriver that you *pushed* me into the water. And if you've got a notion to repeat yourself, I'd think again."

"You know, one of the reasons I'm here is to revisit some of those days, and nights." He took a step forward, she took a step back. "Are you sure it wasn't here that you went in?"

"Yes, I'm sure." He backed her up another step. She slapped a hand on his chest but found herself maneuvered nearer the bank. "Just like I'm sure I'm not going in again."

"Don't be too sure." As her feet skidded on the wet grass, he hauled her back and against him. "Oops." And grinning, locked his arms comfortably around her waist. "Not much to you, is there?"

She gripped his arms firmly, just in case. "There's enough."

"I guess I'll have to take your word for that . . . and anticipate finding out for myself. Anticipation's half the fun."

"What?" She felt her blood drain down to the soles of

her feet. *I'm a big fan of anticipation.* "What did you say?"

"That I'd take your word for it. Hey." He shifted his weight, pulled her closer as she struggled against him. "Watch out, or we're both going to be taking a morning dip."

He managed to pull her back from the edge. Her face had gone sheet-white, and tremors jerked from her so that her skin seemed to bump against his palms.

"Steady," he murmured and gathered her against him. "I didn't mean to scare you."

"No." The fear had come and gone rapidly, and left her feeling like a fool. Because her heart was still thumping, she let herself be held—wondered how long it had been since anyone had put arms around her and let her rest there. "No, it was nothing. Stupid. There was a guy at the campground a couple of nights ago. He said something similar. He scared me."

"I'm sorry."

She let out a long sigh. "Not your fault, really. My nerves are a little close to the surface these days."

"He didn't hurt you?"

"No, no, he never touched me. It was just creepy."

She left her head against his shoulder, started to close her eyes. It would have been so easy to stay there. Being held. Being safe. But easy wasn't always the right way. Or the smart way.

"I'm not going to sleep with you, Nathan."

He waited a moment, letting himself enjoy the feel of her snug against him, the texture of her hair against his cheek. "Well, then, I may as well drown myself in the river right now. You've just shattered my lifelong dream."

He made her want to laugh, and she squelched down the bubble in her throat. "I'm trying to be up front with you."

"Why don't you lie to me for a while instead? Soothe

my ego.'' He gave her ponytail a little tug, and she lifted her head. ''In fact, why don't we start with something simple and work our way up to complications?''

She watched his gaze dip down to her mouth, linger, then slide slowly back up to her eyes. She could almost taste the kiss, feel the hum of it on her lips. It would be simple to close her eyes and let his mouth close over hers. It would be easy to lean forward and meet him halfway.

Instead, she lifted a hand, pressed her fingers to his mouth. ''Don't.''

He sighed, took her wrist and skimmed his lips over her knuckles. ''Jo, you sure know how to make a man work for his pleasures.''

''I'm not going to be one of your pleasures.''

''You already are.'' He kept her hand in his and turned to walk to Sanctuary. ''Don't ask me why.''

Since he didn't seem to expect her to comment on that, or to make small talk, Jo walked in silence. She was going to have to think about this . . . situation, she decided. She wasn't foolish enough to deny that she'd had a reaction to him. That physical, gut-level click any woman recognized as basic lust. It was normal enough to be almost soothing.

She might be losing her mind, but her body was still functioning on all the elemental circuits.

She hadn't felt the click often enough in her life to take it for granted. And when it was so obviously echoed in the man who caused it . . . that was something to think about.

For now, at least, this was something she could control, something she could understand, analyze, and list clear choices about. But she suspected that the trouble with clicks was that they caused itches. And the trouble with itches was that they nagged until she just gave the hell up and scratched.

''We'll have to make this quick,'' she told Nathan and headed toward the side door.

"I know. You're on bed-making detail. I won't keep you long. I'm planning on sniffing around Brian until he feeds me."

"If you're not busy, you might talk him into getting out afterward. Going to the beach, doing some fishing. He spends too much time here."

"He loves it here."

"I know." She turned into a long hallway where a mural of forest and river flowed over the wall. "That doesn't mean he has to serve Sanctuary every hour of every day." She pressed a hinge, and a section of the mural opened.

"That's an odd way to put it," Nathan commented, following her through the opening and up the stairs into what had once been the servants' quarters and was now the private entrance to the family wing. "Serving Sanctuary."

"It's what he does. I suppose it's what all of us do when we're here."

She turned left at the top of the stairs. As she passed the first open door, she glanced into Lexy's room. The huge old canopy bed was empty. Unmade, naturally. Clothes were scattered everywhere—on the Aubusson carpet, the polished floor, the dainty Queen Anne chairs. The scents of lotions and perfumes and powders hung on the air in female celebration.

"Well, maybe not all of us," Jo muttered and kept walking.

Taking a key out of her pocket, she unlocked a narrow door. Nathan's brows lifted in surprise when he walked in. It was a fully equipped and ruthlessly organized darkroom.

An ancient and threadbare rug protected the random-width-pine floor; thick shades were drawn down and snugly fastened to stay that way over twin windows. Shelves of practical gray metal were lined with bottles of chemicals, plastic tubs. On others were boxes of thick black cardboard, which he assumed held her paper, contact sheets, and prints. There was a long wooden work-table, a high stool.

"I didn't realize you had a darkroom here."

"It used to be a bath and dressing room." Jo hit the white light, then moved around the prints she'd developed the night before that were still hanging on the drying line. "I hounded Cousin Kate until she let me take out the wall and the fixtures and turn it into my darkroom. I'd been saving for three years so I could buy the equipment."

She ran a hand over the enlarger, remembering how carefully she'd priced them, counted her pennies. "Kate bought this for me for my sixteenth birthday. Brian gave me the shelves and the workbench. Lex got me paper and developing fluid. They surprised me with them before I could spend my savings. It was the best birthday I've ever had."

"Family comes through," Nathan said, and noted she hadn't mentioned her father.

"Yes, sometimes they do." She inclined her head at his unspoken question. "He gave me the room. After all, it wasn't easy for my father to give up a wall." She turned away to reach up for a box above her matting machine. "I'm compiling prints for a book I'm contracted for. These are probably the best of the lot, though I still have some culling to do."

"You're doing a book? That's great."

"That remains to be seen. Right now it's just something to be worried about." She stepped back as he walked up to the box, then tucked her thumbs in her back pockets.

It took only the first print for him to see that she was well beyond competent. His father had been competent, Nathan mused, at times inspired. But if she considered herself David Delaney's pupil, she had far outreached her mentor.

The black-and-white print shimmered with drama, the lines so clean, so crisp they might have been carved with a scalpel. It was a study of a bridge soaring over churning water—the white bridge empty, the dark water restless, and the sun just breaking the far horizon.

Another showed a single tree, branches wide and spreading and empty of leaves over a deserted, freshly plowed field. He could have counted the furrows. He went through them slowly, saying nothing, struck time after time at what she could see, and freeze and take away with her.

He came to a night shot, a brick building, windows dark but for the top three, which glowed startlingly bright. He could see the dampness on the brick, the faint mist swirling above black puddles. And could all but feel the chilly, moist air on his skin.

"They're wonderful. You know that. You'd have to be ridiculously neurotic and humble not to know how much talent you have."

"I wouldn't say I'm humble." She smiled a little. "Neurotic, probably. Art demands neuroses."

"I wouldn't say neurotic." Curious, he lowered the last print so that he could study her face. "But lonely. Why are you so lonely?"

"I don't know what you're talking about. My work—"

"Is brilliant," he interrupted. "And heartbreaking. In every one of these it's as if someone's just walked away and there's no one there but you."

Uneasy, she took the print from him, put it back in the box. "I'm not terribly interested in portrait photography. It's not what I do."

"Jo." He touched his fingertips to her cheek, saw by the flicker in her eye that the simple gesture had startled her. "You close people out. It makes your work visually stunning and emotional. But what does it do to the rest of your life?"

"My work is the rest of my life." With a sharp slap,

she set the box back on the shelf. "Now, as I said, I've got a full morning."

"I won't take up much more of it." But he turned idly and began to examine the prints on the drying line. When he laughed, Jo hunched her shoulders and prepared to snarl. "For someone who claims to have no interest in portrait photography, you sure hit it dead on."

Scowling, she walked over and saw that he'd homed in on one of the shots she'd taken at the campground. "That's hardly work, it's—"

"Terrific," he finished. "Fun, even intimate. That's the doc with her arm slung around your sister. Who's the woman with the acre of smile?"

"Ginny Pendleton," Jo muttered, trying not to be amused. Ginny's smile was just that, an acre wide, fertile and full of promise. "She's a friend."

"They're all friends. It shows—the affection and that female connection. And it shows that the photographer's connected, not in the picture maybe, but of it."

Jo shifted uncomfortably. "We were drunk, or getting there."

"Good for you. This is undoubtedly wrong for the theme of the book you're doing now, but you ought to keep it in mind if you do another. Never hurts to mix a little fun in with your angst."

"You just like looking at attractive, half-plowed females."

"Why not?" He tipped a hand under her chin, lifting it higher when she would have jerked away. "I'd love to see what you do with a self-portrait the next time you're feeling that loose."

His eyes were warm and friendly, so damned attractive in the way they looked direct and deep into hers. She felt that little click again, sharper this time.

"Go away, Nathan."

"Okay." Before either of them could think about it, he dipped his head and touched his lips lightly to hers. Then touched them there again, a little longer, a little more firmly. Warmer than he'd expected, he thought, and more arousing, as she'd kept her eyes open and unblinking on his throughout. "You shivered," he said quietly.

"No, I didn't."

He skimmed his thumb over her jawline before he dropped his hands. "Well, one of us did."

And she was mortally afraid she would do so again. "You're not going away."

"I guess not—at least not the way you mean." He pressed his lips to her forehead this time. She didn't shiver, but her heart lurched. "No, definitely not the way you mean."

When he left her, she turned to the window, hurriedly unfastening the shade to throw it up and the window behind it. She wanted air, air to cool her blood and clear her mind. Even as she gulped it in, she saw the figure standing near the edge of the dune swale with the wind breezing through his hair, fluttering his shirt.

Alone, as her father was always alone, with every person who would reach out closed off behind that thin, invisible wall of his own making. With a vicious pull, she slammed the window shut again, shot the shade down.

Damn it, she wasn't her father. She wasn't her mother. She was herself. And maybe that was why there were times when she felt as if she was no one at all.

TEN

GIFF WAS WHISTLING AGAIN. Nathan tried to identify the tune as he tackled his French toast at the breakfast counter, but this one eluded him. He could only assume Giff had wandered too deep into country-western territory for Nathan's limited education to follow.

The man was certainly a cheerful worker, Nathan mused. And apparently he could fix anything. Nathan was certain it had taken absolute faith for Brian to ask Giff to take apart the restaurant's dishwasher in the middle of the breakfast shift.

Now Brian was frying and grilling and stirring, Giff was whistling and tinkering with dishwasher guts, and Nathan was downing a second helping of golden French toast and apple chutney.

He couldn't remember when he'd ever enjoyed a meal more.

"How's it coming, Giff?" Brian stepped around Giff to set a completed order under the warmer.

"Fair to middlin'."

"You don't get that thing up and running by end of

shift, Nate here's going to be washing those dishes by hand.''

"I am?" Nathan swallowed the next bite. "I only used one.''

"House rules. You eat in the kitchen, you pick up the slack. Right, Giff?''

"Yep. Don't think it's going to come to that, though. I'll get her.'' He glanced over as Lexy swung through the door. "Yep,'' he said with a grin, "I'll get her, in my own time.''

She spared him a sidelong flick of lashes, annoyed that he managed to look so cute in a silly baseball cap and grubby T-shirt. "Two more specials, one with ham, one with bacon. Two eggs over light, bacon, side of grits, wheat toast. Giff, keep your big feet out of the way,'' she complained, stepping around them to pick up her orders under the warmer.

Giff's grin was already spreading wide as she swung out the door again. "That sister of yours is the prettiest damn thing, Bri.''

"So you say, Giff.'' Brian cracked two eggs, slid them into a skillet.

"She's crazy about me.''

"I could tell. The way she bubbled over when she saw you was embarrassing.''

Giff snorted, tapped the handle of his screwdriver against his palm. "That's just her way. She wants a man sniffing after her like a puppy, gets her nose up in the air when you don't. She'll come around. You just got to understand how a particular female works, is all.''

"Who the hell understands how any females work?'' Brian gestured with his spatula at Nathan. "Do you understand, Nate?''

Nathan contemplated the next bite of French toast, watched the syrup drip lazily. "No,'' he decided. "No, I can't say that I do. And I've done considerable studying on the subject. You could even say I've dedicated a small portion of my life to it, with mixed results.''

"It's not a matter of how they all work." Patiently Giff began replacing screws. "You gotta focus in on the one. It's like an engine. One don't necessarily run the same as another, even if they're the same make and model. They've just got their particular quirks. Now, Alexa . . .''

He trailed off, carefully sending another screw home, selecting the next. "She's almost too pretty for her own good. She thinks about that a lot, worries over it.''

"She's got enough glop on her bathroom counter to paint up a Vegas chorus line," Brian put in.

"Some women feel that's a responsibility. Now, Lex, she gets ticked off if a man's not dazzled by her twenty-four hours a day, and if he is dazzled twenty-four hours a day, she figures he's an idiot 'cause he's not seeing anything but the surface. The trick is to find the line, then choose the right time and place to cross it.''

Brian flipped eggs onto a plate. It was Lexy to a tee, he mused. Contrary and annoying. "Seems like too much work to me.''

"Hell, Bri, women aren't anything but work." Giff flicked up the brim of his hat, dimples flashing. "That's part of the appeal. She'll run for you now," he added, nodding at the dishwasher.

Gauging the time, he calculated that Lexy would be coming back in for her orders any moment. "Ginny and me and some of the others are thinking of having a bonfire on the beach tonight," he said casually. "Down around by Osprey Dunes. I got a lot of scrap wood put by, and it's going to be a clear night." When Lexy pushed through the door, Giff was a satisfied man. "I thought you might want to tell your guests here, let the cottagers and campers know.''

"Know what?" Lex demanded.

"About the bonfire.''

"Tonight?" Her eyes lit as she set dishes on the counter. "Where?''

"Down around Osprey." Giff carefully replaced his tools in his dented metal box. "You'll come on down, won't you, Brian?"

"I don't know, Giff. I've got some paperwork to catch up on."

"Oh, come on, Bri." Lexy nudged him as she reached for the new orders. "Don't be such a stick. We'll all come." Hoping to irritate Giff, she flashed an inviting smile at Nathan. "You'll come down, won't you? There's nothing like a bonfire on the beach."

"Wouldn't miss it." He slid a cautious glance at Giff, hoping the man had put his hammer away.

"Terrific." She beamed at him as she walked by, the full-candlepower smile she saved for special occasions. "I'll start spreading the word."

Giff scratched his chin as he unfolded himself and rose. "No need to look so uneasy, Nate. Flirting comes naturally to Lexy."

"Uh-huh." Nathan eyed the toolbox, thought of all the potential weapons inside.

"Doesn't bother me any." At home, Giff took a biscuit out of a bowl and bit in. "Man decides to take on a beautiful woman, he's got to expect a little flirting on her side, a lot of looking from other men. So you go right on and look." Giff hefted his toolbox and winked. "Now, you do more than look, we'd have to go around some. See you tonight."

He went off whistling.

"You know, Bri . . ." Nathan picked up his plate to carry it to the sink. "That guy has biceps like rock. I don't believe I'm even going to look."

"Good thinking. Now you can pay for that breakfast by loading the dishwasher."

"I don't feel like socializing, Kate. I'm going to do some darkroom work tonight."

"You're not doing any kind of work." Kate marched

over to Jo's dresser, picked up the simple wooden-handled hairbrush, and shook it at her. "You're going to put on some lipstick, fix your hair, and go down to that bonfire. You're going to dance in the sand, drink some wine, and by God, you're going to have a good time."

Before Jo could protest again, Kate held up a hand, traffic-cop style. "Save your breath, girl. I've already had this round with Brian, and won. You might as well just throw in the towel now."

When she tossed the hairbrush, Jo caught it before it beaned her. "I don't see why it matters—"

"It matters," Kate said between her teeth and wrenched open the door on the rosewood armoire. "It matters that people in this house learn how to have a little fun now and then. When I'm through with you, I'm going to go browbeat your father."

Jo snorted, flopped back on the bed. "Not a chance."

"He'll go," Kate said grimly as she studied what there was of Jo's wardrobe. "If I have to knock him unconscious and drag him down to the beach. Don't you have a blouse in here that looks remotely like you care what you have on your back?" Disgusted, she shoved aside hangers. "Something the least bit stylish or attractive?"

Without waiting for an answer, she went to the door, calling out, "Alexa! You pick out a blouse for your sister and bring it down here."

"I don't want one of her shirts." Alarmed now, Jo hopped up. "If I have to go, I'll go in my own clothes. And I'm not going, so it doesn't matter."

"You're going. Put some curl in your hair. I'm tired of seeing it just hang there."

"I don't have anything to put curl in it with if I wanted curl in it, which I don't."

"Hah!" was Kate's only response. "Alexa, you bring that blouse and your hot rollers down here to your sister's room."

"You stay out of here, Lex," Jo shouted. "Kate, I'm not sixteen years old."

"No, you're not." Kate gave a decisive nod, the little gold drops in her ears bobbing at the movement. "You're a grown woman, and a lovely one. It's long past time you took some pride in it. Now, you're going, and you're going to put some effort into your appearance, and I won't take any sass about it. Damn kids, fighting me every which way," she muttered and swung into Jo's bathroom. "Not even a wand of mascara in here. You want to be a nun, enter a convent. Lipstick is not a tool of Satan."

With a blouse slung over her shoulder and a case of hot rollers in her hand, Lexy came in. Her mood was up in anticipation of the night ahead, so she grinned and wiggled her eyebrows at Jo. "On one of her rampages?"

"Big-time one. I don't want my hair curled."

"Oh, loosen up, Jo Ellen." Lexy dumped the rollers on the dresser, then checked out her own appearance in the mirror. She'd kept the makeup subtle to suit the casual event. In any case, firelight was terrifically flattering. Most would be wearing jeans, she knew, so her long, flowing skirt covered with red poppies would make an interesting contrast.

"And I'm not wearing your clothes."

"Suit yourself." Lexy turned, pursed her lips, and gave her sister the once-over. She was feeling just good enough to be companionable. "Hmm. Frills aren't your style."

"Now there's news. Just let me note that down."

Lexy let the sarcasm roll off her perfumed shoulders and walked a slow circle around her sister. "Got a plain black T-shirt that isn't so baggy two of you could slide into it?"

Wary, Jo nodded. "Probably."

"Black jeans?" At Jo's assenting shrug, Lexy tapped her finger to her lips. "That's the way we'll go then. Sleek and hip. Maybe some dangles at the ears and a good belt to accessorize, but that's all. No curls, either."

"No curls?"

"Nope, but you need a new do." Lexy continued to tap her finger, her eyes narrowing, her head nodding. "I can fix that. A little snip here, a little snip there."

"Snip?" Jo put both hands to her hair in defense. "What do you mean, snip? I'm not letting you cut my hair."

"What do you care? It's just hanging there anyway."

"Exactly." Kate breezed back in. "Lexy's got a nice touch with hair. She trims mine up if I can't get over to the mainland. Go wash it, Jo. Lexy, go get your scissors."

"Fine." Defeated, Jo threw up her hands. "Just fine. If she scalps me I won't have to go sit on the sand with a bunch of fools half the night listening to somebody sing 'Kum Ba Yah.' "

Fifteen minutes later, she found herself sitting with a towel bibbed around her and bits of hair falling. "Jesus." Jo squeezed her eyes tight. "I have lost my mind. It's now official."

"Stop squirming," Lexy ordered, but there was a laugh in the order rather than a sting. "I've barely done anything. Yet. And think how long this is going to keep Cousin Kate off your back."

"Yeah." Jo forced her shoulders to relax. "Yeah, there is that."

"You've got great hair, Jo. Good body, a nice natural wave." She pouted a little, studying her own wildly spiraling mane in the mirror. "Don't know why I have to pay such money for curl, myself. My hair's straight as a pin."

With a shrug for life's vagaries, she concentrated again on the job at hand. "A decent cut's all you need. What I'm doing is giving you one that you won't have to do a thing with."

"I already don't do a thing."

"And it looks it. This won't."

"Just don't cut off too . . ." Jo's eyes went huge, her

throat closed as she watched three inches of hair flop into her lap. "Christ! Oh, Christ! What have you done?"

"Relax, I'm giving you bangs, that's all."

"Bangs? Bangs? I didn't ask for bangs."

"Well, you're getting them. A nice fringe to the eyebrow. Your eyes are your best feature. This will highlight them, and it's a nice, casual look that suits you." She continued to comb and snip, stood back, scowled and snipped some more. "I like it. Yes, I like it."

"Good for you," Jo muttered. "You wear it."

"You're going to owe me an apology." Lexy squirted some gel in her palm, rubbed her hands together, then slicked them through Jo's damp hair. "You only need a little of this, about the size of a dime."

Jo scowled at the tube. "I don't use hair gunk."

"You're going to. Just a little," she repeated, then switched on her blow-dryer. "You can air-dry it too, but this'll give it a little more volume. Won't take you more than ten minutes in the morning to fuss with it."

"Doesn't take me more than two now. What's the damn point?" Jo told herself she didn't care about the cut. She was tired of sitting there being fussed with, that was all. She wasn't nervous.

"Fine." Lexy switched off the dryer, tugged out the plug. "All you do is bitch and find fault. Go ahead and look like a hag. I don't give a shit." She stormed out, leaving Jo to tug the towel aside bad-temperedly.

But when she caught her reflection in the mirror, she stopped, stepped closer. It looked . . . nice, she decided, and lifted a hand to brush the tips. Instead of hanging, it skimmed, she supposed, angled over the ears, graduated toward the back. It was sort of . . . breezy, she decided. The bangs weren't such a bad touch after all. Experimentally, she shook her head. Everything fell back into place, more or less. Nothing drooped into her eyes to irritate her.

She picked up her brush, ran it through and watched her hair rise and fall in nice, neat blunt ends. Tidy, she mused. Fuss-free, but with, well, style. She had to admit it had style and the style flattered.

The memory snuck through of sitting on the edge of her bed while her mother brushed her hair.

You've got beautiful hair, Jo Ellen. So thick and soft. It's going to be your crowning glory.

It's the same color as yours, Mama.

I know. And Annabelle laughed and hugged her close. You'll be my little twin.

"I can't be your twin, Mama," Jo whispered now. "I can't be like you."

Wasn't that why she'd never done anything more with her hair than scrape it back into an elastic band? Wasn't that why there was no tube of mascara in the bathroom? Was it stubbornness, Jo wondered, or was it fear, that kept her from spending more than five minutes a day on her appearance? From really looking at herself?

If she was going to keep herself sane, Jo thought, she was going to have to learn how to face what she saw in the mirror every day. And facing it, she realized, she would have to learn to accept it.

Taking a bracing breath, she left her room and walked down to Lexy's.

She found Lexy in the bathroom, choosing a lipstick from among the clutter of cosmetics on the counter.

"I'm sorry." When Lexy said nothing, Jo took the last step forward. "Lexy, I am sorry. You were absolutely right. I was being bitchy, I was finding fault."

Lexy stared down at the little gold tube, watched the slick red stick slide up and down. "Why?"

"I'm scared."

"Of what?"

"Everything." It was a relief to admit it, finally. "Everything scares me these days. Even a new haircut." She managed to work up a smile. "Even a terrific new haircut."

Lexy relented enough to smile back when their eyes

met in the mirror. "It is pretty terrific. It would look better if you had some color, fixed up your eyes."

Jo sighed, looked down at the personal department store of cosmetics. "Why not? Can I use some of this stuff?"

"Anything there would work. We're the same coloring." Lexy turned back to the mirror, carefully painted her lips. "Jo . . . are you scared of being alone?"

"No. I do alone really well." Jo picked up blusher, sniffed at it. "That's about all that doesn't scare me."

"Funny. That's about the only thing that does scare me."

The fire speared up, rose out of white sand and toward a black, diamond-studded sky. Like some Druid ritual fire, Nathan thought, as he sipped an icy beer and watched the flames. He could imagine robed figures dancing around it, offering sacrifices to some primitive and hungry god.

And where the hell had that come from? he wondered, and took another swig to wash the image away.

The night was cool, the fire hot, and the beach, so often deserted, was filled with people and sound and music. He just wasn't quite ready to be part of it. He watched the mating dances, the ebb and flow of male and female as basic as the tide.

And he thought of the photos Jo had shown him that morning, those frozen slices of lonely. Maybe it had taken that, he realized, to make him see how lonely he'd become.

"Hey, handsome." Ginny plopped down on the sand beside him. "Whatcha doing over here all by yourself?"

"Searching for the meaning of life."

She hooted cheerfully. "Well, that's easy. It's living it." She offered him a hot dog, fresh out of the fire and burned to a crisp. "Eat up."

Nathan took a bite, tasted charcoal and sand. "Yum."

She laughed, squeezed his knee companionably. "Well, outdoor cooking's not my strong point. But I whip up a hell of a southern-style breakfast if you ever . . . find your-self in my neighborhood.''

As a come-on it was both obvious and easy. There was her acre of smile, slightly off center now from the tequila she'd been drinking. He couldn't help but smile back at her. "That's a very attractive offer."

"Well, sugar, it's one every single woman on the island between sixteen and sixty would dearly love to make you. I just figure I'm getting to the head of the line."

Not entirely sure how he was supposed to respond now, Nathan scratched his chin. "I'm really fond of breakfast, but—"

"Now don't you fret over it." This time she squeezed his arm as if testing and approving the biceps. "You know what you've got to do, Nathan?"

"What's that?"

"You've got to dance."

"I do?"

"You sure do." She hopped up, shot down a hand. "With me. Come on, big guy. Let's kick up some sand."

He put a hand in hers, found it so warm and alive it was easy to grin. "All right."

"Ginny's got herself a Yankee," Giff commented, watching Ginny pull Nathan toward the damp sand.

"Looks like." Kirby licked marshmallow off her thumb. "She sure knows how to have a good time."

"It isn't so hard." With a beer dangling between his fingers, Giff scanned the beach. Some people were dancing or swaying, others were sprawled around the blazing fire, still others strolled off into the dark to be alone. Kids whooped and hollered, and the old sat in beach chairs exchanging gossip and watching the youth.

"Not everybody wants to have a good time." Kirby glanced toward the dunes again but saw no one coming over them from the direction of Sanctuary.

"You know, you got your eye cocked for Brian, and I've got mine cocked for Lexy." Giff threw a friendly arm around her shoulder. "Why don't we go dance? We'll keep our eyes cocked together."

"That's a fine idea."

Brian came over the dunes, Lexy on one side, Jo on the other. He paused at the top, took a long, slow survey. "And this, my children, all this, will one day be yours."

"Oh, Bri." Lexy elbowed him. "Don't be such a grump." She spotted Giff immediately and felt little toothy nips of jealousy as she saw him slide Kirby into his arms for a slow dance. "I've got a hankering for some crab," she said lightly and started down toward the beach.

"We could probably escape now," Jo began. "Kate's still dragging Daddy down. We could head north, circle around, and be back home before she gets here."

"She'd only make us pay for it later." Resigned, he jammed his hands in his back pockets. "Why do you suppose we're so bad at social occasions, Jo Ellen?"

"Too much Hathaway," she began.

"Not enough Pendleton," he finished. "Guess Lexy got our share of that," he added, nodding down to where their sister was already in the thick of things, surrounded by people. "Let's get it over with."

They'd barely reached the beach before Ginny raced over and greeted them both with loud kisses. "What took y'all so long? I'm half lit already. Nate, let's get these people some beer so they can catch up." She whirled away to do so, ran into someone, and giggled. "Well, hey, Morris, you wanna dance with me? Come on."

Nathan blew out a breath. "I don't know where she gets the energy. She damn near wore me out. Want that beer?"

"I'll get it," Brian told him and walked off.

"I like your hair." Nathan lifted a finger to brush under Jo's bangs. "Very nice."

"Lexy whacked at it, that's all."

"You look lovely." He skimmed his hand over her

shoulder, down her arm until it captured her own hand. "Is that a problem for you?"

"No, I . . . Don't start on me, Nathan."

"Too late." He moved in a little closer. "I already have." Her scent was warm, lightly spicy, intriguing. "You're wearing perfume."

"Lexy—"

"I like it." He leaned in, stunning her by sniffing her hair, her neck. "A lot."

She was having trouble drawing a full breath, and annoyed, she took a step back. "That's not why I wore it."

"I like it anyway. You want to dance?"

"No."

"Good. Neither do I. Let's go sit by the fire and neck."

It was so absurd, she nearly laughed. "Let's just go sit by the fire. If you try anything, I'll have my daddy go get his gun and dispatch you. And you being a Yankee, no one will turn a hair."

He laughed and slipped an arm around her waist, ignoring what he'd come to realize was her instinctive jolt at being touched. "We'll just sit, then."

He got her a beer, poked a stick through a hot dog for her, then settled down beside her. "I see you brought your camera."

Automatically, she laid a hand on the scarred leather bag at her hip. "Habit. I'll wait a while before I take it out. Sometimes a camera puts people off—but after they've had enough beer, they don't mind so much."

"I thought you didn't take portraits."

"As a rule, I don't." Conversation always made her feel pressured. She dipped into her pocket for a cigarette. "You don't have to prime inanimate objects with flattery or liquor to get a shot."

"I've only had one beer." He took the lighter from her, cupped a hand around it to shield it from the wind off the ocean, and lit her cigarette. His eyes met hers over the flame. "And you haven't exactly primed me with flattery. But you can take my picture anyway.''

She considered him through the smoke. Strong bones, strong eyes, strong mouth. ''Maybe.'' She took the lighter back and tucked it in her pocket. What would she see through the lens? she wondered. What would what she saw pull out of her? ''Maybe I will.''

''How uncomfortable will it make you if I tell you I've been waiting here for you?''

Her gaze shifted to his again, then away. ''Very. Very uncomfortable.''

''Then I won't mention it,'' he said lightly, ''or bring up the point that I watched you stand up there between the dunes, and I thought, There she is. What took her so long?''

Jo anchored the stick between her knees to free up a hand for her beer. And the hand was damp with nerves. ''I wasn't that long. The fire hasn't been going more than an hour.''

''I don't mean just tonight. And I don't suppose I should mention how incredibly attracted I am to you.''

''I don't think—''

''So we'll talk about something else altogether.'' He smiled at her, delighted with the baffled look in her eyes, the faint frown on that lovely, top-heavy mouth.

''Lots of faces to study around here. You could do another book just on that. The faces of Desire.'' He shifted slightly so that their knees bumped.

Jo stared at him, amazed at the smoothness of his moves. Certainly that's what they were, just moves. Any man who could get a woman's heart tripping in her chest with no more than a few careless words and a grin must have a trunkful of moves.

''I haven't finished the book I'm contracted for, much less thought about another.''

''But you will eventually. You've got too much talent and ambition not to. But for now why don't you just satisfy my curiosity and tell me about some of these people?''

"Who are you curious about?"

"All of them. Any of them."

Jo turned the dog just over the flames, watched the fat rise and bubble. ''That's Mr. Brodie—the old man there with the white cap and the baby on his lap. That would be his great-grandchild, his fourth if I'm counting right. His parents were house servants at Sanctuary around the turn of the century. He was born on Desire, raised here.''

"And grew up in the house?"

"He'd have spent a lot of time in it, but his family was given a cottage of their own and some land for their long and loyal service. He fought in World War Two as a gunner and brought his wife back from Paris. Her name was Marie Louise, and she lived here with him till she died three years back. They had four children, ten grandchildren, and now four greats. He always carries peppermint drops in his pocket.'' She turned her head. ''Is that what you mean?''

"That's just what I mean." He wondered if she knew how her voice had warmed as she slipped into the story. "Pick another."

She sighed, finding it a little foolish. But at least it wasn't making her nervous. ''There's Lida Verdon, cousin of mine on the Pendleton side. She's the tired, pregnant woman scolding the toddler. This'll be her third baby in four years, and her husband Wally's handsome as six devils and just no damn good. He's a truck driver, goes off on long runs. Makes a decent living, but Lida doesn't see much of it.''

A child ran by screaming with pleasure, chased by an indulgent daddy. Jo crushed her cigarette out in the sand, buried it. ''When Wally's home,'' she continued, ''he's mostly drunk or working on it. She's kicked him out twice now, and taken him back twice. And she's got one baby on leading strings and another under her apron as proof of the reconciliations. We're the same age, Lida and I, born just a couple of months apart. I took the pictures at her wedding. She looks so pretty and so happy and young in them. Now, four years later, she's just about worn out. It's not all fairy tales on Desire," she said quietly.

"No." He slipped his arm around her. "It's not all fairy tales anywhere. Tell me about Ginny."

"Ginny?" With a quick laugh, Jo scanned the beach. "You don't have to tell anything about Ginny. You just have to look at her. See the way she's making Brian laugh? He hardly ever laughs like that. She just brings it out of you."

"You grew up with her."

"Yeah, almost like sisters, though she's closest with Lexy. Ginny was always the first of us to try anything, especially if it was bad. But there was never any harm in it, or in her. It's just a matter of Ginny liking everything, and a lot of it. And—uh-oh. I bet she helped stir that up."

He was too busy looking at Jo to notice. Everything about her had brightened, relaxed. "What?"

"See there?" Jo leaned back against his arm and gestured toward the edge of the water. "Lex and Giff are tangling. They've been blowing hot and cold on each other since they were in diapers. Ginny's mighty fond of both of them and probably did something to have them blowing hot tonight."

"She wants them to fight?"

"No, you pinhead." Laughing, Jo lifted the sizzling hot dog from the fire, anchored the stick in the sand. "She wants them to make up."

Nathan considered, then lifted his brows as Giff scooped Lexy up, hefted her Rhett Butler–style in his arms, and strode—with her kicking and cursing—down the beach. "If that's how it works, I'm going to have to talk to Ginny about stirring things up for me."

"I'm a much harder sell than my sister," Jo said dryly.

"Maybe." Nathan plucked the hot dog off the stick and

tossed it from hand to hand to cool it. "But I've already got you cooking for me."

Despite the struggling woman in his arms, Giff kept his pace steady until the bonfire was a flicker in the distance. Satisfied that they were as private as they were going to get, he set her on her feet.

"Who the hell do you think you are?" She shoved him hard with both hands.

"Same person I've always been," he said evenly. "It's time you took a good look."

"I've looked at you before, and I don't see anybody who's got a right to haul me off when I don't want to go." No matter how exciting it had been, she told herself. No matter how romantic. "I was having a conversation."

"No, you weren't. You were coming on to that guy to piss me off. This time it worked."

"I was being polite and friendly to a man Ginny introduced me to. An attractive man from Charleston. A lawyer who's spending a few days on the island camping with some friends."

"A Charleston lawyer who was just about to drool on your shoulder." Giff's normally mild eyes spit fire. "You've had time to sow your oats, Lexy, and I gave you plenty of space to sow them in. Now you're back, and it's time to grow up."

"Grow up." She planted her hands on her hips, ignoring the water that foamed up the sand inches from her feet. "I've been grown, and you're just one of the many who hasn't had the sense to see it. I do what I want when I want, and with whom I want."

She turned on her heel and began to stalk off, her nose in the air. Giff rubbed his chin and told himself he shouldn't have lost his temper, even if Lexy had been sliding herself around some Charleston lawyer. But the damage was done.

He moved fast. By the time she heard him coming and

turned, she had time only to squeal before he tackled her.

"Why, you flea-brained idiot, you'll ruin my skirt." Furious now, she used elbows, knees, teeth, rolling with him while the surf lapped up and soaked them both. "I hate you! I hate every inch of you, Giff Verdon."

"No, you don't, Lexy. You love me."

"Hah. You can kiss my ass."

"I'll be glad to, honey." He pinned her arms, levered himself up to grin down at her. "But I believe I'll work my way down to it." He lowered his head, and when she turned hers aside, brushed his lips over the soft skin just below her ear. "This is a fine place to start."

Shudders coursed through her, liquid and hot. "I hate you. I said I hate you."

"I know what you said." He nibbled slowly down to her throat, thrilled with the way her body went lax beneath him. "Kiss me, Lexy. Come on and kiss me."

On a sob, she turned her head, found his mouth with hers. "Hold me. Touch me. Oh, I hate you for making me want you."

"I know the feeling." He stroked her hair, her cheeks, while she trembled and strained beneath him. "Don't fret so. I'd never hurt you."

Desperate, she gripped his hair, dragged him down harder. "Inside me. I need you inside me. I'm so empty." She arched up, groaning.

He closed a hand over her breast, filled his palm with her, then giving in to his hunger, tugged the scooped neck of her blouse down so he could take her into his mouth.

The taste of her, hot, damp, pungent, pumped through his blood like whiskey. He wanted it to be slow and sweet, had waited all his life just for that. But she was moving restlessly beneath him, her hands tugging, pulling, reaching. When he closed his mouth over hers again, he couldn't think, could barely breathe. It was all taste and sound.

He was panting as he fought with her wet skirt, yanking

at the thin, clinging material until his hand could skim up her thigh, until he found her, already wet. She jerked against his hand and climaxed before he could do more than moan.

"Jesus. Jesus, Lexy."

"Now. Giff, I'll kill you if you stop. I swear I'll kill you."

"You won't have to," he managed. "I'll already be dead. Get these goddamn clothes off." He tugged at her skirt with one hand, his jeans with the other. "For God's sake, Lexy, help me."

"I'm trying." She was laughing now, trapped in a dripping skirt, still flying on the fast, hard orgasm, her blood singing so high she could barely hear the sea. "I feel drunk. I feel wonderful. Oh, hurry."

"Hell with it." He tossed his jeans aside, dragged off his shirt and pulled her into the water, skirt and all.

"What are you doing? This is brand-new."

"I'll buy you a new one. I'll buy you a dozen. Only for God's sake, let me have you." He dragged the skirt down by the elastic waist and was inside her almost before she could kick her way clear.

She cried out in shock, in delight. She wrapped her legs around him, dug her fingers into his shoulders and watched his face. Dark eyes, never leaving hers, seeing only her.

When the wave swamped her, outside and in, she burrowed against him, and knew he would always bring her back.

"I love you." he murmured it to her as his body raced toward the edge. "I love you, Lexy."

He let himself go, shuddering with her until they both went limp. Then he gathered her close and let the waves rock them. It had been perfect, he thought, free and simple and right. Just as he'd always known it would be.

"Hey, out there."

He glanced over lazily, spotted the figure on the shore

waving both arms. Then he snorted, pressed his lips to Lexy's hair. "Hey, Ginny."

"I see some clothes thrown around here look familiar. Y'all naked out there?"

"Appear to be." He grinned as he felt Lexy chuckle against him.

"Ginny, he drowned my skirt."

"About time, too." She blew them elaborate kisses. "I'm walking a while. Gotta clear my head some. Lexy, Miz Kate got your daddy to drop in down at the bonfire. I'd make sure I had something covering my butt before I went back."

Weaving more than a little, and chuckling herself, Ginny headed down the beach. It made her heart happy to see the two of them together like that. Why, poor old Giff had been pining away for her for years, and Lexy, well, she'd just been chasing her own tail waiting for Giff to catch hold of her.

She had to stop a moment, waiting for her spinning head to settle back on her shoulders. Shoulda skipped the tequila shooters, she told herself. But then, life was too short to go skipping things.

One day she was going to find the right man to catch hold of her too. And until then, she was going to have a high old time looking for him.

As if she'd conjured him, a man walked across the sand toward her. Ginny cocked a hip, aimed a grin. "Well, hey there, handsome. Whatcha doing out here by yourself?"

"Looking for you, beautiful."

She shook her hair back. "Ain't that a coincidence?"

"Not really. I prefer to think of it as fate." He held out a hand and, thinking it was her lucky night, she took it.

Just drunk enough to make it easy, he thought as he led her farther into the dark. And sober enough to make it . . . fun.

PART TWO

What wound did ever heal but by degrees?

—SHAKESPEARE

ELEVEN

For the first time in weeks, Jo woke rested and with an appetite. She felt settled, she realized, and very nearly happy. Kate had been right, Jo decided as she gave her hair a quick finger-comb. She'd needed the evening out, the companionship, the music, the night. And a few hours in the company of a man who apparently found her attractive hadn't hurt a thing. In fact, Jo was beginning to think it wouldn't hurt a thing to spend a bit more time in Nathan's company.

She passed her darkroom on the way downstairs and for once didn't think of the envelope filled with pictures that she'd hidden deep in a file drawer. For once, she didn't think of Annabelle.

Instead she thought of wandering down to the river again and the possibility of bumping into Nathan. Accidentally. Casually. She was getting as bad as Ginny, she decided with a laugh. Plotting ways to make a man notice her. But if it worked for Ginny, maybe it would work for her. What was wrong with a little flirtation with a man who interested her? Excited her?

There now. She paused on the stairs, curious enough to

take stock. It wasn't so hard to admit that he excited her—
the attention paid, the breezy way he would take her hand,
the deliberate way his eyes would meet and hold hers.
The cool and confident way he'd kissed her. Just moved
in, she recalled, sampled, approved, and backed off. As if
he'd known there would be ample opportunity for more
at a time and place of his choosing.

It should have infuriated her, she mused. The cocky and
blatantly male arrogance of it. And yet she found it ap-
pealed to her on the most primitive of levels. She wondered how she would play the game, and if she would
show any skill at it.

She smiled, continued downstairs. She had a feeling she
might just surprise Nathan Delaney. And herself.

"I'd go, Sam, but I have quite a few turnovers here
this morning." Kate glanced over as Jo stepped into the
kitchen. Raking a hand through her hair, she sent Jo a
distracted smile. "Morning, honey. You're up early."

"So's everyone, it seems." Jo glanced at her father as
she headed to the coffeepot. He stood by the door, all but
leaning out of it. The desire to escape was obvious.
"Problem?" Jo asked lightly.

"Just a little one. We've got some campers coming in
on the morning ferry, and some going out on the return.
I just got a call from a family who's packed up and ready
to go, and there's no one to check them out."

"Ginny's not at the station?"

"She doesn't answer there, or at home. I imagine she
overslept." Kate smiled wanly. "Somewhere. I'm sure
the bonfire went on quite late."

"It was still going strong when I left, about midnight."
Jo sipped her coffee, frowning as she tried to remember
if she'd seen Ginny around before she headed back home.

"Girl got a decent night's sleep, in her own bed," Sam
added, "she wouldn't have any trouble getting herself to
work."

"Sam, you know very well this isn't like Ginny. She's

as dependable as the sunrise.'' With a worried frown, Kate glanced at the clock. ''Maybe she isn't feeling well.''

''Hung over, you mean.''

''As some human beings are occasionally in their lives,'' Kate snapped back. ''And that's neither here nor there. The point is, we have people waiting to check out of camp and others coming in. I can't leave here this morning, and even if I could I don't know anything about pitching tents or Porta-Johns. You'll just have to give up a couple of hours of your valuable time and handle it.''

Sam blinked at her. It was a rare thing for her voice to take on that scathing tone with him. And it seemed he'd been hearing it quite a bit lately. Because he wanted peace more than anything else, he shrugged. ''I'll head over.''

''Jo will go with you,'' Kate said abruptly, which caused them both to stare. ''You might need a hand.'' She spoke quickly now, her mind made up. If she could force them into each other's company for a morning, maybe the two of them would hold an actual conversation. ''Jo, you can walk over from the campground and check on Ginny. Maybe her phone's just out, or she's really not feeling well. I'll worry about her until we get in touch.''

Jo shifted the camera on her shoulder, watched her tentative morning plans evaporate. ''Sure. Fine.''

''Let me know when you get it straightened out.'' Kate shooed them to the door and out. ''And don't worry about housekeeping detail. Lexy and I will manage well enough.''

Because their backs were turned, Kate smiled broadly, brushed her hands together. There, she thought. Deal with each other.

Jo climbed in the passenger seat of her father's aged Blazer, snapped her seat belt on. It smelled of him, she realized. Sand and sea and forest. The engine turned over smoothly and purred. He'd never let anything that belonged to him suffer from neglect, she mused. Except his children.

Annoyed with herself, she pulled her sunglasses out of the breast pocket of her camp shirt, slid them on. "Nice bonfire last night," she began.

"Have to see if that boy policed the beach area."

That boy would be Giff, Jo noted, and was aware they both knew Giff wouldn't have left a single food wrapper to mar the sand. "The inn's doing well. Lots of business for this time of year."

"Advertising," Sam said shortly. "Kate does it."

Jo struggled against heaving a sigh. "I'd think word of mouth would be strong as well. And the restaurant's quite a draw with Brian's cooking."

Sam only grunted. Never in his life would he understand how a man could want to tie himself to a stove. Not that he understood his daughters any better than he understood his son. One of them flitting off to New York wanting to get famous washing her hair on TV commercials, and the other flitting everywhere and back again snapping photographs. There were times he thought the biggest puzzle in the world was how they had come from him.

But then, they'd come from Annabelle as well.

Jo jerked a shoulder and gave up. Rolling down her window, she let the air caress her cheeks, listened to the sound of the tires crunching on the road, then the quick splashing through the maze of duckweed that was life in the slough.

"Wait." Without thinking, she reached out to touch Sam's arm. When he braked, she hopped out quickly, leaving him frowning after her.

There on a hummock a turtle sunned himself, his head raised so that the pretty pattern on his neck reflected almost perfectly in the dark water. He paid no attention to her as she crouched to set her shot.

Then there was a rustle, and the turtle's head recoiled

with a snap. Jo's breath caught as a heron rose up like a ghost, an effortless vertical soar of white. Then the wings spread, stirring wind. It flew over the chain of small lakes and tiny islands and dipped beyond into the trees.

"I used to wonder what it would be like to do that, to fly up into the sky like magic, with only the sound of wing against air."

"I recollect you always liked the birds best," Sam said from behind her. "Didn't know you were thinking about flying off, though."

Jo smiled a little. "I used to imagine it. Mama told me the story of the Swan Princess, the beautiful young girl turned into a swan by a witch. I always thought that was the best."

"She had a lot of stories."

"Yes." Jo turned, studied her father's face. Did it still hurt him, she wondered, to remember his wife? Would it hurt less if she could tell him she believed Annabelle was dead? "I wish I could remember all of them," she murmured.

And she wished she could remember her mother clearly enough to know what to do.

She took a breath to brace herself. "Daddy, did she ever let you know where she'd gone, or why she left?"

"No." The warmth that had come into his eyes as he watched the heron's flight with Jo iced over. "She didn't need to. She wasn't here and she left because she wanted to. We'd best be going and getting this done."

He turned and walked back to the Blazer. They drove the rest of the way in silence.

Jo had done some duty at the campground during her youth. Learning the family business, Kate had called it. The procedure had changed little over the years. The large map tacked to the wall inside the little station detailed the campsites, the paths, the toilet facilities. Blue-headed pins were stuck in the sites that were already occupied, red was for reserved sites, and green was for those where campers had checked out. Green sites needed to be checked, the area policed.

The rest room and shower facilities were also policed twice daily, scrubbed out, the supplies renewed. Since it was unlikely that Ginny had done her duty there since before the bonfire, Jo resigned herself to janitorial work.

"I'll deal with the bathrooms," she told Sam as he carefully filled out the paperwork needed to check a group of impatient campers out. "Then I'll walk over to Ginny's cabin and see what's up."

"Go to her cabin first," Sam said without looking up. "The facilities are her job."

"All right. Shouldn't take more than an hour. I'll meet you back here."

She took the path heading east. If she'd been a heron, she thought with a little smile, she'd have been knocking on Ginny's door in a blink. But the way the path wound and twisted, sliding between ponds and around the high duck grass, it was a good quarter mile hike.

She passed a site with a neat little pop-up camper. Obviously no early risers there, she mused. The flaps were zipped tight. A pair of raccoons waddled across the path, eyed her shrewdly, then continued on toward breakfast.

Ginny's cabin was a tiny box of cedar tucked into the trees. It was livened up with two big, bright-red pots filled with wildly colored plastic flowers. They stood by the door, guarded by an old and weathered pair of pink flamingos. Ginny was fond of saying she dearly loved flowers and pets, but the plastic sort suited her best.

Jo knocked once, waited a beat, then let herself in. The single main room was hardly thirty square feet, with the kitchen area separated from the living area by a narrow service bar. The lack of space hadn't kept Ginny from collecting. Knickknacks crowded every flat surface. Water globes, souvenir ashtrays, china ladies in frilly dresses, crystal poodles.

The walls were painted bright pink and covered with really bad prints—still lifes, for the most part, of flowers and fruit. Jo was both touched and amused to see one of her own black-and-white photos crammed in with them. It was a silly shot of Ginny sleeping in the rope hammock at Sanctuary, taken when they were teenagers.

Jo smiled over it as she turned toward the bedroom. "Ginny, if you're not alone in there, cover up. I'm coming in."

But the bedroom was empty. The bed was unmade and it, as well as a good deal of the floor, was covered with clothes. From the looks of it, Jo decided, Ginny had had a hard time picking out the right outfit for the bonfire.

She looked in the bathroom just to be sure the cabin was empty. The plastic shelf over the tiny pedestal sink was crammed with cosmetics. The bowl of the sink was still dusted with face powder. Three bottles of shampoo stood on the lip of the tub, one of them still uncapped. A doll smiled from the top of the toilet tank, her pink and white crocheted gown spread full over an extra roll of toilet paper.

It was so Ginny.

"Whose bed are you sleeping in this morning, Ginny?" Jo murmured, and with a little sigh, left the cabin and prepared to scrub public rest rooms.

When she reached the facilities, Jo took keys out of her back pocket and opened the small storage area. Inside, cleaning paraphernalia and bathroom supplies were ruthlessly organized. It was always a surprise to realize how disciplined Ginny could be about her work when the rest of her life appeared to be an unpredictable and often messy lark.

Armed with mop and bucket, commercial cleaners, rags, and rubber gloves, Jo went into the women's shower. A woman of about fifty was busily brushing her teeth at one of the sinks. Jo sent her an absentminded smile and began to fill her bucket.

The woman rinsed, spat. "Where's Ginny this morning?"

"Oh." Jo blinked her eyes against the strong fumes of the cleaner as it bubbled up. "Apparently among the missing."

"Overpartied," the woman said with a friendly laugh. "It was a great bonfire. My husband and I enjoyed it— so much that we're getting a very late start this morning."

"That's what vacations are for. Enjoyment and late starts."

"It's hard to convince him of the second part." The woman took a small tube out of her travel kit and, squirting moisturizing lotion on her fingers, began to slather it on. "Dick's a real bear about time schedules. We're nearly an hour late for our morning hike."

"The island's not going anywhere."

"Tell that to Dick." She laughed again, then greeted a young woman and a girl of about three who came in. "Morning, Meg. And how's pretty Lisa today?"

The little girl raced over and began to chatter.

Jo used the voices for background music as she went about her chores. The older woman was Joan, and it seemed she and Dick had the campsite adjoining the one Meg and her husband, Mick, had claimed. They'd formed that oddly intimate vacationers' friendship over the past two days. They made a date to have a fish fry that night, then Meg slipped into one of the shower stalls with her little girl.

Jo listened to the water drum and the child's voice echo as she mopped up the floor. This was what Ginny liked, she realized, collecting these small pieces of other people's lives. But she was able to join in with them, be a part of them. People remembered her. They took snapshots with her in them and slipped them into their family vacation albums. They called her by name, and repeaters always asked after Ginny.

Because she didn't hide from things, Jo thought, leaning on her mop. She didn't let herself fade into the background. She was just like her brightly colored plastic flowers. Cheerful and bold.

Maybe it was time she herself took a few steps forward, Jo thought. Out of the background. Into the light.

She gathered her supplies and walked out of the ladies' section, rounding the building to the door of the men's facilities. She used the side of her fist to knock, giving the wooden door three hard beats, waited a few seconds and repeated.

Wincing a little, she eased the door open and shouted. "Cleaning crew. Anyone inside?"

Years before when she'd been helping Ginny, Jo had walked in on an elderly man in a skimpy towel who'd left his hearing aid back at his campsite. She didn't want to repeat the experience. She heard nothing from inside—no sound of water running, urinals whooshing, but she made as much noise as possible herself as she clamored in.

As a final precaution, she propped the door open and hung the large plastic KEEPING YOUR REST ROOMS CLEAN sign in plain sight. Satisfied, she hauled her bucket to the sinks and dumped in cleaner. Twenty minutes, thirty tops, and she'd be done, she told herself. To get through it she began to plan the rest of her day.

She thought she might drive up to the north shore. There were ruins there from an old Spanish mission, built in the sixteenth century and abandoned in the seventeenth. The Spaniards hadn't had much luck converting the transient Indians to Christianity, and the settlement that historians suspected had been planned had never come to pass.

It was a nice day for a drive to the north tip, the light would be excellent by mid-morning for photographing the ruins and the terraces of shells accumulated and left by the Indians. She wondered if Nathan would like to go along with her. Wouldn't an architect be interested in the

ruins of an old Spanish mission? She could ask Brian to
put together a picnic lunch, and they could spend a few
hours with the ghosts of Spanish monks.

And who was she fooling? Jo demanded. She didn't
give a hang about the monks or the ruins. It was the picnic
she wanted, the afternoon with no responsibility, no
agenda, no deadline. It was Nathan she wanted. She
straightened and pressed a hand to her stomach as it fluttered hard and fast. She wanted the time alone with him,
perhaps to test them both. To see what would happen if
she found the courage to just let herself go. To be with
him. To be Jo.

And why not? she thought. She would call his cottage
when she got back home. She'd make it very casual. Impromptu. Unplanned. And whatever happened, happened.

When the lights switched off, she yelped, splashed water all over her feet. She spun around, leading with her
mop like a lance, and heard the echo of the heavy door
closing.

"Hello?" The sound of her own voice, too thin and
too shaky, made her shiver. "Who's there?" she demanded, and in the dim light filtering through the single
high and frosted window, she edged toward the door.

It resisted her first shove. Panic reared up toothily and
snapped at her throat. She shoved again, then pounded.
Then she whirled, heart booming in her ears. She was
certain that someone had slipped in and stood behind her.

She saw nothing—just empty stalls, the dull gleam of
the wet floor. Heard nothing but her own racing breath.
Still, she leaned against the door, terrified to turn her back
on the room, and her eyes wheeled left and right, searching for movement in the shadows.

Sweat began to run down her back, icy panic sweat.
She couldn't draw enough air, no matter how fast and
hard she tried to gulp it in. Part of her mind held firm,
lecturing her: You know the signs, Jo Ellen, don't let it
win, don't let go. If you break down, you'll be back in

the hospital again. Just get a grip. Get a grip.

She pressed a hand to her mouth to hold back the screams, but they came through in whimpers. She could feel herself begin to crack, terror pushing viciously against will until she simply turned her face to the door, slapping it weakly with her palm.

"Please, please, let me out. Don't leave me in here alone."

She heard the sound of feet crunching on the path, opened her mouth to shout. Then the fear grew monstrous, shoved her stumbling back. Her eyes were wide and fixed on the door, her pulse pounding painfully against her skin. There was a scrape and an oath. Her vision spun, grayed, then went blind as the door swung open and brilliant sunlight poured in.

She saw the silhouette of a man. As her knees buckled, she fumbled for the mop again, jabbing it out like a sword. "Don't come near me."

"Jo Ellen? What the hell's going on?"

"Daddy?" The mop clattered to the floor. She nearly followed it, but his hands caught her arms, drew her up.

"What happened here?"

"I couldn't get out. I couldn't. He's watching. I couldn't get away."

At the moment all Sam knew was that she was pale as death and shaking so hard he could almost hear her bones rattle. Moving on instinct, he picked her up and carried her out into the sun. "It's all right now. You're all right, pudding."

It was an old endearment both of them had forgotten. Jo pressed her face to his shoulder, holding tight when he sat on a stone bench with her cradled on his lap.

She was so small still, Sam thought with surprise. How could that be when she always looked so tall and competent? Whenever she'd had nightmares as a child, she'd curled up in his lap just this way, he remembered. She'd always wanted him when her dreams were bad.

"Don't be afraid. Nothing to be afraid of now."

"I couldn't get out."

"I know. Somebody'd braced some wood against the door. Kids, that's all. Playing pranks."

"Kids." She shuddered it out, clung to it as she did to him. "Kids playing pranks. Yes. They turned the lights off, shut me in. I panicked." She kept her eyes closed a moment longer, trained her breathing back to level. "I didn't even have the sense to turn them back on. I just couldn't think."

"You had a scare. Didn't used to scare so easy."

"No." She opened her eyes now. "I didn't."

"Time was you'd have busted down that door and torn the hide off whoever was fooling with you."

It nearly made her smile, his memory image of her. "Would I?"

"Always had a mean streak." Because she'd stopped trembling, and she was a grown woman and no longer the child he'd once comforted, he patted her shoulder awkwardly. "Guess you softened up some."

"More than some."

"I don't know. I thought you were going to run that mop handle clean through me for a minute. Who'd you mean was watching you?"

"What?"

"You said he was watching you. Who'd you mean?"

The photographs, she thought. Her own face. Annabelle's. Jo shook her head quickly and shifted away. Not now, was all she could think. Not yet. "I was just babbling. Scared stupid. I'm sorry."

"No need to be. Girl, you're white as a sheet yet. We'll get you home."

"I left all the stuff inside."

"I'll tend to it. You just sit here until you get your legs back under you."

"I think I will." But when he started to rise, she

reached for his hand. ''Daddy. Thanks for—chasing the monsters away.''

He looked at their joined hands. Hers was slim and white—her mother's hand, he thought with unbearable sadness. But he looked at her face, and saw his daughter. ''I used to be pretty good at it, I guess.''

''You were great at it. You still are.''

Because his hand suddenly felt clumsy, he let hers go and stepped back. ''I'll put the things away, then we'll head home. You probably just need some breakfast.''

No, Jo thought as she watched him walk away. She needed her father. And until that moment, she hadn't had a clue just how much.

TWELVE

⚬⚬⚬

Jo WASN'T IN A PICNIC
mood any longer. Even the thought of food curdled in her
stomach. She would go out alone, she decided. Over to
the salt marsh, or down to the beach. If she'd had the
energy she would have raced down and tried to catch the
morning ferry back to the mainland. She could have lost
herself in the crowds in Savannah for a few hours.

She washed her face with icy water, pulled a fielder's
cap over her hair. But this time when she passed the darkroom she was compelled to go in, to open the file drawer,
dig out the envelope. Her hands trembled a little as she
spread the pictures out on her workbench.

But the photograph of Annabelle hadn't magically reap-
peared. There was just Jo, shot after shot. And eyes, those
artfully cropped studies of her eyes. Or Annabelle's eyes.
How could she be sure?

There had been a photograph of her mother. There *had*
been. A death photo. She couldn't have imagined it. No
one could imagine such a thing. It would make her insane,
it would mean she was delusional. And she wasn't.
Couldn't be. She'd seen it, goddamn it, it had been there.

With a snap of will she forced herself to stop, to close her eyes, to count her breaths, slowly, in and out, in and out, until her heart stopped dancing in her chest.

She remembered too clearly that sensation of cracking apart, of losing herself. She would not let it happen again.

The photo wasn't there. That was fact. It had existed. That was fact, too. So someone had taken it. Maybe Bobby had realized it upset her and gotten rid of it. Or someone else had broken into her apartment while she was in the hospital and taken it away. Whoever had sent it had come back and taken it away.

Briskly, Jo stuffed the photos back in the manila envelope. She didn't care how crazy that sounded, she was holding on to that idea. Someone was playing a cruel joke, and by obsessing over it, she was letting them win.

She stuffed the envelope back in the file drawer, closed it with a slam, and walked away.

But she could confirm or eliminate one possibility with a single phone call. Hurrying back to her room, she pulled her address book out of the desk and thumbed through quickly. She would ask, that was all, she told herself as she dialed the number of the apartment Bobby Banes shared with a couple of college friends. She could keep it casual and just ask if he'd taken the print.

Her nerves were straining by the third ring.

"Hello?"

"Bobby?"

"No, this is Jack, but I'm available, darling."

"This is Jo Ellen Hathaway," she said crisply. "I'd like to speak to Bobby."

"Oh." There was the sound of a throat clearing. "Sorry, Miss Hathaway, I thought it was one of Bobby's ah, well . . . He's not here."

"Would you ask him to get in touch with me? I'll give you a number where I can be reached."

"Sure, but I don't know when he'll be back exactly, or exactly where he is, either. He took off right after finals. Photo safari. He was really hot to put together some new prints before next semester.''

''I'll leave you the number in any case,'' she said and recited it. ''If he checks in, pass that along, will you?''

''Sure, Miss Hathaway. I know he'd like to hear from you. He's been worried about . . . I mean, wondering. He's been wondering about continuing his internship with you in the fall. Um, how's it going?''

There was no doubt in her mind that Bobby's roommate knew about her breakdown. She'd hoped, but hadn't expected, otherwise. ''It's going fine, thanks.'' Her voice was cool, cutting off the possibility of deeper probing. ''If you hear from Bobby, tell him it's important that I speak with him.''

''I'll do that, Miss Hathaway. Ah—''

''Good-bye, Jack.'' She hung up slowly, closed her eyes.

It didn't matter that Bobby had shared her problem with his friends. She couldn't let it matter, couldn't let herself be embarrassed or upset over it. It was too much to expect him to have kept it to himself when his trainer went crazy on him one morning and was carted off to the hospital.

Her pride would just have to stand it, she decided. Shaking off the clinging shame, she headed downstairs. With any luck, Bobby would call within the next couple of weeks. Then she'd have at least one answer.

When she reached the kitchen door, she heard voices inside and paused with her hand on the panel.

''Something's wrong with her, Brian. She's not herself. Has she talked to you?''

''Kate, Jo never talks to anyone. Why would she talk to me?''

''You're her brother. You're her family.''

Jo heard the clatter of dishes, caught the lingering odor of grilled meat from the breakfast shift. A cupboard door opening, shutting.

''What difference does that make?'' Brian's voice was

testy, impatient. Jo could almost see him trying to shrug Kate off.

"It should make all the difference. Brian, if you'd just try, she might open up to you. I'm worried about her."

"Look, she seemed fine to me last night at the bonfire. She hung out with Nathan for a couple of hours, had a beer, a hot dog."

"And she came back from the campground this morning pale as a sheet. She's been up and down like that ever since she got back. And coming back the way she did, out of the blue. She won't talk about what's going on in her life, when she's going back. You can't tell me you haven't noticed how . . . shaky she is."

Jo didn't want to hear any more. She backed away quickly, turned on her heel, and hurried to the front of the house.

Now they were watching her, she thought wearily. Wondering if she was going to snap. If she told them about her breakdown, she imagined there would be sympathetic—and knowing—nods and murmurs.

The hell with it. She stepped outside, into the sunlight, took a long gulp of air. She could handle it. Would handle it. And if she couldn't find peace here, just be left alone to find it, she would leave again.

And go where? Despair washed over her. Where did you go when you'd left the last place?

Her energy drained, bit by bit. Her feet dragged as she descended the stairs. She was too damn tired to go anywhere, she admitted. She walked to the rope hammock slung in the shade of two live oaks and crawled into it. Like climbing into a womb, Jo thought as the sides hugged her and let her sway.

Sometimes on hot afternoons, she had found her mother there and had slipped into the hammock with her. Annabelle would tell stories in a lazy voice. She would smell soft and sunny, and they would rock and rock and look up through the green leaves to the pieces of sky.

The trees were taller now, she mused. They had had more than twenty years to grow—and so had she. But where was Annabelle?

He strode along the waterfront in Savannah, ignoring the pretty shops and busy tourists. It had not been perfect. It had not been nearly perfect. The woman had been wrong. Of course, he'd known that. Even when he'd taken her he'd known.

It had been exciting, but only momentarily. A flash, then over—like coming too soon.

He stood staring at the river and calmed himself. A little game of mental manipulation that slowed his pulse rate, steadied his breathing, relaxed his muscles. He'd studied such mind-over-body games in his travels.

Soon he began to let the sounds in again—piece by piece. The jingle of a passing bicycle, the drone of tires on pavement. The voices of shoppers, the quick laugh of a child enjoying an ice cream treat.

He was calm again, in control again, and smiled out over the water. He made an attractive picture, and he knew it—his hair blowing lightly in the breeze, a man handsome of face and fit of body who enjoyed catching the female eye.

Oh, he'd certainly caught Ginny's.

She'd been so willing to walk with him on the dark beach and over the dunes. Tipsily flirting with him, the southern in her voice slurred with tequila.

She'd never known what hit her. Literally. He had to bite back a chuckle, thinking of that. One short, swift blow to the back of the head, and she'd toppled. It had been nothing to carry her into the trees. He'd been so high on anticipation, she'd seemed weightless. Undressing her had been . . . stimulating. True, her body had been lusher than he'd wanted, but she'd only been practice.

Still, he'd been in too much of a hurry. He could admit that now, he could analyze now. He'd rushed through it, had fumbled a bit with the equipment because he'd been so anxious to get those first shots. Her naked, with hands bound above her head and secured to a sturdy sapling. He hadn't taken the time to fan her hair out just so, to perfect the lighting and angles.

No, he'd been too overwhelmed with the power of the moment and had raped her the instant she regained consciousness. He'd meant to talk to her first, to capture the fear growing in her eyes as she began to understand what he meant to do.

The way it had been with Annabelle.

She struggled, tried to speak. Her lovely, long legs worked, drawing up, pumping. Her back arched. Now I felt that calm, cold control snick into place.

She was subject. I was artist.

The way it had been with Annabelle, he thought again. The way it should have been now, this time.

But the first orgasm had been a disappointment. So . . . ordinary, he thought now. He hadn't even wanted to rape her again. It had been more of a chore than a pleasure, he remembered. Nothing more than an additional step to manipulate the final shot.

But when he'd taken the silk scarf out of his pocket, slipped it around her neck, tightened it, tightened it, watched her eyes go huge, her mouth work for air, for a scream . . .

That had been considerably better. The orgasm then had been beautifully, brutally hard and long and satisfying.

And he thought, the last shot of her, that decisive moment, might be one of his finest.

He'd title it *Death of a Tramp*, for really, what else had she been? Hardly one of the angels. She'd been cheap and ordinary, he decided. Nothing but a throwaway.

That was why it hadn't been even close to perfect. It hadn't been his fault, but hers. It brightened his mood considerably now that it had come clear. She had been flawed—the subject, not the artist.

Yet he had picked her. He'd chosen her, he'd taken her.

He had to remind himself again that she had simply been practice. The entire incident had been no more than a run-through with a stand-in.

It would be perfect next time. With Jo.

With a little sigh, he patted the leather briefcase that held the photographs he'd developed in his rented rooms nearby. It was time to head back to Desire.

Since Lexy was nowhere to be found, again, Brian headed out to the garden to attack more weeds. Lexy had promised to do it, but he was more than certain she'd run off to hunt up Giff and seduce him into a lunchtime roll. He'd seen the two of them the night before from his bedroom window. Soaking wet, sandy, and giggling like children as they came up the path. It had been obvious even to his tired brain that they'd been doing more than taking a midnight swim. He'd been amused, even a little envious.

It seemed so easy for them just to take each other as they were, to live in the moment. Though he imagined that Giff had in mind a great deal more than the moment and that Lexy would do a quick tap dance on his heart on her way.

Still, Giff was a clever and a patient man, and he might have Lexy dancing to his tune before he was done. Brian thought it would be interesting to watch. From a safe distance.

That was really all he wanted, Brian mused. A safe distance.

He glanced down at the columbine, its lavender and yellow trumpets open and celebrational. It was pretty, it was cheerful, and it was up to him to keep it that way. He reached into the pocket of the short canvas apron he'd slung around his waist for the cultivator. And heard the whimper.

He looked over, saw the woman in the hammock. And

his heart skipped. Her hair was darkly red in the green shade, her hand, falling limply over the side, slim and pale and elegant. Shock had him taking a step forward, then she turned her head, restless, and he backed off.

Not his mother, for Christ's sake. His sister. It was staggering how much she looked like Annabelle at times. At the right angle, with the right light. It made it difficult to let go of the memories, and the pain. His mother had loved to swing in the hammock for an hour on a summer afternoon. And if Brian came across her there, he would sometimes sit cross-legged on the ground beside her. She would lay a hand on his head, ruffle his hair and ask him what adventures he'd had that day.

And she would always listen. Or so he'd once thought. More likely she'd been daydreaming while he chattered. Dreaming of her lover, of her escape from husband and children. Of the freedom she must have wanted more than she wanted him.

But it was Jo who slept in the hammock now, and from the looks of her, she wasn't sleeping peacefully.

A part of him—a part he viewed with disdain and something close to hate—wanted to turn around, walk away, and leave her to her own demons. But he went to her, his brow furrowing in concern as she twitched and moaned in her sleep.

"Jo." He laid a hand on her shoulder and shook it. "Come on, honey, snap out of it."

In the dream, whatever it was pursuing her through the forest with its ghost trees and wild wind reached out and dug its sharp nails into her flesh.

"Don't!" She swung out, ripping herself away. "Don't touch me!"

"Easy." He'd felt the wind of her fist brush his face and wasn't sure whether to be concerned or impressed. "I could do without the broken nose."

Her breath ragged, she stared blindly at him. "Brian."

The damn shudders won, so she flopped back down and closed her eyes. "Sorry. Bad dream."

"So I gathered." It was concern after all, and more than he'd expected. Kate was right, as usual. Something was very definitely wrong here. He took a chance and eased himself down on the edge of the hammock. "You want something? Water?"

"No." The surprise showed in her eyes when she opened them and looked down at the hand he'd laid over hers. She couldn't remember the last time he'd taken her hand. Or she his. "No, I'm fine. Just a dream."

"You used to have bad ones as a kid too. Wake up hollering for Daddy."

"Yeah." She managed a weak smile. "You don't grow out of everything, I guess."

"Still get them a lot?" He tried to make it sound casual, but he saw the flicker in her eyes.

"I don't wake up hollering for anyone anymore," she said stiffly.

"No, I don't suppose you would." He wanted to get up, move away. Hadn't her problems stopped being his years ago? But he stayed where he was, rocking the hammock gently.

"It's not a flaw to be self-sufficient, Brian."

"No."

"And it's not a sin to want to handle problems on your own."

"Is that what you're doing, Jo? Handling problems? Well, rest easy. I've got enough of my own without taking on yours."

But still he didn't leave, and they rocked together quietly in the green shade. The comfort of it made her eyes sting. Cautious and needy, she took a tentative step. "I've been thinking a lot about Mama lately."

His shoulders tensed. "Why?"

"I've been seeing her, in my mind." The photograph that isn't there. "Dreaming about her. I think she's dead."

The tears had slipped out without either of them realizing it. When he glanced back, saw them sliding down her cheeks, his stomach clutched. "What's the point of this, Jo Ellen? What's the point in making yourself sick over something that happened twenty years ago and can't be changed?"

"I can't stop it—I can't explain it. It's just there."

"She left us, we lived through it. That's just there too."

"But what if she didn't leave. What if someone took her, what if—"

"What if she was abducted by aliens?" he said shortly. "For Christ's sake. The cops kept the case open more than a year. There was nothing, no evidence she'd been kidnapped, no evidence of foul play. She left. That's that. Stop driving yourself crazy."

She shut her eyes again. Maybe that was what she was doing, slowly driving herself toward insanity. "Is it better to think that every time she told us she loved us it was a lie? Is that more stable, Brian?"

"It's better to leave it alone."

"And be alone," she murmured. "Every last one of us. Because someone else might say they love us, and that might be a lie too. Better to leave it alone. Better not to take the chance. Better to be alone than left alone."

It hit close enough to home to make him bristle. "You're the one with the nightmares, Jo, not me." He made his decision quickly and rose before he could change his mind. "Come on."

"Come on where?"

"We're going for a drive. Let's go." He took her hand again, hauled her to her feet and began to pull her with him to his car.

"Where? What?"

"Just do what you're told for once, goddamn it." He bundled her in, slammed the door, and saw with satisfaction that she was stunned enough to stay put. "I've got Kate on my back," he muttered as he piled in and turned the key. "You crying. I've had just about enough. I've got my own life, you know."

"Yeah." She sniffled, rubbed the back of her hand over her cheeks to dry them. "You're really living it up, Brian."

"Just shut up." The wheels spun as he whipped the car around and headed down the road. "You're going to come back here looking like a sheet-white bag of bones, we're going to get to the bottom of it. Then maybe everybody'll go back to their respective corners and leave me the hell alone."

Eyes narrowed now, she clutched the door handle. "Where are we going?"

"You're going," he corrected, "to the doctor."

"The hell I am." Surprise warred with sick alarm. "Stop this car right now and let me out."

He set his mouth grimly and accelerated. "You're going to the doctor. And if I have to, I'll cart you in. We'll find out if Kirby's half as good as she thinks she is."

"I am not sick."

"Then you shouldn't be afraid to let her look you over."

"I'm not afraid, I'm pissed. And I have no intention of wasting Kirby's time."

He swung up the little drive, squealed to a halt at Kirby's cottage, then clamped a hand on his sister's shoulder. His eyes were hot and dark and level. "You can walk in, or you can embarrass both of us by having me haul you in over my shoulder. Either way, you're going, so choose."

They glared at each other. Jo figured her temper was every bit a match for his. In a verbal battle, she had a decent shot of taking him down. If he decided to get physical—and she remembered from their youth that it was very possible—she didn't have a prayer. Taking the high road, she shifted pride to the forefront.

With a toss of her head, she stepped lightly out of the

car and walked up the steps to Kirby's cottage.

They found Kirby at the kitchen counter, slathering peanut butter on bread. "Hi." She licked her thumb and let her greeting smile stay in place as she scanned first one coldly furious face, then the other. Strange, she thought, how suddenly strong the family resemblance. "Want some lunch?"

"Got any time to do a physical?" Brian demanded and gave his sister a firm shove forward.

Kirby took a small bite of the open-faced sandwich as Jo turned and hissed at her brother. "Sure. My next appointment isn't until one-thirty." She smiled brightly. "Which one of you wants to get naked for me today?"

"She's having her lunch," Jo informed Brian grandly.

"Peanut butter's not lunch unless you're six." He gave her another shove. "Go in there and strip. We're not leaving until she's looked you over, head to foot."

"I see this is my first appointment by abduction." Kirby eyed Brian consideringly. She'd hoped he cared enough about his sister to be tough with her, but she hadn't been sure. "Go ahead, Jo, back in my old room. I'll be right in."

"There's nothing wrong with me."

"Good. That'll make my job easier and give you an excuse to punish Brian afterward." She skimmed a hand over her neat French twist and smiled again. "I'll help you."

"Fine." She spun around and stomped down the hall.

"What's all this about, Brian?" Kirby murmured when the door slammed.

"She's having nightmares, she's not eating. She came back from the campground this morning white as a sheet."

"What was she doing at the campground?"

"Ginny didn't show up for work today."

"Ginny? That's not like her." Kirby frowned, then waved it away. That was a different worry. "I'm glad you brought her in. I've been wanting to take a look at her.''

''I want you to find out what's wrong with her.''

''Brian, I'll give her a physical, and if there's a physical problem, I'll find it. But I'm not a psychiatrist.''

Frustrated, he dug his hands into his pockets. ''Just find out what's wrong with her.''

Kirby nodded, handed him the rest of her sandwich. ''There's milk in the fridge. Help yourself.''

When she stepped into the examining room, Jo was still fully dressed and pacing. ''Look, Kirby—''

''Jo, you trust me, don't you?''

''That has nothing to—''

''Let's just do this, get it done, then everyone will feel better.'' She picked up a fresh gown. ''Go into the bath across the hall, put this on, and pee in the cup.'' She took out a fresh chart and a form as Jo frowned at her. ''I'm going to need some medical history—last period, any physical problems, any prescriptions you're on, any allergies, that sort of thing. You can start filling that out once you've donned the latest fashion there and I'm doing the urinalysis.''

She bent over to print Jo's name on the chart. ''Better give in gracefully,'' Kirby murmured. ''Brian's bigger than you.''

Jo shrugged once, then stalked off to the bathroom.

''Blood pressure's a little high.'' Kirby removed the cuff. ''Nothing major, and likely due to a slight temper fluctuation.''

''Very funny.''

Kirby warmed her stethoscope between her palms, then pressed it to Jo's back. ''Deep breath in, out. Again. You're a tad underweight, too. Which makes the female in me green with envy and the sensible physician cluck her tongue.''

''My appetite's been a little off lately.''

''The cooking at Sanctuary should take care of that.''

And if it didn't, Kirby intended to reevaluate. She took out her ophthalmoscope, began to examine Jo's eyes. "Headaches?"

"Now or ever?"

"Either."

"Now, yes, but I'd say that's a direct result of tangling with Brian the Bully." Then she sighed. "I suppose I've been getting more of them in the last few months than usual."

"Dull and throbbing or sharp and piercing?"

"Mostly the dull and throbbing variety."

"Dizziness, fainting, nausea?"

"I—no, not really."

Kirby leaned back, leaving one hand resting on Jo's shoulder. "No, or not really?" When Jo shrugged, Kirby set the instrument aside. "Honey, I'm a doctor and I'm your friend. I need you to be straight with me, and you need to know that anything you tell me inside this room stays between us."

Jo took a deep breath, clutched her hands hard in her lap. "I had a breakdown." The wind whooshed out of her, part fear, part relief. "About a month ago, before I came back here. I just fell apart. I couldn't stop it."

Saying nothing, Kirby laid both hands on Jo's shoulders, massaged gently. Jo lifted her head and saw nothing but compassion in those soft green eyes. Her own filled. "It makes me feel like such a fool."

"Why should it?"

"I've never felt that helpless. I've always been able to handle things, Kirby, to deal with them as they came. And then everything just piled up, heavier and heavier. And I'm not sure if I was imagining things or if they were really happening. I just don't know. And then I collapsed. Just broke."

"Did you see someone?"

"I didn't have any choice. I fell apart right in front of my assistant. He carted me off to the ER, and they hospitalized me for a few days. A mental breakdown. I don't care if we are nearing the twenty-first century, I don't care how it's intellectualized. I'm ashamed.''

"I'm telling you there's nothing shameful about it and that you have every right to feel whatever you want to feel.''

Jo's lips curved a little. "So I don't have to be ashamed that I'm ashamed.''

"Absolutely not. What was your work schedule like?''

"Tight, but I liked it tight.''

"Your social life?''

"Nil, but I liked it nil. And yes, that pretty much goes for my sex life too. I wasn't depressed or pining over a man or the lack of one. I've been thinking about my mother a lot," Jo said slowly. "I'm nearly the same age she was when she left, when everything changed.''

And your life fell apart, Kirby thought. "And you wondered, worried, if everything was going to change again, beyond your control. I'm not a shrink, Jo, just an old-fashioned GP. That's a friend's speculation. What was the prognosis when you were released?''

"I don't know, exactly.'' Jo shifted, crinkling the paper beneath her. "I released myself.''

"I see. You didn't note any prescriptions down on your form.''

"I'm not taking any. And don't ask me what they prescribed. I never filled anything. I don't want drugs—and I don't want to talk to a shrink.''

"All right, for now we'll handle this the old-fashioned way. We'll eliminate any physical cause. I'll prescribe fresh air, rest, regular meals—and some good, safe sex if you can get it," she added with a smile.

"Sex isn't one of my priorities.''

"Well, honey, then you are crazy.''

Jo blinked, then snorted out a laugh as Kirby dabbed the inside of her elbow with alcohol. "Thanks.''

"No charge for insults. And the last part of the pre-

scription is to talk. With me, with your family, with whoever you can trust to listen. Don't let it build up again.
You're cared for, Jo. Lean a little.''

She shook her head before Jo could speak. "Your
brother cares enough to drag you in here—here to a place
he's avoided like the plague since I moved in. And if I'm
any judge of character, he's out there right now pacing
and muttering and worried sick that I'm going to go out
and tell him his sister has three weeks to live.''

"It would serve him right.'' Jo sighed heavily. "Even
if I do feel better now than I have in weeks.'' Then her
eyes fastened on the syringe and widened. "What the hell
is that for?''

"Just need a little blood.'' Needle poised, Kirby
grinned. "Want to scream, and see how long it takes him
to run in here?''

Jo averted her eyes, held her breath. "I wouldn't give
him the satisfaction.''

When Jo was dressed again, Kirby tossed her a fat plastic
bottle. "They're just vitamins,'' she said. "High-potency.
If you start eating right, you won't need them. But they'll
give you a boost for now. I'll let you know when the
blood work comes back from the lab, but everything else
is within normal range.''

"I appreciate it, really.''

"Show it, then, by taking care of yourself and talking
to me when you need to.''

"I will.'' It always felt a bit odd for her to make an
overtly affectionate move, but she stepped over and kissed
Kirby's cheek. "I will. And I meant what I said. I feel
better than I have in a long time.''

"Good. Follow Doctor Kirby's orders, and you should
feel better yet.'' Keeping her concerns to herself, she led
Jo out.

Brian was exactly where she'd expected, restlessly pacing her living room. He stopped and scowled at them

both. Kirby met the look with a bright smile.

"You have a bouncing one-hundred-and-ten-pound girl, Daddy. Congratulations."

"Very funny. What the hell's wrong with you?" he demanded of Jo.

She angled her head, narrowed her eyes. "Bite me," she suggested, then strolled to the door. "I'm walking back. Thanks for squeezing this idiot's whims into your schedule, Kirby."

"Oh, I've been working on doing just that for months." She chuckled as the screen door slammed.

"I want to know what's wrong with my sister."

"She's suffering from acute brotheritis at the moment. While extremely irritating, it's rarely fatal."

"I want a fucking straight answer," he said between his teeth, and she nodded approvingly.

"I like you even better when you're human." She turned to the coffeepot, pleased to see he'd made himself useful and had brewed fresh. "All right, straight answers. Would you like to sit down?"

His stomach jittered painfully. "How bad is it?"

"Not nearly as bad as you apparently think. You take it black, don't you? Like a real man." Her breath caught when he closed a hand hard over her arm.

"I'm not in the mood for this."

"Okay, so my witty repartee isn't going to relax you. It'll take a couple of weeks to get full test results back, but I can give you my educated opinion from the exam. Jo's a little run-down. She's edgy and she's stressed and she's annoyed with herself for being edgy and stressed. What she needs is exactly what you've shown me you can give her. Support—even when she kicks against it."

The first trickle of relief loosened the pressure in his chest. "That's it? That's all?"

She turned away to finish pouring the coffee. "There's doctor-patient confidentiality. Jo's entitled to her privacy and to my discretion."

"Jo's my sister."

"Yes, and on a personal level I'm happy to see you take that relationship to heart. I wasn't sure that you did. Here." She pressed the cup into his hand. "She came home because she needed to be home. She needed her family. So be there. That's all I can tell you. Anything else has to come from her."

He paced away, sipping coffee without realizing it. All right, he thought, she wasn't suffering from any of the mysterious and deadly diseases he'd conjured up while he'd been waiting. She'd just run herself out of energy. It wasn't cancer or a brain tumor.

"All right." This time he said it aloud. "I can probably browbeat her into eating regularly and threaten Lexy away from picking fights with her."

"You're very sweet," Kirby murmured.

"No, I'm not." He set the cup down abruptly and stepped back. His worry had faded enough to allow him to see Kirby clearly. The way those mermaid eyes were smiling at him. The way she stood there, all cool and composed, all pink and gold. "I'm just looking out for myself. I want my routine back, and I won't get it until she's steadied out."

Eyes warm, Kirby walked toward him. "Liar. Fraud. Softie."

"Back off."

"Not yet." She reached up to catch his face in her hands. He'd stirred more than her lust this time, and she couldn't resist it. "You booked the physical for her, and you haven't paid the bill." She rose to her toes. "My services don't come cheap." And brushed her lips to his.

His hands were at her waist as the taste of her flooded into him. "I keep telling you to back off." He tilted his head, deepened the kiss. "Why don't you listen?"

Her breath was already starting to back up, clog her lungs. A glorious sensation. "I'm stubborn. Persistent. Right."

"You're aggressive." His teeth nipped into her bottom lip, tugged. "I don't like aggressive women."

"Mmm. Yes, you do."

"No, I don't." He pushed her back against the counter until his body was pressed hard and hot to hers, until his mouth could fix firmly and devour. "But I want you. Happy now?"

She tipped her head back, moaning when his mouth raced down her throat. "Give me five minutes to cancel my afternoon appointments and we'll both be ecstatic. Brian, put your hands on me, for God's sake."

"It's not going to be easy." He nipped at her ear where a little emerald stud winked at the lobe, worked his way restlessly back to her mouth to plunder until her nails dug into his shoulders. He saw himself taking her there, where they stood, just dragging down his fly, dragging down her neat trousers and plunging in until this desperate need, this vicious frustration, was behind him.

But he didn't touch her, didn't take her. Instead, he used the ache churning inside him to control them both. He wrapped his hand around her throat, drew her head back until their eyes met. Hers were the green of restless seas, urging him to dive in.

"It's going to be my way. You're going to have to accept that."

Nerves shuddered through desire. "Listen—"

"No, we're done with that. Done with the games too. You could've backed off, but you didn't. Now it's going to be my way. When I come back, we're going to finish this."

Her breath was coming fast, her blood pumping hot. For a moment she hated him for being able to study her with eyes so cool and controlled. "Do you think that scares me?"

"I don't think you've got sense enough to let it scare you." And he smiled, slowly, dangerously. "But it should. When I come back," he repeated and stepped away from her. "And I won't give a damn if you're ready."

She steadied herself and grabbed for some pride. "Why, you arrogant bastard!"

"That's right." He walked toward the door, praying he could make it out before the aching for her made him groan aloud. He shot her a last look, skimming his gaze over the tousled, sunlit hair, the eyes that sparkled with a range of dangerous emotions, the mouth that was still swollen from his. "I'd go tidy myself up a bit, doc. Your next patient just pulled up."

He let the screen slam behind him.

THIRTEEN

❧

L<small>ITTLE</small> D<small>ESIRE</small> C<small>OTTAGE</small>
wasn't much of a detour on the way back to Sanctuary.
In any case, Jo thought, scrambling to justify it, the walk
would do her good.

Maybe she wanted to take some afternoon shots of the
river, see how many more wildflowers had bloomed. And
since she'd be walking by, it would be rude not to at least
stop in.

Besides, it was family property.

She even worked out a little just-passing-by excuse, did
some mental rehearsing to perfect just the right casual
tone. So it was quite a letdown to get to the cottage and
see that Nathan's Jeep was gone.

She stood at the base of the stairs a moment, debating,
then quickly mounted them before she could change her
mind. There was nothing wrong with slipping in, just for
a second, leaving a note. It wasn't as if she would disturb
anything or poke around. She just wanted to—Damn it,
his door was locked.

It was another minor jolt. People on Desire rarely
locked their doors. Too curious now to worry about man-

ners, she pressed her face to the glass panel and peered in.

On the long table that served the kitchen area sat a compact laptop computer, frustratingly and neatly closed. A streamlined printer stood beside it. Long tubes that she assumed held blueprints were stacked nearby. One large square of paper was unrolled and anchored at the corners with a jar of instant coffee, an ashtray, and two mugs. But no matter how she shifted or angled her head, she couldn't make out what was printed on it.

None of my business anyway, she reminded herself, straining to see. At a crash of leaves behind her she stepped back quickly, looked over her shoulder. A wild turkey cut loose with its quick, gobbling call and lumbered into flight. With a roll of her eyes, Jo patted her skipping heart. It would be perfect if Nathan himself strolled out of the trees and caught her spying into his house.

She reminded herself that she had dozens of things she could do, dozens of places she could go. It wasn't as though she'd gone out of her way to see him. By much.

It was probably best that she'd missed him, she told herself, as she jogged back down the stairs and headed home. Taking the Palmetto Trail, she followed the bend of the river into the thick shade where muscadine vines and resurrection ferns turned forest to verdant jungle.

She didn't need the kind of distraction, the kind of complication that Nathan Delaney was bound to bring to her life just now. She was just getting back on her feet.

If she pursued a relationship with him, she'd have to tell him about . . . things. And if she told him, that would be the end of the relationship. Who wanted to get tangled up with a crazy woman on their vacation?

The path twisted, crowded in by the saw palmettos that gave it its name. She heard the turkey call again, and the long, liquid notes of a warbler. Her camera bag thudded at her hip as she quickened her pace and argued with herself.

So, by not starting anything, she was just saving them both time and embarrassment.

Why the hell hadn't he been home?

"Ssh." Giff put a hand over Lexy's mouth when he heard footsteps coming along the path near the clearing that was guarded by thick oak limbs and cabbage palms. "Someone's passing by," he whispered.

"Oh." In a lightning move, Lexy grabbed her discarded blouse and pressed it to her breasts. "I thought you said Nathan had gone over to the mainland for the day."

"He did. I passed him on his way to the ferry."

"Then who—oh." Lexy snickered as she peeked through palm fronds. "It's just Jo. Looking annoyed with the world, as usual."

"Quiet." Giff ducked Lexy's head down with his. "I'd just as soon your sister not catch me with my pants down."

"But you've got such a nice . . ." She made a grab for him, and muffling giggles, they tussled until Jo passed out of sight.

"You're a bad one, Lex." Giff pinned her, grinned down into her face. She still wore her bra—they hadn't quite gotten around to disposing of it—and he enjoyed the sensation of the slick material rubbing against his chest. "Just how would I have explained myself if she'd come over this way?"

"If she doesn't know what's going on, it's time someone showed her."

With a shake of his head, he leaned down to kiss the tip of her nose. "You're too hard on your sister."

"I'm too hard on her?" Lexy snorted. "Let's try that the other way around. It fits much better."

"Well, maybe you're too hard on each other. Looks to me like Jo's had a rough time with something lately."

"Her life's perfect for her," Lexy disagreed, pouting and twirling a lock of Giff's hair around her fingers. "She's got her work, all that traveling. People ooh and aah over her photographs like they were newborn babies. Or they study them like stupid textbooks. And she makes piles of money, enough so that she doesn't have to worry about stingy trust funds."

Love tugged at him as he skimmed his knuckles over her chin. "Honey, it's a pure foolish waste of time for you to be jealous of Jo."

"Jealous?" At the shock of the insult her eyes went dark and wide. "Why in holy hell would I be jealous of Jo Ellen?"

"Exactly." He kissed her, just a little nibbling peck. "The two of you are after the same thing. The way you are and the way you go after it are as different as night and day, but the goal's the same."

"Really?" Her voice was cool and smooth as fresh milk. "And what goal would that be?"

"To be happy. That's what most people want down under the rest of it. And to make their mark. Just because she's made hers before you doesn't make yours less important. And, after all, she had three years' head start."

It didn't placate Lexy in the least. Her voice went from cool to icy. "I don't know why you brought me out here if all you wanted to do was talk about my sister."

"Honey, you brought me." He grinned and kept her pinned under him despite her bad-tempered wiggles. "As I recall, you moseyed on down to Sand Castle Cottage, where I was minding my own business, replacing screens. You whispered a little something in my ear, and as you already had this here blanket in your tote, what was a man to do?"

She lifted her chin, raised a brow. "Why, I don't know, Giff. What is a man to do?"

"I guess I'll have to show you."

He took his time and that left her a little weak and

trembling. The night before, everything had poured over her in a hot rush. Need on top of pleasure, pleasure clawing at need. But today, in the cool air and dim light, his hands were slow, calluses scraping gently over her skin, fingers pressing, then skimming. And though his mouth was hot, it didn't hurry. It came back to hers again and again, as if hers was the only flavor he needed.

When she sighed, it came from deep within.

She could be seduced as well as taken. He'd waited a lifetime to do both, to watch her let him do both. There was nothing about her that wasn't precious to him. Now he could show her, inch by inch. One day soon he would tell her, word by word.

When he slipped inside her, her moan of welcome was sweet and silky. He braced himself over her to give more, to take more, and his pace was as lazy as the river that flowed nearby.

She whimpered when he lowered his head to suck gently on her breasts.

"You come first," he murmured. "So I can see you."

She couldn't have stopped herself. She was being carried along like a weightless leaf on the river's current. The orgasm flowed through her, long and lovely and deep. She could barely sigh out his name as it slid through her system.

His mouth came back to hers as it curved, and he emptied himself into her.

"Mmmm." It was all she could manage as he rolled her over and snuggled her head on his chest. She'd never had a climax like that—one that crept up from the toes like silk-dipped fingers.

And he'd seemed so in control, so completely aware of her. Only the thunder of his heart under her cheek proved that he'd been as undone as she.

She smiled again, and turned her lips to his chest. "You must have done a lot of practicing."

He kept his eyes closed, enjoying the air on his face

and her hair under his hand. "I'm a strong believer that you keep working on a skill until you get it right."

"I'd say you got it right."

"I've wanted you all my life, Lexy."

It made something inside her shiver to hear him say it, so simple, so easy. Caught in the afterglow, she lifted her head, and when she looked at him, that something shivered again. "I guess, deep down, I've always wanted you too."

When his eyes opened, and the look in them made her mouth go dry, she put on a sassy grin. "But you used to be so skinny."

"You used to be flat-chested." She chuckled when he reached down to cup her breasts. "Things do change."

Scooting up, she straddled him. "And you used to pull my hair."

"You used to bite me. I've still got your teeth marks back of my left shoulder."

Laughing, she shook her hair back. It was going to be painful to brush the tangles out, but she had to admit, it had been well worth it. "You do not."

"Hell I don't. Mama calls it my Hathaway brand."

"Let's just see." She tugged at him until he rolled toward his side. She peered down, squinted, though she could see the faint white scar clearly enough. Her brand. It gave her an odd little thrill to know he carried it. "Where? I don't see anything." She shifted closer. "Oh, you mean that little thing? Why, that's nothing. I can do much better now."

Before he could defend himself, she clamped her teeth on his shoulder. He yelped, flipped her over, and rolled until they were tangled in the blanket. His hands managed to reach here, reach there so that she was as breathless with freshening desire as with laughter.

"I'd say it's time I put my mark on you."

"Don't you dare bite me, Giff." She giggled, struggled, rolled. "Ouch! Damn it."

"I didn't bite you yet."

"Well, something did."

He moved fast, visions of snakes slicing into his brain. He rolled her, gained his feet, and scooped her into his arms in one lightning move. Her jaw dropped open as she watched his eyes, suddenly hard and cold, scan the ground.

"Golly," was all she could manage, as her romantic's heart flopped in her chest.

Nothing slithered or crept or crawled. But he saw a glint of silver. He set Lexy on her feet, turned her around. A faint red scrape marred her delicate shoulder blade. "You just rolled over something, that's all." He kissed the scrape lightly, then bent to pick up the dangle of silver. "Somebody's earring."

Bright-eyed, Lexy reached back to rub absently at the little pain. Why, he'd picked her up as if she weighed nothing at all, she thought dreamily. And he'd stood there, holding her, as if he would have defended her against a fire-breathing dragon.

Images of Lancelot and Guinevere, of misty castles, floated into her head before she managed to focus on the earring Giff was holding. It was a bright trail of small silver stars.

"That's Ginny's." With a slight frown, she reached out and took it from him. "It's from her favorite pair. Wonder how it got here."

Giff lifted his brows, wiggled them. "I guess we're not the first people to use the forest for something other than a nature walk."

With a laugh, Lexy sat on the blanket again, setting the earring carefully beside her before she reached for her bra. "I guess you'd be right. Long detour from the camp-ground and her cottage, though. Was she wearing them last night?"

"I don't pay much mind to my cousin's earbobs," Giff said dryly.

"I'm almost sure . . ."

She trailed off, trying to bring back the picture. Ginny'd been wearing a bright-red shirt with silver studs, tight white jeans cinched with a concho belt. And yes, Lexy thought, almost certainly her favorite silver star dangles. Ginny liked the way they swung and caught the light.

"Well, doesn't matter. I'll get it back to her. If I can find her."

He sat down to pull on his Jockeys. "What do you mean?"

"She must have found herself a hot date at the bonfire last night. She didn't show up for work this morning."

"What do you mean she didn't show up? Ginny always shows up."

"Well, she didn't this morning. I heard the hubbub over it when I came down for the breakfast shift." Lexy dug in her tote for a hair pick and began the arduous process of dragging out the tangles. "Ouch, damn it. We had a bunch of check-ins and -outs over at the campground, and no Ginny. Kate sent Daddy and Jo over to handle it."

Giff pulled on his jeans, rising to snap them. "They checked her cabin?"

"I finished up before they got back, but I'd expect so. I can tell you, Kate was in a tizzy."

"That's not like Ginny. She's wild, but she'd never leave Kate in the lurch that way."

"Maybe she's sick." Lexy rubbed the earring between her fingers before tucking it into the little pocket of the tiny shorts she'd put on to drive Giff crazy. "She was knocking back the tequila pretty steady."

He nodded in agreement, but he knew that even hung over, she'd have done her job or seen to her own replacement. He remembered the way she'd looked, staggering over the beach in the dark, waving at him and Lexy, blowing them kisses. "I'll go check on her."

"You do that." Lexy rose, enjoying the way he watched her legs unfold. "And maybe later . . ." She slid her arms around him, up his back. "You'll come check on me."

"I was giving that some thought. I was figuring I'd come by, have dinner at the inn. Let you . . . serve me."

"Oh." Her lips took on a feline curve as she stepped back, slowly pulling the pick through her long corkscrew curls. "Were you figuring that?"

"Yeah. Then I was figuring how about if I just wandered on upstairs afterward, maybe wandered right on into your room. We could try this in a bed for a change."

"Well." She ran her tongue over her top lip. "I might just be available tonight—depending on what kind of tipper you are."

He grinned and captured her just-moistened lips with his in a kiss that rocked her straight back on her heels.

When she could breathe again, she exhaled slowly. "That's a real good start." She bent down to gather the blanket, deliberately turning to tease him with tight buns in tight shorts, then turned her head. "I'm going to give you . . . excellent service."

By the time Giff was back in his truck and on the road to the campground, his heart rate was nearly back to normal. The woman was potent, he thought, and life with her was going to be a continual adventure. He didn't think she was quite ready to have her notions adjusted to a lifetime with him, but he was going to work on that too.

He smiled to himself, flipped the radio up so Clint Black wailed through the speakers. He had it all planned, Giff mused. The courtship—which was progressing just fine in his opinion. The proposal, the marriage, the life.

As soon as he convinced her that he was exactly what she needed, that would be that. Meanwhile, they would give each other a hell of a ride.

He turned into the campground, frowning a little as he saw the teenager inside the booth instead of Ginny. "Hey,

Colin.'' Giff braked, leaned out his window. ''Got you manning the post today?''

''Looks like.''

''Seen Ginny?''

''Not hide nor hair.'' The boy tried out a lascivious wink. ''She musta caught a live one.''

''Yeah.'' But there was an uncomfortable shift in Giff's gut. ''I'm going to look in at her cabin. See what's up.''

''Help yourself.''

Giff drove slowly, mindful of the possibility that a child might dart out·in front of him. With summer just around the corner, he knew more would be coming, stacking up in the campground, the cottages, spreading towels on the beach. Those in the cottages would fry themselves in the sun half the day, then come back and run their ACs to the max. Which usually meant he'd be kept busy replacing coils.

Not that he minded. It was good, honest work. And though he dreamed now and then of taking on something more challenging, he figured his time would come.

He pulled up into Ginny's short drive and climbed out. He hoped to find her in bed, moaning, with her head in a basin. That would explain why it was so damn quiet. When she was home, Ginny always had the radio blaring, the TV on, her voice raised in song or in argument with one of the talk shows she was addicted to. The noises clashed cheerfully. She said it kept her from feeling lonesome.

But he heard nothing except the click of palm fronds in the breeze, the hollow plop of frogs in water. He walked to the door, and because he'd run as tame in her cabin as he did in his own home, he didn't bother to knock.

He nearly jumped out of his skin as he pulled open the door and a man's form filled it. ''Jesus Christ Almighty, Bri, you might as well shoot me as scare me to death.''

''Sorry.'' Brian smiled a little. ''I heard the truck,

thought it might be Ginny.'' His gaze shifted over Giff's shoulder. "She's not with you, is she?"

"No, I just heard she wasn't at work and came to check."

"She's not here. It doesn't look like she's been around today, though it's hard to tell.'' He glanced back over his shoulder. "Woman's messy as three teenage girls on a rampage.''

"Maybe she's at one of the sites.''

Brian scanned the trees that crowded close around the tufts of golden marsh grass. There were a couple of pintail ducks taking a breather in the slough on their trek along the Atlantic flyway. A marsh hawk circled lazily overhead. Near the narrow path, where spiderwort tangled, a trio of swallowtail butterflies flitted gaily.

But he saw no sign of the human inhabitant of this small corner of the island.

"I parked over near number one, circled around to here. I asked after her, but nobody I ran into has seen her since yesterday.''

"That's not right." The discomfort in Giff's stomach escalated into dull pain. "Bri, that's just not right.''

"I agree with you. It's after two o'clock. Even if she'd spent the night somewhere else she should have surfaced by now.'' Worry was a fist pressing at the back of his neck. He rubbed it absently as he looked back into the living mess of Ginny's cabin. "It's time we started to make calls.''

"I'll go by, tell my mother. She'll have half a dozen calls made before either of us can make one. Come on, I'll drop you back at your car.''

"Appreciate it.''

"She was pretty drunk last night,'' Giff added as he slipped behind the wheel. "I saw her—Lexy and I saw her. We were in the water . . . taking a swim,'' he added with a quick glance over.

"Swimming—right.''

Giff waited a beat, tugged at the brim of his cap. "How am I supposed to tell you I'm sleeping with your sister?"

Brian pressed his fingers to his eyes. "I guess that was one way. It's a little difficult for me to get my tongue around the word 'congratulations' under the circumstances."

"You want to know my intentions?"

"I don't." Brian held up a hand. "I really, really don't."

"I'm going to marry her."

"Now I'm never going to be able to say the word 'congratulations' again." Shifting in his seat, Brian aimed a level stare at Giff. "Are you crazy?"

"I love her." Giff slapped the truck into reverse and backed up. "I always have."

Brian got a vividly clear picture of Lexy gleefully kicking Giff's still bleeding heart off a cliff. "You're a big boy, Giff. You know what you're getting into."

"That's right, just like I know that you and everybody else in your family never give Lexy enough credit." Giff's normally mild voice took on a defensive edge that made Brian raise his eyebrows. "She's smart, she's strong, she's got a heart as big as the ocean, and when you shake the nonsense away, she's as loyal as they come."

Brian blew out a long breath. She was also reckless, impulsive, and self-absorbed. But Giff's words had struck a chord and made Brian ashamed. "You're right. And if anyone can polish up her better qualities, I'd say it would be you."

"She needs me." Giff tapped his fingers on the wheel. "I'd appreciate it if you didn't mention any of this to her. I haven't gotten to that part yet."

"Believe me, the last thing I want to discuss with Alexa is her love life."

"Good. Well, I veered off from where I was heading. Like I was saying, I saw Ginny last night. Must have been somewhere around midnight. Wasn't paying much attention to the time. She was walking south on the beach—stopped and waved at us."

"Was she alone?"

"Yeah. Said she needed to clear her head. I didn't notice her walk back, but I was kind of, uh, busy for a while."

"Well, if she passed out on the beach, someone would have come across her by now, so she must have walked back, or cut up over the dunes."

"We found one of her earrings in that clearing on the Sanctuary side of the river."

"When?"

"Little bit ago," Giff said as he pulled up beside Brian's car. "Lexy and I were . . ."

"Oh, please, don't put that image in my brain. What are you, rabbits?" He shook his head. "Are you sure it was Ginny's earring?"

"Lexy was—and she was pretty sure Ginny was wearing it last night."

"That's the kind of thing Lex would notice. But it's a funny way for Ginny to walk if she was heading home."

"That's what I thought. Still, she might have been with someone by then. It's not like Ginny to leave a party before it's over—unless she's got another kind of party planned."

"None of this is like Ginny."

"No, it's not. I'm getting worried, Brian."

"Yeah." He got out of the truck, then turned and leaned in the window. "Go get your mother started on those calls. I'm going to head down to the ferry. Who knows, maybe she met the man of her dreams and eloped to Savannah."

By six there was a full-scale search under way. Through the forest paths, along the rugged hiking trails to the north, down the long curve of beach and around the winding paths that twisted through the sloughs. Some of those who scoured the island remembered another search for another woman.

Twenty years hadn't dimmed the memory. And while they looked for Ginny, many murmured about Annabelle.

Probably she'd taken off just the way Belle had. That was what some thought. She'd gotten an itchy foot and decided to scratch it. The Pendleton girl always had been wild. No, not Annabelle, some said, but Ginny. Annabelle had been still water running deep, and Ginny was all crashing surf.

But both of them were gone, just the same.

Nathan walked in on one of the conversations as he lingered at the dock, tossing his briefcase into the cab, loading his supplies in the back.

It made his heart beat just a little too fast, a little too hard. It made his stomach churn. He heard Annabelle's name tossed back and forth and it made his ears ring. He'd come to face it, Nathan reminded himself, then had tried to ignore it. He wasn't sure how much longer he could do either. Or if he was going to be able to live with whichever path he took.

He drove to Sanctuary.

He saw Jo sitting on the grand front steps, her head resting on her drawn-up knees. She lifted it when she heard his Jeep, and he saw all the ghosts in her eyes.

"We can't find her." She pressed her lips together. "Ginny."

"I heard." Not knowing what else to do, he sat beside her, draped an arm around her shoulders so she could lean against him. "I just came in on the ferry."

"We've looked everywhere. Hours now. She's vanished, Nathan, just vanished, like—" She couldn't say it. Wouldn't say it. And, drawing a breath, slammed the door on even the thought of it. "If she was on the island, someone would have seen her, someone would have found her."

"It's a lot of ground to cover."

"No." She shook her head. "If she was trying to hide, sure, she could keep one step ahead. Ginny knows the island as well as anyone, every trail and cove. But there's no reason for that. She's just gone."

"I didn't see her on the morning ferry. I kicked back and slept most of the way, but she's tough to miss."

"We already checked that. She didn't take the ferry."

"Okay." He ran his hand up and down her arm as he tried to think. "Private boats. There's a number of them around—islanders and outlanders."

"She can pilot a boat, but none of the natives report one missing. No one's reported one missing, or come in to say they took Ginny out."

"A day-tripper?"

"Yeah." She nodded, tried to accept it. "That's what most people are starting to think. She got a wild hair and took off with someone. She's done it before, but never when she was scheduled to work, and never without leaving word."

He remembered the way she'd smiled at him. *Hey, handsome.* "She was hitting the tequila pretty steady last night."

"Yeah, they're saying that too." She jerked away from him. "Ginny's not some cheap, irresponsible drunk."

"I didn't say that, Jo, and I didn't mean that."

"It's so easy to say she didn't care, didn't give a damn. She just left without a word to anyone, without a thought to anyone." Jo sprang up as the words tumbled out. "Left her home and her family and everyone who loved her without a second thought for how sick with worry and hurt they would be."

Her eyes glittered with fury, her voice rose with it. She no longer cared that it was her mother she spoke of now. No longer cared that she could see by the sober and sympathetic look on his face that he knew it.

"I don't believe it." She caught her breath, let it out slowly. "And I've never believed it."

"I'm sorry." He got to his feet, put his arms around her. Though she shoved, strained against him, he kept them firm. "I'm sorry, Jo."

"I don't want your sympathy. I don't want anything from you or anyone else. Let me go."

"No." She'd been let go too often and by too many, Nathan thought. He pressed his cheek to her hair and waited her out.

She stopped struggling abruptly and wrapped her arms tight around him. "Oh, Nathan, I'm so scared. It's like going through it all again, and still not knowing why."

He stared over her head to the rioting garden of snap-dragons and Canterbury bells. "Would it make a difference? Would it help to know why?"

"Maybe not. Sometimes I think it would make it worse. For all of us." She turned her face into his throat, pa-thetically grateful that he was there, that he was solid. "I hate seeing my father remember, and Brian and Lexy. We don't talk about it, can't seem to bring ourselves to talk about it. But it's there. Pushing at us, and I guess it's pushed us away from each other most of our lives." She let out a long sigh, lulled by the steady beat of his heart against hers. "I find myself thinking more about Mama than Ginny, and I hate myself for it."

"Don't." He touched his lips to her temple, her cheek-bone, then her mouth. "Don't," he repeated and slid more easily and more deeply into the kiss than he'd intended.

She didn't pull away, but opened to him. The simple comfort he'd meant to offer grew into something with the backbeat of urgency. His hands came up, framed her face, then slid down her in one long, slow caress that made her stomach drop away to her knees.

The need that rose up in her was so sweet, so ripe, so huge. She wanted nothing more than to fall into it. Where did this come from? she thought dizzily. And where could it go? She wished suddenly and with all her heart that they could just be two people drowning each other in this slow, endless kiss while the sun dipped low in the sky and shadows grew long and deep.

"I can't do this," she murmured.

"I have to." He changed the angle of the kiss and took her under again. "Hold on to me again, for just a minute," he said when her arms dropped limply away. "Need me again, for just a minute."

She couldn't resist it, couldn't deny either of them, so she held close and held tight and let the moment spin out around them. Dimly she heard tires spin on the road below. Reality slipped back in and she drew back.

"I have to go."

He reached out, took her by the fingertips. "Come back with me. Come home with me. Get away from this for a while."

Emotions surged into her eyes, filled them, made them intensely blue. "I can't."

She backed up, then rushed up the stairs, closing the door behind her quickly and without looking back.

FOURTEEN

THIRTY-SIX HOURS AFTER Ginny had failed to show up for work, Brian dragged into the family parlor and stretched out on the ancient davenport. He was exhausted, and there was simply nothing else to be done. The island had been searched in every direction, dozens of calls had been made. Finally, the police had been notified.

Not that they'd seemed terribly interested, Brian thought, as he studied the plaster rosettes edging the coffered ceiling. After all, they were dealing with a twenty-six-year-old woman—a woman with a reputation. A woman who was free to come and go as she pleased, had no known enemies and a predilection for taking strolls on the wild side.

He already knew the authorities would give the matter a glance, do the basics, then file it.

They had done a bit more than that twenty years before, he remembered, when another woman had vanished. They'd worked harder and longer to find Annabelle. Cops prowling the island, asking questions, taking notes, looking soberly concerned. But money had been involved there—trust funds, property, inheritances. It had taken him some time to realize that the police had been pursuing an angle of foul play. And that, briefly, his father had been the prime suspect.

It had scared the hell out of him.

But no evidence of foul play had ever been found, and interest eventually waned. Brian imagined interest would wane in Ginny Pendleton's case much sooner.

And he'd simply run out of things to do.

He thought fleetingly about reaching for the remote, switching on the television or stereo and just zoning out for an hour. The parlor—or the family room, as Kate insisted on calling it—was rarely used.

It was Kate who'd chosen the casual and comfortable furnishings, mixing the deep, wide chairs, the heavy old tables, the stretch-out-and-nap sofa. She'd tossed in colorful floor pillows, with some idea, Brian imagined, that the room might actually be too crowded now and then for everyone to have a traditional seat.

But most often, the room was occupied by no more than one person at a time.

The Hathaways weren't the gather-together-to-watch-the-evening-news type. They were loners, he thought, every one of them, finding more excuses to be apart than to bond together.

It made life less . . . complicated.

He sat up, but lacked the energy to distract himself with someone else's news. Instead, he rose and went to the little refrigerator behind the mahogany bar. That was another of Kate's stubborn fantasies, keeping that bar and cold box stocked. As if the family might stop in after a long day, share a drink, some conversation, a little entertainment. Brian gave a half laugh as he popped open a beer.

Not bloody likely.

With that thought still lying bitter in his head, he glanced up and saw his father in the doorway. It was a toss-up as to who was more surprised to find himself faced with the other.

Silence hung in the air, the thick and sticky kind that only family could brew. At length Brian tipped back his beer, took a long, cold swallow. Sam shifted his feet, hooked his thumbs in his front pockets.

"You finished for the day?" he asked Brian.

"Looks that way. Nothing else to do." Since just standing there made him feel foolish, Brian shrugged his shoulders and said, "Want a beer?"

"Wouldn't mind."

Brian got another bottle from the fridge, popped the top as his father crossed the room. Sam took a swallow and fell back on silence. It had been his intention to relax his mind with a few innings of baseball, maybe knock back a few fingers of bourbon to help him sleep.

He had no idea at all how to have a beer with his son.

"Rain's come in," he said, groping.

Brian listened to it patter against the windows. "It's been a pretty dry spring."

Sam nodded, shifted again. "Water level's dead low on some of the smaller pools. This'll help."

"The outlanders won't like it."

"No." Sam's frown was a reflex. "But we need the rain."

Silence crept in again, stretched until Brian angled his head. "Well, looks like that uses up the weather as a topic. What's next?" he said coolly. "Politics or sports?"

Sam didn't miss the sarcasm, he just chose to ignore it. "Didn't think you had much interest in either."

"Right. What would I know about such manly subjects? I cook for a living."

"That's not what I meant," Sam said evenly. His nerves were scraped raw, his temper closer to the surface than he liked. He concentrated on not losing it. "I just didn't know you had an interest."

"You don't have a clue what interests me. You don't

know what I think, what I want, what I feel. Because that's never interested you.''

"Brian Hathaway." Kate's voice snapped as she stepped into the room with Lexy beside her. "Don't you speak to your father in that tone.''

"Let the boy have his say." Sam kept his eyes on his son as he set his beer aside. "He's entitled.''

"He's not entitled to show disrespect.''

"Kate." Sam shot her one quelling look, then nodded at Brian. "You got something in your craw, spit it out.''

"It would take years, and it wouldn't change a god-damn thing.''

Sam moved behind the bar. He wanted that sour mash after all. "Why don't you just get started anyway?" He poured three fingers of Jim Beam in a short glass, then after a brief hesitation, poured a second and slid it down the bar to Brian.

"I don't drink bourbon. Which probably makes me less of a man as well.''

Sam felt a dull pain center in his gut and lifted his own glass. "A man's drink of choice is his own business. And you've been full grown for a time now. Why should it matter to you what I think?''

"It took me thirty years to get here," Brian shot back. "Where the hell were you for the last twenty?" The lock he'd put on the questions, and the misery behind them, gave way to frustration and snapped open as though it had been rusted through and just waiting for that last kick. "You walked away, just like she did. Only you were worse because you let us know, every fucking day of our lives, that we didn't matter. We were just incidentals that you dumped on Kate.''

War in her eyes, Kate surged forward. "Now you listen to me, Brian William Hathaway—''

"Leave him be," Sam ordered, his voice cold to mask the hot needles pricking at his throat. "Finish it out," he told Brian. "You've got more.''

"What difference will it make? Will it make you go back and be there when I was twelve and a couple of outlander kids beat the hell out of me for sport? Or when I was fifteen and sicked up on my first beer? When I was seventeen and scared shitless because I was afraid I'd gotten Molly Brodie pregnant when we lost our virginity together?"

His fists balled at his sides with a rage he hadn't known lived inside him. "You weren't ever there. Kate was. She's the one who mopped up the spills and held my head. She's the one who grounded me when I needed it and taught me to drive and lectured and praised. Never you. Never once. None of us needs you now. And if you treated Mama with the same selfish disregard, it's no wonder she left."

Sam flinched at that, the first show of emotion during the long stream of bitterness. His hand shook slightly as he reached for his glass again, but before he could speak, Lexy was shouting from the doorway.

"Why are you doing this? Why are you doing this now? Something's happened to Ginny." Her voice shattered on a sob as she raced into the room. "Something terrible's happened to her, I know it, and all you can do is stand here and say these awful things." Tears streaming, she clamped her hands over her ears as if she could block it all out. "Why can't you leave it alone, just leave it all alone and pretend it doesn't matter?"

"Because it does." Furious that even now she wouldn't stand with him, Brian whirled on her. "Because it does matter that we're a pathetic excuse for a family, that you're running off to New York and trying to replace the hole he put in your life with men. That Jo's made herself sick and that I can't be with a woman without thinking I'll end up pushing her away the way he did Mama. It matters, goddamn it, because there's not one of us who knows how to be happy."

"I know how to be happy." Lexy's voice rose and

stumbled as she shouted at him. She wanted to scream out the denial, to make it all a lie. "I'm going to be happy. I'm going to have everything I want."

"What the hell's going on here?" Jo braced a hand on the doorjamb and stared. The raised voices had brought her out of her room, where she'd been trying to nap to make up for the sleep she'd lost worrying over Ginny.

"Brian's hateful. Just hateful." On another wild sob, Lexy turned and rushed into Jo's arms.

The shock of that, and the sight of her brother and her father facing each other across the bar like boxers at the bell, had her gaping. Kate stood in the middle, weeping quietly.

"What's happening here?" Jo managed as her head began to throb. "Is it about Ginny?"

"They don't care about Ginny." Lost in grief, Lexy sobbed into Jo's shoulder. "They don't care."

"It's not about Ginny." Sick now with fury and guilt, Brian stepped away from the bar. "It's just a typical Hathaway evening. And I've had enough of it."

He strode out, pausing briefly by Lexy. He lifted a hand as if to stroke her hair, then dropped it again without making contact.

Jo took a quiet, shallow breath. "Kate?"

Kate brushed briskly at the tears on her cheeks. "Honey, will you take Lexy to your room for a bit? I'll be along shortly."

"All right." Jo took a quick glance at her father—the stony face, the enigmatic eyes, and decided it was best to save her questions. "Come on, Lexy," she murmured. "Come on with me now."

When they'd gone, Kate took a hankie from her pocket and blew her nose. "Not that it's any excuse for his behavior," she began, "but Brian's worried sick and exhausted. All of us are, but he's been talking to the police and still running the inn on top of everything else. He's just worn out, Sam."

"He's also right." Sam sipped, wondering if the liquor would wash the harsh taste of shame out of his throat. "I haven't been a father to them since Belle walked out on us. I left it all up to you."

"Sam . . ."

He looked over at her. "Are you going to tell me that's not true?"

She sighed a little, then because her legs just seemed too tired to hold her up another minute, slid onto a stool at the bar. "No, there's no point in lying."

Sam huffed out what passed for a laugh. "You've always been honest to a fault. It's an admirable—and irritating—quality."

"I didn't figure you paid much notice. I've been chorusing a more polite variation on what Brian's just poured out for years." She angled her head, and though her eyes were red-rimmed, they were steady when they met his. "Never made a dent in you."

"It made a few." He set his glass down to rub his hands over his face. Maybe it was because he was tired, and heartsick, and remembering too damn clearly what he'd let fade, but the words he hadn't known he could say were there. "I didn't want them to need me. Didn't want anyone to. And I sure as hell didn't want to need them."

He started to leave it at that. It was more than he'd ever said before, to anyone other than himself. But she was watching him, so patiently, with such quiet compassion, he found the rest of it pouring out.

"The fact is, Kate, Belle broke my heart. By the time I got over it, you were here and things seemed to run smooth enough."

"If I hadn't stayed—"

"They'd have had nobody. You did a good job with them, Kate. I don't know that I realized that until that boy hit me between the eyes just now. It took guts to do that."

Kate shut her eyes. "I'll never understand men, not if

I live another half century. You're proud of him for shouting at you, swearing at you?''

"I respect him for it. It occurs to me that I haven't shown him the proper respect a grown man deserves.''

"Well, hallelujah,'' she muttered and picked up Brian's untouched bourbon and drank. And choked.

Sam's lips curved. She looked so pretty, he thought, sitting there thumping a fist to her heart with her face red and her eyes wide. "You've never been one for hard liquor.''

She gulped in a breath, hissed it out because it burned like the flames of hell. "I'm making an exception tonight. I'm about worn to the bone.''

He took the glass out of her hand. "You'll just get sick.'' He reached down into the fridge and found the open bottle of the Chardonnay she preferred.

As he poured it for her, she stared at him. "I didn't realize you knew what I like to drink.''

"You can't live with a woman for twenty years and not pick up on some of her habits.'' He heard the way it sounded and felt dull color creep up his neck. "Live in the same house, I mean.''

"Hmm. Well, what are you going to do about Brian?''

"Do?''

"Sam.'' Impatient, she took a quick sip to knock the taste of bourbon out of her mouth. "Are you going to throw this chance away?''

There she was again, was all he could think, poking at him when all he wanted was a little peace. "He's pissed off, and I let him have his say. Now that's done.''

"It is not done.'' She leaned forward on the bar, snagging his arm before he could evade her. "Brian just kicked the door open, Sam. Now you be father enough, you be man enough to walk through it.''

"He doesn't have any use for me.''

"Oh, that's the biggest pile of bull slop I've ever heard.'' She was just angry enough not to notice that his cough disguised a chuckle. "The lot of you are so stubborn. Every gray hair I have is a result of Hathaway muleheadedness."

He skimmed a glance over her neat cap of rich russet. "You don't have any gray hair."

"And I pay good money to keep it away." She huffed out a breath. "Now you listen to me, Sam, and keep your ears open for once. I don't care how old those three children are, they still need you. And it's past time you gave them what you stopped giving them and yourself years ago. Compassion, attention, and affection. If Ginny pulling this awful stunt has brought this to a head, then I'm almost glad of it. And I'm not going to stand by and see the four of you walk away from each other again."

She pushed off the stool, snagged her glass. "Now, I'm going to try to calm Lexy down, which should take me half the night. That gives you plenty of time to find your son and start mending fences with him."

"Kate . . ." When she paused at the door and turned those sparkling eyes back on him, nerves had him reaching for the bottle of Jim Beam, setting it aside again. "I don't know where to start."

"You idiot," she said with such gentle affection that the heat rose up his neck a second time. "You already have."

Brian knew exactly where he was going. He didn't delude himself that he was just taking a long walk to cool off. He could have rounded the island on foot and his blood would still have been hot. He was furious with himself for losing his temper, for saying things it did no good to say. It ripped at him that he'd made both Lexy and Kate cry.

Life was simpler when you kept things inside, he decided, when you just lived with them and went about your business.

Wasn't that what his father had done all these years?

Brian hunched his shoulders against the rain, annoyed that he'd come out without a jacket and was now soaked through. He could hear the sea pounding as he trudged along the soggy sand between the dunes. Lights glowed behind the windows of cottages, and he used them as a compass in the dark.

He heard a drift of classical music as he mounted Kirby's stairs. He saw her through the rain-splattered glass of the door. She wore soft and baggy blue sweats, her feet bare. Her hair swung forward to curtain her face as she bent to poke inside the refrigerator, one dainty foot with sassy pink toenails tapping time to the music.

The quick punch of lust was very satisfying. He opened the door without knocking.

She straightened quickly and with a short, audible gasp. "Oh, Brian. I didn't hear you." Off guard, she balanced a hand on the open refrigerator door. "Is there word on Ginny?"

"No."

"Oh, I thought . . ." Nerves drummed in her fingers as she raked them through her hair from brow to tip. His eyes were dark and direct, with something unquestionably dangerous smoldering in them. Her heart took a rabbit leap into her throat. "You're soaked."

"It's raining," he said and began to walk toward her.

"I, ah—" It didn't matter how ridiculous she told herself it was, her knees were starting to shake. "I was about to have a glass of wine. Why don't you pour some and I'll get you a towel."

"I don't need a towel."

"Okay." She could smell the rain on him now, and the heat. "I'll get the wine."

"Later." He reached out and shut the refrigerator door, then trapped her against it with his body and crushed his mouth to hers in a searing, greedy kiss.

Even as the moan strangled in her throat, his hands snaked under her shirt, closed possessively over her

breasts. His teeth nipped at her tongue, shooting tiny
thrills of pain and fear through her. Then his hands slid
down, around her, cupping her bottom and lifting until
she was inches off the floor, and wet, straining denim was
pressed against the wicked ache between her thighs.

She managed to shudder out a breath when his lips
fastened on her throat. "So much for small talk." Hun-
grily, she attacked his ear. That quick bite of flesh stirred
a craving for more. "The bedroom's down the hall."

"I don't need a bed." His smile sharp-edged and feral,
he lifted his head and looked at her. "My way, remember.
And I do my best work in the kitchen."

Her feet hit the floor again before she could blink. He
pulled her arms over her head, capturing her wrists in one
hand as he pushed her back against the door. "Look at
me," he demanded, then slid his free hand under the elastic of her pants and plunged his fingers into her.

She gave one choked cry—shock and pleasure colliding
in a brutal assault on the system that had her hips jerking
against him, matching his ruthless rhythm in primal response. Her vision narrowed, her breath shortened, and
she came in an explosive gush.

She'd already been wet. He'd found her slick and
ready, and that alone had been brutally arousing. But
when her eyes went blind and she flooded into his hand,
fists of vicious need pounded at his body. His breath was
a snarl as he yanked the shirt over her head, fastened his
mouth to her breast.

She was small and firm and tasted of peaches. He
wanted to devour her, to feed until he was sated or dead.
His murmurs of approval mixed with threats neither of
them could comprehend. Her hands were raking through
his hair, tugging at his wet shirt, those always competent
fingers fumbling in their haste. Her very lack of control
was another layer of arousal for him.

"More," he muttered, dragging her pants over her hips.

"I want more." When his mouth raced down, she gripped his shoulders and sobbed.

"You can't—I can't. Oh, God. What are you doing to me?"

"I'm having you."

Then his mouth was on her, teeth and tongue relentlessly driving her beyond sanity. Her head fell back against the humming refrigerator door as heat swamped her, as it sucked her down, as it coated her skin with sweat. The force of the climax struck her like a runaway train speeding through the tunnel where he held her trapped and helpless.

Her body went limp, her head lolling back when he lifted her. Nothing shocked her now, not even when he laid her on the kitchen table like a main course he had skillfully prepared for his own appetite.

He stripped off his shirt, his eyes never leaving hers. Bracing one foot on the edge of the table, he pulled off one sneaker, then the other, tossing them both aside. He unbuttoned his jeans, dragged the zipper down.

Her eyes were clearing. Good, he thought. He wanted to watch them go blind again. As he stripped off his jeans, he let his gaze wander over her. Rosy, damp skin, delicate curves, her hair tumbled against dark wood. She was beautiful, breathtaking. When he was sure he could form words, he would tell her. Now he mounted her, and feeling her tremble beneath him, smiled.

"Say, Take me, Brian."

She had to concentrate on pulling in enough air to survive, then let it out on a moan as his thumbs brushed over her nipples.

"Say it."

Mindlessly, she arched for him. "Take me, Brian. For God's sake."

He drove inside her in one fast, hard stroke, holding them both on the edge as he watched those mermaid eyes glaze. "Now, take me, Kirby."

"Yes." She lifted a hand to his face, wrapped her legs around him, and gloried in the fast, dark ride.

He was breathless when he collapsed on her, and for the first time in days both his body and his mind were relaxed. He could feel her still quivering lightly beneath him, the solid aftershocks of good, hard sex.

He rubbed his face in her hair, enjoying the scent of it. "That was just to whet the appetite."

"Oh, my God."

He chuckled, and pushing himself up, was delighted to see her smiling at him. "You tasted like peaches."

"I'd just had a bubble bath before you came around to ravish me."

"Good timing on my part."

She reached up to brush the hair back from his face—a casually affectionate gesture that intrigued them both. "As it turned out, I suppose it was. You looked very dangerous and exciting when you walked in here."

"I was feeling dangerous. We had a family scene at Sanctuary."

"I'm sorry."

"Not your problem. I could use that wine now." He shifted, slid off the table, and went to the refrigerator.

Kirby allowed herself to enjoy the view. As a doctor she could give him high marks for keeping in shape. As his lover, she could be grateful for that long, hard body. "Wineglasses are in the second cabinet to the left," she told him. "I'll get a robe."

"Don't bother," he said as she hitched herself off the table.

"I'm not going to stand around the kitchen naked."

"Yes, you are." He poured two generous glasses before his gaze slid in her direction, roamed over her. "And you won't be standing for all that long, anyway."

Amused, she arched a brow. "I won't?"

"No." He turned, handed her a glass, then tapped his

against it. "I figure the counter there will put you at about the right height."

She was grateful she'd yet to sip her wine. "The kitchen *counter*?"

"Yeah. Then there's the floor."

Kirby looked down at the shiny white linoleum her grandmother had been proud to have installed three years before. "The floor."

"I figure we might make it to the bed—if you're set on being traditional—in a couple, three hours." He glanced at the clock on the stove. "Plenty of time. We don't serve breakfast until eight."

She didn't know whether to laugh or gulp. "Awfully confident of your staying power, aren't you?"

"Confident enough. How's yours?"

The thrill of challenge made her smile. "I'll match you, Brian—and more, I'll make sure we live through it." Her eyes laughed at his over the rim of her glass. "After all, I'm a doctor."

"Well, then." He set his glass aside. She squealed when he nipped her around the waist—then yelped when her butt hit the Formica. "Hey, it's cold."

"So's this." Brian dipped a finger into his wine, then let it drip onto her nipple. He bent forward, licked it delicately away. "We'll just have to warm things up."

FIFTEEN

◈

Sam supposed it was a bad sign when a man had to pump up his courage just to speak to his own son. And it was worse when you'd worked yourself up to it, then couldn't find the boy.

The kitchen was empty, with no sign of coffee on the brew or biscuits on the rise. Sam stood there a moment, feeling outsized and awkward, as he always did in what he persisted in thinking of as a woman's area.

He knew Brian habitually took a walk in the morning, but he also knew Brian just as habitually started the coffee and the biscuit or fancy bread dough first. In any case, Brian was usually back by this time. Another half hour, forty minutes, people would be wandering into the dining room and wanting their grits.

Just because Sam didn't spend much time around the house, and as little as possible around the guests, didn't mean he didn't know what went on there.

Sam ran his cap around in his hands, hating the fact that worry was beginning to stir in his gut. He'd woken up on another morning and found a member of his family gone. No preparation then, either. No warning. Just no coffee brewing in the pot and no biscuit dough rising in the big blue bowl under a thick white cloth.

Had he driven the boy off? And would he have more years now to wonder if he was responsible for pushing another out of Sanctuary and away from himself?

He closed his eyes a moment until he could tuck that ugly guilt away. Damned if he'd hang himself for it. Brian was a full-grown man just as Annabelle had been a full-grown woman. The decisions they made were their own. He tugged his cap onto his head, started toward the door.

And felt twin trickles of relief and anxiety when he heard the whistling heading down the garden path.

Brian stopped whistling—and stopped walking—when he saw his father step through the door on the screened porch. He resented having his mood shoved so abruptly from light to dismal, resented having his last few moments of solitude interrupted.

Brian nodded briefly, then moved past Sam into the kitchen. Sam stood where he was for a minute, debating. It wasn't hard for one man to spot when another had spent the night rolling around with a woman on hot, tangled sheets. Seeing that relaxed, satisfied look on his son's face had made him feel foolish—and envious. And he thought of how much easier it would be all around for him to keep walking and just leave things where they lay.

With a grunt, he pulled off his cap again and went back inside.

"Need to have a word with you."

Brian glanced over. He'd already donned a butcher's apron and was pouring coffee beans into the grinder. "I'm busy here."

Sam planted his feet. "I need a word with you just the same."

"Then you'll have to talk while I work." Brian flicked the switch on the grinder and filled the kitchen with noise and scent. "I'm running a little behind this morning."

"Uh-huh." Sam twisted his cap in his hands and decided to wait until the grinder was finished rather than trying to talk over it. He watched Brian measure out coffee, measure out water, then set the big Bunn Omatic on to brew. "I, ah, was surprised you weren't already in here at this."

Brian took out a large bowl and began to gather the basics for his biscuits. "I don't punch a time clock for anybody but myself."

"No, no, you don't." He hadn't meant it that way, and wished to God he knew how to talk to a man wearing an apron and scooping into flour and lard. "What I wanted to say was about yesterday—last night."

Brian poured milk, eyeballing the amount. "I said all I had to say, and I don't see the point in rehashing it."

"So, you figure you can say your piece, but I'm not entitled to say mine."

Brian snatched up a wooden spoon, cradled the bowl in his arm out of habit and began to beat. The dreamy afterglow of all-night sex had dulled to lead. "What I figure is you've had a lifetime to say yours, and I've got work to do."

"You're a hard man, Brian."

"I learned by example."

It was a neat and well-aimed little dart. Sam acknowledged it, accepted it. Then, weary of playing the supplicant, he tossed his cap aside. "You'll listen to what I have to say, then we'll be done with it."

"Say it, then." He dumped the dough on a floured board and plunged his hands into it to knead violently. "And let's be done with it."

"You were right." Sam felt the click in his throat and swallowed it. "Everything you said was right, and true."

Wrist-deep in biscuit dough, Brian turned his head and stared. "What?"

"And I respect you for having the courage to say it."

"What?"

"You got flour in your ears?" Sam said impatiently.

"I said you were right, and you were right to say it. How long does it take that goddamn contraption to make a goddamn cup of coffee?" he muttered, staring accusingly at the machine.

Slowly, Brian began to knead again, but he kept his eyes on Sam. "You could squeeze off a cup if you need one."

"Well, I do." He opened a cupboard door, then scowled at the glasses and stemware.

"Coffee cups and mugs haven't been kept there for eight years," Brian said mildly. "Two cupboards down to the left—right over the coffee beverage area."

"Coffee beverage area," Sam murmured. "Fancy names for fancy drinks when all a man wants is a cup of black coffee."

"Our cappuccino and lattes are very popular."

Sam knew what cappuccino was, right enough—or was mostly sure. But lattes baffled him. He grunted, then carefully slid the glass carafe out to pour coffee into his mug. He sipped, felt a little better, and sipped again. "It's good coffee."

"It's all in the beans."

"I guess grinding them fresh makes some difference."

"All the difference in the world." Brian dropped the dough in the bowl, covered it, then walked to the sink to wash up. "Now, I believe we have what could pass as an actual conversation for the first time in, oh, most of my life."

"I haven't done right by you." Sam stared down into the rich black liquid in his mug. "I'm sorry."

Brian stopped drying his hands and gaped. "What?"

"Damned if I'm going to keep repeating myself." Sam jerked his head up, and his eyes were filled with frustration. "I'm giving you an apology, and you ought to be big enough to take it."

Brian held up a hand before it all descended into an argument again. "You caught me off guard. Knocked me flat,'' Brian corrected, and went to the refrigerator for breakfast meats and eggs. "Maybe I could accept it if I knew what you were apologizing for.''

"For not being there when you were twelve and getting pounded on. When you were fifteen and sicking up your first beer. When you were seventeen and too stupid to know how to make love to a girl without becoming a father.''

More than a little shaky, Brian took out a skillet. "Kate took me over to Savannah and bought me condoms.''

"She did not.'' If the boy had slapped him over the head with the sausage meat, he'd have been less shocked. "Kate bought you rubbers?''

"She did.'' Brian found himself smiling over the memory as he heated the skillet. "Lectured me up one side and down the other about responsibility and restraint, abstinence. Then she bought me a pack of Trojans and told me if I couldn't control the urge, I'd do a damn sight better to wear protection.''

"Sweet Jesus.'' The chuckle escaped as Sam leaned back on the counter. "I just can't picture it.'' Then he straightened, cleared his throat. "It should have been me telling you.''

"Yes, it should have been you.'' As if the arrangement were vital, Brian set sausages in the skillet. "Why wasn't it?''

"I didn't have your mother telling me that I'd better go talk to that boy, something was on his mind. Or that Lexy had new dress shoes and wanted to show them off. I saw those things for myself, but I got used to her prodding me on them. Then when I didn't have her, I let it all go.'' He set the coffee down, shot his hands in his pockets. "I'm not used to explaining myself. I don't like it.''

Brian took out another bowl, broke the first egg for pancake batter. "Your choice.''

"I loved her.'' It seared his throat, and Sam was grateful that Brian continued to focus on his work. "It's not

easy for me to say that. Maybe I didn't tell her enough—
the feeling came a lot easier than the words. I needed her.
Serious Sam, she'd call me, and wouldn't let me stay that
way for long. She loved being around new people, talking
about everything under the sun. She loved this house, this
island. And for a while, she loved me.''

Brian didn't think he'd ever heard a longer speech from
Sam Hathaway. Not wanting to break the flow, he poured
the butter he'd melted into the bowl and said nothing.

''We had our problems. I'm not going to pretend we
didn't. But we always got through them. The night you
were born . . . Jesus, I was scared. Piss-yourself scared,
but Belle wasn't. It was all a big adventure to her. And
when it was over and she had you cuddled right up in her
arms and nursing, she laid back against the pillows, smiling. 'Look what a beautiful baby we made ourselves,
Sam. We'll have to make lots more.' A man's got to love
a woman like that,'' Sam murmured. ''He doesn't even
have a choice.''

''I didn't think you did. Love her.''

''I did.'' Sam picked up his coffee again. All the talk
had dried out his throat. ''It took me a lot of years of
being without her to stop loving her. Maybe I did push
her away, but I don't know how. The not knowing ate at
me bad for a lot of years.''

''I'm sorry.'' He saw the flicker of surprise in his father's eyes. ''I didn't think it mattered to you. I didn't
think any of it really mattered.''

''It mattered. But after a while you learn to live with
what you've got.''

''And you had the island.''

''It was what I could depend on, what I could tend to.
And it kept me from losing my mind.'' He took a deep
breath. ''But a better man would have been around to hold
his son's head when he puked up too much Budweiser.''

''Löwenbräu.''

"Christ, an import? No wonder I don't understand you."

Sam sighed and took a long look at the man his son had become. A man who wore an apron to work and baked pies. A man, he corrected, with cool and steady eyes, and shoulders strong and broad enough to carry more than his own load.

"We've both had our say, and I don't know as it'll make any difference. But I'm glad we said it." Sam held out a hand and hoped it was the right thing.

Jo walked in on the surprising tableau of her father and brother shaking hands in front of the stove. They both looked at her, identical flickers of embarrassment on their faces. Just then she was too damn tired and irritable to analyze it.

"Lex isn't feeling well. I'll be taking her breakfast shift."

Brian grabbed a kitchen fork and hurriedly scooted the sausage around before it burned. "You're going to wait tables?"

"That's what I said." She grabbed a short apron from a peg and tied it on.

"When's the last time you waited tables?" Brian demanded.

"The last time I was here and you were short-staffed."

"You're a lousy waitress."

"Well, I'm all you've got, pal. Lexy's got a crying jag headache, and Kate's heading over to the campground to straighten out the mess there. So live with it."

Sam picked up his cap and edged toward the door. Dealing with his son was one thing, and that had been hard enough. He wasn't about to take on a daughter in the same day. "I've got things to do," he muttered and nearly winced when Jo shot him a killing look.

"Well, so do I, but I'm waiting tables because the two of you decided to go at each other and Kate and I had to spend half the damn night listening to Lexy cry and carry on. Now the two of you, I see, have shaken hands like real men, so everything's fine and dandy. Where are the damn order pads?''

"Top drawer, under the cash register." Out of the corner of his eye, Brian saw his father slip out the door. Typical, he thought grimly, and drained the sausage. "The computer's new," he told Jo. "You ever work a cash register computer?"

"Why the hell would I? I'm not a sales clerk, I'm not a waitress. I'm a goddamn photographer."

Brian rubbed the back of his neck. It was going to be a long morning. "Go up and pour some aspirin down Lexy's throat and get her down here."

"You want her, you get her. I've had more than my fill of Lexy and her drama queen routine. She was wallowing in it." Jo slapped the pad down on the counter and stalked to the coffeepot. "Center of attention, as always."

"She was upset."

"Maybe she was, until she began to enjoy the role, but it wasn't my fault. And I'm the one who was stuck with her. It was after two before Kate and I got her calmed down and out of my room. Now she's the one who claims to have a headache." Jo rubbed hard at the center of her forehead. "Any aspirin down here?"

Brian took a bottle from a cupboard and set it on the counter. "Take the pot in and make the first rounds. Blueberry pancakes are the special. If you have to scowl, scowl in here. Out there you smile. Tell the customers your name and pretend you can be personable. It should offset the slow service."

"Kiss my ass," she snarled but grabbed the pot and the pad and swung through the door.

It didn't get any better.

Brian was slicing a grapefruit and grinding his teeth at the two orders that had been sitting under the warming light for a full five minutes. Another two, he thought, and he'd have to dump them and start again.

Where the hell was Jo?

"Busy morning." Nathan breezed in the back door. "I got a glimpse of the dining room through the windows. Looks like a pretty full house."

"Sunday morning." Brian flipped what he thought must have been the millionth pancake of the day. "People like a big breakfast on Sundays."

"Me, too." Nathan grinned at the grill. "Blueberry pancakes sound perfect."

"Get in line. Goddamn it, what's she doing out there, building the pyramids? You know computers?"

"I'm the proud owner of three. Why?"

"You're now manning the cash register." Brian jerked a thumb behind him. "Go over there and figure it out. I can't keep stopping what I'm doing to fix it every time she fucks up a bill."

"You want me to work the cash register?"

"You want to eat?"

"Why don't I work the cash register?" Nathan decided, and walked over to study it.

Jo rushed in, her face pink and harassed, her arms loaded down with dishes. "She had to know. She had to know what it would be like today. I'm going to kill her if I live through this. What the hell are you doing here?" she shot at Nathan.

"Apparently I've been put on the payroll." He eyed her as she dumped the dishes in the sink and grabbed the waiting orders. "You look real cute today, Jo Ellen."

"Bite me," she muttered and shouldered out the door.

"I imagine she's been just that pleasant to the customers."

"Don't spoil my fantasy," Nathan told him. "I like to believe she saves those ass kicks just for me."

"Going to push her in the river again?"

"She slipped. And I've got something . . . else in mind for me and Jo."

Brian scrubbed a hand over his face. "I don't want to hear about it. I don't want that particular image in my head either."

"I just figured you should know what direction I'm planning to take." To illustrate, Nathan grabbed her when she swung back through the door. Hauling her against him, he kissed her scowling and surprised mouth.

"Are you crazy?" She shoved an elbow in his gut to free herself, then pushed orders and cash and credit cards into his hands. "Here, figure it out." She darted over to snag a fresh pot of coffee and tossed scribbled orders on the counter. "Two specials, eggs, scrambled, side of bacon, whole wheat toast. One I don't remember, but it's written down there, and we're running low on biscuits and cream. And if that monster kid at table three spills his juice one more time, I'm going to strangle him and his idiot parents."

Nathan grinned as she stalked out again. "Bri, I think it could be love."

"More likely insanity. Now keep your hands off my sister and ring up those orders or I'm not feeding you."

At ten-thirty, Jo staggered into her room and fell facedown on the bed. Everything hurt. Her back, her feet, her head, her shoulders. Nobody, she thought, nobody who hadn't been there could possibly know how hard waitressing was. She'd hiked up mountains, waded through rivers, spent sweltering days in the desert—and would do so again for the right shot.

But she would slit her wrists with a smile on her face if she ever had to wait another table.

And she hated having to admit that Lexy not only wasn't a lazy malingerer, but she made the job look easy.

Still, if it hadn't been for Lexy, Jo wouldn't have missed that glorious, watery, after-the-rain light that morning. She wouldn't be gritty-eyed from three hours' sleep. And her feet wouldn't be screaming.

She set her teeth when she felt the mattress give under someone's weight. "Get out, Lexy, or I might find the energy to kill you."

"Don't bother. She's not here."

She turned her head, narrowed her eyes at Nathan. "What are you doing here?"

"You keep asking me that." He reached out to tuck her hair behind her ear and clear his view of her face. "Right now, I'm checking on you. Tough morning, huh?"

She groaned, closed her eyes. "Go away."

"Ten seconds into the foot rub and you're going to beg me to stay."

"Foot rub?"

She pulled her leg back, but he closed his fingers around her ankle, holding it steady as he pried off her shoe. "Ten, nine, eight . . ."

And when he ran the heel of his hand firmly up her arch, sheer pleasure shivered through her system and made her groan.

"See, I told you. Just relax. Happy feet are the key to the universe."

"Galileo?"

"Carl Sagan," he said with a grin. "Did you get anything to eat down there?"

"If I so much as look at another pancake, I'll throw up."

"I thought not. I brought you something else."

She blinked one eye open. "What?"

"Hmm. You've got very attractive feet. Long, narrow, an elegantly high instep. One of these days I'm going to start nibbling on them and work my way up. Oh, you meant what did I bring you to eat." He pressed his fingers against the ball of her foot, worked them down to the heel. "Strawberries and cream, one of Brian's miraculous biscuits with homemade jam, and some bacon for protein.''

"Why?"

"Because you need to eat." He glanced back at her. "Or did you mean why am I going to nibble on your feet?"

"Never mind."

"Okay. Why don't you roll over, sit up, and eat? Then I can do this right."

She started to say she wasn't hungry—an automatic response. But she remembered Kirby's orders to eat. And the idea of strawberries had some appeal. She sat up, trying not to feel foolish when Nathan settled down cross-legged with her foot cradled in his lap. She took the bowl of strawberries and picked one out with her fingers.

She studied him in silence a moment. He hadn't bothered to shave that morning, and his hair was in need of a trim. But the just a bit unkempt style suited him, as did the gold the island sun was teasing out of his thick brown hair.

"You don't have to go to all this trouble," she told him. "I'm thinking about sleeping with you."

"Well, that's a load off my mind."

She took a bite of a strawberry, and the taste was so sweet and unexpectedly bright, she smiled. "I guess I'm a little out of sorts this morning."

"Are you?" He gripped her toes, worked them gently back and forth. "I hadn't noticed."

"Which is your sly Yankee way of saying I'm always bitchy."

"Not always. And I think the word I'd have chosen would have been 'troubled.' ''

"A Hathaway legacy." Because the strawberries had stirred an appetite, she picked up a slice of bacon and bit in. "We had a family brawl last night, which was why Lexy was in bed with her head under the covers and I was waiting tables."

"Do you always pick up the slack?"

Surprised, she shook her head. "No, I wouldn't say I pick up much of anything. I'm rarely here."

"And when you are, you're waiting tables, changing linen, scrubbing toilets."

"How did you hear about that?"

Her voice had gone sharp, puzzling him. "You told me. You were on housecleaning detail here at the inn."

"Oh, that." Feeling foolish, she reached for the biscuit, broke it in half.

"What else?"

"Nothing." She jerked a shoulder. "Just some kids playing a prank a couple of days ago. They locked me in the men's showers over at the campground. I got a little freaked."

"That's not funny."

"No, at the time I didn't find it amusing."

"Did you catch them?"

"No, they were long gone by the time my father came along and got me out. It wasn't a big deal, just annoying."

"So we can add cleaning the men's showers to the list of slack you don't pick up. And in between all that, you're putting a photography book together and finding time to work on new pictures. What about fun?"

"Photography is fun for me." When he only lifted a brow, she sampled another strawberry. "I went to the bonfire."

"And stayed till nearly midnight. You wild woman."

The line formed between her brows. "I'm not much on parties."

"What are you much on besides photography? Books, movies, art, music? This is called the science of getting to know each other," he told her when she said nothing. "It's very handy, especially when one person is thinking about sleeping with the other." He leaned forward, amused when she edged back. "Are you going to share any of those strawberries?"

Jo ordered her pulse to level, and because he was still rubbing her feet, fed him a berry.

He caught the tips of her fingers in his teeth, sucked them in as well. Smiling slowly, he released them. "That's subliminal sensory stimulation. Or what's more commonly known as I'm coming on to you."

"I think I got that."

"Good. Now, movies?"

She tried to think if there was another man who had ever disconcerted her so easily or so often. The answer was a solid no. "I lean to the old black-and-white, especially film noir. The cinematography, the light and shadows are so incredible."

"The Maltese Falcon?"

"The best of the best."

"Look at that." He patted her foot. "Common ground. What about contemporary stuff?"

"There I head for straight action. Art films rarely grab me. I'd rather see Schwarzenegger mow down fifty bad guys than listen to a handful of people expressing their angst in a foreign language."

"This is a big relief for me. We could never have settled down to raise five children and golden retrievers if I'd had to face art films."

It made her laugh, a low, smoky sound he found ridiculously arousing. "If those are my choices, I may reconsider subtitles."

"Your favorite city, anywhere."

"Florence," she said before she'd known it was true. "That bright wash of sunlight, the colors."

"The buildings. The age and grandeur of them. The Pitti Palace, the Palazzo Vecchio."

"I have a wonderful shot of the Pitti, just before sunset."

"I'd love to see it."

"I didn't bring it with me," she said absently, remembering the moment, the slant of light, the quick whoosh of air and noise as a flock of pigeons rose in a wave. "It's back in Charlotte."

"I can wait." Before she had a chance to react, he squeezed her foot. "So, when you've finished breakfast, how about taking me on a real tour of the island?"

"It's Sunday."

"Yeah, I heard a rumor about that."

"No, I mean that's turnover day. Most of the cottages turn over on Sunday. They have to be cleaned and resupplied for incoming guests by three."

"More housekeeping. What the hell did they do when you weren't here?"

"Kate lost the two girls she had on cottage duty the week before I got here. They took jobs on the mainland. And since I'm here, and so's Lexy, she hasn't bothered to replace them yet."

"How many are on your list?"

"Six."

He considered, nodded, rose. "Well, then, we'd better get started."

"We?"

"Sure. I can handle a vacuum cleaner and a mop. And this way you'll get done faster and we'll have time to find the least occupied spot on the beach and neck for a while."

She shifted, slid her feet—her incredibly happy feet, she had to admit—into her shoes. "Maybe I know a couple of spots—if you're as handy with a vacuum cleaner as you are with reflexology."

"Jo Ellen." He put his hands on her hips in a gesture she found shockingly intimate. "There's something you should know."

He was still married. He was under federal indictment. He preferred bondage to straight sex. She let out a little breath, amazed at herself. She hadn't been aware she possessed that much imagination. "What is it?"

"I'm thinking about sleeping with you too."

She snorted a laugh, backed up. "Nathan, that's been a load *on* my mind since you found your way back to Desire."

He was so happy to be back, to be so close to her. Just watching her brought him that quick zing of anticipation for what was to come. In his own good time.

He thought he might prolong it. After all, he'd planned carefully and money was no problem. He had all the time in the world. It would be even more satisfying to lull her into complacency, to watch her relax, bit by bit. Then he would yank her back, a brisk tug on the chain she wasn't aware linked them.

She'd be afraid. She'd be confused. She would be all the more vulnerable because of the calm he'd provided before he rearranged the composition.

Yes, he could wait. He could enjoy the sun and the surf and before long he would know every minute of her routine. Just the way he'd known her habits in Charlotte.

He would let her drift along, maybe even fall in love a little. And what delicious irony that was.

All the while she would have no idea that he was there to control her fate, to grasp his own destiny. And to take her life.

SIXTEEN

"I DON'T SEE WHY YOU CAN'T take one day off, just one, and spend some time with me."

Giff put his nail gun down, sat back on his heels, and studied Lexy's sulky face. It was one of those wicked whims of nature, he supposed, that made that pouty look so damned appealing to a man. "Honey, I told you this was going to be a busy week for me. And it's only Tuesday."

"What difference does it make what day it is?" She threw her hands up in the air. "Every day around here is the same as the other."

"Well, I'll tell you what difference it makes to me." He skimmed a hand over the edge of the decking he'd completed. "I told Miss Kate that I'd have this porch addition finished and screened in by Saturday."

"So you'll have it done by Sunday."

"I told her Saturday." That, to Giff, said everything. But since it was Lexy he was talking to, he worked up the patience to spell out the rest. "The cottage is booked for next week. Since she needs Colin at the campground

full-time right now, and Jed's got this week of school to
finish before the summer break, I've got to see to it on
my own.''

She didn't care about the damn porch. The floor was
nearly finished anyway. How long could it take to put a
silly roof on it and screen it in? ''Just a day, Giff.'' She
crouched down next to him, letting all her charm slide
into her voice as she kissed his cheek. ''Just a few hours.
We can take your boat over to the mainland. Have a nice
lunch in Savannah.''

''Lex, I just can't spare the time. Now if I can get this
done, we can go next Saturday. I can juggle some things
around, and we can take the whole weekend if you want.''

''I don't want to go Saturday.'' Her voice lost its purr
and edged toward mulish. ''I want to go now.''

Giff had a five-year-old cousin who was just as insistent
on having her way and having it now. But he didn't think
Lexy would appreciate the comparison. ''I can't go now,''
he said patiently. ''You can take the boat if you're so
antsy to get gone. Go do some shopping.''

''By myself?''

''Take your sister, take a friend.''

''I can't think of anyone I less want to spend the day
with than Jo. And I don't have any friends. Ginny's
gone.''

He didn't need to see the tears flood her eyes to know
that was the root of the problem and the greatest source
of her newest discontent. There was nothing he could do
about it, just as there was nothing he could do about the
raw spot in his own heart since Ginny's disappearance.

''If you want me to go, you have to wait till Saturday.
I'll get the weekend clear. We can book a hotel room,
and I'll take you out for a fancy dinner.''

''You don't understand anything!'' She thumped a fist
on his shoulder as she sprang to her feet. ''Saturday's not
today, and I'll go crazy if I don't get away from here.

Why won't you make time for me? Why won't you just make time?''

''I'm doing my best.'' Even his patience could wear thin. Giff picked up the nail gun and shot a bolt home.

''You can't even stop work and pay attention for five minutes. You just shuffle me in between jobs. And now a stupid porch is more important than being with me.''

''I gave my word on the porch.'' He rose and, hefting a new board, laid it across the sawhorse to measure. ''I keep my word, Lexy. You still want to go to Savannah on the weekend, I'll take you. That's the best I can do.''

''It's not good enough.'' She jerked her chin up. ''And I'm sure I won't have any trouble finding someone who'd be happy to take me today.''

He scraped his pencil over the board to make his mark, then looked up at her with cool, narrowed eyes. He recognized the threat, and the very real possibility that she'd make good on it. ''No, you won't,'' he said in calm, measured tones. ''And that will be up to you.''

It was like a slap. She'd expected him to rage, to have a jealous fit and tell her exactly what he'd do if she looked at another man. Then they could have had a loud, satisfying fight before she'd let him drag her into the empty house for make-up sex.

Then she would have convinced him to take her to Savannah.

The scene she'd already staged in her head dissolved. Because she wanted to cry, she tossed her head and turned away. ''Fine then, you go right on and build your porch and I'll do what I have to do.''

Giff said nothing as she stalked down the temporary steps. He had to wait until his vision cleared of blind rage before he picked up the skill saw. Temper could cost dearly, he knew, and he didn't want it to cost him a finger. He was going to need all of them, he thought, if she followed through.

It would take four fingers to make the fist he was going to plow into some guy's face.

Lexy heard the saw buzz and gritted her teeth. Selfish bastard, that's all he was. He certainly didn't care about her. She walked fast across the sand, her eyes stinging, her breath short. No one cared about her. No one understood her. Even Ginny . . .

She had to stop a moment as the muscles in her stomach seized. Ginny had left. Just gone away. Everyone she let herself care about left her, one way or another. She never mattered enough to make them stay.

At first she'd been sure something terrible had happened to Ginny. She'd gotten herself kidnapped, or she'd stumbled half drunk into a pond and been eaten by a gator.

That was ridiculous, of course. It had taken her days, but Lexy had resigned herself to the fact that she'd been left behind again. Because no one stayed, no matter how much you needed them to.

But this time . . . She shot a defiant look over her shoulder at the cottage where Giff was working. This time she'd do the leaving first.

She headed for the line of trees. The sun was too hot on her skin, the sand too gritty in her sandals. At that moment she hated Desire and everything on it with a wild and vicious passion. She hated the people who came and expected her to serve them and clean up after them. She hated her family for thinking of her as an irresponsible dreamer. She hated the beach with its blinding white sun and endless lapping waves. And the forest with its pockets of dim shadows and screaming silence.

And most of all she hated Giff because she'd been thinking about falling in love with him.

She wouldn't now. She wouldn't give him the satisfaction. Instead, she thought, as she left sun for shade, she would set her sights on someone else and make Giff suffer.

When she caught sight of Little Desire Cottage, and the figure sitting on the screened porch, she smiled slowly. She didn't know why she hadn't thought of it before. Of him before.

Nathan Delaney. He was perfect. He was successful, sophisticated, educated. He'd been places and done things. He was gorgeous to look at—gorgeous enough that even Jo had taken notice.

She'd bet Nathan Delaney knew how to treat a woman.

Lexy opened the little red bag she wore strapped across her body. After popping a cherry Lifesaver in her mouth to sweeten her breath, she took out her compact, carefully dusted her nose and brow. Her color was up, so her cheeks needed no blusher, but she methodically painted her mouth a young, inviting red. She spritzed on some Joy and fluffed back her hair while calculating exactly how to play the scene.

She wandered closer to the cottage, then looked up with a friendly smile. "Why, hello there, Nathan."

He'd brought his computer out on the picnic table on the porch to enjoy the breeze while he worked. The design he was tinkering with was nearly perfected. At the interruption, he looked up distractedly. And realized his neck had stiffened up again.

"Hello, Lexy." He rubbed at the ache.

"Don't tell me you're working on such a beautiful morning."

"Just fiddling with final details."

"Why, is that one of those little computers? How in the world do you draw whole buildings on that?"

"Painstakingly."

She laughed and, cocking her head, skimmed a finger down her throat. "Oh, now I've interrupted you, and you probably wish I'd scoot."

"Not at all. It gives me an excuse to take a break."

"Really? Would you just hate me if I asked to come

up and take a peek? Or are you temperamental and don't like to show your work in progress?"

"My work's just the beginning of progress, so it's tough to be temperamental about it. Sure, come on up."

He glanced at his watch as she turned to go to the steps. He really wanted a couple of hours more to refine the plans. And he had a date at one. A drive up to the north end of the island, a picnic lunch. And some more time to get to know Jo Ellen Hathaway.

Still, he smiled at Lexy—it was impossible not to. She was pretty as a picture, smelled fresher than the spring breeze teasing through the screens. And the short white skirt she wore hinted that she had legs approximately up to her ears.

"Want something cold?"

"Mmm, I'll just have a sip of yours, okay?" She picked up the large insulated glass on the table and sipped slowly. "Iced coffee. Perfect." She detested iced coffee and had never understood why people chilled a perfectly nice hot drink.

She ran her tongue over her top lip and sat companionably beside him. Not too close. A woman didn't want to be obvious. She glanced at the monitor and was so surprised by the complex and detailed floor plan that she nearly forgot the point of the visit.

"Why, isn't that fantastic? How in the world do you do all that with a computer? I thought architects used pencils and slide rules and calculators."

"Not as much as we used to. CAD makes our lives easier. Computer-assisted drawing," he explained. "You can take out walls, change angles and pitch, widen doorways, lengthen rooms, then change your mind and put it all back the way it was. And you don't wear out erasers."

"It's just amazing. Is this going to be someone's house?"

"Eventually. A vacation home on the west coast of Mexico."

"A villa." Images of hot music, exotic flowers, and white-suited servants popped into her mind. "Bri's been to Mexico. I've never been anywhere." She slanted him a look under her lashes. "You've been all over the world, haven't you?"

"I wouldn't say all over, but here and there." A little alarm bell rang in his brain, but he ignored it as foolish and egocentric. "Wonderful cliffs on the west coast, great vistas. This place will look out over the Pacific."

"I've never seen the Pacific Ocean."

"It can be wild down this way. This area here"—he tapped the monitor—"it'll be the solarium. Arched glass, sides and roof—motorized roof. They'll be able to open it for parties or whatever when the weather's right. The pool goes there. We're keeping it free-form and building up the west side with native rock and flora. Small waterfall trickling down here. It'll look like a lagoon."

"A swimming pool, right inside the house." She gave a long, wistful sigh. "Isn't that something. They must be millionaires."

"And then some."

She filled her eyes with dreamy admiration and stared deeply into his. "You must be the very best, then. So important. So successful. Designing Mexican villas for millionaires." She laid her hand on his thigh. "I can't even imagine what it would be like, being able to build such beautiful things."

Uh-oh. The second alarm bell was louder and impossible to ignore. He considered himself a fairly intelligent man. An intelligent man knew when a woman was hitting on him. "A lot of people work on a project like this. Engineers, landscapers, contractors."

Wasn't he sweet? she thought, and slid a little closer. "But without you, they wouldn't have anything to work on. You're the one who makes it happen, Nathan."

Retreat was often the intelligent man's choice, Nathan decided. He shifted, managed to put the best part of an

inch between them. "Not if I don't get these plans done."
He gave her a quick smile that he hoped wasn't as nervous
as it felt. "And I'm running a bit behind on them, so—"

"They look wonderful." Her hand trailed up a little
higher on his thigh. Intelligent or not, he was also human.
His body reacted as nature dictated.

"Listen, Lexy—"

"I'm just so impressed." She leaned in, inviting. "I'd
just love to see more." Her breath fluttered out onto his
lips. "Lots more." Deciding he was either too much of a
gentleman—or too blockheaded—to make the next move,
she pressed her mouth to his and wound her arms around
his neck.

It took him a minute. She was warm and tasty, and most
of the blood had drained out of his head, making it difficult to think rationally. But he managed to take hold of
her wrists, unwind her, and ease away.

"You know . . ." He found it necessary to clear his
throat. "You know, Lexy, you're a very appealing
woman. I'm flattered."

"Good." Her pulse picked up a little. The image of
Giff's face, enraged with jealousy, slipped into her mind
and the pulse picked up a bit more. "Then why don't we
go inside for a little while?"

"There's this other thing." He drew her arms down,
kept his hands firmly over hers. "I really like my face the
way it is. I've gotten used to it. Hardly ever cut myself
shaving anymore."

"I like it too. It's a wonderful face."

"I appreciate that. And I don't want Giff to feel obliged
to try to remodel it for me."

"Oh, what do I care about Giff?" She gave a careless
toss of her head. "He doesn't own me."

The edge that came into her voice, and the sulky heat
in her eyes amused him, and told him that a lovers' spat

was certainly at the root of this current attempt at seduction. "Have a fight, did you?"

"I don't want to talk about Giff. Why don't you kiss me again, Nathan? You know you want to."

Part of him did, a very primal part that was just a little too close to the surface right then. "Okay, we won't talk about Giff. We'll talk about Jo."

"She doesn't own me either."

"No. I'm . . ." He wasn't quite sure how to put it. "Interested in her," he decided.

"I think you're interested in me." To prove it, she freed a hand and made a beeline for his crotch.

Managing not to yelp, he caught her hand firmly. "Cut that out." His voice took on a lecturing tone that would have made any mother proud. "You're worth more than this, Lexy. A hell of a lot more."

"Why would you want Jo more than me? She's cold and bossy and—"

"Stop it." He gave her captured hands one quick, hard squeeze. "I don't want to hear you talk about her that way. I care about her. And so do you."

"You don't know what I care about. Nobody does."

Because her voice had cracked at the end, he felt suddenly and pitifully sorry for her. Gently he lifted her hands, and when he kissed them had her blinking in surprise. "Maybe that's because you haven't really made up your mind yourself yet." Hoping it was safe, he released one of her hands to brush the hair back from her face. "I like you, Lexy. I really do. That's another reason I'm not taking you up on your very tempting offer."

Shame washed over her, rushing hot to her cheeks. "I made a fool of myself."

"No. I damn near did, though." Steadier at last, he eased back, reached for his now tepid coffee to cool his throat. "Most likely you'd have changed your mind somewhere along the way. Then where would I be?"

She sniffled. "Maybe I wouldn't have. Sex is easy. It's the rest that messes things up."

"Tell me about it." When he offered her the coffee, she managed to smile and shake her head.

"I hate iced coffee. I only drank it to seduce you."

"Nice touch. You want to tell me about your fight with Giff?"

"Doesn't matter." Misery settled over her so heavily she rose and paced, hoping to shake it off. "He doesn't care about me, doesn't care what I do or who I'm with. He couldn't even spare an hour of his precious time for me today."

"Sweetheart, he's crazy about you."

She let out a quick laugh. "Being crazy about somebody's easy too."

"Not always. Not when you're trying to make it all work."

Lips pursed, she looked back at him. "Do you really have feelings for Jo?"

"Apparently."

"She's not easy about anything."

"I'm finding that out."

"Are you sleeping with her?"

"Lexy—"

"Not yet," she decided and her lips curved. "And it's making you twitchy." She came back, sat on the edge of the table. "Want some tips?"

"I don't think it's appropriate for us to discuss . . ." He trailed off, then simply abandoned dignity. "What kind of tips?"

"She likes to be in charge, in control of things, you know? It's how she works, how she lives. And always, she keeps that little space, that maneuvering room between herself and someone else."

He found himself smiling again, and liking Alexa Hathaway even more. "She'd never guess how well you know her."

"Most people underestimate me," Lexy said with a shrug. "And mostly I let them. But I figure you did me a good turn today, so I'll do you a good turn back. Don't let her maneuver too much. When the time comes, you sweep her away, Nathan. I don't think anybody's ever swept Jo Ellen away, and it's just what she needs."

She gave him a long, measuring, and very female look, then smirked. "I figure you can handle that part just fine. And I also figure you're smart enough not to tell her what went on around here."

"Not in this lifetime."

Then the sassy look faded. "Find out what's wrong with her, Nathan."

"Wrong?"

"Something's eating at her, and whatever it is, she came here to get away from it. But she isn't getting away from it. The first week or so she was here, she'd cry in her sleep, or pace the floor half the night. And now and then there's a look in her eye, like she's afraid. Jo's never afraid."

"Have you talked to her?"

"Me?" She laughed again. "Jo wouldn't talk to me about anything important. I'm the silly little sister."

"There's nothing silly about you, Lexy. And I, for one, don't underestimate you."

Touched, she leaned over and kissed him. "I guess that makes us friends."

"I'd like to think so. Giff's a very lucky man."

"Only if I decide to give him a second chance." She tossed her head and rose. "Maybe I will—after he crawls some and begs a lot."

"As a friend, I'd appreciate it if you didn't mention this to Giff either. He'd feel really bad about pounding me."

"Oh, I won't name names." She sauntered to the door, glanced back. "But I think you'd handle yourself, Nathan. I do believe you'd handle yourself just fine. 'Bye now."

Alone, Nathan rubbed his eyes, his heart, then his stomach. Handling that one, he thought, would be a real challenge. And he wished Giff the very best of luck.

Jo was just loading the picnic hamper when Lexy strolled into the kitchen. Her camera bag sat on the counter, carefully packed. Her tripod leaned against it.

"Going on a picnic?" Lexy asked airily.

"I want to shoot some pictures on the north end, thought I'd make an afternoon of it."

"All by yourself?"

"No." Jo tucked the wine she'd decided on into the basket. "Nathan's going along."

"Nathan?" Lexy hitched herself up on the counter to sit, chose a glossy green apple out of the stoneware fruit bowl. "Why, isn't that a coincidence." Smiling, Lexy polished the apple on her blouse, just between her breasts.

"Is it?"

"I just came from his place."

"Oh?" Though her back went stiff, Jo managed to keep her tone casual.

"Mmm-hmm." Enjoying dancing on the edge, and leading her sister to it, Lexy bit into the apple. "I was passing by the cottage, and there he was, sitting out on the screened porch having some iced coffee. He invited me up."

"You don't like iced coffee."

Lexy tucked her tongue in her cheek. "Tastes do change. He showed me some floor plans he's working on. A Mexican villa."

"I wouldn't think you'd be interested in floor plans."

"Oh, I'm interested in all kinds of things." The devil in her eyes, Lexy took another crunchy bite of apple. "Especially good-looking men. That one's prime beef."

"I'm sure he'd be flattered you think so," Jo said dryly and slapped the lid down on the hamper. "I thought you were going to see Giff."

"I saw him too."

"You've been busy." Jo hefted the hamper, slung her camera bag over her shoulder. "I've got to get going or I'll lose the light."

"Toddle on along then and have a nice picnic. Oh, and Jo? Give Nathan my best, won't you?"

When the door slammed, Lexy wrapped an arm around her stomach and howled with laughter. Another tip, Nathan, she thought—rile up that green-eyed monster a bit, then reap the rewards.

She wasn't going to mention it. She would absolutely not lower herself to bring it up in even the most casual manner. Jo shifted her tripod, then bent to look through the viewfinder to perfect the angle she wanted.

The sea beat more violently here, whipping and lashing at the rough beach below the jutting bluff. Gulls wheeled and screamed, white wings slashing across the sky.

Heat and humidity were soaring, making the air shimmer.

The south wall of the old monastery was still standing. The lintel over the narrow doorway had held. Through it, light and shadow tangled and wild vines flourished. She wanted that abandoned look—the tufts of high grass, the hillocks of sand the wind built, then destroyed.

She wanted no movement and had to wait, judge the instants of stillness between gusts of wind. A broad depth of field, she thought, everything in sharp focus—the textures of the stone, the vines, the sand, all the varying shades of gray.

To accomplish it, she had to stop down, decreasing the aperture, slowing the shutter speed. Tilting her lens slightly more toward horizontal, she framed in, careful to block out the ruin of the remaining walls. She wanted it to look as though the building could be whole, yet was still empty and deserted.

Alone.

She took her shots, then carried tripod and camera to the east corner. The texture was excellent there, the pits and scars that wind and sand and time had dug into the stones. This time she used the tumbled walls, capturing desolation and loss.

When she heard a quiet click, she straightened. Nathan stood just to her left, lowering his camera.

"What are you doing?"

"Taking your picture." He'd managed three before she caught him at it. "You had a nice intense look about you."

Her stomach shuddered. Pictures of her, without her being aware. But she forced her lips to curve. "Here, let me have the camera. I'll take yours."

"Better—set the timer on yours and take both of us. In front of the ruins."

"This type of view camera, this light, they aren't made for portraits."

"So, we won't mat it for your next show. It doesn't have to be perfect, Jo." He set his camera down. "It just has to be us."

"If I had a diffuser . . ." Turning her head, she squinted into the sun, then, muttering, changed the camera's viewpoint to cut back on shadows, calculated the aperture, adjusted shutter speed. She shrugged her shoulders.

"Jo." It was a struggle not to laugh. "Think of it as a snapshot."

"I will not. Go stand to the left of the opening in the front wall. About two feet over."

She waited until he'd walked to the spot she'd pointed out. Through the viewfinder she watched him grin at her. She could do so much better, she thought, if she had some control, had the necessary equipment to manipulate the light and shadows. She'd have been able to highlight his windblown hair, bring out all those different shades of light and dark.

The light was hard, she decided. It should have been

softer, just a little romantic to show off those wonderful eyes, that strong bone structure. With a reflector, some backfill, a diffuser, she could have made this shot sing.

God, he was attractive. Standing against that worn and pitted stone, he looked so strong and alive. So male and capable. So sexy with that plain gray T-shirt over a broad chest, those faded and worn jeans snug over narrow hips.

"I see why you don't do portraits as a rule."

She blinked, straightened. "What?"

"Your model would lapse into a coma waiting for you to set the shot." Smiling, he stretched out his arm, giving her a come-ahead curl with his fingers. "It doesn't have to be art."

"It always has to be art," she corrected. She fussed for another moment, then set the timer and went to stand beside him. "Ten seconds. Hey!"

He shifted, pulled her in front of him and wrapped his arms around her waist. "I like this pose. Relax and smile."

She did, leaning back against him as the shutter clicked. When she started to move, he nuzzled her hair.

"I still like this pose." He turned her around, arms sliding and continuing to circle as he lowered his mouth to hers. "And this one even more."

"I have to put my equipment away."

"Okay." He simply moved his mouth from hers and skimmed it down her throat.

Nerves and desire did a pitch and roll inside her. "I— the light's changed. It's not right anymore." Because her knees were going to shake, she drew back. "I didn't mean to take so long."

"It's all right. I liked watching you work. I'll help you stow your gear."

"No, I'll do it. I get edgy when anyone fools with my equipment."

"Then I'll open the wine."

"Yeah, that'd be nice." She walked back to her tripod,

easing out a long, quiet breath. She was going to have to make up her mind, and very soon, she thought, as to whether she was going to advance or retreat.

She unhooked her camera, carefully packed it away. "Lexy said she'd been with you this morning."

"What?" He could only hope the pop of the cork masked part of the shock in his voice.

"She said she went by your cottage." Jo was already cursing herself for bringing it up, and kept her eyes firmly on her work.

Nathan cleared his throat and suddenly wanted a glass of wine very badly. "Ah, yeah, she did. For a minute. Why?"

"No reason." Jo collapsed the tripod. "She said you'd shown her some plans you were working on."

Maybe he'd underestimated Lexy after all, he mused, and poured two hefty portions of wine. "The Mexico job. I was doing some fine-tuning on it when she . . . dropped in."

Jo carried her equipment over, stacked it neatly at the far edge of the blanket he'd spread over the ground. "You sound a little nervous, Nathan."

"No, just hungry." He handed her the wine, took a deep gulp of his own before sitting down and diving into the basket. "So, what do you have to eat?"

Jo's muscles tensed. "Did something happen with Lexy?"

"Something? Happen?" Nathan pulled out a plastic container of cold fried chicken. "I don't know what you mean."

Her eyes narrowed at the all-too-innocent look on his face. "Oh, don't you?"

"What are you thinking?" When you didn't want to defend, he decided, attack. "You think I . . . with your sister?" Insult coated his voice, all the more effective from the desperation that pushed it there.

"She's a beautiful woman." Jo slapped a covered bowl of sliced fruit down on the blanket.

"She certainly is, so of course that means I jumped her at the first opportunity. What the hell kind of man do you take me for?" Temper snapped out, some of it real and, Nathan felt, all of it justified. "I go after one sister in the morning and switch to the other for the afternoon? Maybe I'll give your cousin Kate a roll before nightfall and make my points off the whole family."

"I didn't mean—I was only asking—"

"Just what were you asking?"

"I . . ." His eyes were dark and hot, fury streaking out of them. The jitter of alarm came first, which surprised her, then it was smothered quickly by self-disgust. "Nothing. I'm sorry. She was baiting me." Annoyed with herself, Jo dragged a hand through her hair. "I knew she was baiting me. She knew I was coming up here with you, and that I've been seeing you, more or less, and she wanted to get a rise out of me."

She blew out a breath, cursed herself again for not keeping her mouth shut. "I wasn't going to mention it," she went on when Nathan said nothing. "I don't know why I did. It just slipped out."

He cocked his head. "Jealous?"

She would have been relieved that the heat had died out of his eyes, but the question tightened her up all over again. "No. I was just . . . I don't know. I'm sorry." She reached for his hand, closing the distance. "I really am."

"Let's forget it." Since he had her hand, he brought it to his lips. "It never happened."

When she smiled, leaned over and kissed him lightly on the mouth, he rolled his eyes skyward, wondering if he should thank Lexy or throttle her.

SEVENTEEN

KIRBY CHECKED YANCY Brodie's temperature while his mother looked on anxiously.

"He was up most of the night, Doc Kirby. I gave him Tylenol, but the fever was right back up this morning. Jerry had to leave before dawn to go out on the shrimp boat, and he was just worried sick."

"I don't feel good," Yancy said fretfully and looked up into Kirby's eyes. "My mama said you were gonna make me feel better."

"We'll see what we can do about that." Kirby ran a hand over four-year-old Yancy's straw-colored tuft of hair. "Did you go to Betsy Pendleton's birthday party a couple of weeks ago, Yancy?"

"She had ice cream and cake, and I pinned the tail on the jackass."

"Donkey," his mother corrected.

"Daddy calls it a jackass." Yancy grinned, then laid his head on Kirby's arm. "I don't feel good."

"I know, sweetie. And you know what else, Betsy doesn't feel good today either, and neither do Brandon and Peggy Lee. What we've got here is an outbreak of chicken pox.''

"Chicken pox? But he doesn't have any spots."

"He will." She'd already noted the rash starting under his arms. "And you've got to try really hard not to scratch when it starts to itch, honey. I'm going to give your mom some lotion to put on you that will help. Annie, do you know if you and Jerry ever had the chicken pox?"

"We both did." Annie let out a long sigh. "Fact is, Jerry gave it to me when we were kids."

"Then it's likely you won't get it again. Yancy's incubating now, so you want to keep his exposure to other kids and adults who haven't had it to a minimum. You're quarantined, buster," she said, tapping Yancy on the nose. "Tepid baths with a little cornstarch will help once it breaks out, and I'm going to give you both topical and oral medications. I've only got samples here, so you'll have to get Jerry to fill some prescriptions over on the mainland. Tylenol for the fever's fine," she added, laying a cool hand on Yancy's cheek. "I'll drop by your place in a few days to take a look at him."

Noting the look of distress on Annie's face, Kirby smiled, touched her arm. "He'll be fine, Annie. The three of you are in for a couple of tough weeks, but I don't foresee any complications. I'll go over everything with you before you take him home."

"I just . . . could I talk to you for a minute?"

"Sure. Hey, Yancy." Kirby removed the stethoscope from around her neck and slipped it around his. "You want to hear your heart go thump?" She eased the earpieces in place, guided his hand. His tired eyes went big and bright. "You listen to that for a minute while I talk to your mom."

She led Annie into the hallway, leaving the door open. "Yancy's a strong, healthy, completely normal four-year-old boy," she began. "You have nothing to worry about. Chicken pox is inconvenient, irritating, but it's very rarely complicated. I have some literature if you'd like."

"It's not . . ." She bit her lip. "I took one of those home pregnancy tests a couple of days ago. It was positive."

"I see. Are you happy about that, Annie?"

"Yeah. Jerry and me, we've been trying to make another baby for the best part of a year now. But . . . is it going to be all right? Is it going to get sick?"

Exposure to the virus during the first trimester carried a slight risk. "You had chicken pox when you were a child?"

"Yeah, my mother put cotton gloves on me to stop me from scratching and scarring."

"It's really unlikely you'd contract it again." If she did, Kirby thought with a tug of worry, they would deal with that when it happened. "Even if you did contract the virus, the odds are the baby will be fine. Why don't you let me run a backup pregnancy test now, just to confirm? And give you a quick look. We'll see how far along you are. And go from there."

"It'd make me feel a lot better."

"Then that's just what we'll do. Who's your regular OB?"

"I went to a clinic over to the mainland for Yancy. But I was hoping you could take care of things this time."

"Well, we'll talk about that. Irene Verdon's in the waiting room. Let's see if she can keep an eye on Yancy for a few minutes. Then I want the two of you to go home and get some rest. You're going to need it."

"I feel better knowing you're looking after us, Doc Kirby." Annie laid a hand on her stomach. "All of us."

By one o'clock, Kirby had diagnosed two more cases of chicken pox, splinted a broken finger, and treated a bladder infection. Such, she thought as she grabbed a jar of peanut butter, was the life of a general practitioner.

She had thirty minutes before her next appointment and

hoped to spend it sitting down and stuffing her face. She didn't groan when her door opened, but she wanted to.

This was a stranger. She knew every face on the island now, and she'd never seen this one. She tagged him immediately as a beach rover, one of the type who popped up on the island from time to time in search of sun and surf.

His hair was streaky blond and skimmed his shoulders, his face was deeply tanned. He wore ragged cutoffs, a T-shirt that suggested she sun her buns in Cozumel, and dark-lensed Wayfarer sunglasses.

Late twenties, she judged, clean and attractive. She set her sandwich aside and returned his hesitant smile.

"Sorry." He dipped his head. "Have I got the right place? I was told there was a doctor here."

"I'm Doctor Fitzsimmons. What can I do for you?"

"I don't have an appointment or anything." He glanced at her sandwich. "Should I make one?"

"Why do you need one?"

"I just have this, ah . . ." He shrugged his shoulders, then held out a hand. The palm was badly burned, with a red welt across it oozing with blisters.

"That looks nasty." Automatically she stepped forward, taking his hand gently to examine it.

"It was stupid. Coffee was boiling over and I just grabbed the pot without thinking. I'm down at the campground. When I asked the kid at check-in if there was someplace I could get some salve or something, he told me about you."

"Let's go in the back. I'll clean and dress this for you."

"I'm horning in on your lunch."

"Goes with the territory. So you're camping," she continued as she led him back to the examining room.

"Yeah, I was planning on heading down to the Keys, doing some work. I'm an artist."

"Oh?"

He sat in the chair she indicated, then frowned at his

palm. "I guess this will put the skids on work for a couple of weeks."

"Unless you want to paint left-handed," she said with a smile as she washed up, snapped gloves on.

"Well, I was thinking about hanging out here longer anyway. Great place." He sucked in his breath as she began to clean the burn. "Hurts like a bitch."

"I bet it does. I'd recommend aspirin. And a pot-holder."

He chuckled, then set his teeth against the pain. "I guess I'm lucky there's a doc around. This kind of thing can get infected, right?"

"Mmm. But we'll see that it doesn't. What kind of things do you paint?"

"Whatever strikes me." He smiled at her, enjoying her scent, the way her hair swept down gold over her cheek. "Maybe you'd like to pose for me."

She laughed, then rolled her chair over to a drawer for salve. "I don't think so, but thanks."

"You've got a terrific face. I do good work with beautiful women."

She glanced up. His eyes were hidden by the lenses. Though his smile was wide and friendly, there was something around the edges that made her suddenly ill at ease. Doctor or not, she was a woman and she was alone with a stranger. One who was watching her just a little too closely.

"I'm sure you do. But being the only doctor on the island keeps me pretty busy." She bent her head again to coat the burn with salve.

Foolish, she told herself. She was being ridiculous. He had a second-degree burn on his hand and he was letting a stranger treat it. And he was an artist. Naturally he was watching her.

"If you change your mind, I guess I'm going to be hanging here for a while. Jesus, that feels better." He blew out a long breath, and she felt his hand relax in hers.

Feeling even more foolish now, she offered him a sympathetic smile. "That's what we're here for. I want you to keep this dry. You can put a plastic bag around it when you shower. I wouldn't try swimming for the next week. The dressing should be changed daily. If you don't have someone around to help you with it, just come in and I'll do it."

"I appreciate it. You've got good hands, Doc," he added as she wound gauze around his hand.

"That's what they all say."

"No, I mean it—not just good doctor hands. Artistic hands. Angel hands," he said with another smile. "I'd love to sketch them sometime."

"We'll see about that when you can hold a pencil again." She rose. "I'm going to give you a tube of salve. And I want you to check in with me in two days unless you leave the island. In that case you'll want to have it looked at elsewhere."

"Okay. What do I owe you?"

"Insurance?"

"No."

"Twenty-five for the office visit and ten for the supplies."

"More than fair." He got up, tugged his wallet out of his back pocket with his left hand. Gingerly he plucked bills out with the fingers of his wrapped hand. "Guess it's going to be awkward for a while."

"They'll help you out at the campground if you need it. It's a friendly island."

"So I've noticed."

"I'll get you a receipt."

"No, that's all right." He shifted, and she felt that little jolt of nerves again. "Listen, if you're over that way, maybe you could stop in. You could see some of my work, or we could—"

"Kirby! You back there?"

She felt a warm rush of relief, so fast and full it nearly

made her giddy. "Brian. I'm just finishing up with a patient. You be sure to keep that gauze dry," she said briskly and pulled off her gloves. "And don't be stingy with the salve."

"You're the doctor." He sauntered out ahead of her, then lifted his brows at the man who stood in the kitchen with a bloody rag around his left hand. "Looks like you've got a problem there."

"Good eye," Brian said dryly and glanced at the gauze-wrapped hand. "Looks like I'm not the only one."

"Busy day for the doc."

"The doc," Kirby said as she walked in, "hasn't had five minutes to—Brian, what the hell have you done?" Heart in her throat, she leaped forward, grabbed his wrist, and quickly unwrapped the rag.

"Damn knife slipped. I was just—I'm dripping blood all over the floor."

"Oh, be quiet." Her heart settled back when she studied the long slice on the back of his hand. It was deep and bleeding freely, but nothing had been lopped off. "You need stitches."

"No, I don't."

"Yes, you do, about ten of them."

"Look, just wrap it up and I'll get back to work."

"I said be quiet," she snapped. "You'll have to excuse me, I—" She glanced over, frowned. "Oh, I guess he left. Come into the back."

"I don't want you sewing on me. I only came because Lexy and Kate went half crazy on me. And if Lexy hadn't been pestering me, I wouldn't have cut myself in the first place, so just dump some antiseptic on it, wrap it up, and let me go."

"Stop being a baby." Taking his arm firmly, she pulled him into the back. "Sit down and behave yourself. When's the last time you had a tetanus shot?"

"A shot? Oh, listen—"

"That long ago." She washed up quickly, put the nec-

essary tools in a stainless-steel tray, then sat down in front
of him with a bottle of antiseptic. "We'll take care of that
afterward. I'm going to clean this, disinfect, then I'll give
you a local."

He could feel the wound throbbing in time with his
heart. Both picked up speed. "A local what?"

"Anesthetic. It'll numb the area so I can sew you back
together."

"What is this obsession of yours with needles?"

"Let me see you move your fingers," she ordered.
"Good, good. I didn't think you'd cut through any ten-
dons. Are you afraid of needles, Brian?"

"No, of course not." Then she picked up the hypo and
he felt all the blood drain out of his face. "Yes. Damn it,
Kirby, keep that thing away from me."

She didn't laugh as he'd been dead certain she would.
Instead, she looked soberly into his eyes. "Take a deep
breath, let it out, then take another and look at the painting
over my right shoulder. Just keep looking at the painting
and count your breaths. One, two, three. That's it. Little
stick, that's all," she murmured and slid the needle under
his skin. "Keep counting."

"Okay, all right." He could feel the sweat crawling
down his back and focused on the watercolor print of wild
lilies. "This is the perfect time for you to make some
snotty comment."

"I worked in ER. Saw more blood during that year than
a layman does in three lifetimes. Gunshots, knifings, car
wrecks. I never panicked. The closest I've ever come to
panicking was just now, when I saw your blood dripping
onto my kitchen floor."

He looked away from the print and into her eyes. "I'll
mop it up for you."

"Don't be an idiot." She grabbed a swatch of surgical
paper to make a sterile field, then paused when he touched
his hand to hers.

"I care too." He waited until she looked at him again.

"I care a lot. How the hell did this happen?"

"I don't know. What do you think we should do about it?"

"It's probably not going to work, you know. You and me."

"No." She picked up the suture. "Probably not. Keep your hand still, Brian."

He glanced down, saw her slide the suturing needle under his skin. His stomach rolled. Taking another deep breath, he looked back at the painting. "Don't worry about making it neat. Just make it fast."

"I'm famous for my ladylike little stitches. Just relax and keep breathing."

Since he figured it would be more humiliation than he could stand to pass out on her, he tried to obey. "I'm not afraid of needles. I just don't like them."

"It's a common phobia."

"I don't have a phobia. I just don't like people sticking needles in me."

She kept her head bent so he wouldn't see her smile. "Perfectly understandable. What was Lexy pestering you about?"

"The usual. Everything." He tried to ignore the slight tug as she drew the edges of the wound together. "I'm insensitive. I don't care about her—or anyone else, for that matter. I don't understand her. No one does. If I was a real brother, I'd lend her five thousand dollars so she could go back to New York and be a star."

"I thought she'd decided to stay here through the summer."

"She had some sort of go-round with Giff. Since he hasn't come crawling after her, she's gone from the sulky stage—which was our big treat yesterday—to the nasty stage. Are you almost done?"

"Halfway," she said patiently.

"Half. Great. Wonderful." His stomach rolled again.

Okay, think about something else. "Who was the beach bum?"

"Hmm? Oh, the burn. Tussle with a coffeepot. Says he's an artist, on his way to the Keys. He may be over at the campground for a while. I never did get his name."

"What kind of an artist?"

"A painter, I think. He wanted me to pose for him. Damn it, be still," she said when his hand jerked.

"What did you tell him?"

"That I was flattered, thank you very much, but didn't have time. He made me nervous."

Brian's free hand shot out and grabbed her shoulder, making her curse. "Only a couple more," she began.

"Did he touch you?"

"What?" No, it wasn't fear or pain in his eyes, she realized. It was fury. And that was wonderfully satisfying. "Why, yes, of course, Brian. One-handed, he wrestled me to the floor in a wild burst of lust and ripped off my clothes."

Brian's fingers dug in. "I want a straight answer. Did he put his hands on you?"

"No, of course he didn't. I just got nervous for a minute because the office was empty and he seemed overly interested. Then it turned out he just wanted to sketch my hands." She fluttered the fingers of her left one. "Angel hands. Now be still before you ruin my work and end up with a nasty scar. Not that your jealousy isn't flattering."

"I'm not jealous." He removed his hand and willed the green haze over his vision to subside. "I just don't want some beach bum hassling you."

"He didn't hassle me, and if he had I could have handled it. One more now." She tugged, knotted, snipped, then examined the neat line of stitches carefully. "A lovely job, if I do say so myself." She rose to prepare his tetanus shot.

"How would you have handled it?"

"Handled what? Oh, we're still on that, are we? With a polite rebuff."

"And if that hadn't worked?"

"One good squeeze on that burn and he'd have been on the floor screaming in pain."

When she turned back, careful to keep the hypo behind her back, she saw Brian smiling. "You would have too."

"Absolutely. I once cooled the ardor of an oversexed patient by pressing ever so gently on his larynx. He quickly decided to stop making obscene suggestions to me and the nursing staff. Now you want to look at the lilies again, Brian."

He paled. "What have you got behind your back?"

"Just look at the lilies."

"Oh, Christ." He turned his head, then a moment later yelped and jerked.

"Brian, that was the alcohol swab. This'll be over in ten seconds. You're going to feel a prick."

He hissed. "A prick, my ass. What are you using, an upholstery needle?"

"There, all done." She smoothed a bandage over the needle prick, then sat down to wrap his hand. "Keep this dry. I'll change the dressing for you when it needs it. In about ten days, two weeks, we'll see about taking the stitches out."

"Won't that be fun?"

"Here." She reached in the pocket of her smock and took out a Tootsie Pop. "For being such a good boy."

"I know sarcasm when I hear it, but I'll take the sucker."

She unwrapped it for him, stuck it in his mouth. "Take a couple of aspirin," she advised. "The local's going to wear off quickly and it's going to hurt some. You want to get ahead of the pain, not chase it."

"Aren't you going to kiss it?"

"I suppose." She lifted his hand, touched her lips lightly to the gauze. "Be more careful with your kitchen tools," she told him. "I like your hands just the way they are."

"Then I don't suppose you'd object if I moseyed on over here later tonight, wrestled you one-handed to the floor, and tore your clothes off."

"I don't suppose I would." She leaned forward until her lips met his, then with a little sigh lingered there. "The sooner the better."

Brian glanced over at the examination table, and his grin spread slowly. "Well, since I'm here now, maybe you should give me a complete physical. Haven't had one in a couple, three years. You could wear your stethoscope. Just your stethoscope."

The idea made a nice curl of lust slide into her stomach. "The doctor is in," she began, then came back to earth when she heard the outside door open. "But I'll have to give you an evening appointment." She eased back, then stood to remove the tray. "I've had a morning full of chicken pox, and that's my next patient."

He didn't want to go, he realized. He wanted to sit there and watch her. He wanted to study her, the competent way she handled her instruments, the brisk and graceful way she moved. So he stalled and did just that.

"Who's got the chicken pox?"

"Who under ten doesn't, is more like it. We're at seven and counting." She glanced around. "Have you had it?"

"Oh, yeah, the three of us got it at the same time. I think I was nine, so that would have made Jo about six, Lex just under three. I guess my mother went through a couple of gallons of calamine."

"Must have been great fun for all of you."

"It wasn't so bad, after the first couple of days. My father went over to the mainland and brought back this huge box of Lincoln Logs, at least a dozen coloring books, and that jumbo box of Crayolas, Barbie dolls, Matchbox cars."

Because the memory made him sentimental, Brian

shrugged. "I guess he was desperate to keep us all occupied."

And to give your mother a little peace, Kirby mused. "I imagine three sick kids are pretty hard to handle. Sounds like he had the right idea."

"Yeah, I guess they worked through it together. I used to think that was the way it was with them. Until she took off." Telling himself it didn't matter, he stood up. "I'll get out of your way. Thanks for the repair job."

Because his eyes looked suddenly sad, she framed his face in her hands and kissed him lightly. "I'll bill you. But the physical we've scheduled . . . that's free."

It made him smile. "That's quite a deal."

He turned to the door. He didn't look back at her, and the words just seemed to come out before he considered them or knew they were there. "I think I'm falling in love with you, Kirby. I don't know what we're going to do about that either."

He walked out quickly, leaving her staring. She eased herself down on her stool and decided her next patient was just going to have to wait another moment or two. Until the doctor got her breath back.

Just before sunset, Kirby took a walk on the beach. She needed some quiet time, she told herself, just a little space to think before Brian came back.

He loved her. No, he thought he loved her, she corrected. That was a different level entirely. Still, it was a step she hadn't expected him to take. And one she was afraid of tripping over.

She walked to the water's edge, let the surf foam over her ankles. There, she thought, when the tide swept back and sucked the sand down under her feet. That was exactly the same sensation he was causing in her. That slight and exciting imbalance, that feeling of having the ground shift under you no matter how firmly you planted your feet.

She'd wanted him, and she chipped away at his defenses until she won that battle. Now the stakes had gone up, considerably higher than she'd ever gambled on before.

She'd been very careful to do the picking and choosing in personal relationships. And she'd chosen Brian Hathaway. But somewhere along the way the angle had changed on her.

He wouldn't speak of love lightly, not Brian. She could. But not with Brian, she realized. If she said those words, she would have to mean them. And if she meant them, she would have to build on them. Words were only the foundation.

Home, family. Permanence. She would have to decide if she wanted those things at all, and if she wanted them with him. Then she would have to convince him that he wanted them with her.

It wouldn't be simple. The bruises and scars from his childhood kept anything about Brian from being simple.

She lifted her face to the wind. Hadn't she already decided? Hadn't she known in that split second when she saw him bleeding, when fear swept all professional calm aside, that her feelings for him had gone well beyond lust?

It scared her. She was afraid she would indeed trip over that step. And more, she was afraid to commit to taking it. Better to take it slow, she decided. To be sure of her footing. She handled things better if she was calm and clear-sighted. Certainly something as important as this should be approached with caution and a cool head.

She ignored the little voice snickering inside her head and turned back to walk home. The glint far across the dunes made her frown. The second time it flashed, she realized it was the setting sun's reflection off glass. Binoculars, she thought with a shiver. With a hand shielding her eyes, she could just make out a figure. The distance made it impossible to tell whether it was male or female.

She began to walk more quickly, wanting to be inside again, behind closed doors.

It was foolish, she knew. It was just someone watching the beach at sunset, and she simply happened to be on the beach. But the sensation of being watched, of being studied, stayed with her and hurried her steps toward home.

She'd spotted him, and that only made it more exciting. He'd frightened her, just by being there. Chuckling softly, he continued to frame Kirby in the telephoto lens, snapping methodically as she rushed along the beach.

She had a beautiful body. It had been a pleasure to watch the wind plaster her shirt and slacks to it, outline the curves. The sunlight had glowed on her hair, turning it a rich, burning gold. As the sun had dipped lower at his back, all the tones and hues had deepened, softened. He was pleased that he'd used color film this time.

Oh, and that look in her eyes when she'd realized someone was there. The lens had brought her so close, he'd nearly been able to see her pupils dilate.

Such pretty green eyes, he thought. They suited her. Just as the swing of blond hair suited her, and that soft, soothing voice.

He wondered what her breasts would taste like.

She'd be a hot one in the sack, he decided, snapping quickly before she disappeared around the dunes. The small, delicate types usually were, once you got them revving. He imagined she thought she knew all there was to know about anatomy. But he figured he could show her some tricks. Oh, yes, he could show the lady doctor a few things.

He remembered an excerpt from the journal that seemed to fit the moment and his mood. The rape of Annabelle.

I experimented, allowing myself full range to do things to her that I have never done to another woman. She wept, tears streaming down her cheeks and dampening the gag.

I had her again, again. It was beyond me to stop. It wasn't sex, was no longer rape.

It was unbearable power.

Yes, it was the power he wanted, the full scope of it, which he had not achieved with Ginny. Because Ginny had been defective, he reminded himself. She had been whore instead of angel, and a poor choice.

If he decided to—if he decided he needed just a little more practice before the main event—Kirby, with her pretty eyes and angel hands, would be a fine subject. She would work out just fine.

Something to think about, he mused. Something to consider. But for now he thought he'd wander toward Sanctuary and see if Jo Ellen was out and about.

It was nearly time to remind her he was thinking about her.

Eighteen

As giff drove up the road to Sanctuary, he saw Lexy. She stood on the second-floor terrace, her long legs prettily displayed in cuffed cotton shorts, her hair bundled messily on top of her head. She was washing windows, which he was sure would have her in one of her less hospitable moods.

As appealing a picture as she made, she would have to wait. He needed to talk to Brian.

She saw Giff park his pickup but barely spared him a glance. Her smile was smug as she polished off the mixture of vinegar and water with newspaper until the windowpane shone. She'd known he would come around, though it had taken him longer than she'd expected.

But she decided to forgive him—after he crawled just a little.

She bent to soak her rag again, turning her head a bit, slanting her eyes over and down. Then sprang straight up when she saw Giff was heading not toward the house and her but toward the old smokehouse, where Brian was painting porch furniture.

Why, that rattlesnake, she thought, slapping the cleaning solution on the next window. If he was waiting for her to come to him, he was going to be sorely disappointed. She'd never forgive him now. Not if she lived to be a thousand years old. He could crawl over hot coals, she thought, furiously polishing the window. He could beg and plead and call her name on his deathbed and she would laugh gaily and walk on.

From this moment on, Giff Verdon meant less than nothing to her.

She picked up her bucket and moved three windows down so she could keep an eye on him.

At the moment, Lexy and her moods weren't at the forefront of Giff's mind. He caught the oversweet smell of fresh paint, heard the hiss of the sprayer. He worked up a smile as he rounded the stone corner of the smokehouse and saw Brian.

Little dots of sea-blue paint freckled his arms to past the elbows, and polka-dotted the old jeans he wore. An army-green tarp was spread out and covered with chaises and chairs. Brian was giving the old glider a second coat.

"Nice color," Giff called out.

Brian moved the nozzle slowly back and forth another stroke before disengaging it. "You know Cousin Kate. Every few years she wants something different—and always ends up going with blue."

"Freshens them up nice, though."

"It does." Brian flicked the motor off, set the sprayer down. "She's ordered new umbrellas for the tables, pads for the chairs. Should be in on the ferry in another day or two. She wants the picnic tables painted over at the campground, too."

"I can take care of that if you don't have time."

"I'll probably do it." Brian rolled his shoulders free of kinks. "Gets me out in the air. Gives me some daydreaming time." He'd just been having a nice one, too, replaying his night with Kirby.

He knew he would never think of a stethoscope in quite the same way again.

"How's that porch coming?"

"Got the screening in the truck. The weather looks like it's going to hold, so I should be finished by end of the week, like Miss Kate wanted."

"Good. I'll try to come by and take a look at it."

"How's the hand doing?" Giff asked, nodding toward the bandage.

"Oh." Frowning, Brian flexed his fingers. "A little stiff is all." Brian didn't ask how Giff had heard about it. News simply floated on the island's air—especially the juiciest tidbits. The fact was, he considered it a wonder no one knew that he'd spent most of the night on the good doctor's examining table.

"You and Doc Kirby, huh?"

"What?"

"You and Doc Kirby." Giff adjusted his cap. "My cousin Ned was down to the beach early this morning. You know how he collects shells, polishes them up and sells them off to day-trippers down to the ferry. Seems he saw you leaving the doc's this morning about daybreak. You know how Ned runs his mouth."

So much for wonders, Brian mused. "Yeah, I do. How long did it take him to pass the news?"

"Well . . ." Amused, Giff rubbed his chin. "I was heading down to the ferry to see if the screen came in, saw Ned on Shell Road and gave him a lift. That would make it, oh, about fifty minutes, give or take."

"Ned's slowing down."

"Well, he's getting up in age, you know. Be eighty-two come September. Doc Kirby's a fine woman," Giff added. "Don't know anybody on the island doesn't think high of her. Or you, Bri."

"We've spent a few evenings together," Brian muttered and crouched down to rub the nozzle tip with a rag. "People shouldn't start smelling orange blossoms."

Giff lifted a brow. "Didn't say they were."

"We're just seeing each other some."

"Okay."

"Nobody's thinking about making it a permanent relationship, or tangling it up with strings."

Giff waited a moment. "You trying to convince me, Bri, or is somebody else here?"

"I'm just saying—" Brian caught himself, lifting his hands as if to signal himself to call a halt. He straightened again and tried not to be irritated by the bland and innocent smile on Giff's face. "Did you come by here just to congratulate me on sleeping with Kirby, or is there something else on your mind?"

Giff's smile faded. "Ginny."

Brian sighed, discovered that the tension balled dead center at the back of his neck couldn't be rubbed away. "The cops called here this morning. I guess they talked to you, too."

"Didn't have squat to say. I don't think they'd have bothered to call if I hadn't been hassling them. Damn it, Brian, you know they're not looking for her. They're barely going through the motions."

"I wish I could tell you different."

"They said we could make up flyers, hand them out around in Savannah. What the hell good is that?"

"Next to none. Giff, I wish I knew what to say to you. But you know, Ginny's twenty-six years old and free to come and go as she pleases. That's how the cops look at it."

"That's the wrong way to look at it. Ginny has family here, she has a home and friends. No way she'd have taken off without a word to anyone."

"Sometimes," Brian said slowly, "people do things you never expect they would do. Never believe they could do. But they do them just the same."

"Ginny's not your mama, Brian. I'm sorry this brings

back a bad time for you and your family. But this is now. This is Ginny. It's not the same.''

''No, it's not.'' Brian forced himself to keep his voice and his temper even. ''Ginny didn't have a husband and three children. If she decided to shake the sand out of her shoes, she wasn't leaving lives broken behind her. Now I'll keep talking to the police, I'll see they're called at least once a week to keep Ginny in their heads. We'll make up the flyers for you in the office. I just can't do any more than that, Giff. I'm not having my life turned inside out a second time.''

''That's fine.'' Giff nodded stiffly. ''That's fine, then. I'll get out of your way so you can go about your business.''

Fury lengthened his stride as he stalked back to the truck. He climbed in, slammed the door behind him. Then just lowered his head onto the steering wheel.

He'd been wrong. All the way wrong. Sniping at Brian that way, going stiff and snooty on him. It wasn't Brian's fault or his responsibility. And it wasn't right, Giff added, as he sat back and closed his eyes, for a friend to cut into another that way. He'd just give himself a moment to calm and to settle, then he'd go back and apologize.

Lexy sauntered out of the house. She'd streaked down the inside stairs, nearly breaking her neck in her hurry to be sure Giff didn't drive off before she could taunt him with what he couldn't have. And her heart was still racing. But she moved slowly now, one hand trailing along the banister, a distant smile on her face.

She moseyed up to the truck and, forgetting that her hands smelled of vinegar, propped them on the bottom of the open window. ''Why, hello there, Giff. I was about to take a little walk in the woods to cool off, and saw your truck.''

He opened his eyes, looked into hers. ''Go on then, Lexy,'' he murmured and leaned over to turn the key.

''What is it?'' The misery in his eyes was a balm for

her soul. "You feeling poorly, Giff? Maybe you're feeling blue." She trailed a fingertip up his arm. "Maybe you're wishing you knew how to apologize to me so you wouldn't be so lonely these days."

His eyes remained dark, but the shadows in them shifted from misery to temper. He pushed her hand aside. "You know what, Alexa? Even my limited little world doesn't revolve only around you."

"You've got your nerve, thinking you can talk to me that way. If you think I care what your world revolves around, Giff, you're very mistaken. I couldn't care less."

"Right now that makes two of us. Get away from the truck."

"I will not. Not until I've had my say."

"I don't give a damn what you have to say, now back off before you get hurt."

She did just the opposite, stretching through the open window to turn the key and shut the engine down. "Don't you order me around." She stuck her face in his. "Don't you think for one minute you can tell me what to do, or threaten me into doing it."

She sucked in a breath, prepared to scold him properly. But there was misery in his eyes again, more than she'd ever seen or expected to. Her temper subsided, and she laid a hand on his cheek. "What's the matter, honey? What's hurting you?"

He started to shake his head, but she kept her hand in place. "We can be mad at each other later. You talk to me now. Tell me what's wrong."

"Ginny." He let out an explosive breath that scalded his throat. "Not a word from her, Lexy. Not a single word. I don't know what to do anymore. What to say to my family anymore. I don't even know how to feel."

"I know." She slipped back, opened the door. "Come on."

"I've got work to do."

"You do what I say for once in your life. Now come

on with me.'' She took his hand, tugging until he climbed out. Saying nothing, she led him around the side of the house toward the shade. ''Sit down here.'' She drew him down on the side of the rope hammock and, slipping an arm around him, nudged his head down to her shoulder. ''You just rest your mind a minute.''

''I don't think about it all the time,'' he murmured. ''You go crazy if you do.''

''I know.'' Reaching around, she took his hand in hers. ''It just sneaks up on you now and again, and it hurts so much you don't think you can stand it. But you do, till the next time.''

''I know what people are saying. She just got a wild hair and took off. It'd be easier if I could believe that.''

''It wouldn't, not really. It hurts either way. When Mama left I cried and cried for her. I figured if I cried enough she'd hear me and come back. When I got older I thought, well, she just didn't care enough about me, so I won't care either. I stopped crying, but it still hurt all the same.''

''I keep thinking she'll send some stupid postcard from Disney World or somewhere. Then I could just be mad at her instead of so goddamn worried.''

Lexy tried to imagine that, let herself see it. Perfect. Ginny on some colorful, foolish ride, howling with laughter. ''It'd be just like her to do that.''

''I guess it would.'' He stared down at their joined hands, watching their fingers interlace. ''I just tore a strip off Brian over it. Stupid.''

''Don't you worry about that. Brian's hide's thick enough to take it.''

''How about yours?'' He eased back, absently pushing a loosened bobby pin back into her messy topknot.

''All us Hathaways are tougher than we look.''

''I'm sorry anyway.'' He lifted their joined hands and kissed her knuckles. ''Do we have to be mad at each other later?''

"I guess not." She kissed him lightly, then smiled. The birds were singing in the trees above her, and the flowers smelled so nice and sweet on the air. "Since I've been missing you, just a little bit."

Her breath caught as he pulled her close, pressed his face hard against her throat. "I need you, Lexy. I need you."

When she released her breath, it was unsteady, shuddering from lungs to throat to lips. She put her hands on his shoulders, her fingers pressing once into those hard muscles. Then she pulled back, rose, struggling to grip her own emotions as firmly.

She'd turned her back on him. Giff rubbed his hands over his face, then dropped them helplessly. "What did I say now? What is it I do that always makes you take that step back from me?"

"I'm not." She had to press her fingers to her lips to stop them from trembling before she faced him again. When she did, her heart was swimming in her eyes. "In my whole life, my whole life, Giff, no one's ever said that to me. Unless it was a man meaning sex."

He got to his feet fast. "That's not what I meant. Lexy—"

"I know." She blinked impatiently at the tears. She wanted to see him clearly. "I know it's not what you meant. And I'm not stepping back, I'm just trying to get hold of myself before I act like a fool."

"I love you, Lexy." He said it quietly so she would believe him. "I always have and always will love you."

She closed her eyes tight. She wanted it all engraved on her memory. The moment—every sound, every scent, every feeling. Then she was launching herself into his arms, wrapping herself around him, her breath coming in tiny little hitches that made her dizzy.

"Hold me. Hold on to me, Giff, tight. No matter what I do, no matter what I say, don't ever let me go."

"Alexa." Swamped by her, he pressed his lips into her

hair. "I've always held on to you. You just didn't know it."

"I love you too, Giff. I can't remember when I didn't. It always made me so mad."

"That's all right, honey." He smiled, snuggled her closer. "I don't mind you being mad. As long as you don't stop."

In her bedroom, Jo carefully hung up the phone. Bobby Banes had finally gotten in touch. And had given her at least one answer.

He hadn't taken the print from her apartment.

But you saw the print, didn't you? It was a nude, mixed in with all the shots of me. It looked like me, but it wasn't. I was holding it. I picked it up. You must have seen it.

She could hear her own voice, pitching into panic, and the concern and hesitation in Bobby's when he answered.

I'm sorry, Jo. I didn't see a print like that. Just those ones of you. Ah . . . there wasn't any nude study. At least I didn't notice.

It was there. I dropped it. It fell facedown on the other prints. It was there, Bobby. Just think for a minute.

It must have been there . . . I mean, if you say you saw it.

His tone had been placating, she thought now. Sympathetic. But it hadn't been convinced.

Sick and shaky, she turned away from the phone, told herself it was useless to wish he hadn't called, hadn't told her. It was better, much better, to have the truth. All she had to do now was live with it.

From her bedroom window, Jo looked down on her sister and Giff. They made a pretty picture, she decided. Two young, healthy people locked in each other's arms, with flowers growing wild and ripe all around them. A man and woman sparkling with love and sexual anticipation on a summer afternoon.

It looked so easy, so natural. Why couldn't she let it be easy and natural for herself?

Nathan wanted her. He wasn't pushing, he didn't appear to be angry that she kept that last bit of distance between them. And why did she? Jo wondered, watching as Giff tipped Lexy's face up to his. Why didn't she just let go?

He stirred her. He brought her pleasure and set something to simmering inside her that hinted the pleasure would spread and deepen if she allowed it.

Why was she afraid to allow it?

In disgust she turned away from the window. Because she questioned everything these days. She watched her own moves, analyzed them clinically. Oh, she felt better physically. The nightmares and slick-skinned panic attacks were fewer and farther between.

But . . .

There was always that doubt, the fear that she wasn't really stable. Why else could she still see in her mind that photograph, the photograph of the dead woman? One minute her mother, the next herself. The eyes staring, the skin white as wax. She could still see the texture of the skin, smooth and pale. The shades and sweep of the hair, that artfully spread wave of it. The way the hand had been draped, elbow bent, arm crossed between the breasts. And the head turned, angled down as in shy slumber.

How could she see it so clearly when it had never existed?

And because she could, she had to believe she was still far from well. She had no business even considering a relationship with Nathan—with anyone—until she was solidly on her feet again.

And that, she admitted, was just an excuse.

She was afraid of him—that was the bottom line. She was afraid he would come to mean more to her than she could handle. And that he would expect more of her than she could give.

He was already drawing feelings out of her that no one else ever had. So she was protecting herself with cowardice that wore a mask of logic.

She was tired of being logical and afraid. Would it be so wrong to take a page out of her sister's book for once? To act on impulse, to take whatever she could get?

God, she needed someone to talk to, someone to be with. Someone who could, even for a little while, crowd out all these self-doubts and worries.

Why shouldn't it be Nathan?

She rushed out of her room before she could change her mind, and for once didn't even bother to grab her camera. She paused impatiently when Kate called out her name.

"I'm just heading out." Jo stopped at the door to the office. Kate was behind a desk covered with papers and brochures.

"Trying to get ahead of the fall reservations." Kate pulled a pencil out from behind her ear. "We've got a request to have a wedding here at the inn in October. We've never done that kind of thing before. They want Brian to do the catering, have the ceremony and reception right here. It would be just wonderful if we could figure out how to do it."

"That would be nice. Kate, I'm really on my way out."

"Sorry." She stuck the pencil back behind her ear and smiled distractedly. "Lost my train again. I've been doing that all morning. I've got your mail here. I was going to drop it off in your room, then the phone rang and I haven't budged from this spot in two hours."

As if to punctuate the statement, the phone jingled again, and behind her the second line beeped, signaling an incoming fax. "If it's not one thing, it's two, I swear. There you go, honey, you got a package there." She picked up the phone. "Sanctuary Inn, may I help you?"

Jo heard nothing but the beehive buzz in her own ears. She stepped forward slowly, could feel the air around her thickening like water. The manila envelope felt stiff in her hand when she reached for it. Her name had been printed on it in block letters in thick black marker.

Jo Ellen Hathaway
Sanctuary
Lost Desire Island, Georgia

The warning in the corner stated clearly: PHOTOS. DO NOT BEND.

Don't open it, she told herself. Throw it in the trash. Don't look inside. But her fingers were already tearing at the seal, ripping open the flap. She didn't hear Kate's exclamation of surprise as she upended the envelope, shaking the photographs out onto the floor. With a little keening sound, Jo dropped to her knees, shoving through them, pushing one after another aside in a desperate search for one. The one.

Without hesitation, Kate hung up on the reservation she was taking and rushed around the desk. "Jo, what is it? Jo Ellen, what's wrong? What is all this?" she demanded, holding Jo under one arm as she stared at dozens of pictures of her young cousin.

"He's been here. He's been here. Here!" Jo scrambled through the photos again. There she was, walking on the beach. Asleep in the hammock, on the edge of the dune swale, setting up her tripod at the salt marsh.

But where was the one? Where was the one?

"It's got to be here. It's got to."

Alarmed, Kate hauled Jo up to her knees and shook her. "Stop it. Now. I want you to stop it this minute." Because she recognized the signs, she dragged Jo over to a chair, pushed her into it, then shoved her head between her knees. "You just breathe. That's all you do. Don't you go fainting on me. You sit right there, you hear me? You sit right there and don't you move."

She rushed into the bathroom to run a glass of water

and dampen a cloth. When she dashed back in, Jo was just as she'd left her. Relieved, Kate knelt down and laid the cold cloth on the back of Jo's neck.

"There now, just take it easy."

"I'm not going to faint," Jo said dully.

"That's fine news to me, I'll tell you. Sit back now, slowly, drink a little water." She brought the glass to Jo's lips herself, held it there, grateful when color gradually seeped back into them. "Can you tell me what this is all about now?"

"The photos." Jo sat back, closed her eyes. "I didn't get away. I didn't get away after all."

"From what, honey? From who?"

"I don't know. I think I'm going crazy."

"That's nonsense." Kate made her voice sharp and impatient.

"I don't know that it is. It's already happened once."

"What do you mean?"

She kept her eyes closed. It would be easier to say it that way. "I had a breakdown a few months ago."

"Oh, Jo Ellen." Kate eased down onto the arm of the chair and began to stroke Jo's hair. "Why didn't you tell me you'd been sick, honey?"

"I just couldn't, that's all. Everything just got to be too much and I couldn't hold on anymore. The pictures started to come."

"Pictures like these?"

"Pictures of me. Just pictures of my eyes at first. Just my eyes." Or her eyes, she thought with a shudder. Our eyes.

"That's horrible. It must have frightened you so."

"It did. Then I told myself someone was just trying to get my attention so I'd help them break into photography."

"That's probably just what it was, but it was a terrible way to do it. You should have gone to the police."

"And tell them that someone was sending me, a photographer, pictures?'' Jo opened her eyes again. ''I thought I could handle it. Just ignore it, just deal with it. Then an envelope like that one came in the mail. Full of pictures of me, and one . . . one I thought was of someone else. But it wasn't,'' Jo said fiercely. She was going to accept that. If nothing else, she was going to accept that one thing.

''I imagined it. It wasn't there at all. Just those pictures of me. Dozens of them. And I fell apart.''

''Then you came back here.''

''I had to get away. I thought I could get away. But I can't. These are from here, right here on the island. He's been right here, watching me.''

''And these are going to the police.'' Simmering with fury, Kate rose to snatch up the envelope. ''Postmark's Savannah. Three days ago.''

''What good will it do, Kate?''

''We won't know that till we do it.''

''He could still be in Savannah, or anywhere else. He could be back on the island.'' She ran her hands through her hair, then let them drop into her lap. ''Are we going to ask the police to question everyone with a camera?''

''If necessary. What kind of camera?'' Kate demanded. ''Where and how were they developed? When were they taken? There ought to be a way of figuring some of that out. It's better than sitting here being scared, isn't it? Snap your backbone in place, Jo Ellen.''

''I just want it to go away.''

''Then *make* it go away,'' Kate said fiercely. ''I'm ashamed you'd let someone do this to you and not put up a fight.'' Kate snatched up a photo, held it out. ''When was this taken? Look at it, figure it out.''

Jo's stomach churned as she stared at it. Her palms were damp as she reached out and took the photo. The shot was slightly out of focus, she noted. The angle of light was poor, casting a bad shadow across her body. He was capable of much better work, she thought, then let out a long breath. It helped to think practically, even to critique.

"I think he rushed this one. The marsh at this spot is fairly open. Obviously he didn't want me to know he was taking pictures, so he hurried through it."

"Good. Good girl. Now when were you down there last?"

"Just a couple of days ago, but I didn't take the tripod." Her brow furrowed as she concentrated. "This had to be at least two weeks back. No, three. Three weeks ago, I went out at low tide to do some studies of the tidal pools. Let me see another print."

"I know it's difficult for you, but I like this one." Kate tried a bolstering smile as she offered Jo a photo of herself cradled in Sam's lap. Shade dappled over them in patterns, making the study almost dreamy.

"The campground," Jo murmured. "The day I was locked in the showers and Daddy let me out. It wasn't kids. The bastard. It wasn't kids, it was him. He locked me in there, then he waited around and he took this."

"That was the day Ginny went missing, wasn't it? Nearly two weeks now."

Jo knelt on the floor again, but she wasn't panicking now. Her hands were steady, her mind focused. She went through photo by photo, coolly. "I can't be sure of each and every one, but those I can pinpoint were all taken at least that long ago. So I'll assume they all were. Nothing in the last two weeks. He's held on to them. He's waited. Why?"

"He needed time to print them, to select them. To decide which ones to send. He must have other obligations. A job. Something."

"No, I think he's very flexible there. He had pictures of me on assignment at Hatteras, and others of me in Charlotte. Day-to-day stuff. He isn't worried about obligations."

"All right. Get your purse. We're going to get the boat

and go over to the mainland. We're taking this, all of this, to the police.''

''You're right. That's better than sitting here being afraid.'' Very carefully she slipped photo after photo back into the envelope. ''I'm sorry, Kate.''

''For what?''

''For not telling you. For not trusting you enough to tell you about what happened.''

''And you should be.'' She reached out a hand to help Jo to her feet. ''But that's done now, and behind us. From now on you and everyone else in this house are going to remember we're a family.''

''I don't know why you put up with us.''

''Sweetie pie,'' Kate smiled and patted Jo's cheek, ''there are times when I wonder the selfsame thing.''

NINETEEN

"HEY, WHERE Y'ALL GOING?"
Lexy spotted Kate and Jo as they stepped out the side
door. Her eyes were bright, her smile brilliant. She was
nearly dancing.

"Jo and I have to run over to the mainland on some
business," Kate began. "We'll be back by—"

"I'm going with you." Lexy raced through the door,
zipping by before Kate could grab her arm.

"Lexy, this isn't a pleasure trip."

"Five minutes," Lexy called back. "It's only going to
take me five minutes to get ready."

"That girl." Kate heaved a sigh. "She's always wanting to be someplace she's not. I'll go tell her she has to
stay behind."

"No." Jo tightened her grip on the pair of envelopes
she held. "Under the circumstances it might be better if
she knows what's going on. I think, until we find out
something more, she needs to be careful."

Kate's heart skipped a beat, but she nodded. "I suppose
you're right. I'll tell Brian we're going. Don't you worry,

sweetie." Kate flicked a hand over Jo's hair. "We're going to take care of this."

Because she was afraid of being left behind, Lexy was true to her word. She knew Kate would have balked at the little shorts she'd had on, so she changed in record time to thin cotton pants. She brushed her hair out, tied it back in a mint-green scarf in anticipation of the boat trip. On the drive to Sanctuary's private dock north of the ferry, she freshened her makeup and chattered.

Jo's ears were ringing by the time they boarded the reliable old cabin cruiser.

Once there had been a glossy white boat with bright red trim. The *Island Belle* had been her father's pride and joy, Jo remembered. How many times had the family piled into it, to sail around the island, to streak out over the waves, to take an impromptu run to the mainland for ice cream or a movie?

She remembered steering it, standing on her father's feet to give her a little more height, with his hands laid lightly over hers on the wheel.

A little to starboard, Jo Ellen. That's the way. You're a natural.

But Sam had sold it the year after Annabelle went away. All the replacements since had gone unnamed. The family no longer took dizzying rides together.

Still, Jo knew the routine. She checked the fuel while Lexy and Kate released the lines. Automatically she adjusted her stance to accommodate the slight sway at the dock. Her hands took the wheel easily, and she smiled when the engine caught with a kick and a purr.

"Daddy still keeps her running smooth, I see."

"He overhauled the engine over the winter." Kate took a seat, and her agitated fingers twisted the gold chain that draped over her crisp cotton blouse.

She would let Jo pilot, she thought. It would help her stay calm. "I've been thinking the inn should invest in a new one. Something spiffier to look at. We could offer tours around the island, stop off at Wild Horse Cove, Egret Inlet, that sort of thing. 'Course that means we'd have to hire on a pilot.''

"Daddy knows the island and the water around it better than anyone," Jo pointed out.

"I know." Kate shrugged her shoulders. "But whenever I bring that up, he mutters under his breath and finds something else he has to do. Sam Set-in-His-Ways Hathaway is not an easy man to move."

"You could tell him how he'd be able to keep an eye on things better if he was in charge." Jo glanced at the compass, set her heading, and started across the sound. "He could make sure people didn't trample the vegetation or upset the ecosystem. Put someone else on it, they're not going to care as much, be as vigilant."

"It's a good angle."

"You buy a new boat, he'll have a hard time resisting it." Lexy readjusted the knot in her scarf. "Then you mention how you need to find the right pilot—not only one who's experienced and competent, but somebody who understands the fragility of the environment and how it needs to be explained to the tourists so they understand why Desire has stayed pure all these years."

Both Jo and Kate turned to stare at Lexy in astonishment. Lexy spread her hands. "You just have to know how to work people, is all. You talk about educating the tourists on respecting the island and leaving it as they found it and that sort of thing, he'll not only come around, he'll end up thinking it was his idea to start with."

"You're a sly child, Alexa," Kate told her. "I've always admired that about you."

"The island's what matters to Daddy." Lexy leaned over the rail to let the wind slap her face. "Using that to turn him around isn't sly, it's just basic. Can't you go any faster, Jo? I could swim to Savannah at this rate."

Jo started to suggest that Lexy do just that, then

shrugged. Why not? Why not go fast and free for just a little while? She glanced back at the shoreline of Desire, the white house on the hill, then she gunned the throttle. "Hold on, then."

At the burst of speed, Lexy let out a whoop, then threw back her head and laughed. Oh, God, but she loved going places. Going anywhere. "Faster, Jo! You always handled these buckets better than any of us."

"And she hasn't manned a boat in two years," Kate began, then shrieked as Jo whipped the wheel around, shooting the boat into a fast, wide circle. Heart thumping, she grabbed the rail while Lexy shouted out for more.

"Look there, it's Jed Pendleton's fishing boat. Let's buzz them, Jo. Give them a taste of our wake and rock them good."

"Jo Ellen, you'll do no such thing." Kate conquered the laugh that sprang to her throat. "You behave yourself!"

Jo shared a rare grin with Lexy before she rolled her eyes. "Yes, ma'am," she murmured, tongue in cheek, and cut her speed. She sent out a short hail to the fishing boat. "I was just testing her engines and response."

"Well, now you have," Kate said primly. "And I expect it'll be a smooth ride from here on."

"I just want to get there." Lexy turned around and leaned back on the rail. "I'm dying to see people walking around. And I've just got to do some shopping. Why don't we all buy something new and pretty? Party dresses. Then we'll have us a party. Get all dressed up, have music and champagne. I haven't had a new dress in months."

"That's because your closet's already bursting at the seams," Jo said.

"Oh, those are ancient. Don't you ever have to have something new—just have to? Something wonderful?"

"Well, I have been wanting a new dedicated flash," Jo told her dryly.

"That's because you're more interested in dressing

your camera than yourself.'' Lexy tilted her head. ''Something bold and blue for you for a change. Silk. With silk undies, too. That way if you ever let Nathan get down to them, he'll have a nice surprise. Bet you would, too.''

''Alexa.'' Kate held up a hand and counted slowly to ten. ''Your sister's private life is just that—private.''

''What private life? Why the man's been dying to get inside those baggy jeans she wears since he laid eyes on her.''

''How do you know he hasn't?'' Jo shot back.

''Because,'' Lexy said with a slow, feline smile, ''once he has, you're going to be a whole lot more relaxed.''

''If all it takes to relax a woman is a quick roll, you'd be comatose by now.''

Lexy only laughed and turned her head back into the wind. ''Well, I'm sure feeling serene these days, honey pie. Which is more than I can say for you.''

''Lexy, that's enough.'' Kate spoke quietly, then rose. ''And we're not going to the mainland to shop. We're going because your sister's got troubles. She wanted you to come along so she could tell you about it, so those troubles won't touch on you.''

''What are you talking about?'' Lexy straightened. ''What's wrong?''

''Sit down,'' Kate ordered and picked up the envelopes Jo had stowed. ''And we'll tell you.''

Ten minutes later, Lexy was going through the photos. Her stomach was tight, but her hands were steady and her mind was working. ''He's stalking you.''

''I don't know if I'd call it that.'' Jo kept her eyes on the water, on the faint haze that was the mainland.

''It's exactly that, and that's how you're going to put it to the police. There are laws against it. I knew a woman up in New York. Her ex-boyfriend wouldn't leave her be, kept popping up, calling her, following her around. She lived scared for six months before they did something about it. It's not right you should have to live scared.''

"She knew who he was," Jo pointed out.

"Well, you have to figure out who this is." Because
the pictures spooked her, Lexy set them aside. "Did you
break up with anybody close to the time this started?"

"No, I haven't been seeing anyone in particular."

"You don't have to think it was in particular," Lexy
reminded her. "He has to think it. Who were you dat-
ing—even one date?"

"Nobody."

"Jo, you had dinner with someone, went to a show,
had a quick lunch."

"Not dates."

"Don't be so literal. Problem with you is everything's
just black and white in your head. Just like your pictures.
Even those have shades of gray, don't they?"

Not entirely sure if she was insulted or impressed by
her sister's analogy, Jo frowned. "I just don't see—"

"Exactly." Lexy nodded. "You think up a list, then
you think of another for men you turned down when they
asked you out. Maybe somebody asked you a couple,
three times and you figured he gave up."

"I've been busy this past year. There's hardly anyone."

"That's good. It'll make the odds better on finding the
right one." Lexy crossed her legs, put herself into forming
the plotline. "Maybe there's someone in your building in
Charlotte who tried to draw you out, make conversation
when you bumped into each other in the hallway. Open
your mind now," Lexy said impatiently. "A woman
knows when a man's got an interest in her, even if she's
got none in him."

"I haven't paid much attention."

"Well, pay attention now, and think. You're the one
who has to stay in control here. You're not going to let
him know he's got you scared. You're not going to give
him the satisfaction of thinking he can put you in a hospital again." She reached over, gave Jo's shoulder a hard

shake. "So you think. You've always been the smartest one of us. Use your head now."

"Let me take the wheel, Jo." Gently, Kate pried Jo's tensed hands away. "You sit down, take a breath."

"She can breathe later. Right now she's going to think."

"Lexy, ease off."

"No." Jo shook her head. "No, she's right. You're right," she said to Lexy, taking a good long look at the sister she'd allowed herself to think of as fluff. This time what she saw was substance. "And you're asking the right questions—ones I never thought to ask myself. When I go to the police, they're going to ask the same ones."

"I expect they are."

"Okay." Jo let out an unsteady breath. "Help me out."

"That's what I'm doing. Let's sit down." She took Jo's arm, sat with her. "Now, first think about the men."

"There aren't many. I don't draw them like bees to honey."

"You would if you wanted to, but that's another problem." Lexy waved it away with a flick of her hand. Something to be solved later. "Maybe there's one you come into contact with regularly. You don't pay much attention, but you see him, he sees you."

"The only man I see regularly is my intern. Bobby was the one who took me to the hospital. He was there when the last package came in the mail."

"Well, isn't that handy?"

Jo's eyes widened. "Bobby? That's ridiculous."

"Why? You said he was your intern. That means he's a photographer too. He'd know how to use a camera, develop film. I bet he knew where you'd be and what your schedule was whenever you were on assignment."

"Of course, but—"

"Sometimes he went with you, didn't he?"

"As part of his training, sure."

"And maybe he has a thing for you."

"That's just silly. He had a little crush at first."

"Really?" Lexy lifted a brow. "Did you accommodate him?"

"He's twenty years old."

"So?" Lexy shrugged it off. "Okay, you didn't sleep with him. He was a regular part of your life, he was attracted to you, he knew where you'd be, he knew your routine and he knew how to use a camera. Goes to the top of the short list, I'd say."

It was appalling, even more appalling than the faceless, nameless possibilities. "He took care of me. He got me to the hospital."

He said he hadn't seen the print, Jo remembered as her stomach muscles fisted painfully. It had been only the two of them there, and he said he hadn't seen it.

"Does he know you came back to Sanctuary?"

"Yes, I—" Jo cut herself off, closed her eyes. "Yes, he knows where I am. Oh, God, he knows where I am. I just talked to him this morning. He just called me."

"Why did he call you?" Lexy demanded. "What did he say to you?"

"I'd left a message for him to get in touch with me. Something I . . . I needed to ask him something. He got back to me today."

"Where was he calling from?" Kate flicked a quick glance over her shoulder.

"I didn't ask—he didn't say." With a supreme effort, Jo reined in the thudding fear. "It doesn't make any sense for Bobby to have sent the prints. I've been working with him for months."

"That's just the kind of relationship the police are going to be interested in," Lexy insisted. "Who else knows where you are—that you're sure of?"

"My publisher." Jo lifted a hand to rub her temple. "The post office, the super at my apartment building, the doctor who treated me at the hospital."

"That means anybody who wanted to know could find out. But Bobby stays top of the list."

"That makes me feel sick, sick and disloyal. And it's logical." Pausing, she squeezed the bridge of her nose between her thumb and fingers. "He's good enough to have taken the shots—if he worked at it, took his time. He's got a lot of potential. He still makes mistakes, though—rushes, or doesn't make the right choices in the darkroom. That could explain why some of the photos aren't as high-quality as others."

"What's wrong with them?" Curious, Lexy slipped some of the prints out again.

"Some of them have hard shadows, or the framing's off. See here?" She pointed to the shadow falling over her shoulder in one. "Or this one. It's not crisp, the tones aren't well defined. Some are mottled in a way I'd say means he used fast film, then overenlarged. Or some are thin—underexposed negatives," she explained. "And others just lack creativity."

"Seems pretty picky to me. You look good in most all of them."

"They aren't as carefully composed, certainly not as artfully composed, as the others, as the ones taken in Charlotte or on Hatteras. In fact . . ."—she began to frown as she went through them again, shot by shot—"if I'm remembering right, it looks to me as though the later the photo was taken, the less professional, the less creative it is. As if he's getting bored—or careless.

"See here, a first-year student with some talent and decent equipment could have taken this shot of me in the hammock. The subject is relaxed, unaware, the light's good because it's filtering through the trees. It's an easy shot. It's already laid out. But this one, the beach shot, he should have used a yellow filter to cut the glare, soften the shadows, define the clouds. That's basic. But he didn't bother. You lose texture, drama. It's a careless mistake. He never made them before."

Quickly, she pulled photos out of the other envelope. "Here's another beach shot, from Hatteras this time. Similar angle, but he used a filter, he took his time. The texture of the sand, the lift of my hair in the wind, the position of the gull just heading out over the waves, good cloud definition. It's a lovely shot, really, a solid addition for a show or gallery, whereas the one from home is washed out."

"Was Bobby on assignment with you there? On Hatteras?"

"No. I worked alone."

"But there's a lot of people on Hatteras, compared to Desire. You might not have noticed him. Especially if he wore a disguise."

"A disguise. Oh, Lexy. Don't you think I'd have clued in if I saw some guy walking around in Groucho glasses and a funny nose?"

"With the right makeup, a wig, different body language, I could walk right up to you on the street and you wouldn't recognize me. It's not that hard to be someone else." She smiled. "I do it all the time. It could have been this intern of yours or half a dozen people you know. Dye the hair, wear a hat, sunglasses. Put facial hair on or take it off. All we know for sure is that he was there, and he was here."

Jo nodded slowly. "And he could be back."

"Yeah." Lexy put a hand over Jo's. "But now we're all going to be watching out for him."

Jo looked at the hand covering hers. It shouldn't have surprised her, she realized, to find it there, to find it firm and warm. "I should have told both of you before. I should have told all of you before. I wanted to handle it myself."

"Now there's news," Lexy said lightly. "Cousin Kate, Jo says she wanted to handle something herself. Can you imagine that, the original 'Get out of my way I'll do it myself' girl wanted to handle something on her own."

"Very clever," Jo muttered. "I didn't give you enough credit either, for being willing to be there."

"More news, Kate." Lexy kept her eyes on Jo's. "Why, the bulletins just keep pouring in. Jo didn't give me enough credit for being an intelligent human being with a little compassion. Not that she or anyone else ever has, but that's the latest flash coming off the wire."

"I'd forgotten how good you are at sarcasm—and since I probably deserved both those withering remarks, I won't ruin it by proving I'm better at sarcasm than you can ever hope to be."

Before Lexy could speak, Jo turned her hand over and linked her fingers with Lexy's. "I was ashamed. Almost as much as I was scared, I was ashamed that I'd had a breakdown. The last people I wanted to know about that were my family."

Sympathy flooded Lexy. Still, she kept a smirk on her face and in her voice. "Why, that's just foolish, Jo Ellen. We're southerners. We admire little else more than we admire our family lunatics. Hiding crazy relations in the attic's a Yankee trait. Isn't that so, Cousin Kate?"

Amused, and bursting with pride in her youngest chick, Kate glanced back over her shoulder. "It is indeed, Lexy. A good southern family props up its crazies and puts them on display in the front parlor along with the best china."

Her own quick laugh made Jo Ellen blink in surprise. "I'm not a lunatic."

"Not yet." Lexy gave her hand a friendly squeeze. "But if you keep going you could be right on up there with Great-granny Lida. She's the one, as I recollect, wore the spangled evening dress day and night and claimed Fred Astaire was coming by to take her dancing. Put a little effort into it, you could aspire to that."

Jo laughed again, and this time it was long and rich. "Maybe we'll go shopping after all, and I'll see if I can find a spangled evening dress, just in case."

"Blue's your color." And because she knew it was

easier for her than for Jo, Lexy wrapped her arms around her sister and hugged hard. "I forgot to tell you something, Jo Ellen."

"What's that?"

"Welcome home."

It was after six before they got back to Sanctuary. They'd gone shopping after all and were loaded down with the bags and boxes to prove it. Kate was still asking herself how she'd let Lexy talk her into that frantic ninety-minute shopping spree. But she already knew the answer.

After the hour spent in the police station, they'd all needed to do something foolish.

When they came in through the kitchen, she was already prepared for Brian's tirade. He took one look at them, the evidence of their betrayal heaped in their arms, and snarled.

"Well, that's just dandy, isn't it? That's just fine. I've got six tables already filled in the dining room, I'm up to my elbows in cooking, and the three of you go off shopping. I had to drag Sissy Brodie in here to wait tables, and she hasn't got any more than a spoonful of sense. Daddy's mixing drinks—which we're giving them the hell away to make up for the poor service—and I just burned two orders of chicken because I had to go in there and mop up after that pea-brained Sissy dumped a plate of shrimp fettuccine Alfredo on Becky Fitzsimmons's lap."

"Becky Fitzsimmons is in there, and you got Sissy waiting on her?" Tickled down to her toes, Lexy set her bags aside. "Don't you know anything, Brian Hathaway? Sissy and Becky are desperate enemies since they tangled over Jesse Pendleton, who was sleeping with them both nearly at the same time for six months. Then Sissy found out and she marched right up to Becky outside church after Easter services and called her a no-good toad-faced whore. Took three strong men to pull them apart."

Reliving the scene with gusto, Lexy pulled the scarf loose and shook her hair free. "Why, a plate of shrimp fettuccine's nothing. You're lucky Sissy didn't take up one of your carving knives there and go after Becky good and proper."

Brian drew a breath for patience. "I'm counting my blessings right now. Get your pad and get your butt in there. You're already an hour late for your shift."

"It's my fault, Brian," Jo began and braced herself for the attack when he whirled on her. "I needed Lexy, and I suppose we lost track of time."

"I don't have the luxury of losing track of anything, and I don't need you standing in my kitchen taking up for her when she's too irresponsible to do what she's supposed to." He rattled the lid off the chicken breast he was sautéing and flipped the meat. "And I don't want you trying to smooth it all over," he said to Kate. "I don't have time to listen to excuses."

"I wouldn't dream of offering any," Kate said stiffly. "In fact, I wouldn't dream of wasting my breath on someone who speaks to me in that manner." She jerked her chin up and sailed into the dining room to help Sam with bartending duties.

"It was my fault, Brian," Jo said again. "Kate and Lexy—"

"Don't bother." Lexy waved a hand breezily to mask her simmering temper. "He isn't about to listen—he knows all there is to know, anyway." She snatched up a pad and stomped through the door.

"Flighty, irresponsible bubblehead," Brian muttered.

"Don't talk about her that way. She's none of those things."

"What is this? Suddenly the two of you have bonded over the discount rack at the department store? Women buy shoes together and all at once they're soul mates?"

"You don't think much of the species, do you? Well, it was women I needed, and women who were there for me. If we were a little later getting back than suits you—''

''Suits me?'' He flipped the chicken onto a plate, clenching his teeth as he concentrated on adding side dishes and garnishes. Damned if he'd have women destroying his presentation. ''This isn't about what suits me. It's about running a business, holding on to the reputation we've been building up here for twenty-five years. It's about being left in the lurch with close to twenty people wanting a good meal served in a pleasant and efficient manner. It's about keeping your word.''

''All right, you've every right to be angry, but be angry with me. I'm the one who dragged them off today.''

''Don't worry.'' He filled a basket with fresh, steaming hush puppies. ''I'm plenty angry with you.''

She looked at the pots steaming on the stove, the vegetables already chopped on the cutting board. Dishes were piling up in the sink, and Brian was working awkwardly, hampered by his injured hand.

Left in the lurch was exactly right, she decided. And it had been poorly done by all of them.

''What can I do to help? I could get these dishes—''

''You can stay out of my way,'' he said without looking at her. ''That's what you're best at, isn't it?''

She absorbed the hit, accepted the guilt. ''Yes, I suppose it is.''

She slipped quietly out the back door. Sanctuary wasn't barred to her, she thought, not as it had been in her dreams. But the road to and away from it was forever rocky and full of potholes.

And Brian was right. She'd always been expert at staying away, at leaving the pleasures and the problems that brewed in that house to others.

She wasn't even sure she wanted it to be otherwise.

She cut through the forest. If someone was watching her, let him watch, let him snap his goddamn pictures until his fingers went numb. She wasn't going to live her life afraid. She hoped he was there. She hoped he was close, that he would show himself. Now. This minute.

She stopped, turned in a slow circle, her face grim as she scanned the deep green shadows. A confrontation would suit her mood perfectly. There was nothing she would enjoy better than a good, sweaty physical fight.

"I'm stronger than you think," she said aloud and listened to the furious tone of her own voice echo back. "Why don't you come out, face-to-face, and find out? You bastard." She grabbed a stick, thudded it against her palm. "You son of a bitch. You think you can scare me with a bunch of second-rate photographs?"

She whipped the stick against a tree, pleased by the way the shock wave sang up her arm. A woodpecker sprang from the trunk above her and bulleted away.

"Your composition sucked, your lighting was awful. What you know about capturing mood and texture wouldn't fill a thimble. I've seen better work from a ten-year-old with a disposable Kodak."

Her jaw set, she waited, eager to see someone, anyone, step out onto the path. She wanted him to charge. She wanted to make him pay. But there was nothing but the whisper of wind through the leaves, the clicking of palmetto fronds. The light shifted, dimming degree by degree.

"Now I'm talking to myself," she murmured. "I'll be as loony as Great-granny Lida before I'm thirty at this rate." She tossed the stick, watched it fly end over end, arcing up, then landing with a quiet thump in the thick brush.

She didn't see the worn sneaker inches from where it landed, or the frayed cuffs of faded jeans. When she walked deeper into the forest, she didn't hear the strained sound of breathing struggling to even out, or the harsh whisper that shook with raw emotion.

"Not yet, Jo Ellen. Not yet. Not until I'm ready. But now I'm going to have to hurt you. Now I'm going to have to make you sorry."

He straightened slowly, considered himself in full control. He didn't even notice the blood that welled in his palms as he clenched his fists.

He thought he knew where she was going and, familiar with the forest, he cut through the trees to beat her there.

PART THREE

Love is strong as death;
jealousy is cruel as the grave.

—SONG OF SOLOMON

TWENTY

J O DIDN'T REALIZE SHE'D
made up her mind to go to Nathan's until she was nearly
there. Even as she stopped, considered changing direction,
she heard the pad of footsteps. Adrenaline surged, her fists
clenched, her muscles tensed. She whirled, more than
ready to attack.

Dusk settled around her, dimming the light, thickening
the air. Overhead a slice of twilight moon hung in a sky
caught between light and dark. Water lapped slyly at the
high grass along the banks of the river. With a rush of
wind, a heron rose, soaring away from her and its post.

And Nathan stepped out of the shadows.

He broke stride when he saw her, then stopped a foot
away. His shoes and the frayed hem of his jeans were
damp from the water grasses, his hair tousled from the
quickening breeze. Noting her balls-of-the-feet fighting
stance, he raised an eyebrow.

"Looking for a fight?"

She ordered her fingers to uncurl, one by one. "I might
be."

He stepped forward, then tapped his fist lightly on her

chin. "I say I could take you in two rounds. Want to go for it?"

"Maybe some other time." The blood that was singing in her ears began to quiet. He had broad shoulders, she mused. A nice place to lay your head—if you were the leaning sort. "Brian kicked me out," she said and tucked her hands in her pockets. "I was just out walking."

"Me, too. I'm done walking for a while." The hand he'd fisted uncurled, and the fingers of it brushed over her hair. "How about you?"

"I haven't decided."

"Why don't you come inside . . ." He took her hand, toyed with her fingers. "Think about it."

Her gaze shifted from their hands to his eyes, held steady there. "You don't want me to come inside and think, Nathan."

"Come in anyway. Had any dinner?"

"No."

"I've still got those steaks." He gripped her hand more firmly and led her toward the house. "Why did Brian kick you out?"

"Kitchen crisis. My fault."

"Well, I guess I won't ask you to help grill the steaks." He stepped inside, switched on the lights to cut the gloom. "About all I have to go with them are some frozen fries and a white Bordeaux."

"Sounds perfect to me. Can I use your phone? I should call, let them know I won't be back for . . . a little bit."

"Help yourself." Nathan walked to the fridge, got the steaks out of the freezer. She was jumpy as a spring, he thought, taking the meat to the microwave to defrost it. Angry on top, unhappy underneath.

He wondered why he had such a relentless need to find the reason for all three. He listened to the murmur of her voice as he puzzled over the buttons on the microwave. He was about to make an executive decision and hope for the best when she hung up the phone and came over.

"This part I know," she said and punched a series of buttons. "I'm an expert nuker."

"I do better when the package comes with directions. I'll start the grill. I've got some CDs over there if you want music."

She wandered over to the stack of CDs beside the clever little compact stereo on the end table beside the sofa. It seemed he preferred straight, no-frills rock with a mix of those early rebels Mozart and Beethoven.

She couldn't make up her mind, couldn't seem to concentrate on the simple act of choosing between "Moonlight Sonata" and "Sympathy for the Devil."

Romance or heat, she asked herself impatiently. What do you want? Make up your damn mind what it is you want and just take it.

"The fire shouldn't take long," Nathan began as he stepped back in, wiping his hands on his jeans. "If you—"

"I had a breakdown," she blurted out.

He lowered his hands slowly. "Okay."

"I figure you should know before this goes any farther than it already has. I was in the hospital back in Charlotte. I had a collapse, a mental collapse, before I came back here. I may be crazy."

Her eyes were eloquent, her lips pressed tight together. Nathan decided he had about five seconds to choose how to handle it. "How crazy? Like running-down-the-street-naked-and-warning-people-to-repent crazy? Or I-was-abducted-by-aliens crazy? Because I'm not entirely convinced all those abducted-by-aliens types are actually crazy."

Her mouth didn't exactly relax, but it did fall open. "Did you hear what I said?"

"Yeah, I heard you. I'm just asking for clarification. Do you want a drink?"

She closed her eyes. Maybe lunatics were attracted to lunatics. "I haven't run naked in the streets yet."

"That's good. I'd have to think twice about this if you had." Because she started to pace, he decided touching her wasn't the best next move. He went back to the refrigerator to take out the wine and uncork it. "So, were you abducted by aliens, and if so, do they really look like Ross Perot?"

"I don't understand you," she muttered. "I don't understand you at all. I spent two weeks under psychiatric evaluation. I wasn't functioning."

He poured two glasses. "You seem to be functioning all right now," he said mildly and handed her the wine.

"A lot you know." She gestured with the glass before drinking. "I came within an inch of having another breakdown today."

"Are you bragging or complaining?"

"Then I went shopping." She whirled away, stalking around the room. "It's not a sign of stability to teeter on the brink of an emotional crisis, then go out and buy underwear."

"What kind of underwear?"

Eyes narrowed, she glared at him. "I'm trying to explain myself to you."

"I'm listening." He took a chance, raising his hand to skim his fingers over her cheek. "Jo, did you really think I'd react to this by backing off and telling you to go away?"

"Maybe." She let out the air clogging her lungs. "Yes."

He pressed his lips to her brow and made her eyes sting. "Then you are crazy. Sit down and tell me what happened."

"I can't sit."

"Okay." He leaned back against the kitchen table. "We'll stand. What happened to you?"

"I—it was . . . a lot of things. Work-related stress. But that doesn't really bother me. You can use stress. It keeps you motivated, focused. Pressures and deadlines, I've always used them. I like having my time designated, my routine set out and followed. I want to know when I'm getting up in the morning, what I'm doing first and second and last.''

''We'll say spontaneity isn't your strong suit, then.''

''One spontaneous act and everything else shifts. How can you get a handle on it?''

''One spontaneous act,'' he commented, ''and life's a surprise, more complicated but often more interesting.''

''That may be true, but I haven't been looking for an interesting life.'' She turned away. ''I just wanted a normal one. My world exploded once, and I've never been able to pick up the pieces. So I built another world. I had to.''

He tensed, straightened, and the wine that lingered on his tongue went sour. ''Is this because of your mother?''

''I don't know. Part of it must be. The shrinks certainly thought so. She was about my age when she left us. The doctors found that very interesting. She abandoned me. Was I repeating the cycle by abandoning myself?''

She shook her head and turned back to him. ''But it wasn't just that. I've lived with that most of my life. I coped, damn it. I made my choices and I went for it, straight line, no detours. I liked what I was doing, where I was going. It satisfied me.''

Knowing his hand wouldn't be steady, Nathan set the glass aside. ''Jo Ellen, what happened before, what other people did, no matter who they were to us, can't destroy what we are. What we have. We can't let that happen.''

She closed her eyes, relieved and soothed by his words. ''That's what I'm telling myself. Every day. I started having dreams. I've always had very vivid dreams, but these unnerved me. I wasn't sleeping well, or eating well. I can't even remember if that started before or after the first pictures came.''

''What pictures?''

''Someone started sending me photographs, of me. Just

my eyes at first. Just my eyes." She rubbed a hand over her arm to chase away the chill. "It was creepy. I tried to ignore it, but it didn't stop. Then there was a whole package, dozens of photographs of me. At home, on assignment, at the market. Everywhere I went. He'd been there, watching me." Her hand rubbed slowly, steadily over her speeding heart. "And I thought I saw . . . more. I hallucinated, I panicked. And I broke."

Rage whipped through him, one hard, vicious lash. "Some bastard was dogging you, stalking you, tormenting you, and you're blaming yourself for crumbling?" His hands were steady now as he reached out for her, pulled her against him.

"I didn't face it."

"Stop it. How much is anyone supposed to face? The son of a bitch, putting you through that." He stared over her shoulder, wishing viciously he had something to fight, something to pummel. "What's the Charlotte PD doing about it?"

"I didn't report it in Charlotte." Her eyes went wide when he jerked her back. Widened still more when she saw the wild fury in his.

"What the hell do you mean, you didn't report it? You're just going to let him get away with it? Just do nothing?"

"I had to get away. I just wanted to get away from it. I couldn't cope. I could barely function."

When he became aware that his fingers were digging into her shoulders, he let her go. Snatching up his glass, he paced away from her. And he remembered how she'd looked when he first saw her on the island. Pale, exhausted, her eyes bruised and unhappy.

"You needed sanctuary."

Her breath came out in three jerks. "Yes, I suppose I did. Today I learned I hadn't found it. He's been here." Resolutely she swallowed the fresh panic in her throat.

"He mailed photos of me from Savannah. Photos he'd taken here on the island."

Fresh fury clawed at him with hot-tipped fingers. Drawing on all of his control, Nathan turned slowly. "Then we'll find him. And we'll stop him."

"I don't even know if he's still on the island. If he'll come back, if . . . I don't know why, and that's the worst of it. But I'm facing it now, and I'm going to deal with it."

"You don't have to deal with it alone. You matter to me, Jo Ellen. I won't let you deal with it alone. You're going to have to face that too."

"Maybe that's why I came here. Maybe that's why I had to come here."

He set his wine down again so he could take her face in both hands. "I won't let anyone hurt you. Believe that."

She did, a little too easily, a little too strongly, and tried to backpedal. "It's good knowing you're on my side, but I have to be able to handle this."

"No." He lowered his mouth gently to hers. "You don't."

Her heart began to flutter in a different kind of panic. "The police said—"

"You went to the police?"

"Today. I . . ." She lost her train of thought for a moment as his mouth brushed hers again. "They said they'd look into it, but they don't have a lot to look into. I haven't been threatened."

"You feel threatened." He ran his hands down to her shoulders, over them. "That's more than enough. We're going to make that stop." He skimmed his lips over her cheek, along her temple, into her hair. "I'm going to take care of you," he murmured.

The words revolved in her spinning mind, refused to settle. "What?"

He doubted either one of them was ready to face what

he'd suddenly realized. He needed to take care of her, to soothe away those troubles, to ease her heart. And he needed to be sure that whatever he did wouldn't snap the thin threads of the relationship they were just beginning to weave.

"Put it aside for a little while. Take an evening to relax." He ran his fingers up and down her spine once before drawing back to study her. "I've never seen anyone more in need of a rare steak and a glass of wine."

He was giving her time, she realized. That was good. That was best. She managed to smile. "It does sound pretty good. It would be nice not to even think about all of this for an hour."

"Then I'll put the steaks on, you can dig out the fries. And I'll bore you to tears talking about this new project I have in mind."

"You can try, but I don't cry easily." She turned to the freezer, opened it, then closed it again. "I don't like sex."

He stopped one step away from the microwave. It was necessary to clear his throat before he could face her again. "Excuse me?"

"Obviously that's part of the package we're putting together here." Jo linked her hands together. It was best to be up-front about it, she thought. Practical. Especially since the words were out and couldn't be taken back.

He really had to stop putting his wine down, Nathan decided, and picking it up again, he took one long, slow sip. "You don't like sex."

"I don't hate it," she said, pulling her fingers apart to wave a hand. "Not like coconut."

"Coconut."

"I really hate coconut—even the smell puts me off. Sex is more like, I don't know, flan."

"Sex is like flan."

"I'm ambivalent about it."

"Uh-huh. Meaning, take it or leave it. If it's there, fine, but why go out of your way?"

Her shoulders relaxed. "That's about it. I thought I should tell you so you wouldn't build up any big expectations if we go to bed."

He ran his tongue over his teeth. "Maybe you haven't had any really well-prepared flan . . . in your experience."

She laughed. "It's all pretty much the same."

"I don't think so." He finished off his wine, set the empty glass down. Her eyes went from amused to wary as he walked toward her. "And I'm compelled to debate the subject. Right now."

"Nathan, that wasn't a challenge, it was just a . . ." The words slid down her throat when he swept her off her feet. "Wait a minute."

"I was on the debate team in college." It was a lie, but he thought it too good a line to miss.

"I haven't said I was going to sleep with you."

"What do you care?" He started down the short hallway. "You're ambivalent, remember?" He laid her on the bed, slid his body over hers. "And a little flan never hurt anybody."

"I don't want—"

"Yes, you do." He lowered his mouth, keeping only a breath between them. "So do I, and I have, right along. You're in an honest mood tonight, aren't you, Jo? Tell me you don't wonder, that you don't want?"

His body was warm and solid, his eyes clear and direct. "I wonder."

"That's good enough." He crushed his mouth to hers.

The taste of it, the sudden, sharp demand of it, pushed the worries out of her head. Grateful, knowing he would expect no more than what she had, she lifted her arms to wrap around him.

"Your mouth." He scraped his teeth over that wonderfully overfull top lip. "Christ, I've wanted that mouth. It drives me crazy."

She would have laughed, nearly did. Then his tongue was tangling hotly with hers, and the unexpected burn streaked down to throb between her thighs. It took only her moan to have him diving deeper.

Staggered, she clenched her fists in his hair. He hadn't kissed her like this before. She hadn't known that the pressure of mouth to mouth could cause a thousand wild aches in a thousand places. His hands stayed cupped around her face, as though everything he wanted centered only there.

She moved under him, a tremble, then an arch of hips. He had to tear his mouth from hers and press it to her throat to keep himself from rushing both of them. The scent of her skin, that zing of some early spring fragrance, was another welcome shock to his system. He lingered there, tormenting them both until the pulse under his tongue was racing.

He was undoing her, knot by knot. Moment by moment her body loosened, the shifts and quakes inside her spreading, building. There was excitement in not being quite able to catch her breath, not being quite sure where his mouth would travel next. Enchanted, she ran her hands over his shoulders, down his back, pleased with the bunch and flow of male muscle under her fingers.

When his mouth came greedily back to hers, she met it gratefully, delighting in the edgy jolts that snapped through her system. She arched again, mildly frustrated with the barriers that prevented her from taking him inside her. The need for physical release was greater than she had imagined.

He caught the lobe of her ear between his teeth and bit. "We're not settling for ambivalent this time."

He eased back, straddling her. The last rays of the sun streaked through the west window and set the air on fire. Her hair haloed around her face, the deep, smoky red of autumn leaves. Her eyes were high-summer blue, her skin the delicate rose of spring.

He lifted her hand, kissing the fingers one by one.

"What are you doing?"

"Savoring you. Your hand's trembling, and your eyes are full of nerves. I like that." He scraped his teeth over her knuckle. "It's exciting."

"I'm not afraid."

"No, you're confused." He lowered her hand, unfastened the first button of her blouse. "That's even better. You don't know what I'm going to make you feel next."

When her blouse was undone, he parted it, then slowly let his gaze slip down. Underneath she wore a bra of electric blue, the sheen of satin dipping low over the milk-pale swell of her breasts.

"Well, well." Though his stomach tightened with the need to devour her, he lifted his gaze back to hers. "Who would have thought it?"

"It's not mine." She cursed herself when he smiled. "I mean, I only bought it and wore it out of the store to stop Lexy from hounding me."

"God bless Lexy." Gently, watching her face, he skimmed his thumbs just above the edge of the satin. Her lashes fluttered, lowered. "You're holding back on me." He skimmed his thumbs a fraction lower. "I won't let you. I want to hear you sigh, Jo Ellen. I want to hear you moan. Then I want to hear you scream."

She opened her eyes, but her breath caught when he scraped his thumb over her nipple. "Oh, God."

"You hide too much, and not just this remarkable body. You hide too much of Jo Ellen. I'm going to see it all, and I'm going to have it all before we're finished."

He flicked the front hook of the bra, watched her breasts spill free. Then lowering his head, devoured them.

She did moan, then the sounds she made were quick, wild whimpers. The ache was unbearable, unreasonable. She moved restlessly beneath him to soothe it and only deepened the throb.

She dragged at his shirt, yanking it over his head and

tossing it violently aside so she could feel hot flesh. The storm crashed inside her, tossing her closer and closer to that high, sharp peak, then dragging her back, just inches back, before she could ride it.

His mouth, his hands streaked over her now, daring her to keep pace, making it impossible for her to do anything but stumble blindly. She writhed, tried to roll free. Anywhere there was air, was an anchor to hold her.

But he held her trapped, imprisoned in that terrifying pleasure. And gave her no choice but to endure the violent war of sensation battling sensation. He pulled her slacks over her hips, revealing the blue swatch of satin. His mouth was on her belly, riding low, his labored breathing thickening the air with hers.

She didn't hear herself begging, but he did.

He had only to slide a finger under that satin, had only to touch her to have her explode.

Her body convulsed under his, rocked by wave after molten wave of pleasure. He pressed his face to her belly as it quivered, as his own body shuddered in response.

Thank God, thank God, was all she could think when the tension flooded out of her. Her muscles went lax, and she took one grateful gulp of air. Only to expel it again on a muffled scream as those clever, unmerciful fingers drove her up again.

Did she think that was all? The blood throbbed painfully in his head, his heart, his loins as he tore away the thin barrier. Did she think he would let either of them settle for less than madness now? He yanked her hips high and used his tongue to destroy her.

And she did scream.

Her arms flew back, her fingers bouncing off the glossy painted iron posts of the headboard, then gripping desperately as if to keep her body from being swept away. Behind her closed lids lights pulsed violent red, beneath her skin her blood swam dangerously fast. She shattered again, a thousand pieces of her flying free.

Then his hands gripped hers over the bedposts. He plunged into her, filled her, took her ruthlessly to peak again with long, slow, deliberate strokes. Even as her vision wavered, she could see his eyes, the sharp intensity of them, the pure gray edging toward black.

Helpless, she matched his pace, her breath hitching and tearing when he quickened the tempo. Her hips pumping when he began to thrust inside her, hard and fast.

When his mouth came down on hers, she could do nothing but surrender to it. When her body spun finally and completely out of control, she could do nothing but let herself go.

And he could do nothing but let himself follow.

She didn't know if she'd slept. She almost wondered if she'd simply slid into a coma. But it was full dark when she opened her eyes. That, Jo thought hazily, or she'd been struck blind.

He lay over her, his head resting between her breasts. She could feel the rapid beat of his heart, hear the quiet sigh of the wind fluttering through the window screens.

He felt her shift, just slightly. "I'll stop crushing you in just a second."

"It's all right. I can almost breathe."

His lips curved as he brushed them over the side of her breast, but he rolled over. Before she could move, he'd wrapped an arm around her and pulled her against him. "Flan, my ass."

She opened her mouth, certain that some pithy comment would come. But there was only laughter. "Maybe I've just been off desserts for a while."

"Then you'll just have to have seconds."

She snuggled up against him without thinking. "If we try for seconds, we'll kill each other."

"No, we won't. We'll get to those steaks first, and I'll get you a little drunk. Which was my original plan, by the way. Then we'll have seconds."

"You planned to get me drunk?"

"That was one of my ideas. Then there was the one about climbing up the trellis to your balcony. Sort of the swashbuckle scenario."

"You'd have broken your neck."

"Nah, Brian and I used to monkey up and down that thing all the time."

"Sure, when you were ten." She rose onto her elbow, shook her hair back. "You're about a hundred pounds heavier now, and I doubt you're as agile."

"This is no time to call my agility into question."

She smiled, lowered her brow to his. "You're absolutely right. Maybe you'll surprise me one night."

"Maybe I will. But now . . ." He gave her hair a tug before he sat up. "I'm going to cook you dinner."

"Nathan." She smoothed a hand over the wrinkled spread while he searched for his jeans. "Why are you going to so much trouble for me?"

He didn't speak for a moment. He couldn't be sure of his moves, or his words. After tugging on his jeans he studied her silhouette in the dark. "It only took seeing you again, Jo Ellen. That's all it took. It knocked the wind out of me, and I still don't have my breath back."

"I'm a mess, Nathan." She swallowed hard and was grateful for the dark so he couldn't see her face. The longing that had geysered inside of her had to show. "I don't know what I think or feel about anything. Anyone. You'd be better off shaking loose."

"I've taken the easy way a few times. It usually ends up being dull. So far you've been anything but dull."

"Nathan—"

"You're really wasting your time arguing with me while you're sitting naked on my bed."

She dragged a hand through her hair. "Good point. We'll argue later."

"Fine. I'll just go dump more charcoal on the grill." And since he planned to have her naked and on his bed again before the evening was over, he didn't think they'd have much time to argue.

TWENTY-ONE

"STAY." NATHAN WRAPPED his arms around Jo's waist, nuzzled the back of her neck. Her hair was still damp from the shower they'd shared. Smelling his soap on her skin aroused him yet again. "I'll fix you breakfast in the morning."

She hooked her arm around his neck. It amazed her how easy it was to be this close. "You don't have anything to fix."

"Bread. I have bread." He spun her around so he could feast on that wonderful curve of neck and shoulder. "I'm terrific at toast. I'm famous for my toast."

"As incredibly appetizing as that sounds . . . Nathan." With a sound caught between a laugh and a moan, she tried to wiggle away from his roving hands. "We really will kill each other, and I have to get back."

"It's barely midnight."

"It's after one."

"Well, then, it's practically morning, you might as well stay."

She wanted to. As his mouth found hers, persuasively, she badly wanted to. "I have things to straighten out at home. And I have to make it up to Brian for leaving him in such a mess tonight.''

She put her hands to his face, liking the way it felt under her fingers. Cheekbones, jaw, the scrape of beard. Had she ever explored a man's face this way? Or wanted to?

''And I have to think.'' Firmly, she drew away. ''I'm a thinker, Nathan. A planner. This is new territory for me.''

He rubbed a thumb over the line that formed between her brows. ''You'll just compel me to keep changing directions on you.''

Fresh nerves skidded over her skin. ''Then I'll have to stay a step ahead. But now, I have to go home.''

He could see her mind was made up, and so he forced himself to readjust the pleasant image of waking beside her in the morning. ''I'll drive you.''

''You don't have to—''

''Jo.'' He put his hands on her shoulders, and his voice was quiet and final. ''You're not going out alone in the dark.''

''I'm not afraid. I'm not going to be afraid anymore.''

''Good for you. I'm still driving you. Or we can argue about it, I can maneuver you back into the bedroom, and drive you home in the morning. Does your father have a gun?''

She laughed, pushed at her bangs. ''It's very unlikely he'd shoot you for sleeping with me.''

''If he does, I'm counting on you to nurse me back to health.'' He took his keys from the counter.

''I'm a southern woman,'' she said as they started out the door. ''I'll even find a petticoat to tear into bandages.''

''It would almost be worth getting shot for that.''

As she climbed into his Jeep, she asked, ''Ever been shot?''

''No.'' He slid in beside her and started the engine. ''But I had my tonsils out. How much worse could it be?''

"Considerably, I'd imagine."

She stretched out her legs, leaned back, and shut her eyes. She was tired, but deliciously so. Her muscles were loose, her mind pleasantly fogged. The air felt silky on her skin.

"The nights are best on the island," she murmured, "when the quiet just rings in your ears and no one else is awake. You can smell the trees and the water. The sea's a whisper in the background, like a pulse beating."

"You can be alone and not be lonely."

"Mmm. When I was a little girl I used to imagine what it would be like if I were all alone, had the island all to myself just for a few days. It would all be mine, everywhere I walked, everywhere I looked. I thought I would like that. But then I dreamed it, and I was afraid. In the dream I kept running and running, through the house, out into the forest, over the beach. I wanted to find someone, anyone, to be there with me. But I was all alone. And I woke up crying for Daddy."

"Now you take pictures of being alone."

"I suppose I do." She let out a sigh and opened her eyes. And there, through the dark, she saw the glimmer of light. "Kate left a light on for me."

It was comforting, that flicker of home. She watched it dance through the trees, outdo the shadows. Once she'd run away from that light, and once she'd run toward it. She hoped the time would come when she could walk either way without fear.

As they neared the end of the drive, she saw the figure rise from the porch swing. Her stomach did an ungainly roll before Nathan covered her hand with his.

"Stay here. Lock the doors."

"No, I—" She let out a trembling breath. "It's Brian," she said, feeling foolish at the wave of relief that swamped her.

Nathan nodded, also recognizing the figure as Brian stepped into the light. "Okay, let's go."

"No." She gave the hand that covered hers a quick squeeze. "Let's not complicate it. If he needs to yell at me some more, I deserve it, and I don't want the two of you eyeing each other and trying to figure out how to handle the fact that you're friends and you're sleeping with his sister."

"He doesn't appear to be armed."

It made her laugh, as intended. "Go home." She shifted, finding it simple to just lean over and touch her lips to his. "Let Brian and me deal with our family baggage. We're too polite to do a good job of it in front of you."

"I want to see you tomorrow."

She opened the door. "Come for breakfast—unless you're set on having your world-famous toast."

"I'll be here."

She started toward the porch, waiting until she heard his Jeep reverse before she mounted the stairs. "Evening," she said coolly to Brian. "Nice night for porch sitting."

He stared at her a moment, then moved so quickly she nearly shrieked. His arms strapped tight around her. "I'm sorry. I'm so sorry."

Stunned speechless, she started to pat his back, then yelped as he jerked her away and shook her.

"It's your own goddamn fault. So typical, so goddamn Jo Ellen."

"What?" Insult slapped on top of surprise and had her shoving him. "What the hell are you talking about? Stop manhandling me."

"Manhandling? I ought to kick your butt up to your ears. Why the hell didn't you tell somebody what was going on? Why didn't you let me know you were in trouble?"

"If you don't let go of me right now—"

"No, you just go on the way you always have, pushing people out of the way so you can—"

He broke off with a grunt as her fist plowed into his stomach. The blow was quick and forceful enough to catch him off guard. Dropping his hands, he eyed her narrowly.

"That hasn't changed either. You always packed a decent punch."

"You're lucky I didn't aim for that pretty face of yours." Sniffing, she rubbed her hands over her arms where his fingers had gripped. Damned if she wouldn't have bruises, she thought. "Obviously you're in no state to have a reasonable, civilized conversation. So I'm going up to bed."

"You take one step toward that door and I'll haul you over my knee."

She raised herself up on tiptoe and stuck her face in his. "Don't you threaten me, Brian Hathaway."

"Don't you test me, Jo Ellen. I've been sitting here for better than two hours worried sick, so I'm in the mood to take you on."

"I was with Nathan, which you knew very well. And there's no cause for you to worry about my sex life."

He gritted his teeth. "I don't want to hear about it. I don't want to think about it. I'm not talking about you and Nathan being . . . I'm not talking about that."

Jo bit the inside of her cheek to keep from grinning. Had she known it was so easy to flummox her brother, she would have used that angle years ago.

"Well, then." Pleased with the point scored, she strolled to the porch swing and sat. She cocked her head as she took out a cigarette. "Just what is it you want to hear about, think about, and talk about, Brian?"

"You can't pull off the grand Southern Belle number, Jo. It just doesn't suit you."

She flicked her lighter on. "It's late and I'm tired. If you have something to say, say it so I can go to bed."

"You shouldn't have been alone." His voice had gone quiet and drew her gaze. "You shouldn't have gone through that alone, been in that hospital alone. And I want you to know that the choice of doing that was yours.''

She took a slow drag. ''Yes, it was my choice. It was my problem.''

''That's right, Jo.'' He took a step forward, hooking his thumbs in his front pockets to keep his hands from curling into fists. ''Your problems, your triumphs, your life. You've never seen fit to share any of those things. Why should this be different?''

Her stomach jittered. ''What could you have done?''

''I could have been there. I would have been there. Yeah, that shocks the hell out of you, doesn't it?'' he said before she lowered her eyes. ''I don't care how fucked-up this family is, you wouldn't have gone through that by yourself. And you're not going to go through the rest of it by yourself.''

''I've been to the police.''

''I'm not just talking about the cops, though any pea brain would have gone to them in Charlotte when this started.''

She flicked an ash, took another drag. ''You're going to have to make up your mind whether you want to shame me or insult me.''

''I can do both.''

Annoyed, she flipped the cigarette away, watched the red tip fly through the dark, then disappear into it. ''I came home, didn't I?''

''That, at least, was half sensible. You came home looking like something that had been dragged down five miles of bad road, then you don't tell anybody what's wrong. Except Kirby. You told Kirby, didn't you, after I dragged you over there?'' His eyes flashed. ''I'll deal with her later.''

''You leave her alone. I told her about the breakdown and that was all. That's medical, and she's not obliged to tell her lover about her patients' medical histories.''

''You told Nathan.''

"I told him tonight. I told him all of it tonight, because I thought it was only right and fair." Weary now, she rubbed her forehead. An owl was hooting monotonously somewhere in the cool dark. She wished she could find its tree, climb the branches, and just huddle there in peace.

"Do you want me to go over it all again now, Brian? Do you want chapter and verse and all the little details?"

"No." He let out a sigh and sat beside her. "No, you don't have to go over it again. I guess you'd have told me before if the lot of us weren't so screwed up. I've been thinking about that while I've been sitting out here working myself up to pound on you."

"Couldn't have taken much. You were already mad at me. Kicked me out of the house."

He let out a quick, rough laugh. "Your own fault you let me. It's your house too."

"It's your house, Brian. It always has been more yours than anyone's." It was said gently, with quiet acceptance. "You're the one who cares most, and tends most."

"Does that bother you?"

"No. Well, maybe some, but mostly it's a relief to me. I don't have to worry if the roof's going to leak, because you do."

She tipped her head back, looking up at the glossy white paint of the veranda, then out over the moonlight-sprinkled gardens. The wind chimes were tinkling, the fountain quiet for the night, and the scent of musk roses floated poignantly on the breeze.

"I don't want to live here. For a long time I thought I didn't ever want to be here. But I was wrong. I do. Everything here means more to me than I let myself believe. I want to know I can come back now and then. I can sit here on a warm, clear night like this and smell the sweet peas and the jasmine and Mama's roses. Lexy and me, we just can't stay here the way you do. But I guess we both need to know that Sanctuary stands on the hill like always and nobody's going to lock the door on us."

"No one would."

"I dreamed the doors were locked and I couldn't get inside. No one came when I called, and all the windows were dark and empty." She closed her eyes, wanting it to play back in her mind, wanting to know she could stand against it now. "I lost myself in the forest. I was alone and scared and couldn't find my way. Then I saw myself standing on the other side of the river. Only it wasn't me at all. It was Mama."

"You've always had strange dreams."

"Maybe I've always been crazy." She smiled a little, then looked out into the night. "I look like her, Brian. Sometimes when I see my face in the mirror, it gives me such a jolt. In the end, that's what pushed me over the edge. When those pictures came, all those pictures of me. I thought one of them was Mama. Only she was dead. She was naked and her eyes were open and staring and lifeless as a doll's. I looked just like her."

"Jo—"

"But the picture wasn't there," she said quickly. "It wasn't even there. I imagined it. I've always hated seeing pictures of myself, because I see her in them."

"You may look like her, Jo, but you're not like her. You finish what you start, you stick."

"I ran away from here."

"You got away from here," he corrected. "You went out to make your own life. That's different from leaving a life you'd already started and all the people who needed you. You're not Annabelle." He draped an arm over her shoulder and let the swing slide into motion. "And you're only about as crazy as the rest of us around here."

She laughed. "Well, that's comforting, isn't it?"

It was late when Susan Peters marched out of the rented cottage and stalked toward the cove. She'd had a nasty fight with her husband—and had had to do it in undertones so as not to disturb their friends who'd taken the cottage with them for the week.

The man was an idiot, she decided. She couldn't even think why she'd married him, much less why she'd stayed married to him for three years—not to mention the two they'd lived together before making it legal.

Every time, every single time, she so much as mentioned buying a house, he got that closed-in look on his face. And he started going on about down payments and taxes and maintenance and money, money, money. What the hell were both of them working their butts off for? Was she supposed to live in an apartment in Atlanta forever?

The hell with the conveniences, she thought, and tossed back her curly mop of brown hair. She wanted a yard, a little garden, a kitchen where she could practice cooking the gourmet dishes she'd taken classes for.

But all she got out of Tom was one day. One day. Well, when was one day going to get here?

Disgusted, she plopped down on the beach, slipping off her shoes so she could dig her toes in the sand while she stared out at the quiet water that lapped and lapped against the hull of the little outboard they'd rented.

He didn't have any problems spending money on a silly boat so he could go fishing every stupid day they were on Desire.

They had enough for a down payment. She propped her elbow on her knee and watched sulkily as the moon floated overhead. She'd done all the research on financing and balloon payments and interest rates. She wanted that sweet little house on Peach Blossom Lane.

Sure, it would be tight for the first couple of years, but they could manage. She'd been so positive that when she talked to him about building equity and breaking out of the endless cycle of renting month after month, he would come around.

And, oh, it was just about killing her that Mary Alice

and Jim were about to settle on that pretty place in the development. A magnolia tree in the front yard and a little patio off the kitchen.

She sighed and wished she'd waited until they'd gotten back home to start working on Tom again. That would have been smarter. She knew how important timing was when dealing with her husband. But she'd gotten so damned upset, she hadn't been able to stop herself.

When they got back to Atlanta, Tom was going to look at that house on Peach Blossom if she had to drag him by the ear.

She heard the footsteps behind her and stared straight ahead. "No point in coming down here to try to make up, Tom Peters. I'm not nearly finished being mad at you yet. I may never be."

Furious that he didn't attempt to talk her out of it, she wrapped her arms around her knees. "You just go on back up and balance your checkbook, since money is all you want. I don't have another thing to say to you."

As the silence dragged on, she gritted her teeth and turned her head. "Listen here, Tom—Oh." Embarrassment heated her cheeks as she looked up into a stranger's face. "I'm sorry. I thought you were someone else."

He smiled, charmingly, and with a gleam of laughter in his eyes. "That's all right. I'm going to think of you as someone else, too."

Even as the first streak of alarm sent a scream toward her throat, he struck.

It wasn't going to be perfect, he decided, studying her as she lay crumpled at his feet. He hadn't planned on this impromptu practice session, but he hadn't been able to sleep. His mind was so full of Jo, and the sexual need was unexpectedly sharp tonight.

He was very, very annoyed with her. And that only made him want her more.

Then the pretty brunette had just been there, like a gift,

sitting all alone by the water under the shifting light of the moon.

A wise man didn't look a gift horse in the mouth. So to speak, he thought with a chuckle as he hauled her up into his arms. They would just move off a bit, he decided. In case old Tom—whoever he might be—wandered down to the cove.

She was a light load, and he didn't mind the exercise. He whistled tunelessly as he carried her over the sand and up through a narrow break in the dunes. He would need the moonlight, so he settled on the verges of the swale. It was picturesque, with the moon-silvered bushes, he thought, as he laid her down.

And it was deserted.

He used his belt to tie her hands and one of the silk scarves he always carried to gag her. He stripped her first, pleased to find that her body was trim and athletic. She moaned a little as he pulled off his jeans.

"Don't worry, darling, you look very pretty, very sexy. And the moonlight flatters you."

He took out his camera—the Pentax single-lens reflex he liked for portraits—pleased that he'd loaded it with slow film. He wanted fine detail now, knife-edged sharpness. Likely he'd have to do some burning in and dodging in the darkroom to get the contrasts and textures just so.

He would look forward to that, to perfecting the prints.

Whistling under his breath, he fixed his flash and ran off three shots before her eyelids fluttered.

"That's right, that's right, I want you to come around now. Slow. A few nice close-ups of that pretty face. The eyes are the best. They always are."

He grew hard as they opened, dulled with pain and confusion. "Beautiful, just beautiful. Look here, look right here now. That's the way, baby. Focus."

Delighted, he captured understanding and fear. He set the camera down as she began to stir. Her movement would blur the shot, and he didn't have any backup film

of faster speed. Still smiling, he picked up the gun he'd
laid on his neatly folded jeans. And showed it to her.

"Now, I don't want you to move. I want you to stay
still, really still, and do everything I tell you. The last
thing I want to do is use this. Now you understand that,
don't you?"

Tears began to swim in her eyes, then leak out. But she
nodded. Terror bubbled in her brain, and though she tried
to remain motionless, shudders racked her.

"I'm just going to take your picture. We're having a
photo shoot. You're not afraid of having your picture
taken, a pretty woman like you."

He exchanged gun for camera and smiled winningly.
"Now here's what I want you to do. Bend your knees.
Come on now, that's the way, and move them over to
your left side. You've got a lovely body. Why don't we
show it off to its best advantage?"

She did what he asked, her eyes wheeling over to stare
at the gun. The chrome glinted and shone. He just wanted
pictures, she told herself, as her breath hitched and shuddered. He would leave her alone then. He'd go away. He
wouldn't hurt her.

Terror bulged in her eyes, turned her skin milky white
and had him throbbing viciously. His hands began to
tremble, signaling him that he could no longer wait for
the next stage.

His heart thudded in his head as he carefully set his
camera down on his shirt. Very gently he put a hand on
her throat and looked deeply into her eyes.

"You're beautiful," he murmured. "And you're helpless. You know that, don't you? There's nothing you can
do. I'm in control. I have all the power. Don't I?"

She jerked her head down in a nod, small sobs muffling
against the silk. When his hand closed over her breast and
squeezed, she moaned out pleas and tossed her head
wildly. Her heels dug into the sand as she tried to escape.

He straddled her. "It won't do you any good." He

shuddered as she bucked and twisted under him. "The more fight you put up, the better I like it. Try to scream." He squeezed her breasts again, then bent down to bite at them. "Scream, goddamn it. Scream."

A harsh keening sound ripped out of her, burned her throat. Desperate, she fought against the gag, struggled to use her teeth, her tongue, her lips to drag it aside.

He pried her thighs apart, deliberately bruising the flesh. And thought of Jo as he raped her. Thought of Jo Ellen's long legs. Jo Ellen's sexy mouth. Jo Ellen's heavy-lidded blue eyes, while he pounded himself with sweaty violence into her substitute.

The orgasm was towering, brought tears of surprise and triumph to his eyes. So much better than the last one, he realized, and absently closed a hand over her throat, pressing down only until she stopped fighting.

He'd chosen well this time, he thought, as the climax eased off into sweetness. He'd found his practice angel. The breeze cooled his damp skin when he rose for the camera.

He remembered how the process had been outlined in his journal and reminded himself not merely to duplicate but to improve.

"I may rape you again, I may not." He smiled, attractive creases forming around his mouth and eyes. "I may hurt you, I may not. It all depends on how you behave. Now you just lie there, angel, and think about that."

Satisfied that she was quiescent for a while, he changed lenses. Her pupils were enormous black moons with only a sliver of pale brown encircling them, her breathing was short and shallow. He whistled contentedly as he loaded fresh film. He shot the entire roll before he raped her a second time.

And he'd decided to hurt her. After all, the choice, the mood, the control were all completely in his hands.

She stopped fighting him. In all but a physical sense she'd stopped being there. Her body was numb, belonged to someone else. In her mind she was safe, with Tom, sitting together on the patio of their pretty new house on Peach Blossom Lane.

She barely felt him remove the gag. She managed a quiet sob, made a pitiful effort to draw in breath enough to scream.

"You know it's too late for that." He said it gently, almost lovingly, as he wound the scarf around her throat. "You'll be my angel now."

He tightened the scarf, slowly, wanting to draw out the moment. He watched her mouth open, struggle to suck in air. Her heels drummed on the sand, her body jerked.

His breath became labored, the power flooding him, screaming in his head, racing through his blood. He lost track of the times he stopped, let her claw back to consciousness before he took her to the brink again. He would rise, aim the camera again. Not just one decisive moment, he thought. But many. The fear of death, the acceptance, the flicker of hope as life pumped back. The surrender when it blinked out again.

Oh, he regretted the lack of a tripod and remote.

Finally his system roared past control and he finished it.

Gasping, he murmured endearments, kissed her gratefully. She had shown him a new level, this unexpected angel that fate had tossed at his feet. It had been meant to be, of course. He understood that now. He'd had more to learn before he met his destiny with Jo. So much more to learn.

He removed the scarf, folded it, and laid it reverently over the gun. He took time to pose her, adjusting her hands after he'd freed them. The welts on the wrists troubled him a little until he slid her hands under her head like a pillow.

He thought he would title this one *Gift of an Angel.*

He dressed, then bundled her clothes. The marsh was too far, he decided. Whatever the gators and other predators had left of Ginny was buried deep there. He didn't have time for the hike, or energy for the labor.

There were conveniently deep spots in the river, however, and that would do well enough. He would take her to her final resting place, weigh her body down so that it would rest on the slippery bottom.

And then, he decided with a wide yawn, he'd call it a night.

TWENTY-TWO

WHEN GIFF SLIPPED OUT of Lexy's room and down the back steps, the sky was pearled with dawn. He'd meant to be out of the house and on his way before sunup. But then, he thought with a lazy smile, Lexy had a way of persuading a man to tarry.

She'd needed him. First to work off her mad at Brian, then to tell him about her sister's troubles. They could talk about things like that, and all manner of other things, tucked in her room, their voices hushed with secrets.

That ease of talking, Giff mused, was just one of the advantages of being in love with someone you'd known since childhood.

Then there was the electric jolt, the unexpected sizzle of surprise, as you got to know that very familiar person on other, more intimate levels. Giff puffed out a breath as he reached for the door. It sure wasn't any hardship to study Lexy Hathaway on those other levels. The way she'd looked in that little silk nightie she'd bought in Savannah had been enough to make a strong man sink to his knees and praise God for coming up with the brilliant notion of creating Eve.

Getting her out of that sheer little concoction hadn't been a worrisome task either. In fact, he decided that when he took her to Savannah on Saturday he'd buy her another one, just so he could . . .

The erotic image of Lexy in buttermilk silk fled as he found himself faced with her father. It was a toss-up as to which one of them was more disconcerted, Lexy's lover, with his hair still tumbled from sex and sleep, or Lexy's father, with a bowl of cornflakes in his hand.

Both cleared their throats.

"Mr. Hathaway."

"Giff."

"I . . . ah . . . I was . . ."

"That plumbing need seeing to again upstairs?"

It was an out, offered as desperately as it was nearly taken. But Giff straightened his shoulders, told himself not to take the coward's way, and met Sam's eyes directly. "No, sir."

Miserably uneasy, Sam set his bowl down and dumped milk onto the cereal. "Well, then," was all he could think to say.

"Mr. Hathaway, I don't want you to think I'm sneaking out of your house." Which of course, Giff admitted, was exactly what he was doing.

"You've been running tame in Sanctuary since you could walk." Leave it alone, boy, Sam prayed. Leave it lie and move along. "You're welcome to come and go as you please, just like you ever were."

"I've been walking a lot of years now, Mr. Hathaway. And for most of them I've been . . . I figure you know how I feel about Lexy. How I always have."

Damn cereal was going to get soggy, Sam thought with regret. "I guess you didn't grow out of it like most thought you would."

"No, sir. I'd say it's more I grew into it. I love her, Mr. Hathaway. My feelings for her are long-standing and steady. You've known me and my family all my life. I'm not feckless or foolish. I've got some savings put by. I can make a good living with my hands and my back.''

"I don't doubt it." But Sam frowned. Maybe he'd barely sipped through his first cup of coffee, but his mind was clear enough to catch the drift. ''Giff, if you're asking me for permission to . . . call on my daughter, seems to me you've already opened that particular door, walked in, and made yourself to home.''

Giff flushed and hoped his swallow wasn't audible. ''Yes, sir, I can't deny the truth of that. But it's not that particular door I'm speaking of, Mr. Hathaway.''

''Oh.'' Sam opened a drawer for a spoon, hoping Giff would take the hint and mosey on before things got any stickier. Then he put the spoon down with a clatter and stared. ''Sweet Jesus, boy, you're not talking about marrying her?''

Giff's jaw set, his eyes glinted. ''I'm going to marry her, Mr. Hathaway. I'd like to have your blessing over it, but either way, I'm having her.''

Sam shook his head, rubbed his eyes. Life just flat refused to be simple, he reflected. A man went along, minding his own business, wanting nothing more than for other people to mind theirs in return, but life just kept throwing tacks under your bare feet.

''Boy, you want to take her on, I'm not going to stand in your way. Couldn't anyhow, even if I planted my boots in concrete. The two of you are of age and ought to have the sense to know your own minds.'' He dropped his hands. ''But I've got to say, Giff, as I've always been fond of you, I think you're taking on a sack of trouble there. You'll be lucky to get one moment's peace from the time you say 'I do' till you take your last breath.''

''Peace isn't a priority of mine.''

''She'll run through every penny you've put by and won't have a clue where she spent it.''

''She's not near as foolish as you think. And I can always make more money.''

"I'm not going to waste my breath talking you out of something you've got your mind set on."

"I'm good for her."

"No question about it. Fact is, you might be the making of her." Resigned to it, Sam offered a hand. "I'll wish you luck."

Sam watched Giff go off with a spring in his step. He didn't doubt the boy was in love, and if he let himself he could remember what it was like to feel that light in the head, that edgy in the gut. That hot in the blood.

Sam settled in the breakfast nook with his second cup of coffee and his soggy cereal and watched the sky lighten to a bold summer blue. He'd been just as dazed and dazzled by Annabelle as Giff was now with Lexy. It had only taken one look for his heart to jolt straight out of his chest and fall at her feet.

Christ, they'd been young. He was barely eighteen that summer, coming to the island to work on his uncle's shrimp boat. Casting nets, sweating under a merciless sun until his hands were raw and his back a misery.

He enjoyed every second of it.

He fell in love with the island, first glance. The hazy greens, the pockets of solitude, the surprises around every bend of the river or road.

Then he saw Belle Pendleton walking along the beach, gathering shells at sunset. Long golden legs, willowy body, the generous fall of waving red hair. Eyes as clear as water and blue as summer.

The sight of her hazed his vision and closed his throat.

He smelled of shrimp and sweat and engine grease. He wanted a quick swim through the waves to loosen the muscles the day's work had aching. But she smiled at him and, holding a pink-lined conch shell, began to talk to him.

He was tongue-tied and terrified. He'd always been intimidated by females, but this vision who had already captured his heart with one smile left him grunting out responses like an ill-mannered ape. He never knew how he'd managed to stutter out an invitation to take a walk the next evening.

Years later, when he asked her why she'd said yes, she just laughed.

You were so handsome, Sam. So serious and stern and sweet. And you were the first boy—and the last man—to make my heart skip a beat.

She'd meant it. Then, Sam thought. After he had worked enough, saved enough money to satisfy him, he'd gone to her father to ask permission for her hand. A great deal more formal that had been, Sam mused, sipping his coffee, than the meeting just now with Giff. There'd been no sneaking out of Annabelle's bedroom at dawn either. Though there had been stolen afternoons in the forest.

Even when a man's blood had been cool for years, he remembered what it was like to have it run hot. For the first few years that Annabelle was gone, his blood had heated from time to time. He'd taken care of that in Savannah.

It hadn't shamed him to pay for sex. A professional woman didn't require conversation or wooing. She simply transacted business. It had been some time since he'd required that particular service, though. And since AIDS and other potential horrors of impersonal sex scared him, Sam was relieved to have weaned himself away from it.

Everything he needed was on the island. He'd found the peace that young Giff claimed not to want.

Sam sat back to enjoy the rest of his coffee in the quiet. He had to struggle with a hard twinge of irritation when the door opened and Jo walked in. The fact that she hesitated when she saw him and a slight flicker of annoyance moved over her face both shamed and amused him.

Peas in a pod, he decided, who don't much care to share the pod.

"Good morning." Damn it, all she'd wanted was a quick slug of coffee before she went out to work. Not just wander or brood, but work. She'd awakened for the first time in weeks refreshed and focused, and she didn't want to waste it.

"Clear morning," Sam said. "Thunderstorms and strong winds by evening, though."

"I suppose." She opened a cupboard.

Silence stretched between them, long and complete. The trickle of coffee as Jo poured it from pot to cup was loud as a waterfall. Sam shifted, his khakis hissing against the polished wood of the bench.

"Kate told me . . . she told me."

"I imagined she would."

"Um. You're feeling some better now."

"I'm feeling a great deal better."

"And the police, they're doing what they can do."

"Yes, what they can."

"I was thinking about it. It seems to me you should stay here for the next little while. Until it's settled and done, you shouldn't plan on going back to Charlotte and traveling like you do."

"I'd planned to stay, work here, for the next few weeks anyway."

"You should stay here, Jo Ellen, until it's settled and done."

Surprised at the firm tone, as close to an order as she could remember receiving from him since childhood, she turned, lifted her brows. "I don't live here. I live in Charlotte."

"You don't live in Charlotte," Sam said slowly, "until this is settled and done."

Her back went up, an automatic response. "I'm not having some wacko dictate my life. When I'm ready to go back, I'll go back."

"You won't leave Sanctuary until I say you can leave."

This time her mouth dropped open. "I beg your pardon?"

"You heard me right enough, Jo Ellen. Your ears have

always been sharp and your understanding keen. You'll stay here until you're well enough, and it's safe enough for you to leave and go about your business.''

"If I want to go tomorrow—"

"You won't," Sam interrupted. "I've got my mind set on it."

"You've got your mind set?" Stunned, she strode over to the table and scowled down at him. "You think you can just set your mind on something that has to do with me after all this time, and I'll just fall in line?"

"No. I reckon you'll have to be planted in line and held there, like always. That's all I have to say." He wanted to escape, he wanted the quiet, but when he started to slide down the bench to get up, Jo slapped a hand onto the table to block him.

"It's not all I have to say. Apparently you've lost track of some time here. I'm twenty-seven years old."

"You'll be twenty-eight come November," he said mildly. "I know the ages of my children."

"And that makes you a sterling example of fatherhood?"

"No." His eyes stayed level with hers. "But there's no changing the fact that I'm yours just the same. You've done well enough for yourself, by yourself, up to now. But things have taken a turn. So you'll stay here, where there are those who can look out for you, for the next little while."

"Really?" Her eyes narrowed to slits. "Well, let me tell you just what I'm going to continue to do for myself, by myself."

"Good morning." Kate breezed in, all smiles. She'd had her ear to the door for the last two minutes and calculated it was time to make an entrance. It pleased her to enter a room in that house and not find apathy or bitterness. Temper, at least, was clean.

"That coffee smells wonderful. I'm just dying for some."

354 *Nora Roberts*

In a calculated move, she brought a cup and the pot to the table, sliding in beside Sam before he could wriggle away. "Just let me top this off for you, Sam. Jo, bring your cup on over here. I swear I don't know the last time we sat down for a quiet cup of coffee in the morning. Lord knows, after that chaos in the dining room last night, we need it."

"I was on my way out," Jo said stiffly.

"Well, honey, sit down and finish your coffee first. Brian'll be coming in soon enough to tell us all to scat. You look like you got a good night's sleep." Kate smiled brilliantly. "Your daddy and I were worried you'd be restless."

"There's no need to worry." Grudgingly, Jo got her coffee and brought it to the table. "Everything that can be done's being done. In fact, I'm feeling so much calmer about it all, I'm thinking about going back to Charlotte." She shot a challenging look at Sam. "Soon."

"That's fine, Jo, if you want to send the lot of us to an early grave with worry." Kate spoke mildly as she spooned sugar into her coffee.

"I don't see—"

"Of course you see," Kate interrupted. "You're just angry, and you have a right to be. But you don't have the right to take that anger out on those who love you. It's natural to do just that," Kate added with a smile, "but it's not right."

"That's not what I'm doing."

"Good." Kate patted her hand, as if the matter were settled. "You're planning to take some pictures today, I see." She glanced over at the camera bag Jo had set on the counter. "I got out that book that Nathan's father did on the island. Put it in the public parlor after I'd looked through it again. My, there are some pretty photographs in there."

"He did good work," Jo muttered, struggling not to sulk.

"He sure did. I found one in there of Nathan, Brian, and I suppose Nathan's younger brother. Such handsome little boys. They were holding up a couple of whopping trout and had grins on their faces that stretched a mile wide. You ought to take a look at it."

"I will." Jo found herself smiling, thinking of Nathan at ten with a trout on the line.

"And you could think about doing a photo book on the island yourself," Kate went on. "It would be just wonderful for business. Sam, you take Jo over to the marsh, that spot where the sea lavender's full in bloom. Oh, and if the two of you go through the forest, along the southwest edge, the path there's just covered with trumpet vine petals. That would make such a nice picture, Jo Ellen. That narrow, quiet little path just dusted with fallen blossoms."

She went on and on, chattering out suggestions without giving father or daughter a chance to interrupt. When Brian trooped in the back door and stared, baffled, at the cozy family group, Kate beamed him a smile.

"We'll be out of your way in just a shake, sweetie. Jo and Sam were just deciding which route they were going to take around the island today for Jo's pictures. Y'all better get started."

Kate got up quickly, gathering Jo's camera bag. "I know how fussy you are about the light and such. You just tell your daddy when it strikes you as right. I can't wait to see what kind of pictures you get. Hurry along now, before Brian starts to fuss at us. Sam, you get a chance, you take Jo down to where those baby terns hatched a while back. Goodness, look at the time. You two scoot."

She all but dragged Sam to his feet, kept nudging and talking until she'd shoved them both out the door.

"Just what the hell was that, Kate?" Brian asked her.

"That, with any luck at all, was the beginning of something."

"They'll go their own ways when they're five feet from the house."

"No, they won't," Kate disagreed as she started toward the ringing phone on the wall. "Because neither one of them will want to be the first to take that step away. While they're each waiting for the other one to back off first, they'll be heading in the same direction for a change. Good morning," she said into the receiver. "The Inn at Sanctuary." Her smile faded. "I'm sorry, what? Yes, yes, of course." Automatically, she grabbed a pencil and began scribbling on the pad by the phone. "I'll certainly make some calls right away. Don't worry now. It's a very small island. We'll help in every way we can, Mr. Peters. I'll come on down there to the cottage myself, right now. No, that's just fine. I'll be right along."

"Mosquitoes getting in through the screen again?" Brian asked. But he knew it was more than that, much more.

"The Peterses took Wild Horse Cove Cottage with some friends for the week. Mr. Peters can't seem to find his wife this morning."

Brian felt a quick stab of fear at the base of his spine. He couldn't ignore it, but told himself it was foolish over-reaction. "Kate, it's not quite seven A.M. She probably got up early and took a walk."

"He's been out looking for almost an hour. He found her shoes down by the water." Distracted, she ran a hand through her hair. "Well, it's probably just as you say, but he's terribly worried. I'll run down there and calm him down, help him look around until she comes wandering home."

She managed a thin smile. "I'm sorry, sweetie, but this means I'm going to have to wake Lexy up so she can take the breakfast shift in my place this morning. She's liable to be snappish about it."

"I'm not worried about Lexy. Kate," he added as she

headed for the door, "give me a call, will you, when Mrs. Peters gets home?"

"Sure I will, honey. Like as not she'll be there before I make it down to them."

But she wasn't. By noon Tom Peters wasn't the only one on Desire who was worried. Other cottagers and natives joined in the search, Nathan among them. He'd seen Tom and Susan Peters once or twice during their stay and had a vague recollection of a pretty brunette of medium height and build.

He left the others to comb the beach and the cove while he concentrated on the swath of land between his cottage and Wild Horse Cove. There was barely an eighth of a mile between them. The verge of his end forested then, giving way to dune and swale. He covered the ground slowly and saw, when he reached the stretch of sand, the crisscrossing footprints of others who had come that way to look.

Though he knew it was useless, he climbed over the dunes. The cove below was secluded, but anyone there would have been spotted half a dozen times by now by others who were searching.

There was only one figure there now, a man who paced back and forth. "Nathan?"

He turned and, seeing Jo mounting the incline between the dunes, held out a hand to help her up.

"I went by your cottage," she began. "I see you've heard."

"That must be the husband down there. I've seen him a couple of times before."

"Tom Peters. I've been all over the island. I was out working this morning, from about seven. One of the Pendleton kids tracked us down an hour or so ago and told us. He said her shoes were down there, by the water."

"That's what I heard."

"People are thinking she might have gone in to swim,

and . . . The current's fairly gentle here, but if she cramped or just swam out too far . . .''

It was a grim scenario, one that had already occurred to him. "Shouldn't the tide have brought her in by now if that's what happened?"

"It may yet. If the current carried her along for a while, they could find her down the island at the next tide change. Barry Fitzsimmons drowned like that. We were about sixteen. He was a strong swimmer, but he went out by himself one night during a beach party. He'd been drinking. They found him the next morning at low tide, half a mile down."

Nathan shifted his gaze to the south, where the waves were less serene. He thought of Kyle, sinking under blue Mediterranean waves. "Where are her clothes, then?"

"What?"

"It seems to me if she'd decided to go swimming, she'd have stripped down."

"I suppose you're right. But she might have come down in her bathing suit."

"Without a towel?" It didn't quite fit, he decided. "I wonder if anyone's asked him if he knows what she was wearing when she left the house. I'm going down to talk to him."

"I don't think we should intrude."

"He's alone and he's worried." Nathan kept her hand in his as he started down. "Or he had a fight with his wife, killed her, and disposed of her body."

"That's horrid and ridiculous. He's a perfectly decent, normal man."

"Sometimes perfectly decent, normal men do the unthinkable."

Nathan studied Tom Peters as they approached. Late twenties, he decided, about five ten. He looked fit in wrinkled camp shorts and a plain white T-shirt. Probably worked out at the gym three or four mornings a week, Nathan thought. He had a good start on his vacation tan, and though the stubble on his chin gave him an unkempt appearance, his dark blond hair had been cut recently, and cut well.

When he raised his head and Nathan saw his eyes, he saw only sick fear.

"Mr. Peters. Tom."

"I don't know where else to look. I don't know what to do." Saying the words out loud brought tears swimming into his eyes. He blinked them back, breathing rapidly. "My friends, they went to the other side of the island to look. I had to come back here. To come back here, just in case."

"You need to sit down." Gently Jo took his arm. "Why don't we go back up to your cottage and you can sit down for a while? I'll make you some coffee."

"No, I can't leave here. She came down here. She came down last night. We had a fight. We had a fight, oh, God, it's so stupid. Why did we have a fight?"

He covered his face with his hands, pressing his fingers against his burning eyes. "She wants to buy a house. We can't afford it yet. I tried to explain to her, tried to show her how impractical it is, but she wouldn't listen. When she stormed out I was relieved. I was actually relieved and thought, Well, now, at least I can get some sleep while she goes out and sulks."

"Maybe she took a swim to cool off," Nathan prompted.

"Susan?" Tom let out a short laugh. "Swim alone, at night? Not hardly. She'd never go in water past her knees anyway. She doesn't like to swim in the ocean. She always says she hears cello music the minute it hits her knees. You know," he said with a faint smile, *"Jaws."*

Then he turned back, staring out at the water. "I know people are thinking she might have gone swimming, she might have drowned. It's just not possible. She loves to sit and look at the ocean. She loves to listen to it, to smell it, but she won't go in. Where the hell is she? Goddamn it, Susan, this is a hell of a way to scare me into buying a house. I've got to go somewhere, look somewhere. I can't just stand here.''

He raced back toward the dunes and sent sand avalanching down as he rushed up and over them.

''Do you think that's what she's doing, Nathan? Putting a scare into him because she's angry?''

''We can hope so. Come on.'' He slipped an arm around her waist. ''We'll take the long way back to the cottage, keep our eyes peeled. Then we'll take a break from this.''

''I could use a break. From just about everything.''

The wind was rising as they headed through the trough between the surfside dune hummocks and the higher, inland dunes where beach elders and bayberry stabilized the sand. Tracks scored the ground, the scratches from scudding ghost crabs, the three-toed prints from parading wild turkeys, the spots where deer had meandered to feed on seeds and berries.

Human tracks had churned up the sand as well, and the wind would take them all.

Despite the grazing, thousands of white star rush and fragile marsh pinks spread their color.

Would she have walked this way, Jo wondered, alone, at night? It had been a clear evening, and a lonely beach drew troubled hearts as well as contented ones. The wind would have been stiff and fresh. And even after the tide receded, leaving the sand wet, the wind would have chased it along in streamers that scratched at the ankles.

''She could have left her shoes down there,'' Jo considered. ''If she'd wanted to walk. She was angry, upset, wanted to be alone. It was a warm night. She might have headed down the shoreline, just following the water. That's more likely than anything else.''

She turned, looking out over the low hillocks to the sea. The wind lifted sand and salt spray, sending the sea oats waving, sifting a fresh coat over the pennywort and railroad vines that tangled.

"Maybe they've found her by now." Nathan laid a hand on her shoulder. "We'll call and check when we get to the cottage."

"Where else would she have gone?" Jo shifted, to stare inland where the dunes crept slowly, relentlessly, toward the trees in smooth curves. "It would have been foolish to wander into the forest. She'd have lost the moonlight—and she'd have wanted her shoes. Would she be angry enough with her husband to stay away, to worry him like this because of a house?"

"I don't know. People do unaccountable things to each other when they're married. Things that seem cruel or indifferent or foolish to outsiders."

"Did you?" She turned her head to study his face. "Did you do cruel, indifferent, and foolish things when you were married?"

"Probably." He tucked the hair blowing across her face behind her ear. "I'm sure my ex-wife has a litany of them."

"Marriage is most often a mistake. You depend on someone, you inevitably lean too hard or take them for granted or find them irritating because they're always there."

"That's remarkably cynical for someone who's never been married."

"I've observed marriage. Observing's what I do."

"Because it's less risky than participating."

She turned away again. "Because it's what I do. If she's out somewhere, walking, avoiding coming back, letting her husband suffer like this, how could he ever forgive her?"

Suddenly she was angry, deeply, bitterly angry. "But he will, won't he?" she demanded, whirling back to him. "He'll forgive her, he'll fall at her feet sobbing in relief, and he'll buy her the fucking house she wants. All she had to do to get her way was put him through hell for a few hours.''

Nathan studied her glinting eyes, the high color that temper had slapped into her cheeks. ''You may be right.'' He spoke mildly, fascinated that she could shift from concern to condemnation in the blink of an eye. ''But you're heaping a lot of blame and calculation on a woman you don't even know.''

''I've known others like her. My mother, Ginny, people who do exactly what they choose without giving a damn for the consequences or what they do to others. I'm sick to death of people. Their selfish agendas, their unrelenting self-concern.''

There was such pain in her voice. The echo of it rolled through him, leaving his stomach raw and edgy. He had to tell her, he thought. He couldn't keep blocking it out, couldn't continue to shove it aside, no matter how hard he'd worked to convince himself it was best for both of them.

Maybe Susan Peters's disappearance was a sign, an omen. If he believed in such things. Whatever he believed, and whatever it was he wanted, eventually he would have to tell her what he knew.

Was she strong enough to stand up to it? Or would it break her?

''Jo Ellen, let's go inside.''

''Yeah.'' She folded her arms as clouds rolled over the sun and the wind kicked into a warning howl. ''Why the hell are we out here, worrying ourselves over a stranger who has the bitchiness to put her husband and friends through this?''

''Because she's lost, Jo. One way or another.''

''Who isn't?'' she murmured.

It would wait another day, he told himself. It would wait until Susan Peters had been found. If he was daring the gods by taking another day, stealing another few hours before he shattered both their lives, then he'd pay the price.

How much heavier could it be than the one he'd already paid?

When he was sure she was strong, when he was sure she could bear it, he would tell her the hideous secret that only he knew.

Annabelle had never left Desire. She had been murdered in the forest just west of Sanctuary on a night in high summer, under a full white moon. David Delaney, the father he had grown up loving, admiring, respecting, had been her killer.

Jo saw lightning flash and the shimmering curtain of rain form far out to sea. "Storm's coming," she said.

"I know."

TWENTY-THREE

THE FIRST DROPS HIT THE
ground with fat plops, and Kirby quickened her pace. The
search group she'd joined had parted ways at the fork of
the path. She'd chosen the route to Sanctuary, and now
she shivered a bit as the rain fell through the overhanging
limbs and vines to soak her shirt. By the time she reached
the verge it was coming down hard, wind-whipped and
surprisingly cold. She saw Brian, hatless, shoulders
hunched, trooping up the road to her right.

She met him on the edge of the east terrace. Saying
nothing, he took her hand and pulled her onto the screened
porch. For a moment they simply stood dripping as lightning stabbed the sky in pitchforks and thunder boomed in
answer.

"No word?" Kirby shifted her medical bag from hand
to hand.

"Nothing. I just came over from the west side. Giff has
a group that took the north." Weary, Brian rubbed his
hands over his face. "This is getting to be a habit."

"It's been more than twelve hours since she was seen."
Kirby looked out into the driving rain. "That's too long.

They'll have to call off the search until the storm passes. God, Brian, we're going to find her washed up after this. It's about the only explanation left. Her poor husband.''

"There's nothing to do now but wait it out. You need a dry shirt and some coffee.''

"Yeah.'' She dragged her wet hair away from her face. "I do. I'll take a look at your hand while I'm here and redress it for you.''

"It's fine.''

"I'll decide that,'' she said, following him in, ''after I take a look.''

"Suit yourself. Go on up and get something out of Jo's closet.''

The house seemed so quiet, isolated in the violent rain. "Is she here?''

"As far as I know, she's out too.'' He went to the freezer, took out some black bean soup he'd made weeks before. ''She'll take shelter, like everybody else.''

When Kirby came back fifteen minutes later, the kitchen smelled of coffee and simmering soup. The warmth eased away the last of the tension in her shoulders. Leaning against the doorway a moment, she indulged herself by watching him work.

Despite his bandaged hand, he was neatly slicing thick slabs from a loaf of brown bread he'd undoubtedly baked himself. His wet shirt clung to him, displaying an attractive outline of muscle and rib. When he looked over at her, his eyes were a cool, misty blue that made her stomach flutter pleasantly.

"It smells wonderful.''

"Figured you hadn't eaten.''

"No, I haven't—not since a stale Danish this morning.'' She held out the shirt she'd taken from his closet. "Here, put this on. You shouldn't stand around in wet clothes.''

"Thanks.'' He noted that she'd changed into some of Jo's dull gray sweats. They bagged on her and made her seem all the more delicate. "You look lost in those."

"Well, Jo's a good six inches taller than I am." She lifted a brow as he tugged the wet shirt off over his head. His skin was damp and brown and smooth. "God, you're attractive, Brian." She laughed when his brows drew together in what was obviously confused embarrassment. "I get to appreciate your wonderful build on two levels, as a doctor and as a woman. Better put that shirt on, or I might lose control, on both counts."

"That could be interesting." Letting the shirt dangle from his fingers, he stepped toward her. "Which would come first?"

"I never let personal leanings interfere with professional obligations." She trailed a finger up his arm, then down to his wrist. "Which is why I'm going to examine that wound first thing."

"And second thing?" Before she could answer, he cupped his hands under her elbows and lifted her. When their mouths were level, he leaned forward to toy with her lips.

"Excellent upper body strength." Her voice was just a little breathless as she wrapped her legs around his waist. "Your pulse is a little elevated," she murmured, checking the one at his throat with her mouth. "Just a little fast."

"I've got a case on you, Doc Kirby." Brian turned his face into her hair. It smelled of rain and lemons. "It doesn't seem to be passing. Fact is, I'm starting to think it's terminal." When she went very still, he shifted her until he could see her eyes. "What do you want from me, Kirby?"

"I thought I knew." Her fingers tingled when she skimmed them over his face. "I'm not sure anymore. Maybe whatever case you've got is contagious. Do you have this ache around your heart?"

"Just like it's being squeezed."

"And this lifting and sinking sensation in your stomach?"

"All the time lately. So what's wrong with us, Doc?"

"I'm not sure, but—" She broke off as the screen door slammed. Voices rose and invaded the kitchen. Sighing, Kirby laid her brow against Brian's until he shifted her hips and set her down.

"Sounds like Lexy and Giff are back." He kept his eyes on Kirby. "Some of the others are likely with them, and they'll be looking for a hot meal."

"Then I'll help you dish up some soup."

"I'd appreciate it." He lifted the lid on the pot, letting steam and scent escape. "We're going to have to finish this conversation sometime or other."

"Yes, we are." She opened a cupboard to get bowls. "Sometime or other."

From Nathan's porch, Jo watched the rain and smoked restlessly. He'd tried the television when they came in, hoping for a weather report. The cable was already out, so they settled for the radio. Static hissed out, along with the announcer's listings of small-craft advisories and flash-flood warnings.

They'd lose power if it kept up much longer, she thought. And the ponds and rivers would certainly flood. Already she could see puddles forming and deepening.

"No word yet." Nathan joined her on the porch. "Some of the search party's taken shelter at Sanctuary to wait this out." He laid a towel over her shoulders. "You're shivering. Why don't you come inside?"

"I like to watch." Lightning stabbed the sky and sent an answering jolt into her stomach. "Quick squalls like this are hell to be out in, but they're exciting from the right vantage point." She took a deep breath when the sky went hot and white. The sting of ozone lingered on the air. "Where's your camera? I took mine back home."

"In the bedroom. I'll get it for you."

Impatient, she stabbed out her cigarette in a broken shell. Too much energy, she thought. It was pumping through her, pounding at her. She all but snatched the camera from Nathan when he brought it out. "What kind of film do you have in here?"

"Four hundred," he said quietly, watching as she quickly examined it.

"Good. That's fast. I want fast." She lifted, aimed at the rain-lashed trees, the swinging moss. "Come on, come on," she muttered, then snapped with the next burst of lightning. "Another, I want another." Thunder rattled the air as she changed angles, her finger as itchy as if it were on the trigger of a gun.

"I need to get down, shoot up at that tree."

"No." Nathan bent to pick up the towel that had fallen from her shoulders. The overhang offered little protection. The two of them were rapidly getting soaked. "You're not going out there. You don't know where or when we could have a lightning strike."

"That's half of it, isn't it? The not knowing. The not caring." She tossed back her head. Recklessness streaked through her, glowed dangerously in her eyes. "I don't know what I'm doing with you, or when I might get hit next. I don't seem to care. How much are you going to hurt me, Nathan, and how long will it take me to get over it? And how long before one of us does something cruel, indifferent, or foolish?"

Before he could speak, she grabbed a handful of his hair and dragged his mouth to hers. "I don't care." She dug her teeth into his lip.

"You need to care." Enraged with fate, he caught her face in his hands, pulled her back. His eyes were as dark and violent as the storm whipping the air. "I want you to understand that when I do hurt you, I won't have a choice."

"I don't care," she repeated, pulling his mouth back to hers. "I only want now. Right now. I want you. I don't want to think, I don't want either of us to think. I just want to feel."

His mind was already hazed as they stumbled through the door. She bobbled the camera, laughing and moaning as he tore at her shirt. "Fast," she managed. "I still want fast."

He tumbled with her to the floor, and the camera thudded lightly on the carpet as they ripped off clothes and shoes. Her hands were tangled in her shirt when he thrust inside her. She grappled to free them, the momentary thrill of being helpless and bound adding another layer of excitement. Then she was free, and her fingers dug into his hips to urge him to drive deeper, and harder.

He couldn't stop himself, and let the speed, the heat, the fury of mating rule them both. If her need was frantic, his was desperate. To take her, to have her, to keep her. One more day, one more hour. A dozen lifetimes.

If his punishment for his father's sin was to fall in love, so terribly in love, and lose, he would take every moment he could steal before payment came due.

She cried out in grateful relief when the orgasm stabbed through her. His body plunged violently in hers, then stilled. His breath was ragged as he pushed himself back to stare down at her. "Is that what you wanted?"

"Yes."

"Fast, and heartless."

"Yes."

His hand closed in a fist. It was exactly what he'd given her. "Do you think it's going to stop at that?"

She closed her eyes briefly, then willed herself to open them. "No."

"Good." He relaxed his hand, brushed it over her cheek. Another moment stolen, he thought when her eyes opened and met his. "I'd hate to have to argue with you when I'm still wanting you. Give me more, Jo Ellen." His mouth lowered to tease her. "Don't make me take it this time."

Her arms lifted, wrapped around him. "I'm so afraid of you."

"I know. Give me more anyway. Take a chance."

His mouth stayed gentle, waiting for hers to answer, then to demand. He wanted more, much more, than that rough and edgy release they'd offered each other. More than the animal lunge of hot blood. When she sighed out his name he knew he had the beginnings of it.

Her mouth grew more hungry, her hands began to roam. Fresh need built in her quickly, as though it had never been met. She craved the taste of his skin and took her mouth on a journey over his face and throat. With a murmur of approval, she rolled with him until she stretched across his body with the freedom to do as she pleased.

The wind kicked, rattling the screen door on its hinges. The house shuddered beneath them. In contrast they moved slowly, almost languidly. Touch and taste, sigh and murmur. She lost herself in the easy sway of it, the shift and glide of bodies, rhythms set and matched.

She thought she could float over him, inch by inch, and wonder as she set each separate muscle to quivering.

He eased her back, sitting up to slide her into his lap. It was tenderness he needed for both of them now, to soothe the pain already suffered. And the pain yet to come.

Their eyes held as he lowered his mouth to hers, took the kiss deep, gradually deep so that the warmth from it flushed over her. The intimacy of it shimmered through her. She might have resisted, she lifted a hand to his chest as if to do so. But her limbs went limp, and she was lost.

And she gave him more.

It was surrender he wanted, for both of them. His and hers. A yielding. Soft, liquid kisses filled them both, nudged them lazily toward excitement. When he cupped her, her moan was quiet and ended on a little gasp of pleasure. He took her up slowly so that the orgasm was long and sleek.

They each trembled, and when she reached for him,

thrilling to find him hard and ready, her lips curved
against his.

"Again," she murmured. "Just like that. Again."

The pleasure rolled through her, layer by layer to whirl
in her head like wine. Still shimmering from it, she
shifted, until her body was over his and the thick beat of
his heart was under her mouth.

"I love what you can do to me." She slid down,
spreading light, open-mouthed kisses down to his belly.
"I want to know I can do it to you."

His skin quivered when she closed that hot, generous
mouth over him. Dark pleasure blurred his vision, and the
roar in his head drowned out the rain. She drove him to
the brink, where he clung to pleasure and control and
sanity only by slippery fingertips.

She rose up over him, her body glimmering in the
murky light. She lowered to him, took him in, arched
back, took him deeper. Her arms lifted up, folded behind
her head as if in triumph. Her eyes met his, stared intently
into that smoky gray as she began to move.

Slowly, torturously. And her body shivered when his
hands closed hard and possessive over her breasts.
Smoothly, silkily. His breath caught and strangled as she
braced her own hands on his chest.

Her head fell back, her body going arrow-taut and her
muscles clamping hard around him as she rode herself to
peak. Yet even as her heart tripped, her brain staggered,
her system revved greedily for more. She couldn't bear
it, couldn't stop it. Her body drove, forward, back, racing
for new pleasure.

Sweat dewed her skin. When he levered himself up to
surround her nipple with his mouth, he tasted salt and
heat. She came again, crying out in shock and near panic.
Holding tight to her, he let go of the edge and took them
both flying.

Her lungs were burning, her throat dry as dust. She
tried to swallow, then gave up and dropped her head on

his shoulder. When her ears stopped ringing, she heard the silence.

"It's stopped raining."

"Mmm-hmm."

With a laugh she nearly managed to take a full breath. "We're going to have a hell of a time explaining these rug burns." Enjoying the sensation, she ran her hands over his damp back. "I need about a gallon of water."

"I'll get it."

"Okay, I'll wait right here."

"Though it pains me to admit it, I think I'm a little too weak as yet to cart you over to the sink." He shifted her weight and grinned as she rolled limply onto the rug.

He got up to fill a glass, then stopped and looked at her. Her skin was rosily flushed all over, her hair a tangled red halo around her face. Her mouth was soft, still swollen and slightly curved in contentment. On impulse he set the glass down and lifted his camera.

Her eyes flew open when she heard the click of the shutter. She yelped, instinctively crossing her arms over her breasts. "What the hell are you doing?"

Stealing moments, he thought. He was going to need them. "Christ, you look good." He crouched, clicked off another shot as her eyes widened.

"Stop that. Are you crazy? I'm naked."

"You look incredible. All rumpled and flushed and freshly fucked. Don't cover yourself. You've got beautiful breasts."

"Nathan." She only folded her arms more protectively. "Put that camera down."

"Why?" He lowered it but continued to grin. "You can develop them yourself. Who's to see? There's nothing much more artistic and visually stunning than a nude study."

"Fine." Keeping one arm strategically bent, she held out a hand. "Let me take you."

"Sure." He offered the camera, amused to see her frown of surprise.

"You aren't the least bit embarrassed."

"No."

She angled her head toward the camera he still held. "I want that roll of film."

"Well, I wasn't planning on taking it in to Fotomat, darling." He glanced down, checked the number of shots left. "Just one more in here. Let me take it. Just your face."

"Just my face," she agreed and relaxed enough to smile at him. "There. Now I want that film."

"Okay." He moved quickly when she lowered her arm and got off the last shot.

"Damn it, you said it was out."

"I lied." Roaring with laughter, he rose and set the camera on the table. "But it's out now. I'll want to see the contacts so I can pick out the prints I want."

"If you think I'm going to develop that film, you're mistaken." She got up and grabbed the camera.

"The pictures you took of the storm are in there." He said it with a smile on his face that widened as he saw her struggle between the urge to rip out the roll and ruin it and the need to preserve her own shots.

"That was very sneaky, Nathan."

"I thought so. Don't put that back on," he said when she bent down to retrieve her shirt. "It's still damp. I'll get you a dry one."

"Thanks." She watched him walk to the bedroom, pursing her lips as she studied his tight, muscular buns. Next time, she decided as she tugged on her slacks, she'd make sure she had her own camera handy.

And with that thought in mind, she unloaded the film and tucked it into her back pocket.

He tossed her a T-shirt when he came back out, then fastened the dry jeans he'd pulled on. "I'll walk back to Sanctuary with you. We'll check on the status of things."

"All right. The search parties will probably be heading out again." She combed her fingers through her hair to untangle it. "It's going to be a mess out there from the storm. I'd put some boots on if I were you."

He glanced down at her olive-green sneakers. "You're not wearing any."

"I would if I had them handy."

"So we'll both get sloppy." He took her hand and watched surprise flicker into her eyes when he lifted it to kiss her knuckles. "Then tonight, I'll take you out to dinner."

"Out to dinner?"

"Well, in to dinner. We'll sit in the dining room, look at menus, order wine. I'm told people do that all the time."

"It's silly. I live there."

"I don't. I want to have dinner with you. The kind of evening where you sit across from each other at a table, with candles inbetween, have conversation. Where other people pretend they're not watching us and thinking what an attractive couple we make." He picked up a ball cap from the coffee table and snugged it over her hair. "And I can look at you all through the meal and think about making love to you again. It's called romance."

"I'm not any good at romance."

"You said that about sex. You were wrong." He took her hand and walked to the door. "Let's see how this works out. Maybe Brian will whip up some flan."

She had to laugh. "People are going to think it's pretty strange for me to take a table at the inn."

"It'll give them something to talk about." Their feet squelched into the soggy ground when they reached the bottom of the stairs.

The heat was rolling back, sending the steam rising, turning the air thick. The forest looked ripe, fertile, and darkly green. Water dripped and plopped from leaves, sending fresh showers over their heads as they turned toward the river.

"Churned everything up," Jo commented. "Water's running high and fast. It may crest over the banks, but I doubt it'll cause any damage here."

She detoured for a closer look, philosophically accepting ruined shoes as she sank past her ankles in muck. "Daddy'll want to take a look, I imagine, but there's not much to be done. It'll be more worrisome over at the campground. The beach should be fine, though. The winds weren't high enough to take down the dunes. We'll have a nice crop of shells washed up from it."

"You sound like your father's daughter."

Distracted, she looked over her shoulder. "No. I rarely give a thought to what goes on here. During hurricane season I might pay more attention to the weather reports for this area, but we haven't been hit hard that way in years."

"Jo Ellen, you love this place. It shouldn't worry you to admit that."

"It's not the center of my life."

"No, but it matters to you." He stepped closer. "A lot of things, a lot of people can matter to you without taking over your life. You matter to me."

Alarm jingled in her heart, and she took a hasty step back. "Nathan—" She nearly fell as the ground sucked at her feet.

"You're going to end up back in the river." He took her arms in a firm grip. "Then you'll accuse me of pushing you in again. That's not what I'm doing. I'm not pushing you, Jo Ellen. But I'm not going to be sorry if you slip."

"I like keeping my feet under me, and knowing where the ground gives before I step on it."

"Sometimes you've got to try new territory. This is unexplored ground for me, too."

"That's not true. You've been married, you—"

"She wasn't you," he said quietly and Jo went still in his arms. "I never felt about her the way I'm feeling about you, right now. She never looked at me the way you're looking at me. And I never wanted her as much as I want you. That was what was wrong with it all along. I didn't know it, didn't understand how much of it was my fault until I saw you again."

"You're moving too fast for me."

"Then keep up. And goddamn it, Jo Ellen," he said with an impatient sigh as he tipped her head back. "Give in a little."

She tasted the impatience when his mouth met hers, and the need that went deeper than she'd allowed herself to see. The quick flare of panic inside her fought with a shiver of delight. And the warm stream that shimmered in her blood felt like hope.

"Maybe you're not pushing." She didn't resist when he gathered her closer. "But I feel like I'm sinking." She rested her head on his shoulder, willed her brain to clear. "Part of me just wants to let it happen, and another part keeps fighting to kick back to the surface. I don't know which is best, for me or for you."

He needed that glimmer of hope, the whisper in his heart that promised if she loved him enough, if they loved each other enough, they could survive what had happened. And what was to come.

"Why don't you think about which makes you happier instead of which may be best?"

It sounded so simple that she started to smile. She watched the river flow, wondered if it was time for her just to dive in and see where it took her. She could almost see herself riding that current. See herself rushing along it.

Trapped under the surface, staring up. Dragged down away from air and light.

The scream ripped from her throat, had her sinking to her knees before he could catch her.

"Jo, for God's sake!"

"In the water. In the water." She clamped a hand over her mouth to hold back the bubbling hysteria. "Is it Mama? Is it Mama in the water?"

"Stop it." He knelt beside her, dragged her around by the shoulders until her face was close to his. "Look at me. I want you to stop it. I'm not letting you fall apart. I'm not letting it happen, so you just look at me and pull back."

"I saw—" She had to gulp for air. "In the water, I saw—I'm losing my mind, Nathan. I can't hold on to it."

"Yes, you can." Desperately he pulled her close. "You can hold on to me. Just hold on to me." As she shuddered against him, he looked down grimly at the surface of the river.

And saw the pale ghost staring up at him.

"Jesus God." His arms tightened convulsively on Jo. Then he shoved her back and slid heedlessly into the rising river. "She's in here," he shouted, grabbing on to a downed limb to keep himself from being swept clear. "Give me a hand with her."

"What?"

"You're not losing your mind." Panting with the effort, Nathan reached out with his free hand and gripped hair. "There's someone in here! Help me get her out."

"Oh, my God." Without hesitation now, Jo bellied up to the edge, fighting to anchor her toes in the slippery bank. "Give me your hand, Nathan. Try to hold on to her and I'll help pull you up. Is she alive? Is she breathing?"

He'd gotten a closer look now, a clearer look. And his stomach lurched with horror and pity. The river hadn't been kind. "No." He spoke flatly, shifting his grip on the limb. His gaze lifted to Jo's. "No, she's not alive. I'll hold on here, keep her from going downriver. You get to Sanctuary for help."

She was calm now, cold and calm. "We'll get her out together," she said and stretched out her hand.

TWENTY-FOUR

It was a hideous, grisly task. Twice Nathan lost his grip as he tried to free Susan Peters's hair from the spearing branches that had trapped her body. He went under, fiercely blanking out his mind when her arms knocked into his belly. He could hear Jo calling him, concentrated on the desperate calm in her voice, as together they struggled to free what was left of Susan from the river.

Ignoring her lurching stomach, Jo slid farther over the bank, with the water lapping and rushing over her chin when she hooked her arms under the body. Her breath came short and shallow as for one gut-wrenching moment she was face-to-face with death.

She knew the shutter in her mind had clicked, capturing the image, preserving it. Making it part of her forever.

Then she hauled, grunting, digging knees and feet into the soggy ground. She let the body roll, couldn't bear even to watch. She thrust her hands out, felt Nathan's grip them, slip, clutch again. When he was chest-high out of the water, squirming his way free from the river, she rolled away and retched.

"Go back to the cottage." He coughed violently, spat to clear the taste of river and death from his mouth.

"I'll be all right." She rocked back on her heels, felt the first hot tears flow down her icy cheeks. "I just need a minute. I'll be all right."

She had no more color than what they had pulled from the river did, and she was shaking so hard he was surprised he couldn't hear her bones clattering. "Go back to the cottage. You need dry clothes." He closed a hand over hers. "You have to call Sanctuary for help. We can't leave her like this, Jo."

"No. No, you're right." Steeling herself, she turned her head. The body was paste gray and bloated, the hair dark and matted and slick with debris. But she had once been a woman. "I'll get something to cover her. I'll get her a blanket."

"Can you make it on your own?"

She nodded, and though her body felt hollowed out and frighteningly brittle, she pushed herself to her feet. She looked down at him. His face was pale and filthy, his eyes reddened from the water. She thought of the way he'd gone into the angry river, without hesitation, without a thought for anything but what needed to be done.

"Nathan."

He used the heel of his hand to wipe the mud off his chin, and the gesture was sharp. "What?"

"Nothing," she murmured. "Later."

He waited until he heard her footsteps recede, waited until he heard nothing but the roar of the river and the thud of his own laboring heart. Then he pulled himself over to the body, forced himself to turn it, to look. She'd been pretty once—he knew that. She would never be pretty again. Gritting his teeth, he touched her, easing her head to the side until he could see, until he could be sure.

There, scoring her neck, were livid red bruises. He snatched his hand away, drew up his knees and pressed his face into the filthy denim of his jeans.

Sweet Jesus, sweet Jesus. What was happening here?

Fear was worse than grief, sharper than guilt. And when one rolled into the other, it left the soul sickened.

Still, he had himself under control when Jo came back. She hadn't changed her clothes, but he said nothing, just helped her spread the thin yellow blanket over the body.

"They're coming." She scrubbed her fingers over her mouth. "Brian and Kirby. I got Bri on the phone, told him . . . told him. He said he'd bring her, a doctor, but wasn't going to tell anyone else until . . ."

She trailed off, looked helplessly into the trees. "Why would she have come up here, Nathan? Why in God's name would she have gone into the river? Maybe she fell in the dark, hit her head. It's horrible. I was prepared that we'd find her drowned, washed up on the beach. Somehow this is worse."

Only yards from his door, was all he could think. Only yards from where he'd just made love to Jo. Where he had dared the gods, he thought with a hard shudder.

Had the body come downriver, or had it been put in here, so close he could almost have seen it from his kitchen window on a clear afternoon?

She slipped her hand into his, concerned that it was still icy and as lifeless as the body that lay on the bank. "You're soaked through and frozen. Go get into dry clothes. I'll wait for them."

"I'm not leaving. I'm not leaving you. Or her."

Thinking of warmth and comfort, she put her arms around him. "That was the kindest and bravest thing I've ever seen anyone do." She pressed her lips to his throat, wanting to feel him give, respond. "You went in for her. You could have left her, but you went in. Getting her out wouldn't have mattered to some."

"It mattered."

"To you. You're a good man, Nathan. I'll never forget what you did."

He closed his eyes tight, then drew away without touching her. "They're coming," he said flatly. Even as he turned, Brian and Kirby came hurrying down the path.

Kirby took a quick look at both of them. "Go inside, get in a hot shower. I'll take a look at you shortly." She moved past them and knelt by the blanket.

Jo stood her ground. "It has to be Mrs. Peters. She was caught up on that branch. She must have fallen in sometime last night, and the storm brought her downriver."

Jo steadied herself, reached for Nathan's hand again as Brian knelt beside Kirby. Brian nodded grimly when Kirby folded the blanket down.

"That's her. They came in for meals a couple of times. Goddamn it." He sat back on his heels, scrubbed his hands over his face. "I'll go find her husband. We need to take her somewhere—somewhere better than this."

"No, she can't be moved." Kirby fought her words out over the thick beat of her heart. "You need to call the police and tell them to get out here quickly. I don't believe she drowned." Gently, she lifted the chin, exposed the raw bruising. "It looks as though she was strangled. She was murdered."

"How could this be? How could this happen?" Lexy curled up tight in the corner of the couch in the family parlor. She gripped her hands together to keep herself from biting her nails. "People don't get murdered on Desire. People just don't. Kirby has to be wrong."

"We'll find out soon enough." Kate switched the ceiling fan up to high to try to stir the heavy air. "The police will tell us. Either way, that poor woman's dead, and her husband . . . Jo Ellen, stop prowling so and sit, drink that brandy. You're bound to catch a terrible chill."

"I can't sit." Jo continued to pace from window to window, though she couldn't have said what she was looking for.

"I wish you would sit." Lexy spoke plaintively. "You're about to drive me to distraction. I wish Giff was here. I don't see why he has to be down there with the others instead of here with me.''

"Oh, stop whining for five minutes," Jo snapped. "Hold your own hand for a change."

"Don't. Don't the two of you start." Kate threw up her hands. "I can't stand it just now."

"And I can't stand this waiting. I'm going back out." Jo walked to the door. "I've got to see what's happening. I've got to do something."

"Jo! Don't go out alone." Kate pressed a hand to her head. "I'm already worried sick. Please don't go out there alone."

Seeing her cousin look suddenly old and shaky, Jo changed her mind. "You're right. None of us should go out. We're just in the way. You sit down, Kate. Come on, now." She took Kate's arm and led her toward the sofa beside Lexy. "You sit down and have a brandy. You're worn out."

"I'll get the brandy," Lexy said.

"Just give her mine," Jo told Lexy as she rose. "I don't want it."

"If fussing over me will keep the two of you from snapping at each other, then fuss away." She took the brandy Lexy offered her and smiled weakly. "We should have fresh coffee for when they come in. I don't know when Brian last made any."

"I'll take care of it." Lexy leaned down to kiss Kate's cheek. "Don't you worry." But when she straightened she saw Giff in the doorway.

"They're coming in. They want to talk to Jo."

"All right." Jo closed a hand gratefully over the one Lexy touched to her arm. "I'm ready."

"How much longer will they peck at her?" Brian stood on the front porch, listening to the jungle sounds of cicadas and peepers filling the air.

"It can't be much longer," Kirby said quietly.

"They've had her in there nearly an hour. They didn't keep Nathan more than an hour."

"She shouldn't have to go through this. It's bad enough she found the body, helped drag it out of the water, without having to go over and over it again."

"I'm sure they'll make it as easy on her as they can." She only sighed when he whirled and scalded her with a look. "Brian, there's nothing else to be done, no other choices to be made. A woman's been murdered. Questions have to be asked."

"Jo sure as hell didn't kill her." He threw himself down on the porch swing. "It's easier for you. Big-city doctor. Seen it all, done it all."

"Maybe that's true." She spoke coolly to mask the hurt. "But easier or harder doesn't change the facts. Someone decided not to let Susan Peters live any longer. They used their hands and they choked the life out of her. Now questions have to be asked."

Brian brooded into the dark. "They'll look toward the husband now."

"I don't know."

"They will. It's the logical step. Something happens to the wife, look to the husband. Odds are, he's the one who did it. They looked to my father when my mother left. Until they were satisfied she'd just . . . left. They'll take that poor bastard into some little room. And questions will have to be asked. Who knows, maybe he's the one who decided not to let Susan Peters live."

He shifted his gaze to Kirby. She stood very straight, very composed under the yellow glow of the porch light. She still wore Jo's baggy sweats. But he'd seen her with the police, watched her relay information, rolling clinical terms off her tongue, before huddling over the body with the team from the coroner's office.

There was nothing delicate about her.

"You should go home, Kirby. There's nothing else for you to do here now."

She wanted to weep. She wanted to scream. She wanted to pound her fists against the clear, thin wall he'd suddenly erected between them. "Why are you shutting me out, Brian?"

"Because I don't know what to do about you. And I never meant to let you in in the first place."

"But you did."

"Did I, Kirby? Or did you just jimmy the door?"

Jo's shadow fell between them before she stepped out. "They're finished here. The police."

"Are you all right?" Kirby moved over to her. "You must be exhausted. I want you to go upstairs and lie down now. I can give you something to help you sleep."

"No, I'm fine. Really." She gave Kirby's hand a quick squeeze. "Better, in fact, for having gone through it step by step. I just feel sad and sorry, and grateful to be whole. Did Nathan go back?"

"Kate talked him into going upstairs." Brian rose, walked closer to study her for himself. She looked steadier than he'd expected. "I don't think it would take much to persuade him to stay here tonight. Cops may be tromping around the river for hours yet."

"Then we'll persuade him. You should stay too," she said to Kirby.

"No, I'll be better at home." She looked at Brian. "There's no need for me here. I'm sure one of the detectives will drive me back. I'll just get my bag."

"You're welcome to stay," Brian told her, but she flicked a cool, composed glance over her shoulder.

"I'll be better at home," she repeated and let the screen door slam shut behind her.

"Why are you letting her go?" Jo asked quietly.

"Maybe I need to see if I can. Might be for the best."

Jo thought of what Nathan had said just before the world had gone mad again. "Maybe we all should start thinking about what makes us happy instead of what might be best. I know I'm going to try, because you start running out of chances after a while. I've got something to say to you that I've passed up plenty of chances to say before.''

He shrugged his shoulders, tucked his hands in his pockets in what Jo thought of as his gloomy Hathaway stance. ''Spill it, then.''

''I love you, Brian.'' The warmth of saying it was nearly eclipsed by the sheer delight of watching the astonishment on his face.

He decided it was a trick, a feint to distract the eye before she delivered the jab. ''And?''

''And I wish I'd said it sooner and more often.'' She rose on her toes to press a brief, firm kiss on his suspicious mouth. ''Of course, if I had I wouldn't have the satisfaction of seeing you goggle like a trout on the line right now. I'm going up and make Kate go to bed so she can pretend not to know Nathan's going to sleep in my room tonight.''

''Jo Ellen.'' Brian found his voice by the time she reached the door, then lost it again when she looked back at him.

''Go ahead.'' She smiled broadly. ''Just say it. It's so much easier than you think.''

''I love you too.''

''I know. You've got the best heart of all of us, Bri. That's what worries you.'' She closed the door quietly, then went upstairs to the rest of her family.

She dreamed of walking through the gardens of Sanctuary. The high summer smells, the high summer air. Overhead the moon was as full and clear as a child's cutout. White on black. Stars were a streaming sea of light.

Monkshood and Canterbury bells nodded gently in the breeze, their blossoms glowing white. Oh, how she loved the pure-white blooms, the way they shone in the dark. Fairy flowers, she thought, that danced while mortals slept.

She felt immortal herself—so strong, so vivid. Raising her arms high, she wondered she didn't simply lift off the ground and soar. The night was her time as well. Her alone time. She could drift along the garden paths like a ghost, and the ring of the wind chimes was music to dance by.

Then a shadow stepped out of the trees. And the shadow became a man. Immortal, only curious, she walked toward him.

Now running, running through the forest in the blinding dark, with rain lashing viciously at her face. The night was different now, she was different now. Afraid, pursued. Hunted. The wind was a thousand howling wolves with fangs bared and bloody, the raindrops tiny bright-edged spears aimed to tear the flesh. Limbs whipped at her mercilessly. Trees sprang up to block her path.

She was pathetically mortal now, terrifyingly mortal. Her breath caught on a little sob as she heard her hunter call her name. But the name was Annabelle.

Jo ripped away the sheets that tangled around her legs and bolted upright. Even as the vision cleared away, Nathan laid a hand on her shoulder. He wasn't lying beside her, but standing, and his face was masked in the dark.

"You're all right. Just a dream. A bad one."

Not trusting her voice, she nodded. The hand on her shoulder rubbed it once, absently, then dropped away. The gesture was a distant comfort.

"Do you want something?"

"No." The fear was already fading. "It's nothing. I'm used to it."

"It'd be a wonder if you didn't have nightmares after today." He moved away from her, walked to the window, turned his back.

She could see he'd pulled on his jeans, and when she ran her head over the sheets beside her, she found they were cool. He hadn't been sleeping beside her. Hadn't wanted to, Jo realized. He'd only stayed over at Sanctuary because Kate had made it impossible to refuse. And he was only sharing the bed here because it would have been awkward otherwise.

But he hadn't touched her, hadn't turned to her.

"You haven't slept, have you?"

"No." He wasn't sure he would ever close his eyes peacefully again.

Jo glanced at the clock. 3:05. She'd experienced her share of restless three A.M.s. "Maybe you should take a sleeping pill."

"No."

"I know this was hell for you, Nathan. There's nothing anyone can say or do to make it better."

"Nothing's ever going to make it better for Tom Peters."

"He might have killed her."

Nathan hoped it was true—with all his heart he hoped it. And felt filthy for it.

"They argued," Jo said stubbornly. "She walked out on him. He could have followed her down to the cove. They kept arguing and he snapped. It would only take a minute, a minute of rage. Then he panicked and carried her away. He'd have wanted the distance, so he put her in the river."

"People don't always kill in rage or panic," he said softly. Bitterness rose into his throat, threatening to choke him. "I have no business being in this house. Being with you. What was I thinking of? Going back. To fix what? What the hell did I think I could do?"

"What are you talking about?" She hated the quaver in her voice. But the sound of his, so hard and cold, chilled her.

He turned back to stare at her. She sat in the big, feminine bed, her knees drawn up defensively, her face a pale shadow. He'd made mistakes all along, he realized. Selfish and stupid mistakes. But the biggest had been to fall in love with her, and to nudge her into love with him.

She would hate him before it was done. She would have to.

"Not now. We've both had enough for now." Walking toward her, he thought, was as hard as it would be to walk away. He sat on the side of the bed, ran his hands down her arms. "You need to sleep."

"So do you. Nathan, we're alive." She took his hand, pressed it to her heart. "Getting through and going on— that's important. It's a lesson I learned the hard way." Leaning forward, she touched her lips to his. "Right now, let's just help each other get through the night." Her eyes were dark and stayed on his as she tilted her head to warm the kiss. "Make love with me. I need to hold you."

He let her draw him down, let himself sink. She would hate him before it was done, but for now love would be enough.

In the morning he was gone, from her bed, from Sanctuary, and from Desire.

"He left on the morning ferry?" Jo stared at Brian, wondering how he could fry eggs when the world had just turned upside down again.

"I passed him at dawn, heading back to his cottage." Brian checked his order sheet and spooned up grits. Crises came and went, he thought, but people always managed to eat. "He said he had some business to take care of on the mainland. He'd be a couple of days."

"A couple of days. I see." No good-bye, no see you around. No anything.

"He looked pretty ragged around the edges. And so do you."

"It hasn't been an easy twenty-four hours for anyone."

"No, but I've still got an inn to run. If you want to be useful, you could sweep off the terraces and patios, see that the cushions are put back out."

"Life goes on, right?"

"There's nothing we can do about that." He scooped the eggs up neatly, the glimmering yolks trembling. "You just do what has to be done next."

He watched her drag the broom out of the closet and head outside. And he wondered just what in the hell he was supposed to do next.

"I'm surprised people can eat, the way their mouths are running." Lexy breezed in, exchanged an empty coffeepot for a full one, then slapped down new orders. "One more person asks me about that poor woman, I'm going to scream."

"There's bound to be talk, there's bound to be questions."

"You don't have to listen to them." She gave herself a break, resting a hip against the counter. "I don't think I got more than ten minutes' sleep all night. I don't guess any of us did. Is Jo up yet?"

"She's out clearing off the terraces."

"Good. Keep her busy. Best thing for her." She huffed out a breath when Brian sent her a speculative look. "I'm not brainless, Bri. This has to be harder on her than the rest of us. Harder yet, after what she's already been through. Anything that keeps her mind off it for a five-minute stretch is a blessing."

"I never thought you were brainless, Lex. No matter how hard you pretend to be."

"I'm not going to worry about your insults this morning, Brian. But I am worried about Jo." She turned to peek out the window and was satisfied to see her sister sweeping violently. "Good manual labor should help. And thank God for Nathan. He's just exactly what she needs right now."

"He's not here."

She spun back around so fast that the coffee sloshed to the rim of the pot. "What do you mean he's not here?"

"He went over to the mainland for a few days."

"Well, what in blue hell for? He should be right here, with Jo Ellen."

"He had some business to see to."

"Business?" Lexy rolled her eyes and grabbed the tray of new orders. "Why, isn't that just like a man, just exactly like one? All of you, useless as a three-titted bull, every last one of you."

She stormed out, hips twitching. And for some reason Brian found himself in a much lighter mood. Women, he thought. Can't live with them, can't dump them off a cliff.

An hour later Lexy marched outside. She found Jo opening the last of the patio table umbrellas. "Everything's nice and tidy here, I see. Fine and dandy. Go on up and get a bathing suit. We're going to the beach."

"What for?"

"Because it's there. Go on and change. I've got sunscreen and towels here already."

"I don't want to sit on the beach."

"I don't think I asked what you wanted to do. You need some sun. And if you don't come along with me for an hour, Brian or Kate will find something else for you to sweep up or scrub."

Jo looked at the broom with distaste. "There is that. All right. Why not? It's hot. I could use a swim."

"Get a move on, then, before somebody catches us and puts us to work."

Jo cut through the breakers, took the roll, then began to swim with the current. She'd forgotten how much she loved being in the ocean—fighting against it, drifting with it. She could hear a girlish squeal in the distance as a couple laughed and wrestled in the surf. Farther out, a young boy, brown as a berry, struggled to catch a wave and ride his inflatable raft back to shore.

When her arms tired, she flipped onto her back. The sun burned down through hazy skies and stung her eyes.

It was easy to close them, to float. When her mind drifted to Nathan, she cut it off.

He had a life of his own, and so did she. Maybe she'd started to lean just a little too much. It was good that he'd jerked that shoulder away so abruptly, forced her to regain her own balance.

When he came back—if he came back—she'd be steadier.

With a moan of disgust, she flipped again, letting her face sink into the water.

Goddamn it, she was in love with him. And if that wasn't the stupidest thing she'd ever done, she didn't know what topped it. There was no future there, and why would she even think of futures? She turned her head, gulped in air, and began to swim again.

They had come together by accident, through circumstance, and had simply taken advantage of it. If they'd gotten closer than they intended, that was a matter of circumstance too. And circumstances changed. She'd changed.

If coming back to Sanctuary had brought some pain and some misery, it had also brought back to her a strength and clear-sightedness that she'd been missing for far too long.

She planted her feet, let the sand shift under her as she walked through the waves to shore.

Lexy was posed on a blanket, stretched out to show off her generous curves. She rested lazily on an elbow, turning the pages of a thick paperback novel. On the cover was a bare-chested man with amazing and improbable pecs, black hair that swirled over his gleaming shoulders, and an arrogant smile on his full-lipped mouth.

Lexy gave a low, murmuring sigh and flipped a page. Her own hair rippled in the breeze. The curves of her generous breasts rose in smooth, peach-toned swells over the minuscule bikini top on which neon shades of green and pink warred. Her long legs were slicked with lotion, and her toenails were a glitter of coral.

She looked, Jo decided, like an ad for some sexy resort. Dropping down beside her, Jo picked up a towel and rubbed it over her hair. "Do you do that on purpose, or is it just instinct?"

"What's that?" Lexy tipped down her rose-lensed sunglasses and peered over the top.

"Arrange yourself so that every male in a hundred yards strains his neck to get a look at you."

"Oh, that." Lips curving, Lexy nudged her glasses back in place. "That's just instinct, sugar. And good luck. You could do the same, but you'd have to put your mind to it some. You've gotten your figure back since you've been home. And that black tank suit's not a bad choice. Looks athletic and sleek. Some men go for that." She tipped her glasses down again. "Nathan seems to."

"Nathan hasn't seen me in this suit."

"Then he's in for a treat."

"If he comes back."

" 'Course he'll come back. You're smart, you'll make him pay just a little for going off."

Jo scooped up a handful of sand, let it drift through her fingers. "I'm in love with him."

"Of course you are. Why wouldn't you be?"

"In love with him, Lexy." Jo frowned at the glittering grains of sand that clung to her hand.

"Oh." Lexy sat up, crossed her pretty legs, and grinned. "That's nice. You sure took your time falling, but you picked a winner."

"I hate it." Jo grabbed more sand and squeezed it into her fist. "I hate feeling this way, being this way. It ties my stomach up in knots."

"It's supposed to. I've had mine tied up dozens of times. It was always real easy to loosen it up again." Her mouth went into a pout as she looked out to sea. "Until now. I'm having a harder time of that with Giff."

"He loves you. He always has. It's different for you."

"It's different for everybody. We're all built different inside. That's what makes it so interesting."

Jo tilted her head. "You know, Lex, sometimes you're absolutely sensible. I never expect it, then there it is. I guess I need to tell you what I told Brian last night."

"What's that?"

"I love you, Lexy." She bent over and touched her lips to her sister's cheek. "I really do."

"I know that, Jo. You're ornery about it, but you always loved us." She let out a breath as she decided to make her own confession. "I guess that's why I got so mad at you when you went away. And I was jealous."

"You? Of me?"

"Because you weren't afraid to go."

"Yes, I was." Jo rested her chin on her knee and watched the waves batter the shore. "I was terrified. Sometimes I'm still scared of being out there, of not being able to do what I need to do. Or doing it but failing at it."

"Well, I failed, and I can tell you, it sucks."

"You didn't fail, Lexy. You just didn't finish." She turned her head. "Will you go back?"

"I don't know. I was sure I would." Her eyes clouded, misted between gray and green. "Trouble is, it gets easy to stay here, let time go by. Then I'll just get old and wrinkled and fat. Oh, what are we talking about this for?"

Annoyed with herself, Lexy shook her head, picked out a cold can of Pepsi from the little cooler beside her. "We should be talking about something interesting. Like, I was wondering . . ."

She popped the top, took a long, cooling sip. Then ran her tongue lazily over her top lip. "Just how is sex with Nathan?"

Jo snorted out a laugh. "No," she said definitely and rolled over to lie on her stomach.

"On a scale of one to ten." Lexy poked Jo's shoulder.

"Or if you had to pick one adjective to describe it."

"No," Jo said again.

"Just one little bitty adjective. I mean, would it be 'incredible'?" she asked, leaning down close to Jo's ear. "Or would it be 'fabulous'? Maybe 'memorable'?"

Jo let out a small sigh. " 'Stupendous,' " she said without opening her eyes. "It's stupendous."

"Oh, stupendous." Lexy waved a hand in front of her face. "Oh, I like that. Stupendous. Does he keep his eyes open or closed when he kisses you?"

"Depends."

"He does both? That gives me the shivers. You'd never know which. I just love that. So, how about when he—"

"Lexy." Though a giggle escaped, Jo kept her eyes tightly closed. "I'm not going to describe Nathan's lovemaking technique for you. I'm going to take a nap. Wake me up in a bit."

And to her surprise, she dropped like a stone into sleep.

TWENTY-FIVE

NATHAN PACED THE AG-
ing Turkish carpet in the soaring two-level library of Dr.
Jonah Kauffman's brownstone. Outside, and two dozen
stories down, New York was sweltering under a massive
heat wave. Here in the dignified penthouse all was cool
and polished and worlds away from the bump and grind
of the streets.

It never felt like New York inside Kauffman's realm.
Whenever Nathan walked into the grand foyer with its
golden woods and quiet colors, he thought of English
squires and country houses.

One of Nathan's earliest commissions had been to design the library, to shift walls and ceilings to accommodate Kauffman's enormous collection of books in the
understated and traditional style that suited one of the top
neurologists in the country. The warm chestnut wood, the
wide, intricately carved moldings, the tall sweep of triple
windows set back to form a cozy alcove had been Nathan's choices. Kauffman had left it all up to him, chuckling whenever Nathan would ask for an opinion.

You're the doctor on this case, Nathan. Don't ask me

to collaborate on the choice of structural beams, and I won't ask you to assist in brain surgery.

Now Nathan struggled to compose himself as he waited. This time around, Kauffman was the doctor, and Nathan's present, his future, every choice, large or small, that he would ever make were in Kauffman's skilled hands.

It had been six days since he'd left Desire. Six desperately long days.

Kauffman strode in, slid the thick pocket doors shut behind him. "Sorry to make you wait, Nathan. You should have helped yourself to a brandy. But brandy's not your drink, is it? Well, I'll have one and you can pretend to join me."

"I appreciate your seeing me here, Doctor. And your doing all . . . this yourself."

"Come now, you're part of the family." Kauffman lifted a Baccarat decanter from a sideboard to pour two snifters.

He was tall, nearly six five, an imposing man both straight and trim after seventy years of living. His hair remained thick, and he allowed himself the vanity of wearing it brushed back like a flowing white mane. He sported a neat beard and moustache that surrounded his somewhat thin mouth. He preferred the no-nonsense lines of British suits, the elegance of Italian shoes, and he never failed to appear perfectly and elegantly turned out.

But it was his eyes that drew the onlooker's attention first, and most often held it. They were dark and keen under heavy lids and sweeping black brows. Those eyes warmed as he offered Nathan a snifter. "Sit down, Nathan, and relax. It won't be necessary to drill into your brain anytime in the foreseeable future."

Nathan's stomach did a long, slow turn. "The tests?"

"All of them, and you requested—rather, you insisted on—quite an extensive battery of tests, are negative. I've gone over the results myself, as you asked. You have no tumors, no shadows, no abnormalities whatsoever. What you have, Nathan, is a very healthy brain and neuro system. Now sit down.''

"I will." His legs gave way easily enough, and he sank into the buttery-soft leather of a wingback, man-size chair. "Thank you for all the time and trouble, but I wonder if I shouldn't get a second opinion."

Kauffman raised those dramatic black brows. As he sat down across from Nathan, he automatically lifted the pleats of his trousers so they would fall correctly. "I consulted with one of my associates on your tests. His opinion corroborates with mine. You're welcome, of course, to go elsewhere."

"No." Though he didn't care for brandy, Nathan took a quick swallow and let it slide through his system. "I'm sure you covered all the bases."

"More than. The CT and the MRI scans were both perfectly normal. The physical you underwent, the blood work and so forth, only served to prove that you're a thirty-year-old man in excellent health and physical condition." Kauffman swirled his snifter, brought it to his lips. "Now, it's time you told me why you felt the need to put yourself through such intensive testing."

"I wanted to be sure there wasn't anything physically wrong. I thought I might be having blackouts."

"Have you lost time?"

"No. Well, how would I know? There's a possibility that I've been blanking out, doing . . . something during— what would you call it—a fugue state."

Kauffman pursed his lips. He'd known Nathan too long to consider him an alarmist. "Have you any evidence of that? Finding yourself in places without remembering how you got there?"

"No. No, I haven't." Nathan allowed the relief to trickle through, slowly. "I'm all right, then, physically."

"You're in excellent, even enviable physical condition. Your emotional condition is another matter. You've had a hideous year, Nathan. The loss of your family is bound to have taken its toll on you. A divorce not long before that. So much loss, so much change. I miss David and Beth so much myself. They were very dear to me.''

''I know.'' Nathan stared into those dark, compelling eyes. Did you know? he wondered. Did you suspect? But all he saw on Kauffman's face was sympathy and regret. ''I know they were.''

''And Kyle.'' Kauffman sighed deeply. ''So young, his death so unnecessary.''

''I've had time to cope, to start to accept that my parents are gone.'' Even to thank God for it, Nathan thought. ''As for Kyle, we hadn't been close in a long time. Their deaths didn't change that.''

''And you feel guilty that you don't grieve for him as you do for them.''

''Maybe.'' Nathan set the snifter aside, rubbed his hands over his face. ''I'm not sure where the guilt's rooted anymore. Doctor Kauffman, you were friends with my father for thirty years, you knew him before I was born.''

''And your mother.'' Kauffman smiled. ''As a man who has three ex-wives, I admired their dedication to each other and their marriage. To their sons. You were a lovely family. I hope you can find comfort in the memory of that.''

And that, Nathan thought with a sinking heart, was the crux of it. There could be no comfort in the memories now, and never would be again. ''What would make a man, a seemingly normal man living a perfectly normal life, plan and commit an obscene act? An unspeakable act.''

The pressure on his chest forced Nathan's heart to beat too hard, too thickly. He picked up the snifter again, but without any desire to drink. ''Would he be insane, would he be ill? Would there be some physical cause?''

''I couldn't say, Nathan, on such general speculation.

Do you believe your father committed an unspeakable act?''

"I know he did.'' Before Kauffman could speak, Nathan shook his head and rose to pace again. "I can't— I'm not free to explain it to you. There are others I have to talk to first.''

"Nathan, David Delaney was a loyal friend, a loving husband, and a devoted father. You can rest your mind on that.''

"I haven't been able to rest my mind on that since the month after he was killed.'' Emotions swirled in his eyes, turning them to smoke. "I buried him, Doctor Kauffman, him and my mother. And I'm very tempted to bury the rest. If I could be sure,'' he said softly, "that it's not happening again.''

Kauffman leaned forward. He'd been treating the human condition for half a century and knew there was no healing of the body or the brain without healing of the heart. "Whatever it is you believe he did, you can't bear the weight of it.''

"Who else can? Who else will? I'm the only one left.''

"Nathan.'' Kauffman let out a little sigh. "You were a bright, interesting child, and you have become a talented and intelligent young man. Too often when you were growing up, I saw you shoulder the responsibilities of others. You took on your brother's far too often for your own good, or for Kyle's. Don't make that mistake now over something you can neither change nor repair.''

"I've been telling myself that for the last couple of months. 'Leave it alone, live your own life.' I'd decided not to dig into the past, to try to concentrate on the present and forge a future. There's a woman.''

"Ah.'' Kauffman relaxed, eased back.

"I'm in love with her.''

"I'm delighted to hear it and would love to meet her. Has she been vacationing on that island you took yourself off to?''

"Not exactly. Her family lives there. She's spending some time. She's had . . . difficulties of her own. Actually I met her when we were children. When I saw her again . . . well, to simplify, one thing led to another. I could have prevented it." He moved to the window, to the view of Central Park, which was thick and green with summer. "Perhaps I should have."

"Why would you deny yourself happiness?"

"There's something I know that affects her. If I tell her, she'll despise me. More, I don't know what it will do to her, emotionally." Because the park made him think of the forest on Desire, he turned away from it. "Would it be better for her to go on believing something that hurts her but isn't true, or to know the truth and have to live with pain she might not be able to bear? I'll lose her if I tell her, and I don't know if I can live with myself if I don't."

"Is she in love with you?"

"She's beginning to be. If I let things go on as they are, she will be." A ghost of a smile flitted around his mouth. "She'd hate hearing me say that, as if it were inevitable. As if she had no control over it."

Kauffman heard the warmth come back into Nathan's voice. The boy had always been his favorite, he admitted privately. Even among his own grandchildren. "Ah, an independent woman. Always more interesting—and more difficult."

"She's fascinating, and she certainly isn't easy. She's strong, even when she's wounded, and she's been wounded enough. She's built a shell around herself, and since I've seen her again I've watched it crack, watched her open up. Maybe I've even helped that happen. And inside she's soft, giving."

"You haven't once said what she looks like." Kauffman found that to be the telling mark. Physical attraction had led him into three hot marriages, followed by three chilly divorces. More was needed for the long, often sweaty, haul.

"She's beautiful," Nathan said simply. "She'd prefer to be ordinary, but it's impossible. Jo doesn't trust beauty. She trusts competency. And honesty," Nathan finished, staring down into the brandy he'd barely touched, "I don't know what to do."

"Truth is admirable, but it isn't always the answer. I can't tell you what choice to make, but I've always believed that love, when genuine, holds. Perhaps you should ask yourself which would be more loving, giving her the truth or remaining silent."

"And if I remain silent, the foundation we build on will already have a crack. Still I'm the only one alive who can tell her, Doctor Kauffman." Nathan lifted his gaze, and his eyes stormed with emotion. "I'm the only one left."

Nathan didn't return to the island the next day, or the day after. By the third day Jo had convinced herself it didn't matter. She was hardly sitting around waiting for him to sail across the sound and scoop her up like a pirate claiming his booty.

On the fourth day she was weepy, despising herself for wandering down to the ferry twice a day, hoping to catch sight of him.

By the end of a week she was furious, and spent a great deal of her time snapping at anyone who risked speaking to her. In the interest of restoring peace, Kate bearded the lion in Jo's room, where she had gone to sulk after a hissing match with Lexy.

"What in the world are you doing holed up indoors on such a pretty morning?" Moving briskly, Kate whisked back the curtains Jo had pulled over the windows. Sunlight beamed in.

"Enjoying my privacy. If you've come in here to try

to convince me to apologize to Lexy, you're wasting your time.''

''You and Lexy can fight your own battles, just like always, as far as I'm concerned.'' Kate put her hands on her hips. ''But you'll mind your tone when you speak to me, young lady.''

''I beg your pardon,'' Jo said coolly, ''but this is my room.''

''I don't care if you're sitting on top of your own mountain, you won't bare your claws on me. Now I've been as patient as I know how to be these last few days, but you've mooned around and snarled around here long enough.''

''Then maybe it's time I should think about going home.''

''That's your decision to make. Oh, shake yourself loose, Jo Ellen,'' Kate ordered with a snap in her own voice. ''The man's only been gone a week, and he'll certainly be back.''

Jo firmed her jaw. ''I don't know what, or whom, you're referring to.''

Before she could stop herself, Kate snorted. ''Don't think you can out la-de-da me. I've been at it more years.'' Kate sat down on the bed where Jo was sprawled under the pretense of selecting the final prints for her book. ''A blind man on a galloping horse could see that Nathan Delaney's got you in a dither. And it's likely the best thing to happen to you in years.''

''I am not, in any way, any shape, any form, in a dither.''

''You're more than halfway in love with him, and it wouldn't surprise me in the least if he'd gone off like this to nudge you over the rest of the way.''

Since that hadn't occurred to her, Jo felt her blood heat to a boil. ''Then he's made a very large miscalculation. Going off without a word is hardly the way to win my affections.''

"Then do you want him to know you've been moping around here the whole time he's been gone?" Kate lifted a brow as she saw the flush of anger heat Jo's cheeks. "There are plenty who'd be happy to tell him so if you keep this up. I'd hate for you to give him that satisfaction."

"I don't intend to give him so much as the time of day, should he decide to come back."

Kate patted Jo's knee. "I couldn't agree more."

Wary of a trap, Jo narrowed her eyes. "I thought you liked him."

"I do. I like him very much, but that doesn't mean I don't think he deserves a good swift kick in the rear end for making you unhappy. And I'd be mighty disappointed in you if you gave him the opportunity to crow over it. So get up," she ordered, rising herself. "Go on about your business. Take your camera and go along. And when he comes back, all he'll see is that your life went on without him."

"You're right. You're absolutely right. I'm going to call my publisher and give them the final go-ahead on the last prints. Then I'm going to go out, take some new shots. I've got an idea for another book."

Kate smiled as Jo scrambled up and began to pull her shoes on. "That's wonderful. You'll have pictures of the island in it, then."

"All of them. People this time, too. Faces. No one's going to accuse me of being lonely, of hiding behind the lens. I've got more than one facet to me."

"Of course you do, sweetie pie. I'll get out of your way so you can get to work." All but vibrating with the pleasure of success, Kate strolled out. Maybe now, she thought, they'd have some peace.

The adrenaline carried Jo through that day and into the next. It fueled her, this new ambition. For the first time in her career, she hunted up faces with enthusiasm, began to study and dissect them. She thrilled at the way Giff's eyes twinkled under the brim of his cap, the way his hand gripped a hammer.

She hounded Brian in the kitchen, using charm when she could, threats when she couldn't, to draw the right expression, to produce the right body language.

Lexy was easy. She would pose endlessly. But Jo's favorite shot was one of Lexy and Giff, the foolishly happy expressions on their faces as Giff swept Lexy up to spin her in circles just on the edge of the garden.

She even trooped after her father, using silence to lull him into relaxing, then capturing the quiet thoughtfulness in his face as he looked out over the salt marsh.

"It's time you put that thing away." Sam's brows drew together in irritated embarrassment as she aimed the camera at him again. "Run along and play with that somewhere else."

"It stopped being play when they started paying me. Turn just a little to the right and look out toward the water."

He didn't move a muscle. "I don't recollect you ever being such a pest before."

"I'll have you know I'm a very famous photographer. Thousands cheer when I aim my lens." She clicked quickly when a faint smile tugged at his mouth. "You're so handsome, Daddy. And you look so masterful out here."

"You're so damned famous, you shouldn't have to flatter people to get their picture."

She laughed and lowered the camera. "True enough. But you are handsome. I was taking some shots over at Elsie Pendleton's. The Widow Pendleton," Jo added, wiggling her eyebrows. "She made a point to ask after you. Several times."

"Elsie Pendleton's been looking for a man to replace the one she buried since she tossed the first handful of dirt on his coffin. It ain't by any means going to be me."

"For which good sense your family thanks you."

He found his lips trembling again, shook his head as much over the reaction as the cause. "You're awfully chipper today."

"A nice change, don't you think? I got tired of myself." She crouched down to change lenses. "And it occurred to me that a corner needed to be turned. Maybe coming here was the start of it." She paused for a moment, just to look out over the shimmering marsh. "Facing some things, myself included. And realizing that maybe if I didn't feel loved, it was because I hadn't let anyone love me."

She glanced up, saw that he was watching her, searching her face. "Don't look for her in me, Daddy." Jo closed her eyes as the pain stabbed through her. "Don't look for her in me anymore. It hurts me when you do."

"Jo Ellen—"

"All my life I've tried to stop looking like her. In college when the other girls were fussing and primping, I held back. If I fussed I'd have to look in the mirror. And I'd see her, just the way you do when you look at me." Her eyes swam as she straightened. "What do I have to do, Daddy, to make you see who I am?"

"I do see. I can't help but see her too, but I do see you, Jo Ellen. Don't go spilling over on me here. I'm useless with that female stuff." He stuffed his hands in his pockets and turned away. "You get hold of yourself now. It's Lexy who leaks at the drop of a hat, not you. Damn girl'll leak if you look cross-eyed, and if she isn't leaking she's flouncing. She don't marry that Giff soon and get on with things, I'll lose my mind."

Jo gave a watery chuckle. "Why, Daddy, I didn't know you loved her enough to let her drive you crazy."

" 'Course I love her. She's mine, isn't she?" He spoke gruffly and made himself turn back to face Jo. "So are you."

"Yes." She smiled and let the ache pass away. "So am I."

When the light no longer pleased her, Jo locked herself in her darkroom. There was excitement there as well. From film to negatives, from negatives to contacts. These she pored over, scrutinizing details, flaws, shadows through her loupe.

Out of a dozen she might select one that satisfied her strict requirements. Still, her drying line filled rapidly with prints she felt were worthy. When she came to an unmarked roll of film, she clicked her tongue in annoyance.

Careless of her, she thought. She set the timer, flicked off the lights, and began the developing process. The dark soothed her. She could move competently, even mechanically, by feel alone. Anticipation hummed. What would she see here, what would she find? What frozen moment would be preserved forever simply because she had chosen it?

She turned on the red bulb, washed the room in that eerie workman's lighting. And gave a choked cry that was part shock, part laughter as she stared at the negative of herself, nude, sprawled on Nathan's carpet.

"Jesus, that'll teach me not to mark film."

She held up the roll, studying the other negatives. The ones she'd taken of the storm looked promising. And her mouth pursed as she examined the earlier shots, ones Nathan must have taken along the way.

There was one of dunes, across the meadow where the flowers were blooming and the sea beyond rolled in a high, frothy crest.

Decent composition, she mused. For an amateur. Of course if she bothered to take it to contact stage, she'd undoubtedly find several major flaws.

Her eyes were drawn back to the end of the roll. Her own face, her own body. Even as her hand reached for the scissors to destroy the negatives, she paused. Was she going to be that prudish, that stubborn, and not satisfy her own curiosity?

She was the only one who had to see them, after all.

On impulse, she set back to work. It couldn't hurt to make a set of contacts from the roll. She could destroy the ones of herself later. After she'd taken a good look at them.

She didn't hum along with the radio as she worked now. She felt too uneasy, and too excited, to hear the music that tinkled out.

The sheet was barely dry when she slapped it onto her light table and applied the loupe. She caught her breath as the images enlarged and focused.

She looked so . . . wanton, she supposed would be the word. Her eyes half closed, her lips just curved in obvious sexual satisfaction. Her body looked almost ripe. Apparently she had gotten her figure back without even noticing. She certainly had curves.

In the next her eyes were fully open and round with shock. Her hands were halfway up to her breasts, movement frozen by the fast film. There was no denying that she looked—how had he put it? Rumpled and sexy?

Oh, God, she had never allowed herself to be that exposed to anyone before. She'd let that happen, and now for just a moment, she could admit she wanted to let it happen again.

She wanted to let him touch her, to make her feel desired and reckless. There was a yearning deep in the pit of her stomach to be that woman again, the woman he'd seen and captured on film. To let him take control of her, and to know that she had the power to take control of him.

He'd given that to her, and by preserving that moment, had made her look straight at it and see what she could have with him. And what she could lose without him.

"You bastard, Nathan. I hate you for this."

She got up quickly, stuffed the sheet deep into a

drawer. No, she wouldn't destroy it. She would keep it, as a reminder. Whenever she felt herself tempted to trust a man again, to give that much to a man, she would take it back out, study it.

And remind herself how easily they walked away.

"Jo Ellen." Lexy's voice came through the door as her knock sounded sharp and loud.

"I'm working in here."

"Well, I know that. But you might want to finish up quick, fast, and in a hurry. Guess who came in on the late ferry?"

"Brad Pitt."

"Don't I wish? But you might like this better. Nathan Delaney just walked in the kitchen, big as life and twice as handsome. And he's looking for you."

Jo lifted a fist to her heart and firmly shoved it back in place. "Tell him I'm busy."

"I already gave him the cold shoulder for you, sugar. Told him I didn't see why you should drop what you were doing and come running just because he blew back onto Desire like an ill wind." .

Jo found her lips curving in appreciation. She could easily visualize the scene, with Lexy playing the chilly Southern Belle to the hilt. "I appreciate it."

"But I have to tell you—oh, open this door, Jo. I'm tired of talking through it."

Because Lexy had just climbed to the top of Jo's most favored list, she obliged, snicking open the lock, and opening the door enough that she could lean on the jamb.

"I'd appreciate it if you'd tell him I'm not interested in adjusting my schedule to suit his whims."

"I will. That's nicely put. But Jo, he looks so wind-blown and sexy and on the edge of something." Lexy rolled her eyes in pure female appreciation. "It gave my heart a nice flutter just to look at him."

"Well, you can just stop fluttering. Whose side are you on?"

"Yours, honey lamb, absolutely one hundred percent."
She kissed Jo's cheek to prove it. "He has to be punished,
no doubt about it. And if you need some advice on how
to go about it, I'm more than happy to give you some
ideas."

"I've got plenty of my own, thanks." But she rolled
her shoulders to ease the tension. "Tell him I have no
desire to see or speak to him, and that I expect to be busy
with a great many more important matters than him for
quite some time."

"I wish you'd tell him that yourself, just that way. I
believe you've got a real knack for this." Lexy's grin
spread wide as she wound a lock of hair around her finger.
"I'll go down and tell him, then I'll come back up here
and tell you what he has to say to that."

"This isn't high school."

"No, it's more interesting and more fun. Oh, I know
you're scalded good and proper, Jo." She patted her sister's cheek. "I'd be as spitting mad as a stomped-on cat
myself. But just think how satisfying it's going to be when
he crawls. Don't you take him back until he does. And
he comes up with at least two bouquets of flowers and a
nice, expensive present. It should be jewelry."

Jo's humor made a rapid return. "Lexy, you're a ma-
nipulative and materialistic woman."

"And proud of it, honey. You listen to your baby sister
and you'll end up *owning* that man. Now I figure he's
been down there waiting and sweating long enough for
the next slap." She rubbed her hands together. "I'll make
it count for you, don't you worry."

Jo stayed leaning against the doorjamb as Lexy
flounced away. "I bet you will," she murmured. "And
I'll owe you big for it."

Satisfied, Jo turned back into the darkroom. She tidied
her workbench, rearranged her bottles of chemicals, then
put them back in their original positions. She examined

her nails and wondered if she should let Lexy give her a
manicure after all.

When she heard the footsteps, she turned toward the
door, prepared to hear Lexy's report. When Nathan filled
the doorway, his temper shot straight into hers.

"I need you to come with me." His voice was clipped
and anything but apologetic.

"I believe you were informed I'm busy. And you
haven't been invited into this room."

"Save it, Scarlett." He grabbed her hand and pulled.
When her free one reared back, whipped forward, and
cracked hard across his face, he narrowed his eyes and
nodded. "Fine, we do it the hard way."

The room turned upside down so rapidly she didn't
even get out the curse burning on her tongue. He was
halfway out of the room with her slung over his shoulder
before she got past the shock enough to fight.

"Get your goddamn belly-crawling Yankee bastard
hands off me." She punched at his back, furious that she
couldn't manage a full swing.

"You think you can send your sister to brush me off?
In a pig's eye." He shoved open the door with his shoulder and started down the narrow stairway. "I've been
traveling the whole fucking day to get here, and you'll
have the courtesy to listen to what I need to say."

"Courtesy? Courtesy? What does a snake oil New York
hotshot know about courtesy?" In the confines of the
stairway, her struggles only resulted in her rapping her
head against the wall. "I hate you." Her ears rang from
both the blow and the humiliation.

"I've prepared myself for that." Grim and determined,
he hauled her into the kitchen. Both Lexy and Brian froze
and gaped. "Excuse me," he said shortly, and carried her
outside while she left a trail of threats and curses behind
them.

"Oh." Lexy sighed, long and deep, holding a hand to

her heart. "Wasn't that the most romantic thing you've ever seen in all your life?"

"Shit." Brian set down the pie he'd just taken out of the oven. "She'll rip his face off first chance she gets."

"A lot you know about romance." Lexy leaned against the counter. "Twenty dollars says he's got her in bed, fully willing, within an hour."

Brian heard Jo scream out something about castrating a certain Yankee son of a bitch and nodded. "You're on, darling."

TWENTY-SIX

Jo sat in simmering silence as Nathan drove the Jeep hissing across Shell Road. She wouldn't give him the satisfaction of leaping out of a moving vehicle, or of running away once he stopped it. She would simply tear his skin into bloody shreds when they were no longer in danger of running off the road.

"This isn't the way I wanted to go about this," Nathan muttered. "I need to talk to you. It's important. A hell of a time you pick to pull some lame female cold-shoulder routine."

Ignoring her low, purring sound of warning, he dug a deeper hole for himself. "I don't mind a fight. Under any reasonable circumstances I don't mind a good kick-ass fight. Clears the air. But these aren't reasonable circumstances, and you having your nose out of joint is only complicating an already painful situation."

"So it's my fault." She sucked in her breath as he jerked the Jeep to a halt at the cottage. "This is my fault?"

"It's not a matter of fault, Jo. That's the whole—" He

broke off abruptly, too busy defending himself to bother with more words.

She didn't go at him with teeth and nails and heated accusations. She waded in with balled-up fists, and the first several blew right past his guard.

"Jesus! Jesus Christ!" He wished he could laugh at them. He wished to God he could just drag her close, pin those surprisingly well-toned arms with his and just howl at the pair of them.

He tasted blood in his mouth, wasn't entirely sure his jaw wouldn't turn out to be broken, and finally managed to hold her down on the seat while both of them panted for breath.

"Would you stop it? Would you pull out some modicum of control and stop trying to beat my brains—which I'm assured are in perfect working order—to a bloody pulp?" He tightened his grip, shifting fast as she tried to bring her knee up and render him helpless. "I don't want to hurt you."

"Well, that's too bad because I want to hurt you. I want to send you off limping for treating me this way."

"I'm sorry." He lowered his brow to hers and tried to catch his breath. "I'm sorry, Jo."

She refused to soften, refused to acknowledge the little trip her heart experienced at the utter despair in his voice. "You don't even know what you're sorry for."

"For more than you know." He eased back, met her eyes. "Please come inside. I have things to tell you. Things I wish I didn't have to tell you. After I do, you can beat me black and blue and I won't lift a hand to stop you. I swear it."

Something was wrong, horribly wrong. The anger dropped away into fear. She kept her voice cool before her imagination ran wild. "That's quite an arrangement. I'll come in, and you can say what you have to say. Then we're finished, Nathan."

She shoved him away and pushed open her car door.

"Because nobody walks away from me," she said in a low, vibrant voice. "Nobody ever again."

His heart sank, but he led the way inside, switched on the lights. "I'd like you to sit down."

"I don't need to sit down, and what you'd like doesn't interest me. How could you go that way?" Even as she rounded on him, she wrapped her arms around herself in defense. "How could you leave my bed and just go, without a word? And stay away when you had to know how it would make me feel. If you were tired of me, you still could have been kind."

"Tired of you? Sweet Jesus, Jo, there hasn't been a minute of the past eight days that I haven't thought of you, wanted you."

"Do you think I'm stupid enough, or needy enough, to believe that kind of lie? If you'd thought of me, wanted me, you couldn't have turned your back on me as if none of it mattered. Had ever mattered."

"If it hadn't mattered, didn't matter more than anything else in my life, I could have stayed. And we wouldn't be having this conversation."

"You hurt me, you humiliated me, you—"

"I love you."

She jerked back as if to avoid a blow. "You expect my knees to go weak now? You think you can say that and make me run into your arms?"

"No. I wouldn't love you if you couldn't stand there and spit at me after I'd said it." He walked to her, gave in to the need to touch her. Just a brush of his fingertips over her shoulders. "And I do love you, Jo Ellen. Maybe I always did. Maybe that seven-year-old girl ruined me for anyone else. I don't know. But I need you to believe me. I need to say it, and I need you to believe it before I start the rest."

She stared into his eyes, and now her knees did start to tremble. "You do mean it."

"Enough to put my past, present, and future in your

hands." He took hers in his for a moment, studied them, memorized them, then let them go. "I went back to New York. There's a friend of the family, a doctor. A neurologist. I wanted him to run some tests on me."

"Tests?" Baffled, she pushed at her hair. "What kind of—Oh, my God." It struck her like a fist, hard in the heart. "You're sick. A neurologist? What is it? A tumor." Her blood shivered to ice in her veins. "But you can have treatment. You can—"

"I'm not sick, Jo. There's no tumor, there's nothing wrong with me. But I had to be sure."

"There's nothing wrong?" She folded her arms again, hugged them to her body. "I don't understand. You went back to New York to have tests run on your brain when there's nothing wrong with you?"

"I said I needed to be sure. Because I thought I might have had blackouts or been sleepwalking or had fugues. And have maybe killed Susan Peters."

She lowered herself gingerly, bracing a hand on the back of the chair as she sat on the arm. She never took her eyes off his. "Why would you think such a crazy thing?"

"Because she was strangled here on the island. Because her body was hidden. Because her husband, her family, her friends, might have gone the rest of their lives not knowing what had happened."

"Stop it." She couldn't get her breath, had to fight back the urge to clap her hands over her ears. Her heart was beating too fast, making her head spin, her skin damp. She knew the signs, the panic waiting slyly to spring. "I don't want to hear any more of this."

"I don't want to tell you any more. But neither one of us has a choice." He braced himself not only to face it but to face her. "My father killed your mother."

"That's insane, Nathan." She willed herself to get up and run, but she couldn't move. "And it's cruel."

"It's both. And it's also the truth. Twenty years ago, my father took your mother's life."

"No. Your father—Mr. David—was kind, he was a friend. This is crazy talk. My mother left." Her voice shuddered and broke, then rose. "She just left."

"She never left Desire. He . . . he put her body in the marsh. Buried her in the salt marsh."

"Why are you saying this? Why are you doing this?"

"Because it's the truth, and I've avoided it too long already." Nathan forced himself to say the rest, to finish it while she shut her eyes and shook her head fiercely. "He planned it from the minute he saw her, when we arrived that summer."

"No. No, stop this."

"I can't stop what's already happened. He kept a journal and . . . evidence in a safe-deposit box. I found it all after he and my mother died."

"You found it." Tears leaked through her lashes as she wrapped her arms tight around her body and rocked. "You came back here."

"I came back here to face it, to try to remember what that summer had been like. What he had been like . . . then. And to try to decide whether to leave it all buried or to tell your family what my family had done."

The familiar flood of sick panic rushed through her, roared in her head, raced through her blood. "You knew. You knew all along, and you came back here. You took me to bed knowing." Nausea made her dizzy as she surged to her feet. "You were inside me." Rage sliced through her an instant before her hand cracked across his cheek. "I let you inside me." She slapped him again, viciously. He neither defended himself nor evaded the blows. "Do you know how that makes me feel?"

He'd known she would look at him just like this, with hate and disgust, even fear. He had no choice but to accept it. "I didn't face it. My father . . . he was my father."

"He killed her, he took her away from us. And all these years . . ."

"Jo, I didn't know until after he'd died. I've been trying to come to grips with it for months. I know what you're going through now—"

"You can't know." She flung the words out. She wanted to hurt him, to scar him, to make him suffer. "I can't stay here. I can't look at you. Don't!" She jerked back, hands fisted when he reached out. "Don't put your hands on me. I could kill you for ever putting them on me. You bastard, you stay away from me and my family."

When she ran, Nathan didn't try to stop her. He couldn't. But he followed her erratic dash, keeping her in sight. If he could do nothing else, he would make certain she arrived safe at Sanctuary.

But it wasn't to Sanctuary that she fled.

She couldn't go home. Couldn't bear it. She couldn't get her breath, couldn't clear her vision. Part of her wanted to simply fall to the ground, curl up and scream until her mind and body were empty of grief. But she was terrified that she'd never find the strength to get up again.

So she ran, without thought of destination, through the trees, through the dark, with images flipping hideously through her head.

The photograph of her mother, coming to life. The eyes opening. Confusion, fear, pain. The mouth stretching wide for a scream.

Pain stabbed into Jo's side like a knife. She gripped it, whimpering, and kept running.

On the sand now, with the ocean crashing. Her breath heaved out of her lungs. She fell once, hitting hard on her hands and knees, only to scramble up and stumble back into a run. She only knew she had to get away, to run away from the pain and this horribly tearing sorrow.

She heard someone call her name, and the sound of

feet pounding the sand behind her. She nearly tripped again, righted herself, then turned to fight.

"Jo, honey, what is it?" Clad in only a robe, her hair streaming wet from the shower, Kirby hurried toward her. "I was out on the deck and saw you—"

"Don't touch me!"

"All right." Instinctively, Kirby lowered her voice, gentled it. "Why don't you come up to the house? You've hurt yourself. Your hands are bleeding."

"I . . ." Confused, Jo looked down, saw the scrapes and the slow trickle of blood on the heels of her hands. "I fell."

"I know. I saw you. Come on up. I'll clean them for you."

"I don't need—they're all right." She couldn't even feel her hands. Then her legs began to tremble, her head began to spin. "He killed my mother. Kirby, he murdered my mother. She's dead."

Cautiously, Kirby moved closer until she could slide a supporting hand around Jo's waist. "Come with me. Come home with me now." When Jo sagged, she led her across the sand. Glancing back, she saw Nathan standing a few yards away. In the moonlight their eyes met briefly. Then he turned and walked away into the dark.

"I feel sick," Jo murmured. Sensation was creeping back, tiny needle pricks all over her skin, and with it the greasy churning in her stomach.

"It's all right. You need to lie down. Lean on me and we'll get you inside."

"He killed her. Nathan knew. He told me." It felt as if she were floating now, up the steps, in the door of the cottage. "My mother's dead."

Saying nothing, Kirby helped Jo onto the bed, put a light blanket over her. She was beginning to tremble with shock now. "Slow breaths," Kirby ordered. "Concentrate on breathing. I'm just going in the other room for a moment. I'm going to get something to help you."

"I don't need anything." Fresh panic snaked through her, and she gripped Kirby's hand hard. "No sedatives. I can get through this. I can. I have to."

"Of course you can." Kirby eased onto the bed and took Jo's wrist to check her pulse. "Are you ready to tell me about it?"

"I have to tell someone. I can't tell my family yet. I can't face that yet. I don't know what to do. I don't even know what to feel."

The pulse rate was slowing, and Jo's pupils were returning to normal. "What did Nathan say to you, Jo?"

Jo stared at the ceiling, focused on it, centered herself on it. "He told me that his father had murdered my mother."

"Dear God." Horrified, Kirby lifted Jo's hand to her cheek. "How did it happen?"

"I don't know. I don't know. I couldn't listen. I didn't want to listen. He said his father killed her, that he kept a journal. Nathan found it, and he came back here. I slept with him." Tears trickled out of her eyes, slid away. "I slept with the son of my mother's murderer."

Calm was needed now, Kirby knew. And cool logic. The wrong word, the wrong tone, and she was afraid Jo would break in her hands. "Jo, you slept with Nathan. You cared for Nathan, and he for you."

"He knew. He came back here knowing what his father had done."

"And that must have been terribly hard for him."

"How can you say that?" Furious, Jo pushed herself onto her elbows. "Hard for him?"

"And courageous," Kirby said softly. "Jo, how old would he have been when your mother died?"

"What difference does it make?"

"Nine or ten, I imagine. Just a little boy. Are you going to blame the little boy?"

"No. No. But he's not a little boy now, and his father—"

"Nathan's father. Not Nathan."

A sob choked out, then another. "He took her away from me."

"I know. I'm so sorry." Kirby gathered Jo close. "I'm so terribly sorry."

As Jo wept in her arms, Kirby knew this storm was only the beginning.

It took an hour before she could think again. She sipped the hot, sweet tea Kirby made her. The sick panic had flowed away in a wash of grief. Now, for a moment, the grief was almost as soothing as the tea.

"I knew she was dead. Part of me always knew, from the time it happened. I would dream of her. As I got older I pushed the dreams away, but they would always come back. And they only got stronger."

"You loved her. Now, as horrible as things are, you know she didn't leave you."

"I can't find comfort in that yet. I wanted to hurt Nathan. Physically, emotionally, in every possible way to cause him pain. And I did."

"Do you think that's an abnormal reaction? Jo, give yourself a break."

"I'm trying to. I nearly cracked again. I would have if you hadn't been there."

"But I was." Kirby squeezed Jo's hand. "And you're stronger than you think. Strong enough to get through this."

"I have to be." She drank more tea, then set the cup down. "I have to go back to Nathan's."

"You don't have to do anything tonight but get some rest."

"No, I never asked why or how or . . ." She shut her eyes. "I have to have the answers. I don't think I can live with this until I have the answers. When I go to my family, I have to know it all."

"You could go to them now, I'll go with you. You could ask the questions together."

"I have to do it alone. I'm at the center of this, Kirby." Jo's head throbbed nastily. When she opened her eyes they were brutally dark in a colorless face. "I'm in love with the man whose father murdered my mother."

When Kirby dropped her off at Nathan's cottage, Jo could see his silhouette through the screen door. She wondered if either of them would ever do a harder thing in their lives than facing the past and each other.

He said nothing as she climbed the steps, but opened the door, stepped back to let her in. He'd thought he would never see her again, and he wasn't sure whether that would have been harder to live with, or if seeing her like this—pale and stricken—was worse.

"I need to ask you . . . I need to know."

"I'll tell you what I can."

She rubbed her hands together so that the small pain of her scratched palms would keep her centered. "Did they—were they involved?"

"No." He wanted to turn away but forced himself to face the pain in her eyes. "There was nothing like that between them. Even in the journal, he wrote that she was devoted to her family. To her children, her husband. Jo—"

"But he wanted there to be. He wanted her." She opened her hands. "They fought? There was an accident." Her breath shuddered, and the words were a plea. "It was an accident."

"No. God." It was worse, he thought, by every second that passed it grew worse. "He knew her habits. He studied them. She used to walk, at night, around the gardens."

"She . . . she loved the flowers at night." The dream she'd had the night they'd found Susan Peters spun back into her mind. "She loved the white ones especially. She loved the smells and the quiet. She called it her alone time."

"He chose the night," Nathan continued. "He put a sleeping pill into my mother's wine so she . . . so she wouldn't know he'd been gone. Everything he did he documented step by step in his journal. He wrote that he waited for Annabelle at the edge of the forest to the west of the house." It was killing him by degrees to say it, to look into Jo's face and say it. "He knocked her unconscious and took her into the forest. He had everything set up. He'd already set up his lights, his tripod. It wasn't an accident. It was planned. It was premeditated. It was deliberate."

"But why?" She had to sit. On legs stiff and brittle as twigs, she stumbled to a chair. "I remember him. He was kind to me. And patient. Daddy took him fishing. And Mama would make him pecan pie now and then because he was fond of it." She made a helpless sound, then pressed her fingers to her lips to hold it back. "Oh, God, you want me to believe he murdered her for no reason?"

"He had a purpose." He did turn away now and strode into the kitchen to drag a bottle of Scotch from a cupboard. "You could never call it a reason."

He splashed the liquor into a glass, tossed it back quickly, and hissed through the sting. With his palms braced on the counter, he waited for his blood to settle.

"I loved him, Jo. He taught me how to ride a bike, how to field a grounder. He paid attention. Whenever he traveled, he'd call home not just to talk to my mother but to all three of us. And he listened—not just the pretense of listening some adults think a child can't see through. He cared."

He turned back to her, his eyes eloquent. "He would bring my mother flowers for no reason. I'd lie in bed at night and listen to them laughing together. We were happy, and he was the center of it. Now I have to face that there was no center, that he was capable of something monstrous.''

''I feel carved out,'' she managed. Her head seemed to be floating somewhere above her shoulders. ''Scraped out. Raw. All these years.'' She squeezed her eyes tight a moment. ''Your lives just went on?''

''He was the only one who knew, and he was very careful. Our lives just went on. Until his ended and I went through his personal papers and found the journal and photographs.''

''Photographs.'' The floating sensation ended with a jerk. ''Photographs of my mother. After she was dead.''

He had to say it all, no matter how even the thought ripped through his brain. '' 'The decisive moment,' he called it.''

''Oh, my God.'' Lectures heard, lectures given, whirled in her head. *Capturing the decisive moment, anticipating when the dynamics of a situation will reach peak, knowing when to click the shutter to preserve that most powerful image.* ''It was a study, an assignment.''

''It was his purpose. To manipulate, to cause, to control, and to capture death.'' Nausea churned violently. He downed more Scotch, pitting the liquor against the nausea. ''It wasn't all, it can't be. There was something warped inside him. Something we never saw. Something no one ever saw, or suspected. He had friends, a successful career. He liked to listen to ball games on TV and read mystery novels. He liked to barbecue, he wanted grandchildren.''

It was tearing him apart, every word, every memory. ''There is no defense,'' he said. ''No absolution.''

She stepped forward. Every emotion inside her coalesced and focused on one point. ''He took photographs of her. Of her face. Her eyes. Of her body. Nudes. He posed her, carefully. Her head tilted down toward her left shoulder, her right arm draped across her midriff.''

''How do you—''

"I did see." She closed her eyes and spun away. Relief was cold, painfully cold. An icy layer over hot grief. "I'm not crazy. I was never crazy. I didn't hallucinate. It was real. All of it."

"What are you talking about?"

Impatient, she dug her cigarettes out of her back pocket. But when she struck the match, she only stared down at the flame. "My hand's steady," she muttered. "It's perfectly steady. I'm not going to break now. I can get through it. I'm never going to break again."

Worried that he had pushed her over some line, he moved toward her. "Jo Ellen."

"I'm not crazy." Her head snapped up. Calmly she touched the flame to the tip of her cigarette. "I'm not going to shatter and fall ever again. The worst is just the next thing you have to find room for and live with." She blew out smoke, watched it haze, then vanish. "Someone sent me a photograph of my mother. One of your father's photographs."

His blood chilled. "That's impossible."

"I saw it. I had it in my hands. It's what snapped me, what I couldn't find room for. Then."

"You told me someone was sending you pictures of yourself."

"They were. It was with them, in the last package I got in Charlotte. And afterward, when I was able to function a little, I couldn't find it. Whoever sent it got into my apartment and took it back. I thought I was hallucinating. But it was real. It existed. It happened."

"I'm the only one who could have sent it to you. I didn't."

"Where are the pictures? The negatives?"

"They're gone."

"Gone? How?"

"Kyle wanted to destroy them, them and the journal. I refused. I wanted time to decide what to do. We argued about it. His stand was that it had been twenty years. What good would it do to bring it all out? It could ruin both of us. He was furious that I would even consider going to the police, or to your family. The next morning he was gone. He'd taken the photographs and the journal with him. I didn't know where to find him. The next I heard he'd drowned. I have to assume he couldn't live with it. That he destroyed everything, then himself.''

''The photographs weren't destroyed.'' Her mind was very clear and cold. ''They exist, just like the ones of me exist. I look like my mother. It's not a large leap to shift an obsession with her to one with me.''

''Do you think I haven't thought of that, that it hasn't terrified me? When we found Susan Peters, and I realized how she'd died, I thought . . . I'm the only one left, Jo. I buried my father.''

''But did you bury your brother?''

He stared, shook his head slowly. ''Kyle's dead.''

''How do you know? Because the reports say he got drunk and fell off a boat? And what if he didn't, Nathan? He had the photographs, the negatives, the journal.''

''But he did drown. He was drunk, stumbling drunk, depressed, moody, according to the people who were with him on the yacht. They didn't realize he was missing until well into the next morning. All of his clothes, his gear were still on the boat.''

When she said nothing, he spun around her and began to pace. ''I have to accept what my father did, what he was. Now you want me to believe my brother's alive, that he's capable of all this. Of stalking you, pushing you until you collapse. Of following you here and . . .'' As the rest slammed into him, he turned back. ''Of killing Susan Peters.''

''My mother was strangled, wasn't she, Nathan?''

''Yes. Christ.''

She had to stay cold, Jo warned herself, and go to the next step. ''Susan Peters was raped.''

Understanding the question she was asking, Nathan closed his eyes. "Yes."

"If it wasn't her husband—"

"The police haven't found any evidence to hold the husband. I checked before I came back. Jo Ellen." It scraped his heart to tell her. "They're going to be looking more closely into Ginny's disappearance now."

"Ginny?" With understanding came horror. The cold that had shielded her melted away in it. "Oh, no. Ginny."

He couldn't touch her, could offer her nothing. He left her alone, stepped out onto the porch. He put his hands on the rail and leaned out, desperate for air. When the screen door squeaked, he made himself straighten.

"What was your father's purpose, Nathan? What were the photographs to accomplish if he would never be able to show them to anyone?"

"Perfection. Control. Not simply to observe, and preserve, but to be a part of the image. To create it. The perfect woman, the perfect crime, the perfect image. He thought she was beautiful, intelligent, gracious. She was worthy."

He watched fireflies light up the dark in quick, flirtatious winks. "I should have told you, all of you, as soon as I came here. I told myself I wanted—needed—time to try to understand it. I justified keeping it to myself because you had all accepted a lie, and the truth was worse. Then I kept it to myself because I wanted you. It got easier to rationalize it. You'd been hurt, you were wounded. It could wait until you trusted me. It could wait until you were in love with me."

His fingers flexed and released on the railing as she stood silent behind him. "Rationalizations are usually self-serving. Mine were. After Susan Peters, I couldn't ignore the truth anymore, or your right to know it. There's nothing I can do to change it, to atone for what he did. Nothing I can say can heal the damage he did to you and your family."

"No, there's nothing you can do, nothing you can say. He took my mother, and left us all to think she had abandoned us. That single selfish act damaged all of our lives, left a rift in our family we've never been able to heal. He must have hurt her." Jo's voice quavered so she bit down hard on her lip until she could steady it. "She must have been so frightened, so confused. She'd done nothing to deserve it, nothing but be who she was."

She drew a long breath, tasted the sea, and released it. "I wanted to blame you for it, Nathan, because you're here. Because you had your mother all your life. Because you touched me and made me feel what I'd never felt before. I needed to blame you for it. So I did."

"I expected you to."

"You never had to tell me. You could have buried it, forgotten it. I never would have known."

"I'd have known, and every day I'd have had with you would have been a betrayal." He turned to her. "I wish I could have lived with that, spared you this and saved myself. But I couldn't."

"And what now?" Lifting her face to the sky, she searched her heart. "Am I to make you pay what can't be paid, punish you for something that was done to both of us when we were children?"

"Why shouldn't you?" Bitterness clogged his throat as he looked out into the trees, where the river flowed in secret silence. "How could you look at me and not see him, and what he did? And hate me for it."

It was exactly what she had done, Jo thought. She had looked at him, seen his father, and hated. He had taken it, the verbal and physical blows, without a word in his own defense.

Courageous, Kirby had called him. And she'd been right.

How badly he'd been damaged, she realized. She wondered why it had taken her even this long to realize that however much harm had been done to her, an equal share had been done to him. "You don't give me much credit for intelligence or compassion. Obviously you have a very low opinion of me."

He hadn't known he had the strength left to be surprised. He stared at her in disbelief. "I don't understand you."

"No, you certainly don't if you think that after I'd had time to accept it, to grieve, I would blame you, or hold you accountable."

"He was my father."

"And if he was alive, I'd kill him myself for what he did to her, to all of us. To you. I'll hate him for the rest of my life. There will never be forgiveness in me for him. Can you make room to live with that, Nathan, or are you just going to walk away? I'll tell you what I'm going to do." She rushed on before he could speak, her words fast and hot. "I'm not going to let myself be cheated. I'm not going to let the chance of real happiness be stolen from me. But if you walk away, I'll learn to hate you. I can do it if I have to. And no one will ever hate you more than I will."

She stormed back into the house, slamming the door behind her.

He stood where he was for a moment, struggling to absorb the shock, the gratitude. But it wasn't possible. He stepped back into the house and spoke quietly. "Jo Ellen, do you want me to stay?"

"Isn't that what I just said?" She dragged out another cigarette, then furious, hurled it away. "Why should I have to lose again? Why should I have to be alone again? How could you come here and make me fall in love with you, then cut yourself out of my life because you think it's best for me? Because you think it's the honorable thing to do. Well, the hell with your honor, Nathan, the hell with it if it cheats me out of having what I need. I've been cheated before, lost what I needed desperately before, and was helpless to stop it. I'm not helpless anymore.''

She was vibrating with fury, her eyes fired with it, her color high and glowing. He'd never seen anything, or anyone, more magnificent. "Of all the things I imagined you'd say to me tonight, this wasn't it. I'd prepared myself to lose you. I hadn't prepared myself to keep you.''

"I'm not a damn cuff link, Nathan.''

The laugh came as a surprise, felt rusty in his throat. "I can't decide what I should say to you. All I can think of is that I love you.''

"That might be enough, if you were holding on to me when you said it.''

His eyes stayed on hers as he walked toward her. His arms were tentative at first, then tightened, tightened until he buried his face in her hair. "I love you.'' Emotions swamped him as he drew in the scent of her, the taste of her skin against his lips. "I love you, Jo Ellen. Every part of you.''

"Then we'll make it enough. We won't let this be taken away.'' Her voice was low and fierce. "We won't.''

He lay very still, hoping she slept.

The woman beside him, the woman he loved, was in danger, the source of which was too abhorrent to him to name. He would protect her, with his life if necessary. He would kill to keep her safe, whatever the cost.

And he would hope that what they had together survived it.

There was no avoiding it. They had stolen a moment, taken something for themselves. But what haunted them, from twenty years before and now, would have to be faced.

"Nathan, I have to tell my family.'' In the dark she reached for his hand. "I need to find the right time and the right way. I want you to leave that to me.''

"You have to let me be there, Jo. It should be done your way, but not alone."

"All right. But there are other things that need to be handled, need to be done."

"You need protection."

"Don't try to go white knight on me, Nathan. I find it irritating." The lazy comment ended on a gasp when he hauled her up to her knees.

"Nothing happens to you." His eyes gleamed dangerously in the dark. "Whatever it takes, I'm going to see to that."

"You'd better start by calming yourself down," she said evenly. "I'm of a mind that nothing happens to either of us. So we have to start thinking, and we have to start doing."

"There are going to be rules, Jo. The first is that you don't go anywhere alone. You don't step off your own porch by yourself until this is over."

"I'm not my mother, I'm not Ginny, I'm not Susan Peters. I'm not defenseless, or stupid or naive. I will not be hunted for someone's sport."

Because a show of temper would only wound her pride and make her angry, he latched on to calm. "If necessary, I'll haul you off the island just the way I hauled you here tonight. I'll take you somewhere safe and I'll lock you in. All it'll take to avoid that unhappy event is your promise not to go anywhere alone."

"You have an inflated image of your own capabilities."

"Not in this case I don't." He caught her chin in his hand. "Look at me, Jo. Look at me. You're everything. I'll take anything else, I'll face anything else, but I won't face losing you. Not again."

She trembled once, not from anger or fear but from the swift, hard flood of emotion. "No one's ever loved me this much. I can't get used to it."

"Practice—and promise."

"I won't go anywhere by myself." She let out a sigh. "This relationship business is nothing but a maze of concessions and compromises. That's probably why I've managed to avoid it all this time." She sat back on her heels. "We're not going to stand around and just let things happen. I'm not the only woman on the island." She trembled again. "I'm not Annabelle's only daughter."

"No, we're not going to stand around and wait. I'm going to make some calls, gather any information on Kyle's accident that I might have missed before. I wasn't thorough. It wasn't an easy time, and I might have let something slip by."

"What about his friends, his finances?"

"I don't know a lot about either. We weren't as close the last few years as we used to be." Nathan rose to open the windows and let in the air. "We drifted into different places, became different people."

"What kind of a person did he become?"

"He was . . . I guess you'd call him a present-focused sort. He was interested in now—seize the moment and wring it dry. Don't worry about later, about consequences or payment. He never hurt anyone but himself."

It was vitally important that she understand that. Just as important, Nathan realized, that he understand it himself. "Kyle just preferred the easy way, and if the easy way had a shortcut, all the better. He had a lot of charm, and he had talent. Dad was always saying if Kyle would put as much effort into his work as he did his play, he'd be one of the top photographers in the world. Kyle said Dad was too critical of his work, never satisfied, jealous because he had his whole life and career ahead of him."

He paused, listened to the words replay in his head. And suffered their implication. Was it competition? A twisted need for the son to outdo the father? His head began to pound again, hard beats at the temples.

"I'll make the calls," Nathan said flatly. "If we can

eliminate that possibility, we can concentrate on others. Kyle might have gotten drunk, showed the photos to a friend, an associate.''

''Maybe.'' It wasn't an area Jo wanted to push just then. ''Whoever is responsible has a solid knowledge of photography, and quite a bit of skill. It's inconsistent, occasionally lazy, but it's skill.''

Nathan only nodded. She'd just described his brother perfectly.

''He would have to be doing his own developing,'' she continued, relieved to be able to concentrate on practical steps. ''Which means access to a darkroom. He must have had one in Charlotte, and then when he came down here, he'd have needed to arrange for another. The package I got here was mailed from Savannah.''

''You can rent darkroom time.''

''Yeah, and that might be what he did. Or he rented an apartment, a house, brought in his own equipment. Or bought new. He would have more control, wouldn't he, if it was his own place, his own equipment?'' Her eyes met Nathan's. ''That's what drives this. The control. He could go back and forth between the mainland and the island. He'd be in control.''

To control the moment, to manipulate the mood, the subject, the outcome. That is the true power of art. His father's words, he remembered, neatly written on the page.

''Yes, it's about control. So we check photo supply outlets, find out if someone ordered equipment to outfit a darkroom and had it shipped to Savannah. It won't be easy, and it won't be quick.''

''No, but it's a start.'' It was good to think, to have a tangible task. ''He'd likely be alone. He needs the freedom to come and go as he pleases. He took pictures of me all over the island, so he's wandering around freely. We can keep our eye out for a man alone with a camera, though we're just as likely to jump some harmless bird-watcher.''

"If it was Kyle, I'd know him. I'd recognize him.''

"Would you, Nathan? If he didn't want you to? He'd know you're here. And he'd know that I've been with you. Annabelle Hathaway's daughter with David Delaney's son. There are some who might see that as coming full circle. And if that's so, I don't believe you're any safer than I am.''

Twenty-Seven

Jo slept into midday and woke alone. She couldn't remember the last time she'd slept until ten, or when she had enjoyed such a deep and dreamless sleep.

She wondered if she should have been restless, edgy, or weepy. Perhaps she'd been all of those things long enough, and there was no need to go on with them now that she knew the truth. She could grieve for her mother. And for a woman the same age as Jo was now who had faced the worst kind of horror.

But more, she could grieve for the years lost in the condemnation of a mother, a wife, a woman who had done nothing more sinful than catch the eye of a madman.

Now there could be healing.

"He loves me, Mama," she whispered. "Maybe that's fate's way of paying us all back for being cruel and heartless twenty years ago. I'm happy. No matter how crazy the world is right now, I'm happy with him."

She swung her legs over the side of the bed. Starting today, she promised herself, they were going to stand together and fight back.

• • •

In the living room, Nathan finished up yet another call, this one to the American consulate in Nice. He hadn't slept. His eyes were gritty, his soul scorched. He felt as if he were running in circles, pulling together information, searching for any hint, any whisper that he'd missed months before.

And all the while he dealt with the dark guilt that his deepest hope was to confirm that his own brother was dead.

He looked up as he heard footsteps mounting his stairs. Working up a smile when he saw Giff behind the screen, he waved him in as he completed the call.

"Didn't mean to interrupt you," Giff said.

"No problem. I'm finished, for now."

"I was heading out to do a little work on Live Oak Cottage and thought I'd drop off these plans. You said how you wouldn't mind taking a look at the design I've been working up for the solarium at Sanctuary."

"I'd love to see it." Grateful for the diversion, Nathan walked over to take the plans and unroll them on the kitchen table. "I had some ideas on that myself, then I got distracted."

"Well." Giff tucked his tongue in his cheek as Jo walked out from the bedroom. "Understandable enough. Morning, Jo Ellen."

She could only hope she didn't flush like a beet and compound the embarrassment as both men stared at her. She'd pulled on one of Nathan's T-shirts and nothing else. Though the bottom of it skimmed her thighs, she imagined it was obvious that she wore nothing under it.

This would teach her, she supposed, to follow the scent of coffee like a rat to the tune of the pipe. "Morning, Giff."

"I was just dropping something off here."

"Oh, well, I was just . . . going to get some coffee."

She decided to brazen it out and walked to the counter to pour a mug. "I'll just take it with me."

Giff couldn't help himself. It was such a situation. And since he was dead sure Lexy would want all the details, he tried for more. "You might want to take a look yourself. Kate's got that bee in her bonnet about this sunroom add-on. You always had a good eye for things."

Manners or dignity. It was an impossible decision for a woman raised on southern traditions. Jo did her best to combine both and stepped over to study the drawing. She puzzled over what appeared to be a side view of a long, graduated curve with a lot of neatly printed numbers and odd lines.

Nathan ordered himself to shift his attention from Jo's legs back to the drawing. "It's a good concept. You do the survey?"

"Yeah, me and Bill. He does survey work over to the mainland, had the equipment."

"You know, if you came out at an angle"—he used his finger to draw the line—"rather than straight, you could avoid excavating over here, and you'd gain the benefit of using the gardens as part of the structure."

"If you did that, wouldn't you cut off this corner, here? Wouldn't it make it tight and awkward coming out from the main house? Miss Kate'd go into conniptions if I started talking about moving doorways or windows."

"You don't have to move any of the existing structure." Nathan slid the side view over to reveal Giff's full view. "Nice work," he murmured. "Really nice. Jo, get me a sheet of that drawing paper over there." Nathan gestured absently. "I've got men in my firm who don't have the skill to do freehand work like this."

"No shit?" Giff forgot Jo completely and goggled at the back of Nathan's head.

"You ever decide to go back for that degree and want to apprentice, you let me know."

He picked up a pencil and began to sketch on the paper

Jo had put in front of him. "See, if you hitch it over this
way, not so much of an angle as a flow. It's a female
house, you don't want sharp points. You keep it all in the
same tone as the curve of the roof, then instead of lining
out into the gardens, it pours through them."

"Yeah, I see it." He realized that his working drawing
seemed stiff and amateurish beside the artist's. "I couldn't
think of something like that, draw like that, in a million
years."

"Sure you could. You'd already done the hard part. It's
a hell of a lot easier for somebody to look at good, detailed work and shift a couple of things around to enhance
it than it is to come up with the basic concept in the first
place."

Nathan straightened, contemplated his quick sketch
through narrowed eyes. He could see it, complete and
perfect. "Your way might suit the client better. It's more
cost-effective and more traditional."

"Your way's more artistic."

"It isn't always artistic that the client wants." Nathan
put his pencil down. "Anyway, you think about it, or
show the works to Kate and let her think about it. Whichever choice, we can do some refining before you break
ground."

"You'll work with me on it?"

"Sure." Without thinking, Nathan picked up Jo's coffee mug and drank. "I'd like to."

Revved, Giff gathered up the drawings. "I think I'll
just swing by and drop these off for Miss Kate now. Give
her some time to mull it over. I'm really obliged, Nathan." He tugged on the brim of his cap. "See you, Jo."

Jo leaned against the counter and watched as Nathan
got another sheet of drawing paper. Finishing off her coffee, he started another sketch.

"You don't even know what you just did," she murmured.

"Hmm. How far is that perennial bed with the tall blue

flowers, the spiky ones? How far is that from the corner here?"

"Nope." She got herself another mug. "You don't have a clue what you've done."

"About what? Oh." He looked down at the mug. "Sorry. I drank your coffee."

"Besides that—which I found both annoying and endearing." She slid her arms around his waist. "You're a good man, Nathan. A really good man."

"Thanks." Normality, he promised himself. Just for an hour, they would take normality. "Is that because I didn't give you a little swat on the bottom when you strolled out here in my shirt—even though I wanted to?"

"No, that just makes you a smart man. But you're a good one. You didn't see his face." She lifted her hands to his cheeks. "You didn't even notice."

At sea, he shook his head. "Apparently I didn't. Are you talking about Giff?"

"I don't know anyone who doesn't like Giff, and I don't know many who think of him as anything more than an affable and reliable handyman. Nathan—" She touched her lips to his. "You just told him he was more, and could be more yet. And you did it so casually, so matter-of-factly, he can't help but believe you."

She rose up on her toes to press her cheek to his. "I really like you right now, Nathan. I really like who you are."

"I like you, too." He closed his arms around her and swayed. "And I'm really starting to like who we are."

Kirby had a firm grip on her pride as she walked into Sanctuary. If Jo was there, she would find a way to speak to her privately. Her strict code of ethics wouldn't permit her to tell any of the Hathaways what she'd learned the night before. If Jo had come home after speaking with Nathan again, Kirby imagined the house would be in an uproar.

If nothing else, she could stand as family doctor.

But that wasn't why she'd been summoned.

She had planned her visit to avoid Brian, using that window of time between breakfast and the midday meal. And she'd used the visitors' front door rather than the friends' entrance through the kitchen.

Since they had managed to avoid each other for a week, she thought, they could do so for another day. She wouldn't have come at all if Kate hadn't hailed her with an SOS after one of the guests slipped on the stairs. Even as she turned toward them, Kate came hurrying down.

"Kirby, I can't tell you how much I appreciate this. It's a turned ankle, no more than that, I swear. But the woman is setting up such a to-do you'd think she'd broken every bone in her body in six places at once."

One glance at Kate's distracted face and Kirby knew that Jo had yet to speak of Annabelle. "It's all right, Kate."

"I know it's your afternoon off, and I hated to drag you over here, but she won't budge out of bed."

"It's no problem, really." Kirby followed her up the stairs. "It's better to have a look. If I think it's more than a strain, we'll x-ray and ship her off to the mainland."

"One way to get her out of my hair," Kate muttered. She knocked briskly on a door. "Mrs. Tores, the doctor's here to see you. Bill the inn," Kate added to Kirby in an undertone, "and add whatever you like for a nuisance fee."

Thirty minutes later, and more than a little frazzled, Kirby closed the bedroom door behind her. Her head was aching from the litany of complaints Mrs. Tores had regaled her with. As she paused to rub her temples, Kate peeked around the corner.

"Safe?"

"I was tempted to sedate her, but I resisted. She's perfectly fine, Kate. Believe me, I know. I had to give her what amounts to a complete physical before she was satisfied. Her ankle is barely strained, her heart is as strong as a team of oxen, her lungs even stronger. For your sake, I hope she's planning on a very short stay.''

"She leaves day after tomorrow, thank the Lord. Come on down. Let me get you a nice glass of lemonade, a piece of that cherry pie Brian made yesterday."

"I really need to get back. I've got stacks of paperwork to wade through."

"I'm not sending you back without a cold drink. This heat's enough to fell a horse."

"I like the heat," she began, then came to a dead halt as Brian walked in the front door.

His arms were full of flowers. They should have made him look foolish. She wanted him to look foolish. Instead he looked all the more male, all the more attractive, with his tanned, well-muscled arms loaded down with freshly cut blossoms.

"Oh, Brian, I'm so glad you got to that." Kate hurried down with her mind racing at light-speed. "I was going to cut for the fresh arrangements myself this morning, but this crisis with Mrs. Tores threw me off my stride."

She chattered on as she transferred flowers from his arms to hers. "I'll just take it from here. You don't have any sense at all about how to arrange them. I swear, Kirby, the man just stuffs them into a vase and thinks that's all there is to it. Brian, you go fix Kirby a lemonade, make her eat a piece of pie. She's come all the way out here just to do me a favor, and I won't have her going off until she's been paid back. Run along now, while I take this upstairs."

She headed up the steps, willing the two of them not to behave like fools.

"I don't need anything," Kirby said stiffly. "I was just on my way out."

"I imagine you can spare five minutes to have a cold drink and avoid hurting Kate's feelings."

"Fine. It's a quicker trip home through the back anyway.'' She turned and started down the hall at a brisk pace. She wanted to be away from him. When he found out about his mother, she would do what she could for him. But for now she had her own pain to cope with.

''How's the patient?''

''She could dance a jig if she wanted to. There's not a thing wrong with her.'' She pushed through the door and stood stubbornly while he got out a pitcher of golden-yellow lemonade swimming with mint and pulp. When her mouth watered, she swallowed resolutely. ''How's your hand?''

''It's all right. I don't really notice it.''

''I might as well look at it while I'm here.'' She set her bag down on the breakfast table. ''The sutures should have been removed a couple of days ago.''

''You were leaving.''

''It'll save you a trip out to see me.''

He stopped pouring her lemonade and looked at her. The sun was streaming through the window at her back, licking light over her hair. Her eyes were a dark, stormy green that made his loins tighten.

''All right.'' He carried her glass to the table and sat down.

Despite the heat, her hands were cool. Despite her anger, they were gentle. She saw no swelling or puffiness, no sign of infection. The edges of the wound had fused neatly. He would barely have a scar, she decided, and opened her bag for her suture scissors.

''This won't take long.''

''Just don't put any new holes in me.''

She clipped the first suture, tugged it free with tweezers. ''Since we both live on this island, and it's likely we'll be running into each other on a regular basis for the rest of our lives, perhaps you'd do me the courtesy of clearing the air.''

''It's clear enough, Kirby.''

''For you, apparently. But not for me.'' She clipped,

tugged. "I want to know why you turned away from me. Why you decided to end things between us the way you did."

"Because they'd gone farther than I'd intended them to. Neither one of us thought it would work. I just decided to back off first, that's all."

"Oh, I see. You dumped me before I could dump you."

"More or less." He wished he couldn't smell her. He wished she'd had the decency not to rub that damned peach-scented lotion all over her skin to torment him. "I'd see it more as just a matter of simplifying."

"And you like things simple, don't you? You like things your way, in your time and at your pace."

Her voice was mild, and though he wasn't sure he could trust it, particularly when she had a sharp implement in her hand, he nodded. "That's true enough. You're the same, but your way, your time, and your pace are different from mine."

"I can't argue with that. You prefer a malleable woman, a delicate woman. One who sits patiently and waits for your move and your whim. That certainly doesn't describe me."

"No, it doesn't. And the fact is I wasn't looking for a woman—or a relationship, whatever you choose to call it. You came after me, and you're beautiful. I got tired of pretending I didn't want you."

"That's fair. And the sex was good for both of us, so there shouldn't be any complaints." She removed the last suture. "All done." She lifted her eyes to his. "All done, Brian. The scar will fade. Before long, you won't even remember you were hurt. Now that the air's all clear, I'll be on my way."

He remained where he was when she rose. "I appreciate it."

"Don't give it a thought," she said with a voice like frosted roses. "I won't." She left by the back, quietly and deliberately closing the screen behind her.

She didn't start to run until she was into the shelter of the trees.

"Well, that was fun." Brian picked up Kirby's untouched lemonade and downed it in several long gulps. It hit his tortured stomach like acid.

He'd done the right thing, hadn't he? For himself and probably for her. He'd kept things from stringing out, getting too deep and complicated. All he'd done was nick her pride, and she had plenty of it to spare. Pride and class and brains and a tidy little body with the energy of a nuclear warhead.

Christ, she was a hell of a woman.

No, he'd done the right thing, he assured himself, and ran the cold glass over his forehead because he suddenly felt viciously hot inside and out. She would have set him aside eventually and left him slack-jawed and shot in the knees.

Women like Kirby Fitzsimmons didn't stay. Not that he wanted any woman to stay, but if a man was going to start fantasizing, if he was going to start believing in marriage and family, she was just the type to draw him in, then leave him twisting in the wind.

She had too much fuel, too much nerve to stay on Desire. The right offer from the right hospital or medical institute or whatever, and she'd be gone before the sand settled back in her footprints.

God, he'd never seen anything like the way she'd handled Susan Peters's body. The way she'd turned from woman to rock, clipping out orders in that cool, steady voice, her eyes flat, her hands without the slightest tremor.

It had been an eye-opener for him, all right. This wasn't some fragile little flower who would be content to treat poison ivy and sunburn on a nowhere dot in the ocean for long. Hook herself up with an innkeeper who made the best part of his living whipping up soufflés and frying chicken? Not in this lifetime, he told himself.

So it was done, and over, and his life would settle back quietly into the routine he preferred.

Fucking rut, he thought on a sudden surge of fury. He nearly hurled the glass into the sink when he spotted her medical bag on the table. She'd left her bag, he mused, opening it and idly poking through the contents.

She could just come back and get it herself, he decided. He had things to do. He couldn't be chasing after her just because she'd been in a snit and left it behind.

Of course, she might need it. You couldn't be sure when some medical emergency would come along. It would be his fault, wouldn't it, if she didn't have her needles and prodding things. Someone could up and die, couldn't they?

He didn't want that on his conscience. With a shrug, he picked the bag up, found it heavier than he'd imagined. He thought he'd just run it over to her, drop it off, and that would be that.

He decided to take the car rather than cut through the forest. It was too damn hot to walk. And besides, if she'd dawdled at all he might beat her there. He could just leave the bag inside her door and drive off before she even got home.

When he pulled up in her drive, he thought he had accomplished just that and was disgusted with himself for being disappointed. He didn't want to see her again. That was the whole point.

But when he was halfway up the steps, he realized she'd beaten him back after all. He could hear her crying.

It stopped him in his tracks, the sound of it. Hard, passionate sobs, raw gulps of air. It shook him right to the bone, left him dry-mouthed and loose at the knees. He wondered if there was anything more fearful a man could face than a weeping woman.

He opened the door quietly, eased it shut. His nerves were shot as he started back to her bedroom, shifting her bag from hand to hand.

She was curled up on the bed, a tight ball of misery with her hair curtaining her face. He'd dealt with wild female tears before. A man couldn't live with Lexy half his life and avoid that. But he'd never expected such unrestrained weeping from Kirby. Not the woman who had challenged him to resist her, not the woman who had faced the result of murder without a quiver. Not the woman who had just walked out of his kitchen with her head high and her eyes cold as the North Atlantic.

With Lexy it was either get the hell out and bar the door or gather her up close and hold on until the storm passed. He decided to hold on and, sitting on the side of the bed, he reached out to bundle her to him.

She shot up straight as an arrow, slapping out sharply at the hands that reached for her. Patiently, he persisted—and found himself holding on to a hundred pounds of furious woman.

"Get out of here! Don't you touch me." The humiliation on top of the hurt was more than she could stand. She kicked, shoved, then scrambled off the far side of the bed. Standing there, she glared at him through puffy eyes even as fresh sobs choked her.

"How dare you come in here? Get the hell out!"

"You left your doctor's bag." Because he felt foolish half sprawled over her bed, he straightened up and faced her across it. "I heard you crying. I didn't mean to make you cry. I didn't know I could."

She pulled tissues out of the box on the bedside table and mopped at her face. "What makes you think I'm crying over you?"

"Since I don't expect you ran into anyone else in the last five minutes who would set you off like this, it's a reasonable assumption."

"And you're so reasonable, aren't you, Brian?" She yanked out more tissues, littering the floor with them. "I was indulging myself. I'm entitled to that. Now I'd like you to leave me alone."

"If I hurt you—"

"*If* you hurt me?" Out of desperation she grabbed the box of tissues and threw it at him. "If you hurt me, you son of a bitch. What am I, rubber, that you can slap at me and it bounces off? You say you're falling in love with me, then you turn around and calmly tell me that it's over."

"I said I thought I was falling in love with you." It was vital, he thought with a little squirm of panic, to make that distinction. "I stopped it."

"You—" Rage really did make you see red, she realized. Her vision was lurid with it as she grabbed the closest thing at hand and heaved it.

"Jesus, woman!" Brian jerked as the small crystal vase whizzed by his head like a glittering bullet. "You break open my face, you're just going to have to stitch it up again."

"The hell I will." She grabbed a favorite perfume atomizer from her dresser and let it fly. "You can bleed to death and I won't lift a finger. To fucking death, you bastard."

He ducked, dodged, and was just fast enough to tackle her before she cracked him over the head with a silver-backed mirror. "I can hold you down as long as it takes," he panted out as he used his weight to press her into the mattress. "Damned if I'm going to let you take a chunk out of me because I bruised your pride."

"My pride?" She stopped struggling and her eyes went from hot to overflowing. "You broke my heart." She turned her head, closed her eyes, and let the tears slide free. "Now I don't have any pride to bruise."

Staggered, he leaned back. She simply turned on her side and curled up again. She didn't sob now but lay silent with tears wet on her cheeks.

"Leave me alone, Brian."

"I thought I could. I thought you'd want me to do just that sooner or later. So why not sooner? You won't stay."

He spoke quietly, trailing a finger through her hair. "Not here, not with me. And if I don't step back, it'll kill me when you leave."

She was too tired even to cry now. She slipped a hand under her cheek for comfort and opened her eyes. "Why won't I stay?"

"Why would you? You can go anywhere you want. New York, Chicago, Los Angeles. You're young, you're beautiful, you're smart. A doctor in any of those places is going to make piles of money, go to the country club every week, have a fancy office in some big, shiny building."

"If I'd wanted those things, I would already have them. If I wanted to be in New York or Chicago or L.A., I'd be there."

"Why aren't you?"

"Because I love it here. I always have. Because I'm practicing the kind of medicine here that I want to practice and living my life the way I want to live it."

"You come from a different place," he insisted. "A different lifestyle. Your daddy's rich—"

"And my ma is good-looking." She sniffled and didn't see the quick, involuntary quiver of his mouth.

"What I mean is—"

"I know what you mean." Her head felt like an overblown balloon ready to burst. Idly, she told herself she'd take something for it. In just a minute. "I don't care much for country clubs. They're usually stuffy and burdened with rules. Why would I want that when I can sit on my deck and see the ocean every day of my life? I can walk in the forest and spot a deer, watch the mists rise off the river."

She shifted just a little so she could see his face. "Tell me, Brian, why do you stay here? You could go to any of those places you named, run the kitchen in a fine hotel, or own your own restaurant. Why don't you?"

"It's not what I want. I have what I want here."

"So do I." She turned her cheek back against the bed-spread. "Now go away and leave me alone."

He got up and stood looking down at her. He felt big and awkward and out of his depth. Hooking his thumbs in his front pockets, he paced away, paced back, turned to stare out the window, to stare back at her. She didn't move, didn't speak. He cursed under his breath, hissed out a breath, and started for the door. Turned back.

"I wasn't truthful with you before. I didn't stop it, Kirby. I wanted to, but I couldn't. And it wasn't just thinking, it was . . . being. I'd rather not be, I'll tell you that straight out. I'd rather not be, because it's bound to be a mess somewhere along the line. But there it is."

She brushed a hand over her cheek and sat up. No, he did not have the look of a happy man, she decided. There was resentment in his eyes, stubbornness in his mouth, and annoyance in his stance. "Is this your charming way of telling me you're in love with me?"

"That's what I said. It so happens I'm not feeling very charming at the moment."

"You boot me out of your life, you humiliate me by catching me at a weak moment, you insult me by denying my feelings and my character, then you tell me you love me." She shook her head, pushed her damp hair back from her face. "Well, this is certainly the romantic moment every woman dreams of."

"I'm just telling you the way it is, the way I feel."

She let loose a sigh. If in a corner of her heart joy was blooming, she decided to hold it in check, just for a while. "Since for some reason that I can't quite remember I seem to be in love with you too, I'm going to make a suggestion."

"I'm listening."

"Why don't we take a walk on the beach, a nice long walk? The air might clear your brain enough for you to find a few drops of charm. Then you can try to tell me again, the way it is, and the way you feel.''

He considered her, discovered his head was already clearing. ''I wouldn't mind a walk,'' he said and held out a hand for hers.

TWENTY-EIGHT

SOMETHING BAD WAS IN the air. Sam could sense it. It was more than the thick heat, more than the hard look to the sky. He had some worries about Hurricane Carla, which was currently kicking the stuffing out of the Bahamas. The forecasters claimed she was primed to dance her way out to sea, but Sam knew hurricanes were essentially female. And females were essentially unpredictable.

Odds were she'd give Desire a miss and take out her temper on Florida. But he didn't like the feel to the air. It was too damn tight, he thought. Like it was ready to squeeze over your skin.

He was going to go in and check the little weather station Kate had gotten him last Christmas, do a run on the shortwave. There was a storm coming, all right. He wished he knew when it was coming.

As he crested the hill he saw the couple at the edge of the east garden. The sun was slanting over them, turning Jo's hair into glittering flame. Her body was angled forward, balanced against the man's with a kind of yearning it was impossible not to recognize.

The Delaney boy, Sam thought, grown up to a man. And the man had his hands on Sam's daughter's butt. Sam blew out a breath, wondered just how he was supposed to feel about that.

Their eyes were full of each other, and with a fluid shift of bodies their mouths tangled. It was the kind of hotly intimate kiss that made it obvious they'd been spending time doing a lot more to each other.

And how was he supposed to feel about that?

Time was, young people wouldn't neck right out in the open that way. He remembered when he'd been courting Annabelle, the way they'd snuck off like thieves. They'd done their groping in private. Why, if Belle's daddy had ever come across them this way, there'd have been hell to pay.

He walked on, making sure his footsteps were loud enough to wake the dead and the dreaming. Didn't even have the courtesy to jerk apart and look guilty, Sam thought. They just eased apart, linked hands, and turned toward him.

"There's guests inside the house, Jo Ellen, and they ain't paying for a floor show."

Surprised, she blinked at him. "Yes, Daddy."

"You want to be free with your affections, do it someplace that won't set tongues wagging from here to Savannah."

Wisely, she swallowed the chuckle, lowered her eyes before he caught the gleam of laughter in them, and nodded. "Yes, sir."

Sam shifted his feet, planted them, and looked at Nathan. "Seems to me you're old enough to strap down your glands in a public place."

Following Jo's lead and warned by the quick squeeze of her hand, Nathan kept his tone sober and respectful. "Yes, sir."

Satisfied, if not completely fooled, by their responses, Sam frowned up at the sky. "Storm coming," he muttered. "Going to give us a knock no matter what the weatherman says."

He was making conversation, Jo realized, and shoved her shock aside to fall in. "Carla's category two, and on dead aim for Cuba. They're saying it's likely she'll head out to sea."

"She doesn't care what they say. She'll do as she pleases." He turned his gaze on Nathan again, measuring. "Don't get knocked by hurricanes much in New York City, I expect."

Was that a challenge? Nathan wondered. A subtle swing at his manhood?

"No. I was in Cozumel when Gilbert pummeled it, though." He nearly mentioned the tornado he'd watched sweep like vengeance across Oklahoma and the avalanche that had thundered down the mountain pass near his chalet when he'd been working in Switzerland.

"Well, then, you know," Sam said simply. "I hear that you and Giff got a mind to do that sunroom Kate's been pining for."

"It's Giff's project. I'm just tossing in some ideas."

"Guess you got ideas enough. Why don't you show me then what y'all have in mind to do to my house?"

"Sure, I can give you the general layout."

"Fine. Jo Ellen, I suspect your young man figures on finagling dinner. Go tell Brian he's got another mouth to feed."

Jo opened her mouth, but her father was already walking away. She could do no more than shrug at Nathan and turn to the house.

When she stepped into the kitchen, Brian was busy at the counter de-heading shrimp. And singing, she realized with a jolt. Under his breath and off-key, but singing.

"What's come over this place?" she demanded. "Daddy's holding full conversations and asking to see solarium plans, you're singing in the kitchen."

"I wasn't singing."

"You were too singing. It was a really lousy rendition of 'I Love Rock and Roll,' but it could be loosely described as singing."

"So what? It's my kitchen."

"That's more like it." She went to the fridge for a beer. "Want one of these?"

"I guess I wouldn't turn it down. I'm losing weight just standing here." He swiped the back of his hand over his sweaty forehead and took the bottle she'd opened for him. He took a long swallow, then tucked his tongue in his cheek. "So, is Nathan able to walk without a limp today?"

"Yeah, but I bloodied his lip." She reached into the white ceramic cookie jar and dug out a chocolate-chip. "A brother with any sense of decency would have bloodied it for me."

"You always said you preferred fighting your own battles. How in God's name can you chase cookies with beer? It's revolting."

"I'm enjoying it. You want any help in here?"

It was his turn to experience shock. "Define 'help.' "

"Assistance," she snapped. "Chopping something, stirring something."

He took another pull on his beer as he considered her. "I could use some carrots, peeled and grated."

"How many?"

"Twenty dollars' worth. That's what you cost me."

"Excuse me?"

"Just a little wager with Lexy. A dozen," he said and turned back to his shrimp.

She got the carrots out, began to remove the peels in slow, precise strips.

"Brian, if there was something you believed all your life, something you'd learned to live with, but that something wasn't true, would you be better off going on the way you'd always gone on, or finding out it was something different? Something worse."

"You can let a sleeping dog lie, but it's hard to rest easy. You never know when it's going to wake up and go for your throat." He slid the shrimp into a boiling mixture of water, beer, and spices. "Then again, you let the dog lie long enough, it gets old and feeble and its teeth fall out."

"That's not a lot of help."

"That wasn't much of a question. You're getting peelings all over the floor."

"So, I'll sweep them up." She wanted to sweep the words up with them, under the first handy rug. But she would always know they were there. "Do you think a man, a perfectly normal man, with a family, a job, a house in the suburbs, a man who plays catch with his son on a Sunday afternoon and brings his wife roses on a Wednesday evening, could have another side? A cold, dark side that no one sees, a side that's capable of doing something unspeakable, then folding back into itself so he can root at the Little League game on Saturday and take the family out for ice cream sodas afterward?"

Brian got the colander out for the shrimp and set it in the sink. "You're full of odd questions this evening, Jo Ellen. You writing a book or something?"

"Can't you just tell me what you think? Can't you just have an opinion on a subject and say what it is?"

"All right." Baffled, he tipped the lid to the pot to give the shrimp a quick stir. "If you want to be philosophical, the Jekyll and Hyde theme has always fascinated people. Good and evil existing side by side in the same personality. There's none of us without shadows."

"I'm not talking about shadows. About a man who gives in to temptation and cheats on his wife one afternoon at the local motel, or who skims the till at work. I'm talking about real evil, the kind that doesn't carry a breath of guilt or conscience with it. Yet it doesn't show, not even to the people closest to it."

"Seems to me the easiest evil to hide is one with no

conscience tagged to it. If you don't feel remorse or responsibility, there's no mirror reflecting back.''

"No mirror reflecting back," she repeated. "It would be like black glass, wouldn't it? Opaque.''

"Do you have any other cheerful remarks or suppositions to discuss?"

"How's this? Can the apple fall far from the tree?"

With a half laugh, Brian hefted the pot and poured shrimp and steaming water into the colander. "I'd say that depended entirely on the apple. A firm, healthy one might take a few good bounces and roll. You had one going rotten, it'd just plop straight down at the trunk.''

He turned, mopping his brow again and reaching for his beer when he caught her eye. "What?" he demanded as she stared at him, her eyes dark and wide, her face pale.

"That's exactly right," she said quietly. "That's so exactly right.''

"I'm hell on parables.''

"I'm going to hold you to that one, Brian.'' She turned back to her grating. "After dinner, we need to talk. All of us. I'll tell the others. We'll use the family parlor.''

"All of us, in one place? Who do you want to punish?"

"It's important, Brian. It's important to all of us.''

"I don't see why I have to twiddle my thumbs around here when I've got a date.'' Looking at her image in the mirror behind the bar, Lexy fussed with her hair. "It's nearly eleven o'clock already. Giff's liable to just give up waiting and go to bed.''

"Jo said it was important,'' Kate reminded her. She fought to make her knitting needles click rhythmically rather than bash together. She'd been working on the same afghan for ten years and was bound and determined to conquer it before another decade passed.

"Then where is she?'' Lexy demanded, whirling around. "I don't see anybody here but you and me.

Brian's probably snuck off to Kirby's, Daddy's holed up with his shortwave tracking that damned hurricane—and it isn't even coming around here."

"They'll be along. Why don't you fix us all a nice glass of wine, honey?" It was one of Kate's little dreams, having her family all gathered together, cooling off after a hot day, sharing the events of it.

"Seems like I'm always waiting on somebody. I swear, the last thing I'll do to keep the wolf away from the door when I go back to New York is wait tables."

Sam ducked his head and stepped in. He glanced at Kate with amusement. That blanket never seemed to grow by much, he thought, but somehow or other it got uglier every time she dragged it out. "You know what the girl's got on her mind?"

"No, I don't," Kate said placidly. "But sit down. Lexy's getting us some wine."

"Sooner have a beer, if it's all the same."

"Well, place your orders," Lexy said testily. "I live to serve."

"I can fetch my own."

"Oh, sit down." She waved a hand at him. "I'll get it."

Feeling chastised, he lowered himself to the couch beside Kate, drummed his fingers on his knee. He looked up when Lexy held out a brimming pilsner. "Guess you want a tip now." When she arched a brow, he nodded soberly. "Recycle. The world is your backyard."

Kate's needles stilled, Lexy stared. As color crept up his throat, Sam stared into his beer.

"My God, Sam, you made a joke. Lexy, you be sure to remind me to mark this down on my Year-at-a-Glance calendar."

"Sarcastic woman's the reason I keep my mouth shut in the first place," he muttered, and Kate's laugh tinkled out.

She patted Sam's knee affectionately while Lexy grinned down at them.

That's what Jo saw when she came in. Her father, her cousin, and her sister sharing a moment together while Kate's laughter rang out.

Her heart sank. It was an image she'd never expected to see, one she hadn't known could be so precious to her. Now she, and the man who stood behind her, could destroy it.

"There she is." Kate continued to beam, and when she spotted Nathan, her idea of what Jo had wanted the family to hear took on the hint of orange blossoms and bridal lace. Fluttering, she set her knitting aside. "We were just having some wine. Maybe we should make it champagne instead, just for fun."

"No, wine's fine." Her nerves screaming, Jo hurried in. "Don't get up, Kate, I'll get it."

"I hope this won't take long, Jo. I've got plans."

"I'm sorry, Lexy." Jo clinked glasses together in her hurry to have it done.

"Sit down," Kate hissed, rolling her eyes, wiggling her brows to try to give Lexy a hint. "Make yourself comfortable, Nathan. I'm sure Brian will be right along. Oh, here he is now. Brian, turn up the fan a little, will you? This heat's just wilting. Must be cooler at your place by the river, Nathan."

"Some." He sat, knowing he had to let Jo set the pace. But he looked at Sam. They'd spend twenty minutes together that evening, outlining plans, discussing structure and form. And all the while Nathan had tasted the bitter tang of deceit.

It was time to open it up, spread it out, and accept the consequences. "I'm sorry?" he said, realizing abruptly that Kate was speaking to him.

"I was just asking if you're finding it as easy to work here as you do in New York."

"It's a nice change." His eyes met Jo's as she brought

him a glass of wine. Get it done, he asked her silently.
Get it finished.

"Would you sit down, Brian?" she murmured.

"Hmm." She'd interrupted his daydream about wandering over to Kirby's shortly and waking her up in a
very specific and interesting manner. "Sure."

He settled into a chair and decided he'd never been
more relaxed or content in his life. He even gave Lexy a
quick wink when she sat on the arm beside him.

"I don't know how to begin, how to tell you." Jo took
a bracing breath. "I wish I could take the chance and let
sleeping dogs lie." She caught Brian's eye, saw the flicker
of confusion in his. "But I can't. Whether it's the best
thing or not, I have to believe it's the right thing. Daddy."
She walked over, sat on the coffee table so that her eyes
were on a level with Sam's. "It's about Mama."

She saw his mouth harden and, though he didn't move,
felt him pull back from her. "There's no point in stirring
up old waters, Jo Ellen. Your mother's been gone long
enough for you to deal with her going."

"She's dead, Daddy. She's been dead for twenty
years." As if to anchor them both, she closed a hand over
his. "She didn't leave you, or us. She didn't walk away
from Sanctuary. She was murdered."

"How can you say such a thing?" Lexy surged to her
feet. "How can you say that, Jo?"

"Alexa." Sam kept his eyes on Jo's. "Hush." He had
to give himself a moment to stand up to the blow she'd
delivered. He wanted to dismiss it, slide over or around
it. But there was no evading that steady and sorrowful
look in her eyes. "You've got a reason for saying that.
For believing it."

"Yes."

She told him calmly, clearly, about the photograph that
had been sent to her. The shock of recognition, the un-
deniable certainty that it was Annabelle.

"I worked it out a hundred different ways in my head,"

she continued. "That it had been taken years later, that it was just a trick of the camera, just a horrible joke. That I'd imagined it altogether. But none of those were true, Daddy. It was Mama, and it was taken right here on the island on the night we thought she left."

"Where's the picture?" he demanded. "Where is it?"

"It's gone. Whoever sent it came back and took it while I was in the hospital. But it was there, I swear it. It was Mama."

"How do you know? How can you be sure of that?"

She opened her mouth, but Nathan stepped forward. "Because I've seen the photograph. Because my father took it, after he killed her."

With a storm raging in his head, Sam got slowly to his feet. "You're going to stand there and tell me your father killed Belle. Killed a woman who'd done him no harm, and then took pictures of it. He took pictures of her when he'd done with her, and showed them to you."

"Nathan didn't know, Daddy." Jo clung to Sam's arm. "He was just a boy. He didn't know."

"I'm not looking at a boy now."

"I found the photographs and a journal after my father died. Everything Jo told is true. My father killed your wife. He wrote it all down, locked the journal and the prints, the negatives in a safe-deposit box. I found them after he and my mother died."

When the words trailed away there was no sound but the whisk of the blades from the ceiling fan, Lexy's weeping, and the harsh breaths Sam pushed in and out of his lungs.

He could see her now, shimmering at the front of his mind, the wife he'd loved, the woman he'd cursed. All the lights and shadows of her shifted together to form rage. To form grief.

"Twenty years he kept it to himself." Sam clenched his fists, but there was nothing to strike. "You find out and you come back here and put your hands on my daughter. And you let him.'' He burned Jo with a look. ''You know, and you let him.''

''I felt the same way when he told me. Just the same. But when I had time to think it through, to understand . . . Nathan wasn't responsible.''

''His blood was.''

''You're right.'' Nathan moved so that Jo no longer stood between him and Sam. ''I came back here to try to find a way through it, or around it, or to just bury it. And I fell in love where I had no right to.''

Brian set Lexy aside so that she could weep into her hands instead of on his shoulder. ''Why?'' His voice was as raw as his soul. ''Why did he do it?''

''There's no reason that can justify it,'' Nathan said wearily. ''Nothing she'd done. He . . . selected her. It was a project to him, a study. He didn't act out of anger, or even out of passion. I can't explain it to myself.''

''It's best if you go now, Nathan.'' Kate spoke quietly as she rose. ''Leave us alone with this for a while.''

''I can't, until it's all said.''

''I don't want you in my house.'' Sam's voice was dangerously low. ''I don't want you on my land.''

''I'm not going until I know Jo's safe. Because whoever killed Susan Peters and Ginny Pendleton wants her.''

''Ginny.'' To steady herself, Kate gripped Sam's arm.

''I don't have any proof of Ginny, but I know. If you'll listen to the rest of it, hear me out, I'll leave.''

''Let him finish it.'' Lexy sniffed back her tears and spoke in a voice that was surprisingly strong. ''Ginny didn't just run off. I've known that in my heart all along. It was just like Mama, wasn't it, Nathan? And the Peters woman, too.''

She folded her hands in her lap to compose herself and turned to Jo. ''You were sent photos here, to the house, pictures taken here, on the island. It's all happening again.''

"You're handy with a camera, Nathan." Brian's eyes were hot blue slits.

It stung, coming from a man who had been friend in both the past and the present. "You don't have any reason to trust me, but you have plenty of reason to listen."

"Let me try to explain it, Nathan." Jo picked up her wine to cool her throat.

She left nothing out, picking her way from detail to detail, question to question, and leading into the steps she and Nathan had agreed upon taking to find the answers.

"So his dead father's responsible for killing our mother," Brian cut in bitterly. "Now his dead brother's responsible for the rest. Convenient."

"We don't know who's responsible for the rest. But if it is Nathan's brother, it doesn't make Nathan culpable." Jo stepped up to Brian. "There's a parable about apples falling from the tree someone told me recently. And how some are strong enough to roll clear and stay whole, and others aren't."

"Don't throw my own words back at me," he said furiously. "His father killed our mother, destroyed our lives. Now another woman's dead, maybe two. And you expect us to pat him on the back and say all's forgiven? Well, the hell with that. The hell with all of you."

He strode out, leaving the air vibrating in his wake.

"I'll go after him." Lexy paused in front of Nathan, studied him out of red-rimmed eyes. "He's the oldest, and maybe he loved her best, the way boys do their mamas. But he's wrong, Nathan. There's nothing to forgive you for. You're a victim, just like the rest of us."

When she slipped out, Kate said in surprised admiration, "You never expect her to be the sensible one." Then she sighed. "We need some time here, Nathan. Some wounds need private tending."

"I'm going with you," Jo began, but Nathan shook his head.

"No, you stay with your family. We all need time."

He turned to face Sam. "If you have more to say to me—"

"I'll find you right enough."

With a nod, Nathan left them alone.

"Daddy—"

"I don't have anything to say to you now, Jo Ellen. You're a grown woman, but you're living under my roof for the time being. I'm asking you to go to your room for now and let me be."

"All right. I know what you're feeling, and just how it hurts. You need time to deal with it." She kept her eyes level with his. "But after you've had that time, if you still hold to this stand, you'll make me ashamed. Ashamed that you would blame the son for the father's deed."

Saying nothing, he strode past her.

"Go ahead to your room, Jo." Kate laid a hand on Jo's knotted shoulder. "Let me see what I can do."

"Do you blame him, Kate? Do you?"

"I can't get my mind clear on what I think or feel. I know the boy's suffering, Jo, but so is Sam. My first loyalty is to him. Go on now, don't pester me for answers until I can sort things through."

Kate found Sam on the front porch, standing at the rail, staring out into the night. Clouds had rolled in, covering moon and stars. She left the porch light off and stepped quietly up beside him.

"I have to grieve again." He ran his hands back and forth over the railing. "It isn't right that I should have to grieve for her again."

"No, it's not."

"Do I take comfort that she never meant to leave me and the children? That she didn't run off and forget us? And how do I take back all the hard thoughts of her I had over the years, all the nights I cursed her for being selfish and careless and heartless?"

"You can't be faulted for the hard thoughts, Sam. You believed what was set in front of you. Believing a lie doesn't make you wrong. It's the lie that's wrong.''

He tightened up. ''If you came out here to defend that
boy to me, you can turn right around and go back inside.''

''That's not why I came out, but the fact is that you're
no more at fault for believing what you did about Belle
than Nathan was for believing in his father. Now you've
both found out you were wrong in that belief, but he's
the one who has to accept that his father was the selfish
and heartless one.''

''I said you could go on back inside.''

''All right, then, you stubborn, stiff-necked mule. You
just stand out here alone and wallow in your misery and
think your black thoughts.'' She spun around, shocked
when his hand shot out and took hers.

''Don't leave.'' The words burned his throat like tears.
''Don't.''

''When have I ever?'' she said with a sigh. ''Sam, I
don't know what to do for you, for any of you. I hate
seeing the people I love hurt this way and not knowing
how to give them ease.''

''I can't mourn for her the way I should, Kate. Twenty
years is a long stretch. I'm not the same as I was when I
lost her.''

''You loved her.''

''I always loved her, even when I thought the worst of
her, I loved her. You remember how she was, Kate, so
bright.''

''I always envied her the way she would light up everything and everyone around her.''

''A soft light's got its own appeal.'' He stared down at
their joined hands and missed the shock that bolted into
her eyes. ''You always kept that light steady,'' he said
carefully. ''She'd have been grateful for the way you
mothered the children, looked after things. I should have
told you before that I'm grateful.''

''I started out doing it for her, and stayed for myself.
And Sam, I don't think Belle would have wanted you to

grieve all over again. I never knew her to nurse a hurt or cling to a grudge. She wouldn't have blamed a ten-year-old boy for what his father was.''

''I'm cut in two on this, Kate. I'm remembering that when Belle went missing, David Delaney joined in the search for her.'' He had to close his eyes as the rage rose up black again. ''The son of a bitch walked this island with me. And all the while he'd done that to her. His wife came and got the children, took them back with her to mind all that day. I was grateful to him, God forgive me for that. I was grateful to him.''

''He deceived you,'' she said quietly. ''He deceived his own family.''

''He never missed a step. I can't go back to that day, knowing what I know now, and make him pay for it.''

''Will you make the son pay instead?''

''I don't know.''

''Sam, what if they're right? What if someone wants to do to Jo what was done to Annabelle? We need to protect what we have left, to use whatever we have to protect what we have left. If I'm any judge, Nathan Delaney would step in front of a moving train to keep her safe.''

''I can see to my own this time. I'm prepared this time.''

The edge of the woods on a moonless night was an excellent vantage point. But he hadn't been able to resist creeping a little closer, using the dark to conceal his movements.

It was so exciting to be this close to the house, to hear the old man's words so clearly. It was all out now, and that was just another arousal. They thought they knew it all, understood it all. They probably believed they'd be safe in that foreknowledge.

And they couldn't be more wrong.

He tapped the gun he'd tucked, combat-style, in his boot. He could use it now if he wanted, take both of them out. Like shooting ducks in a barrel. That would leave the two women alone in the house, since Brian had driven off in a stone-spitting fit of temper.

He could have both of Annabelle's daughters, one after the other, both at once. A delicious ménage à trois.

Still, that would be a detour from the master plan. And the plan was serving him so well. Sticking to it would prove his discipline, his ability to conceive and execute. And if he wanted to duplicate the Annabelle experience, he would have to be patient just a little longer.

But that didn't mean he couldn't stir things up a bit in the meantime. Scared rabbits, he mused, were so much easier to trap.

He melted back into the trees and spent a pleasant hour contemplating the light in Jo's window.

TWENTY-NINE

KIRBY JOGGED ALONG THE beach, hugging her solitude. The sky to the east was wildly red, gloriously, violently vivid with sunrise. She supposed that if the old adage were true, sailors better take warning, but she could only think how beautiful the morning was with its furious sky and high, wild winds.

Maybe they were in for a backslap from Carla after all, she thought, as her feet pounded the hard-packed sand. It might be exciting, and it would take Brian's mind off his troubles for a little while.

She wished she knew what to say to him, how to help him. All she'd been able to do when he'd roared into her cottage the night before was listen, as she had listened to Jo. But when she'd tried to comfort him, as she had comforted Jo, it hadn't been the soft, soothing words she'd offered that he wanted. So she'd given him the heat instead and had held on for dear life as he pounded out his misery in sex.

She hadn't been able to convince him to stay and sleep past dawn. He was up and gone before the sun peeked over the horizon. But at least he gathered her close, at least he pulled her to him. And she knew she'd steadied him for the return to Sanctuary.

Now she wanted to clear her head. If the man she loved was in trouble, if he was in distress, then so was she. She would gear herself up to stand by him, to see him through this, and she hoped, to guide him toward some peace.

Then she saw Nathan standing near where the booming breakers hammered the shoreline. Loyalty warred against reason as she slowed her pace. But in the end her need to help, to heal, overrode everything else. She simply couldn't turn her back on pain.

"Some morning." She had to lift her voice over the thunder of surf and wind. Puffing only a little, she stopped beside him. "So, is your vacation living up to your expectations?"

He laughed. He couldn't help it. "Oh, yeah. It's the trip of a lifetime."

"You need coffee. As a doctor, I'm supposed to tell you that caffeine isn't good for you, but I happen to know it often does the trick."

"You offering?"

"I am."

"I appreciate it, Kirby, but we both know I'm persona non grata. Brian wouldn't appreciate you sharing a morning cup with me. I can't blame him for it."

"I do my own thinking, form my own impressions. That's why he's crazy about me." She laid a hand on his arm. No, she couldn't turn her back on pain. Even the air around Nathan was hurting. "Come on up to the house. Think of me as your kindly island doctor. Bare your soul." She smiled at him. "I'll even bill you for an office visit if you want."

"Such a deal." He took a long breath. "Christ, I could use a cup of coffee. I could use the ear too."

"And I've got both. Come on." She tucked her arm in his and walked away from the shore. "So, the Hathaways gave you a rough time."

"Oh, I don't know, they were fairly gracious all in all. That southern hospitality. My father raped and murdered your mother, I tell them. Hell, nobody even tried to lynch me."

"Nathan." She paused at the base of her steps. "It's a hell of a mess, and a terrible tragedy all around. But none of them will blame you once they're able to think it through."

"Jo doesn't. Of all of them, she's the most vulnerable because of it, but she doesn't."

"She loves you."

"She may yet get over that. Lexy didn't," he murmured. "She looked me straight in the eye, her cheeks still wet from crying, and told me none of it was my responsibility."

"Lexy uses pretenses and masks and foolishness and uses them expertly. So she can see through them and cut to the bone faster than most." She opened her door, turned back to him. "And Nathan, none of it is, or was, your responsibility."

"I know that intellectually, and I'd almost convinced myself of it emotionally—I wanted to because I wanted Jo. But it's not over, Kirby. It's not finished. At least one other woman is dead now, so it's not over."

She nodded and held the door open for him. "We'll talk about that too."

Carla teased the southeast coast of Florida, giving Key Biscayne a quick and violent kiss before shimmying north. In her capricious way, she did a tango with Fort Lauderdale, scattered trailers and tourists and took a few lives. But she didn't seem inclined to stay.

Her eye was cold and wide, her breath fast and eager. She'd grown stronger, wilder since her birth in the warm waters of the West Indies.

Like a vengeful whore, she spun back out to sea,

stomping her sharp heels over the narrow barrier islands in her path.

Lexy hurried into the guest room where Jo was just smoothing the spread on the walnut sleigh bed. The sun beamed hot and brilliant through the open balcony doors, highlighting the shadows under Jo's eyes that spoke of a restless night.

"Carla just hit St. Simons," Lexy said, a little breathless from her rush up two flights of stairs.

"St. Simons? I thought she was tracking west."

"She changed her mind. She's heading north, Jo. The last report said if she keeps to course and velocity, her leading edge will hit here before nightfall."

"How bad is she?"

"She's clawed her way up to category three."

"Winds of over a hundred miles an hour. We'll need to batten down."

"We're going to evacuate the tourists before the seas get too rough for ferry crossings. Kate wants you to help down at checkout. I'm going out with Giff. We'll start boarding up."

"All right, I'll be down. Let's hope she heads out to sea and gives us a pass."

"Daddy's on the radio getting updates. Brian went down to see that the boat's fueled and supplied in case we have to leave."

"Daddy won't leave. He'll ride it out if he has to tie himself to a tree."

"But you will." Lexy stepped closer. "I went by your room earlier, saw your suitcases open and nearly packed."

"There's more reason for me to go than to stay."

"You're wrong, Jo. There's more for staying, at least until we find the way to settle this for everyone. And we need to bury Mama."

"Oh, God, Lexy." Jo covered her face, then stood there with her fingers pressed to her eyes.

"Not her body. But we need to put a marker up in the cemetery, and we need to say good-bye. She loved us. All my life I thought she didn't, and that maybe it was because of me."

When Lexy's voice broke, Jo dropped her hands. "Why would you think something like that?"

"I was the youngest. I thought she hadn't wanted another child, hadn't wanted me. So I spent most of my life trying so hard to make people love me, people want me. I'd be whatever I thought they'd like best. I'd be stupid or I'd be smart. I'd be helpless or I'd be clever. And I'd always make sure I left first."

She walked over, carefully shut the balcony doors. "I've done a lot of hateful things," she continued. "And it's likely I'll do plenty more. But knowing the truth's changed something inside me. I have to say good-bye to her. We all do."

"I'm ashamed I didn't think of it," Jo murmured. "If I go before it can all be arranged, I'll come back. I promise." She bent down to gather up the linens she'd stripped from the bed. "Despite everything, I'm glad I came back this time. I'm glad things have changed between us."

"So am I." Lexy aimed a sidelong smile. "So, now maybe you'll fancy up some of the pictures you took that I'm in, and take a few more. I could use them for my portfolio. Casting directors ought to be pretty impressed with glossies taken by one of the top photographers in the country."

"If we shake loose of Carla, you and I will have a photo shoot that'll knock every casting director in New York on his ass."

"Really? Great." She scowled out at the sky. "Goddamn hurricane. Something's always coming along to postpone the good stuff. Maybe we can do it in Savannah. You know, rent a real studio for a couple of days, and—"

"Lexy."

"Oh, all right." Lexy waved her hands. "But thinking

about that's a lot more fun than thinking about nailing up sheets of plywood. Of course, maybe Giff'll think I'm plain useless at it, and I can whisk back inside and check through my wardrobe for the right outfits. I want sexy shots, sexy and moody. We could get us a little wind machine for—''

''Lexy,'' Jo said again on an exasperated laugh.

''I'm going, I'm going. I've got this terrific evening gown I got wholesale in the garment district.'' She started toward the door. ''Now, if I can just talk Kate into letting me borrow Grandma Pendleton's pearls.''

Jo laughed again as Lexy's voice carried down the hall-way. Things shouldn't change too quickly, she decided, or too much. Bundling the linens more securely, she carted them out to the laundry chute. Through an open door she could see the couple who had come in for the week from Toronto packing, and making quick work of it. She imagined most of the other guests were doing the same.

Checkout, usually a breezy and relaxed process, was going to be frantic.

The minute she came downstairs, she saw she hadn't exaggerated. Luggage was already piled by the front door. In the parlor, half a dozen guests were milling around or standing by the windows staring at the sky as if they expected it to crack open at any moment.

Kate was at the desk, surrounded by a sea of paperwork and urgent demands. Her hospitable smile was frayed around the edges when she looked up and spotted Jo.

''Now don't you worry. We'll get everyone safely to the ferry. We have two running all day, and one leaves for the mainland every hour.'' At the flood of voices, questions, demands, she lifted her hand. ''I'm going to take the first group down right now. My niece will take over checkout.''

She sent Jo an apologetic, slightly desperate look. ''Mr. and Mrs. Littleton, if you and your family would go out to the shuttle. Mr. and Mrs. Parker. Miss Houston. I'll be right there. Now if the rest of you will be patient, my niece will be right with you."

Having no choice, she waded through the bodies and voices and gripped Jo's arm. "Out here for a minute. I swear, you'd think we were about to be under nuclear attack."

"Most of them probably haven't dealt with a hurricane before."

"Which is why I'm glad to help them on their way. For heaven's sake, this island and everything on it have stood up to hurricanes before, and will again."

Since privacy was needed, Kate took it where she could get it, in the powder room off the foyer. With a little grunt of satisfaction, she flipped the lock. "There. That ought to hold for two damn minutes. I'm sorry to leave you surrounded this way."

"It's okay. I can run the next group down in the Jeep."

"No." Kate spoke sharply, then blowing out a breath, she turned to the sink to splash cold water on her face. "You're not to leave this house, Jo Ellen, unless one of us is with you. I don't need another thing to worry about."

"For heaven's sake. I can lock the doors to the Jeep."

"No, and I won't stand here and argue about it. I just don't have the luxury of time for it. You'll help most right here, keeping these people calm. I have to swing around and pick up some of the cottage people. Brian was going by the campground. We'll have another flood of them in shortly."

"All right, Kate. Whatever you want."

"Your father brought the radio down to the kitchen." She took Jo by the arms. "He's well within hailing distance. You take no chances, you understand me?"

"I don't intend to. I need to call Nathan."

"I've already done that. He didn't answer. I'll go by

before I bring the next group. I'd feel better if he was here, too.''

''Thanks.''

''Don't thank me, honey pie. I'm about to leave you with the world's biggest headache.'' Kate sucked in a breath, braced her shoulders, and opened the door.

Jo winced at the din of voices from the parlor. ''Hurry back,'' she said and mustered a weak smile as she walked straight into the line of fire.

Outside, Giff muscled a sheet of plywood over the first panel of the wide dining room bay. Lexy crouched at his feet, hammered a nail quickly and with easy skill into the lower corner. She was chattering away, but Giff heard only about every third word. The wind had died, and the light was beginning to take on a brutish yellow hue.

It was coming, he thought, and faster than they'd anticipated. His family had their home secure and would likely ride it out there. He'd delegated one of his cousins and two friends to begin boarding up the cottages, starting on the southeast and moving north.

They needed more hands.

''Has anyone called Nathan?''

''I don't know.'' Lexy plucked another nail from her pouch. ''Daddy wouldn't let him help anyway.''

''Mr. Hathaway's a sensible man, Lexy. He wants what's his secured. And he's had a night to think things through.''

''He's as stubborn as six constipated mules, and him and Brian together are worse than that. Why it's like blaming that bastard Sherman's great-grandchildren for burning Atlanta.''

''Some do, I imagine.'' Giff hefted another sheet.

''Those who haven't a nickel's worth of brains, I imagine.'' Her teeth set, Lexy whacked the hammer onto a nailhead. ''And it's going to be mighty lowering for me if I have to admit my own daddy and brother got short-changed in the brain department. And that they're half blind to boot. Why, an eighty-year-old granny without her cheaters could see how much that man loves Jo Ellen. It's sinful to make the two of them feel guilty over it."

She straightened, blowing the hair out of her eyes. Then frowned at him. "Why are you grinning at me that way? Is my face all sweaty and grimy already?"

"You're the most beautiful thing I've ever seen in my lifetime, Alexa Hathaway. And you always surprise me. Even knowing you inside out, you surprise me."

"Well, honey . . ." She tilted her head, batted her lashes. "I mean to."

Giff slid his hand into his pocket, fingered the small box he'd tucked there. "I had different plans for doing this. But I don't think I've ever loved you more than I do right this second."

He tugged the box out of his pocket, watching her eyes go huge and wide as he flipped open the lid with his thumb. The little diamond centered on the thin gold band winked out points of fire in the sun.

"Marry me, Alexa."

Her heart swelled and butted against her ribs. Her eyes misted so that the light shooting from the diamond refracted and blinded her. Her hand trembled as she pressed it to her mouth.

"Oh, how could you! How could you spoil it all this way?" Spinning around, she thumped the hammer against the edge of the wood.

"Like I said," he murmured, "you're always a surprise to me. You want me to put it away until we have candle-light and moonbeams?"

"No, no, no." With a little sob, she struck the wood with the hammer again. "Put it away. Take it back. You know I can't marry you."

He shifted his feet, planted them. "I don't know any such thing. Why don't you explain it to me?"

Furious and heartsick, she whirled back to him. "You

know I will if you keep asking. You know I'll give in because I love you so much. Then I'll have given up everything else. I'll stay on this damn island, I won't go back to New York, and I won't try to make it in the theater again. Then I'll start to hate you as the years pass and I start to think, if only. If only. I'll just shrivel up here wondering if I could ever have been something.''

''What makes you think I'd expect you to give up on New York and the theater, that I'd expect you to give up everything you want? I'd hate to think you'd marry a man who wants less for you than you want for yourself. Whatever you want for Lexy, I want twice that much.''

She wiped a hand over her cheeks. ''I don't understand you. I don't know what you're saying.''

''I'm saying I've got plans of my own, wants of my own. I don't plan on swinging a hammer on Desire my whole life.''

Mildly irritated, he took off his cap to wipe the sweat off his forehead, then shoved it back on again. ''Things need to get built in New York, don't they? Things need fixing there just like anywhere else.''

She lowered her hands slowly, staring into his eyes, wishing she could read them. ''You're saying you'd go to New York. You'd live in New York. For me.''

''No, that's not what I'm saying.'' Impatient, he snapped the lid closed and shoved the box back into his pocket. ''If I was to do that, I'd just end up resenting you, and we'd be right back where we started. I'm saying I'd go for both of us. And that even with the money I've been putting by, we'd live pretty tight for a while. I'd probably have to take some classes if I wanted Nathan to give me a chance at a job in his firm.''

''A job with Nathan? You want to work in New York?''

''I've had a hankering to see it. And to see you, on-stage, in the spotlight.''

''I might not ever get there.''

"Hell you won't." His dimples winked down, and his eyes went from sulky brown to golden. "I've never seen anybody who can play more roles. You'll get there, Lexy. I believe in you."

Tears gushed out even as she laughed and threw herself at him. "Oh, Giff, how'd you get to be so perfect? How'd you get to be so right?" She leaned back, catching his face in her hands. "So absolutely right for me."

"I've been studying on it most of my life."

"We'll have a time, we will. And I'll wait damn tables until you're out of school or I get my break. Whatever it takes. Oh, hurry up, hurry up and put it on." She jumped down, held out her hand. "I can't hardly stand to wait."

"I'll buy you a bigger one someday."

"No, you won't." She thrilled as he slipped the ring onto her finger, as he lowered his head and kissed her. "You can buy me all the other bright, shiny baubles you want when we're rich. Because I want to be good and rich, Giff, and I'm not ashamed to say so. But this . . ." She held up her hand, turning it so the little stone winked and danced with light. "This is just perfect."

After two hours, Jo's head throbbed and her eyes were all but crossed. Kate had come and gone twice, hauling guests to and from, swinging by various cottages. Brian had dropped off a dozen campers, then headed back to make another sweep in case there were any lingering. Her only news of Nathan was that he was helping board up cottages along the beachfront.

Except for the monotonous *thwack* of hammers, the house was finally quiet. She imagined Kate would be back shortly with the last of the cottagers. The windows on the south and east sides were boarded, casting the house into gloom.

When she opened the front door, the wind rushed in. The cool slap of it was a shock after the thick heat of the closed house. To the south, the sky was bruised and dark.

She saw the flicker of lightning but heard no answering thunder.

Still far enough away, she decided. She would check shortly and see what track they were predicting Carla to take. And as a precaution, she would get all of her prints and negatives out of her darkroom and into the safe in Kate's office.

Because she wanted to avoid her father for a while yet, she took the main stairs, checking rooms automatically to see that nothing had been left behind by a harried guest. She flicked off lights, moving briskly toward the family wing. The sound of hammering was louder now, and she found it comforting. Tucking us in, she thought. If Carla lashed out at Sanctuary, it would hold, as it had held before.

She caught the sound of voices as she went by Kate's office. Plywood slipped over the window, blanking it as she passed. Either Brian was back or her father had gone out to help Giff, she decided.

She snapped on the lights in her darkroom, then turned on the radio.

"Hurricane Carla has been upgraded to category three and is expected to make landfall on the barrier island of Little Desire off the coast of Georgia by seven P.M. Tourists have been evacuated from this privately owned island in the Sea Islands chain, and residents are being advised to leave as soon as possible. Winds of up to one hundred and twenty miles an hour are expected, with the leading edge striking the narrow island near high tide."

Her earlier confidence shaken, Jo dragged her hands through her hair. It didn't get much worse than this, she knew. Cottages would be lost, by wind or water. Homes flattened, the beach battered, the forest ripped to pieces.

And their safety net was shrinking, she thought, with a glance at her watch. She was going to get Nathan, and Kirby, and if she had to knock her father unconscious, she was going to get him and her family off the island.

She yanked open a drawer. She could leave the prints, but damned if she'd risk losing all her negatives. But as she started to reach for them, her hand froze.

On top of her neatly organized files was a stack of prints. Her head went light, her skin clammy as she stared down into her mother's face. She'd seen this print before, in another darkroom, in what almost seemed like another life. Over the roaring in her head, she could hear her own low moan as she reached out for it.

It was real. She could feel the slick edge of the print between her fingers. Breathing shallowly, she turned it over, read the carefully written title.

DEATH OF AN ANGEL

She bit back a whimper and forced herself to look at the next print. Grief swarmed over her, stinging like wasps. The pose was nearly identical, as though the photographer had sought to reproduce one from the other. But this was Ginny, her lively, friendly face dull and lax, her eyes empty.

"I'm sorry," Jo whispered, pressing the print to her heart. "I'm sorry. I'm so sorry."

The third print was certainly Susan Peters.

Jo shut her eyes, willed the sickness away, and gently set the third print aside. And her knees went to water.

The last print was of herself. Her eyes were serenely closed, her body pale and naked. Sounds strangled in her throat as she dropped the photo, backed away from it.

She groped behind her for the door, the adrenaline pumping through her, priming her to run. She backed sharply into the table, knocked the radio onto its side. Music jangled out, making her want to scream.

"No." She fisted her hands, digging her nails into her palms until the pain cut through the shock. "I'm not going to let it happen. I'm not going to believe it. I won't let it be true."

She rocked herself, counting breaths until the faintness passed, then grim and determined, she picked up the photo again.

Her face, yes. It was her face. Taken before Lexy had cut her hair for the bonfire. Several weeks, then. The bonfire had been at the very start of summer. She carried the photo closer to the light, ordered herself to study it with an objective and trained eye.

It took her only seconds of clear vision to realize that while the face was hers, the body wasn't. The breasts were too full, the hips too round. She set the photo of Annabelle beside it. Was it more horrifying, she wondered dully, to realize her face had been imposed on her mother's body? Making them one, she thought.

That's what he'd wanted all along.

Brian steered the Jeep down the maintenance road of the campground. Several of the sites had been left in disarray. With the way the storm was rolling in, he figured that wasn't going to matter much. The wind was already ripping like razors through the trees. A gust shook the Jeep around him, had him gripping the wheel tighter. He calculated they had perhaps an hour to finish preparations.

He had to fight not to hurry this check run. He wanted to get to Kirby, lock her safely inside Sanctuary. He'd have preferred shipping her off to the mainland, but knew better than to waste his breath or his energy arguing with her. If one resident stayed put to ride it out, she would stay put to treat any injuries.

Sanctuary had stood for more than a hundred years, Brian thought. It would stand through this.

There were dozens of other worries. They would undoubtedly be cut off from the mainland. The radio would help, but there would be no phone, no power, and no transportation once they were hit. He'd fueled the generator to provide emergency power, and he knew Kate kept an ample supply of bottled water.

They had food, they had shelter, they had several strong backs. And after Carla did her worst, strong backs were going to be a necessity.

He continued to tick off tasks and options in his mind, growing calmer as he assured himself there were no stragglers in the camping areas. He only hoped there weren't any idiots hiding out in the trees, or staking in near the beach, thinking a hurricane was a vacation adventure.

He cursed and stomped on the brakes as a figure stepped out on the road in front of the Jeep.

"Jesus Christ, you idiot." Disgusted, Brian slammed out of the vehicle. "I damn near ran you over. Haven't you got the sense to stay out of the middle of the road, much less the path of an oncoming hurricane?"

"I heard about that." His grin spread wide. "Amazing timing."

"Yeah, amazing." Resenting every second wasted, Brian jerked a thumb at the Jeep. "Get in, I might be able to get you down for the last ferry, but there isn't much time."

"Oh, I don't know about that." Still smiling, he lifted the hand he'd held behind his back and fired the gun.

Brian jerked back as pain exploded in his chest. He staggered, fought to keep the world from revolving. And as he fell, he saw the eyes of a childhood friend laughing.

"One down." Using his boot, he nudged Brian's limp body over. "I appreciate the opportunity to fix the odds a bit, old pal. And the loan of the Jeep."

As he hopped in, he gave Brian one last glance. "Don't worry. I'll see it gets back to Sanctuary. Eventually."

Rain began to lash at the windows as Kirby gathered medical supplies. She was dead calm as she tried to anticipate every possible need. If she was forced into triage, it would work best at Sanctuary. She'd already faced the very real possibility that the cottage might not survive the night.

She understood that most of the islanders would be too

stubborn to leave their homes. By morning, there could be broken bones, concussions, gashes. The house trembled under a hard gust, and she set her jaw. She would be there to treat any and all injuries.

She was hefting a box, heading out to load it in her car, when her front door swung open. It took her a moment to recognize the figure in the yellow slicker and hood as Giff.

"Here." She shoved the box into his arms. "Take this out, I'll get the next one."

"Figured you'd be putting this kind of thing together. Make it fast. The bitch is coming in."

"I've nearly got everything packed." She pulled on her own slicker. "Where's Brian?"

"He was checking the campground. Isn't back yet."

"Well, he should have been," she snapped. Worry dogged her heels as she ran in for the rest of her supplies. The wind shoved her backward when she tried to step out on her porch. It whistled past her ears as she bent low and fought her way forward.

"You all secure here?" Giff shouted over the pounding of the surf. He grabbed the box from her and shoved it into the Jeep.

"As much as possible. Nathan helped me with it this morning. Is he back at the house?"

"No. Haven't seen him either."

"For God's sake." She pushed back her already streaming hair. "What in hell could they be doing? We're going by the campground, Giff."

"We don't have a lot of time here, Kirby."

"We're going by. Brian could be in trouble. This wind could have taken some trees down. If he wasn't at Sanctuary when you left, and you didn't pass him along the way here, he could still be over there. I'm not going in until I make sure."

He yanked open the Jeep door and bundled her inside. "You're the doctor," he shouted.

•   •   •

"Goddamn son of a bitch." Nathan beat the heel of his hand against the steering wheel. He'd loaded the most precious of his work and equipment into the Jeep, and now it wouldn't start. It didn't even have the decency to cough and sputter.

Furious, he climbed out, hissing as the rising wind slapped hard pricks of rain into his face. He hauled up the hood, cursed again. He didn't have time for the pretense of fixing whatever was wrong.

He needed to get to Jo and he needed to get to her now. He'd done everything else he could.

He slammed the hood down and, abandoning his equipment, began to trudge toward the river. He'd have to go a quarter of a mile upstream before he could cross, and the hike over to Sanctuary through the woods promised to be miserable.

He heard the ominous creak of trees being shoved and tortured by the wind, felt the hard hands of it playfully pushing him back as he lurched forward. Lightning snapped overhead, turning the sky to an eerie orange.

The wind stung his eyes, blurred his vision. He didn't see the figure step out from behind a tree until he was almost upon it.

"Christ, what the hell are you doing out here?" It took him nearly ten baffled seconds to see past the changes and recognize the face. "Kyle." Horror tripped over shock. "My God, what have you done?"

"Hello, bro'." As if they were meeting on a sunny street, Kyle offered a hand. And as Nathan shifted his gaze for a blink to stare at it, Kyle smashed the butt of the gun into his temple.

"Two down." This time, he threw back his head and roared. The storm empowered him. The violence of it aroused him. "I didn't feel quite right about shooting my own brother, irritating bastard though he is, in what some would call cold blood." He crouched down, whispering as if Nathan could hear. "The river's going to rise, you know, trees are going to go down. Whatever happens, bro', we'll just figure it's fate."

He straightened and, leaving his brother lying on ground soaked with rain and blood, started off to claim the woman he'd decided belonged to him.

THIRTY

～∞～

RAIN GUSHED OVER THE windshield of the Jeep, overpowering the wipers. The road was turning to mush under the wheels, so Giff had to fight for every yard of progress.

"We're heading in," he told Kirby. "Brian's got more sense than to be out in this, and so do I."

"Just take the west route back." She prayed it was the storm making her heart thump and freezing her bones. "That's the way he'd have gone. Then we'll be sure."

"South road's quicker."

"Please."

Abandoning his better judgment, Giff muscled the Jeep to the left. "If we get back in one piece, he's going to skin me for keeping you out here five minutes longer than necessary."

"That's all it'll be, five extra minutes." She leaned forward, struggling to see through the waterfall streaming down the windshield. "What is that? Something on the side of the road up ahead."

"Probably some gear that fell out of somebody's

camper. People were scrambling to get the hell off before—''

"Stop!" Shouting, she grabbed the wheel herself and sent them into a skid.

"Jesus Christ, you aiming to send us into a ditch? Hey—'' Though he reached out to stop her, he only caught the tip of her slicker as she bolted out into the torrent of rain. "Goddamn women." He shoved open the door. "Kirby, get back in here, this wind's liable to blow you clean to Savannah."

"Help me, for God's sake, Giff! It's Brian!" Her frigid hands were already tearing open the bloody shirt. "He's been shot."

"Where could they be?" While the wind pounded the walls, Lexy paced the main parlor. "Where could they be? Giff's been gone nearly an hour, and Brian twice that long."

"Maybe they took shelter." Kate huddled in a chair and vowed not to panic. "They might have decided not to try to get back and took shelter."

"Giff said he'd be back. He promised."

"Then he will be." Kate folded her hands to keep from wringing them. "They'll be here in a minute. And they'll be tired and wet and cold. Lexy, let's go in and get coffee into thermoses before we lose power."

"How can you think about coffee when—'' She cut herself off, squeezed her eyes shut. "All right. It's better than just standing here. Windows all boarded, you can't even look out for them."

"We'll get hot food, hot coffee, dry clothes." Kate reeled off the practicalities, picking up a flashlight as a precaution as she took Lexy with her.

When they were gone, Jo rose. Her father stood across the room, his back to her, staring at the boarded-up window as if he could will himself to see through the plywood.

"Daddy, he's been in the house."

"What?"

"He's been in the house." She kept her voice calm as he turned. "I didn't want to say anything to Lexy and Kate yet. They're both frightened enough. I'd hoped they'd get on the last ferry, but with Brian still out . . ."

Sam's stomach began to burn. "You're sure of this."

"Yes. He left—he's been in my darkroom, sometime in the last two days. I can't be sure when."

"Nathan Delaney's been in this house."

"It's not Nathan."

Sam kept his gaze hard and steady. "I'm not willing to take a chance on that. You go in the kitchen with Kate and Lexy, and you stay with them. I'll go through the house."

"I'm going with you."

"You're going to do what I tell you and go in the kitchen. Not one of you takes a step without the other two."

"It's me he wants. If they're with me, they're only in more danger."

"No one's going to touch anyone of mine in this house." He took her arm, prepared to drag her into the kitchen if necessary. The front door burst open, letting in wild wind and flooding rain.

"Upstairs, Giff, get him upstairs." Breathing fast, Kirby side-stepped to keep the pressure firm on Brian's chest as Giff staggered under his weight. "I need my supplies out of the Jeep. Now," she ordered as Sam and Jo raced forward. "I need sheets, towels, I need light. Hurry. He's lost so much blood."

Kate dashed down the hall. "God, sweet God, what happened?"

"He's been shot." Kirby kept deliberate pace with Giff, never taking her eyes off Brian's face. "Radio the mainland, find out how long it'll take to get a helicopter in. We need to get him to a hospital, and we need the police. Hurry with the supplies. I've already lost too much time.''

Without bothering with rain gear, Sam ran out into the storm. He was blind before he'd reached the Jeep, deaf but for the roar of blood in his head and the scream of the wind. He dragged the first box free, then found Jo shoving past him for the next.

They shouldered the weight and fought their way back into the house together.

''She's putting him in the Garden Suite. It's the closest bed.'' Lexy put her back into it and managed to shut the door behind them. ''She won't say how bad it is. She won't say anything. Kate's on the radio.''

Jo gripped the box until her knuckles were white as they hurried up the steps.

Kirby had stripped off her blood-smeared slicker, tossed it aside. She didn't hear the rain pound or the wind scream. She had only one goal now: to keep Brian alive.

''I need more pillows. We need to keep his trunk and legs higher than his head, keep the site of the bleeding elevated. He's in shock. He needs more blankets. It went through. I found the exit wound.''

She pressed padding high on the back of his right shoulder. Her ungloved hand was covered with blood. ''I can't tell what the internal damage might be. But the blood loss is the first concern. His BP is very low, pulse is thready. What's his blood type?''

''It's A negative,'' Sam told her. ''Same as mine.''

''Then we'll take some of yours for him. I need someone to draw it, I'll talk you through, but I don't have enough hands.''

''I'll do it.'' Kate hurried in. ''They can't tell us on the helicopter. Nothing can get on or off the island until Carla's done with us. Everything's grounded.''

Oh, God. She wasn't a surgeon. For the first time in her life, Kirby cursed herself for not heeding her father's wishes. The entrance wound was small, easily dealt with, but the exit wound had ripped a hole in Brian's back nearly as big as her fist. She felt the panic scraping at her nerves and shut her eyes.

"Okay, all right. We need to get him stabilized. Giff, for now keep pressure here, right here, and keep it firm. If it bleeds through don't remove the padding. Add more. Use your other hand to hold this arterial pressure point. Keep your fingers flat and firm. Kate, get my bag. You'll see the rubber tube. You're going to make a tourniquet."

As she readied a syringe, her voice went cool. She'd chosen to heal, and by God, she would heal. She took one long look at Brian's waxy face. "I'm keeping you with me, you hear?"

As she slid the needle under his skin, the house went black.

Nathan struggled toward the surface of a red mist, slid back. It seemed vital that he break through it, though the pain whenever he got close to the thin, shimmery skin was monstrous. He was chilled to the bone, felt as though he was being pulled down into a vat of icy water. He clung to the edge again, felt those mists close in and thicken and with a vicious leap, cut through.

He found himself in a nightmare, dark and violent. The wind screamed like a thousand demons set loose, and water gushed over him, choking him when he tried to gulp in air. With his head reeling, he rolled over, got on his hands and knees. The water from the rising river beside him was up over his wrists. He tried to gain his feet, slid toward unconsciousness. The cold slap of water as his face hit the ground jerked him back.

Kyle. It had been Kyle. Back from the dead. This Kyle had streaming blond hair rather than brown, an almost brutal tan rather than city-pale skin. And lively madness in his eyes.

"Jo Ellen." He choked it out as he began to crawl away from the sucking water of the river. Murmured it like a prayer as he dug his fingers into the streaming bark of a tree to fight his way to his feet. And as he began a stumbling, wind-whipped run to Sanctuary, he screamed it.

"I'm not going to lose him." Kirby spoke matter-of-factly as she worked by the light of a lantern. Her mind was rigidly calm, forcing out the screaming fears and doubts. "Stay with me, Brian."

"You'll need more light." Giff stroked a hand over Lexy's hair. "If you can spare me here, I'll go down and get the generator started."

"Whoever did this . . ." Lexy gripped his hand. "They could be anywhere."

"You stay right here." He lifted her hand to kiss it. "Kirby may need some help." He moved to the bed, bending low as if to study Brian, and spoke softly to Sam. "You got a gun in the house?"

Sam continued to stare at the tubing that was transferring his blood to his son. "My room, top of the closet. There's a metal box. Got a thirty-eight, and ammo." His gaze shifted briefly, measured the man. "I'll trust you to use it if you have to."

Giff nodded, turned to give Lexy a quick smile. "I'll be back."

"Is there another lantern, more candles?" Kirby lifted Brian's eyelid. His pupils were fully dilated with shock. "If I don't close this exit wound, he's going to lose more blood than I can get into him."

Kate rushed over with a flashlight, beamed it onto the ripped flesh. "Don't let him go." She fought to blink back the tears. "Don't let my boy go."

"We're keeping him here."

"We won't lose him, Kate." Sam reached out, took the hand she had balled up at her side.

"Giff may have trouble with the generator." Jo spoke quietly, laying a hand on Lexy's shoulder. "I'm going to go down and get more emergency lights."

"I'll go with you."

"No, stay here. Kirby may need another pair of hands. Daddy can't help, and Kate's not going to hold up much longer. I'll be quick." She gave Lexy's shoulder a squeeze.

She took a flashlight and slipped out quietly. She had to do something, anything to help hold back the fear for Brian, for Nathan. For all of them.

What if Nathan was shot too, lying out there bleeding, dying? There was nothing she could do to stop it. And how could she live if she only stood by?

He's taken shelter, she promised herself, as she hurried down the stairs. He'd taken shelter, and when the worst of the storm had passed, she'd find him. They'd get Brian to the mainland, to a hospital.

She jolted at the loud crack, the crashing of glass. Her mind froze, envisioning another bullet, more flesh ripped by steel. Then she saw the splintered plywood in the parlor window, the flood of rain that poured in where the tree limb had snapped through it.

She grabbed a lantern, lighting it and holding it high. She would have to find Giff. As soon as she took the light to Kirby, they would have to get more wood, block the damage before it was irreparable.

When she whirled back, he was there.

"This is nice." Kyle stepped forward into the light. "I was just coming up to get you. No, don't scream." He lifted the gun so she could see it clearly. "I'll kill whoever comes down to see what was wrong." He smiled widely. "So, how's your brother doing?"

"He's holding on." She lowered the lantern so the shadows deepened. Beside her, the storm blasted through the splintered wood and spit rain into her face. "It's been a long time, Kyle."

"Not all that long, in the grand scheme of things. And I've been in close touch, so to speak, for months. How did you like my work?"

"It's . . . competent."

"Bitch." The word was quick and vicious, then he shrugged. "Come on, be honest, that last print. You have to admit the creativity of the image, the blending of old and new. It's one of my best studies."

"Clichéd at best. Where's Nathan, Kyle?"

"Oh, I imagine he's just where I left him." He darted a hand out, quick as a snake, and gripped her by the hair. "For once, I'm not going to worry about taking my big brother's leftovers. The way I look at it, he was just . . . tenderizing you. I'm much better than he is, at everything. Always have been."

"Where is he?"

"Maybe I'll show you. We're going for a little ride."

"Out in this?" She feigned resistance as he pulled her to the door. She wanted him out, away from Sanctuary, whatever it took. "You have to be crazy to go out in a category three."

"What I am, darling, darling Jo, is strong." He skimmed his lips over her temple. "Powerful. Don't worry, I won't let anything happen to you until everything is perfect. I've planned it out. Open the door."

The lights flashed on. Using the split second of diversion, she swung back with the flashlight, aiming for the groin, but bouncing hard off his thigh. Still, he grunted in pained surprise and loosened his grip. Ripping away, Jo tore open the front door and rushed out into the teeth of the storm. "You want me, you son of a bitch, you come get me."

The minute he barreled through the door, she was pitting her will against the gale, and fighting to lead him away from Sanctuary.

The rain-lashed darkness swallowed them.

It was less than a minute later when Giff climbed the steps from the basement. He felt the wild gust of wind the instant he turned into the hall. The front door was open wide to the driving rain. With his blood cold, he pulled out the gun he'd tucked in the waistband of his jeans, flicked off the safety, and moved forward. His finger wrapped around the trigger, trembled a breath away from full pressure when Nathan fell through the door.

"Jo Ellen. Where is she?"

"What happened to you?" Hating himself, but unwilling to risk, Giff kept the gun aimed as he walked forward.

"I was coming, my brother . . ." He swayed to his feet, brushed a hand over the raw wound on his temple as his vision doubled. "It was my brother."

"I thought you said he was dead."

"He's not." Shaking his head clear, Nathan focused on the gun. "He's not," he repeated. "Where's Jo?"

"She's fine and safe and going to stay that way. Brian was shot."

"God. Oh, God. Is he dead?"

"Kirby's working on him. Step away from the door, Nathan. Close it behind you. Keep your hands where I can see them."

"Goddamn it." He bit off the words as he heard the scream. The blood that had risen to his head to throb blindingly drained. "That's Jo. She's out there."

"You move, I'll have to shoot you."

"He's going to kill her. I'm not going to let that happen to her. I'm not letting it happen again. For God's sake, Giff, help me find her before he does."

It was a choice between instinct and caution. Giff prayed the choice was the right one and held the gun butt out. "We'll find her. He's your brother. You do what you have to do."

Jo bit back another scream as a limb as thick as a man's torso crashed inches from her feet. It was all swirling dark, roaring sound and wild, tearing wind. Tattered hunks of moss bulleted past her face. Saw palmettos rattled like sabers. Stumbling, she fought for another inch, another foot while the wind raked at her.

Finally, she dropped to her knees, wrapped her arms around the base of a tree, afraid she would simply be ripped apart.

She'd led him away, she prayed she'd led him away, but now she was lost. The forest was shuddering with greedy violence. Rain came at her like knives, stabbing her flesh. She couldn't hear her own breathing now, though she knew it must be harsh and fast because her lungs were on fire.

She had to get back, she had to get back home before he gave up his search. If he got back before she did, he would kill them all. As he'd surely killed Nathan. Sobbing, she began to crawl, digging her hands into the mud to pull her body along inch by straining inch.

Inside, Kirby clamped off the tube that was transferring Sam's blood to Brian. She couldn't risk taking any more until Sam had rested. "Sam needs fluids, and some protein. This has sapped his strength. Juice," she began, wearily stretching her back before she lowered her hand to take Brian's pulse. When his fingers bumped hers, her eyes flew to his face. She caught the faint flutter of his lashes.

"He's coming around. Brian, open your eyes, Brian. Come back now. Concentrate on opening your eyes."

"Is he all right? Is he going to be all right?" Lexy crowded closer, her shoulder bumping Kirby's.

"His pulse is a little stronger. Get me the BP cuff. Brian, open your eyes now. That's the way." Her throat burned as she watched his eyes open, struggle to focus. "Take it easy, take it slow. I don't want you to move. Just try to bring my face into focus. Can you see me?"

"Yeah." The pain was outrageous, an inferno in his chest. Dimly he thought he heard someone weeping, but Kirby's eyes were dry and clear.

"Good." Her hand trembled a little, but she steadied

it to shine a light in his eyes. "Just lie still, let me check you over."

"What happened?"

"You were hurt, baby." Weeping helplessly, Kate took his hand and lowered her cheek to it. "Kirby's fixing you up."

"Fuzzy," he managed, turning his head restlessly. He saw his father's face, pale and exhausted, then the tube that connected them. "Hurts like a bitch," he said, then watched in amazement as Sam covered his face with his hands and shook with sobs. "What the hell's going on. What?" He sank back, weak as a baby under Kirby's firm hands.

"I said lie still. I'm not having you undo all my work here. I'll give you something for the pain in just a minute. Blood pressure's coming back up. He's stabilizing."

"Can I get some water or something? I feel like I've been . . ." He trailed off as it snapped back to his mind. The figure on the road, the dull glint of a gun, the explosion in his chest. "Shot. He shot me."

"Kirby and Giff found you," Lexy told him, struggling to reach around and take his other hand. "They brought you home. She saved your life."

"It was Kyle. Kyle Delaney." The pain was coming in waves now, making his breath short. "I recognized him. His eyes. He had sunglasses on before. He was . . . the day I cut my hand. It was Kyle in there with you. He was with you."

"The artist?" Kirby lowered the hypo she'd prepared. "The beach bum?"

"It was Kyle Delaney. He's been here all along."

"Hold still. Hold him still, Lexy. Damn it, Brian." Frightened by his struggles to get up, Kirby plunged the needle into him with more haste than finesse. "You'll start the bleeding up again, damn it. Help me here, Kate, he'll hurt himself before the drug can take effect."

Kate pressed her hand on Brian's shoulder and looked

with frightened eyes around the room. "Where's Jo? Where is Jo Ellen?"

Lost, lost in the dark and the cold. She wondered if the wind was dying down or if she was just so used to its nasty buffeting that she no longer felt it trying to kill her. She tried to imagine herself springing to her feet and running, she wanted to will herself to try it, but was too weak, too tired to do more than belly along the ground.

She'd lost all sense of direction, and was afraid she would end up crawling blindly into the river to drown. But she wouldn't stop, couldn't stop, as long as there was a chance of reaching home.

And if she was lost, he might be lost as well. Another tree crashed somewhere behind her, falling with a force that shook the ground. She thought she heard someone call her name, but the wind ripped the sound away. He would call her, she thought, as her teeth began to chatter. He would call her hoping she'd give herself away so that he could kill her as he had the others. As his father had killed her mother.

She was nearly tired enough to let him. But she wanted him dead more.

For her mother, she thought, pulling herself along another foot. For Ginny, for Susan Peters. She gritted her teeth and dragged herself. And for Nathan.

She saw the light, just the narrow beam of it, and curled herself into a ball behind a tree. But the light held steady, didn't waver as a flashlight or a lantern held in the hand of a man would.

Sanctuary, she realized, pressing her muddy hands to her mouth to hold back a sob. That narrow beam of light, from the parlor, breaking through the broken window. Gathering her strength, she forced herself to her feet. She had to brace a hand on the tree until her head stopped spinning. But she concentrated on the light and put one foot in front of the other.

When she reached the edge of the trees, she began to run.

"I knew you'd come back." Kyle stepped into her path, pressed the barrel of the gun against her throat. "I've been studying you long enough to know how you think."

She couldn't stop the tears this time. "Why are you doing this? Isn't what your father did enough?"

"He never thought I was good enough, you know. Not as good as him, certainly not as good as Golden Boy. All I needed was the right inspiration." He smiled as rain streamed down his face and his hair blew madly. "We're going to have to clean you up quite a bit. No problem. I've got plenty of supplies back at the campground. Men's showers, remember?"

"Yes, I remember."

"I love practical jokes. I've been playing them on Nathan all our lives. He never knew. Oh, did Mister Kitty-Cat run away? No, indeed, Mr. Kitty took a little dip in the river. Inside a plastic bag. Why, Nathan, how could you be so careless as to cover all the holes in the lightning bug jar with your classic boy's novel?" With a laugh, Kyle shook his head. "I used to drive him crazy doing stuff like that—making him wonder how the hell it had happened."

He gestured with the gun. "Jeep's at the base of the road. What's left of the road. We'll have to walk that far."

"You hated him."

"Oh, definitely." He gave her a playful nudge to get her going. "My father always favored him. But then, my father wasn't the man we always thought he was. That was a real eye-opener. David Delaney's little secret. He was good, but I'm better. And you're my masterpiece, Jo Ellen, the way Annabelle was his. They'll blame Nathan for it, too. That's so wonderfully satisfying. If he survives, they'll lock him away."

She stumbled, righted herself. "He's alive?"

"It's possible. He'll start screaming about his dead brother. Then sooner or later, they'll look in his cottage. I took the time to drop some photographs off there. All the angles. Too bad I won't be able to slip one of yours in with them."

He could be alive, she thought. And she was going to fight to stay alive. Turning, she pushed her sopping hair back. She'd been right, she realized, the sharpest edge of the storm was dulling. She could stand up to it. And to him.

"The trouble is, Kyle, your father was a first-rate photographer. His style was, perhaps, a bit conservative and in some cases pedestrian. But you're third-rate at best. Your composition is poor, your discipline spotty. You have no knack for lighting whatsoever."

When his hand swung out, she was ready. She ducked under it and, leading with her head, rammed his body. His feet slid out from under him, sent him skidding down on his knees. She grabbed his wrist, inching her hand up toward the gun, but he swept an arm under her legs and took her down.

"You bitch. Do you think I'm going to take your insults? Do you think I'm going to let you spoil this after all the trouble I've gone to?"

He grabbed for her hair, but his hand closed on nothing but rain as she twisted her body around and used her feet to knock him back. Shells bit into her hands as she crab-walked back, fought for purchase.

She saw him lift the gun.

"Kyle."

Kyle's attention bolted to the right, and so did his aim. "Nathan." His grin spread, the lip Jo Ellen had split leaked blood onto his chin. "Well, this is interesting. You won't use that." He nodded at the gun Nathan had leveled at him. "You don't have the spine for killing. You never did."

"Put the gun down, Kyle. It's over."

"Wrong again. Our father started it, but I'll finish it."
He got slowly to his feet. "I'll finish it, Nathan, in ways
even he couldn't have imagined. My decisive moment,
my triumph. He only planted the seeds. I'm reaping
them."

He took a careful step forward, the grin never wavering.
"I'm reaping them, Nathan. I'm making them my own.
Think of how proud he'd be of what I've accomplished,
not just following in his footsteps. Enlarging them."

"Yeah." Despite the cold on his skin, a hot sickness
churned in Nathan's gut. "You've outdone him, Kyle."

"It's about time you admitted it." Kyle cocked his
head. "This is what we call a Mexican standoff. Do you
shoot me, or do I shoot you?" He gave a quick, brittle
laugh that raked along Nathan's brain. "Since I know
you're gutless, I already know the answer to that. How
about if I change the game, shift the rules like I used to
do when we were kids. And shoot her first."

As he swung the gun toward Jo, Nathan squeezed the
trigger. Kyle jerked back, his mouth dropping open as he
pressed a hand to his chest and it came away wet with
blood. "You killed me. You killed me for a woman."

Nathan lowered the gun as Kyle crumpled. "You were
already dead," he murmured. He walked toward Jo,
watching as she got to her feet. Then his arms were
around her. "He was already dead."

"We're all right." She pressed her face to his shoulder,
hanging on. "We're all right now."

Giff came skidding down the pitted road. His eyes
hardened when he saw the figure crumpled on the ground.
He lifted his gaze to Nathan. "Get her inside. You need
to get her inside."

Nathan shifted Jo to his side and walked through the
weakening storm toward Sanctuary.

EPILOGUE

"HELICOPTERS ARE ON THEIR way. One's bringing the police. They'll medevac you to the mainland."

"I don't want to go to the hospital."

Kirby walked to the bed, lifted Brian's wrist to check his pulse yet again. "Too bad. You're not in any position to argue with your doctor."

"What are they going to do there that you haven't already done?"

"A great deal more than my emergency patch job." She checked his bandages, pleased that there was no fresh bleeding. "You'll have a couple of pretty nurses, some dandy drugs, and in a few days you'll be on your feet and back home."

He considered. "How pretty are the nurses?"

"I'm sure they're—" Her voice broke, and though she turned away quickly, he saw the tears spring to her eyes.

"Hey, I was only kidding." He fumbled for her hand. "I won't even look at them."

"I'm sorry. I thought I had it under control." She turned back, sliding to her knees to drop her head on the side of the bed. "I was so scared. So scared. You were bleeding so badly. Your pulse was just slipping away under my hands."

"But you didn't let it." He stroked her hair. "You brought me back, stayed with me. And look at you." He nudged until she lifted her face. "You haven't had any sleep."

"I'll sleep later." She pressed her lips to his hand over and over. "I'll sleep for days."

"You could pull some strings, share my hospital room."

"Maybe."

"Then you could come back here, share my room while I'm recuperating."

"I suppose I could."

"Then when I'm recovered, you could just share the rest of my life."

She knuckled a tear away. "If that's a proposal, you're supposed to be the one on your knees."

"But you're such an aggressive woman."

"You're right." She turned her cheek into his hand. "And since I feel at least somewhat responsible that you have a rest of your life, it seems only right that I share it with you."

"The gardens are ruined." Jo looked down at the sodden, beaten blooms drowning in mud. "It'll take weeks to clean them out, save what can be saved and start again."

"Is that what you want to do?" Nathan asked her. "Save what can be saved and start again?"

She glanced over. The bandage Kirby had applied to his temple was shockingly white against his skin. His eyes were deeply shadowed, still exhausted.

She wrapped her arms around herself, turned in a slow circle. The sun was radiant, the air stunningly fresh. She could see the wreckage—the toppled trees, the broken pottery that had been the little fountain, the now roofless smokehouse. Branches and leaves and glass littered the patio.

Above them, Giff and Lexy worked on prying off the protective plywood, and opening the windows to the light. She saw her father and Kate at the edge of the trees, then with wonder and amazed joy, saw him drape an arm around Kate's shoulders.

"Yes, I'd like that. I'd like to stay a while longer, help them put things back. It won't be exactly as it was. But it might be better."

She shielded her eyes with the flat of her hand to block the sun and see him clearly. "Brian asked to see you."

"I went in to see him before I came out. We put things back. They might not be the same." He smiled a little. "But they might be better."

"And you spoke with my father."

"Yeah. He's very glad his children are safe." He slid his hands into his pockets. He hadn't touched her since the night before, when Kate had whisked her off for a hot bath, whiskey-soaked tea, and bed. "He thinks it took courage for me to kill my brother."

"It took courage for you to save my life."

"It had nothing to do with courage." He walked away from her, down the muddy path. "I didn't feel anything when I pulled the trigger. He was already gone for me. It was nothing but a relief to end it."

"Don't tell me it didn't take courage. You were hurt, in every way it's possible to be hurt. And you fought your way through it, and through that storm for me. You faced what no one should ever have to face and did what no one should ever have to do. When the police get here, I'm going to tell them you're a hero."

She laid a hand on his arm. "I owe you my life, the lives of my family, and the memory of my mother."

"He was still my father. He was still my brother." His eyes were dark with the truth of that as he looked down at her. "I can't change that."

"No, you can't. And now they're gone." She glanced up, hearing the distant *whirr* of the helicopter. She wanted it said and settled before the ugliness came back. Before the police got there, with their questions, their investigations. "You said you loved me."

"I do, more than anything."

"Isn't that what you'd call a foundation? I'd think a man with your talents would be good at seeing what needs to be dug under, what can be rebuilt, what has to be reinforced to make it stand. Do you want to save what can be saved, Nathan, and start over?"

"I do." He took a step toward her. "More than anything."

She looked back at him, held out a hand. "Then why don't we get started on the rest of our lives?"

#1 *New York Times* Bestselling Author
NORA ROBERTS

__MONTANA SKY   0-515-12061-8/$7.99
"A sweeping tale of three sisters who learn to live, and love, as a family when they jointly inherit their father's ranch."
                                        —New Woman

__TRUE BETRAYALS   0-515-11855-9/$7.99
A breathtaking story of a mother's secret, a daughter's love, and a shattering crime—set in the fascinating world of championship thoroughbred racing.

__HONEST ILLUSIONS   0-515-11097-3/$7.50
From carnival tents to the world's greatest stages, Nora Roberts sweeps through the decades to create a shimmering novel of glamour, mystery, and intrigue.

__PRIVATE SCANDALS   0-515-11400-6/$7.99
Set in the captivating arena of television talk shows, *Private Scandals* reveals the ambitious dreams of a savvy young woman, and the dark obsessions that threaten all she's worked to achieve.

__HIDDEN RICHES   0-515-11606-8/$7.99
Within the intriguing world of antiques, Philadelphia dealer Dora Conroy discovers the price of desire—and the deadly schemes of a professional smuggler.

Prices slightly higher in Canada

Payable by Visa, MC or AMEX only ($10 00 min), No cash, checks or COD. Shipping & handling: US/Can. $2.75 for one book, $1.00 for each add'l book; Int'l $5 00 for one book, $1.00 for each add'l Call (800) 788-6262 or (201) 933-9292, fax (201) 896-8569 or mail your orders to:

| Penguin Putnam Inc.
P.O. Box 12289, Dept. B
Newark, NJ 07101-5289
Please allow 4-6 weeks for delivery
Foreign and Canadian delivery 6-8 weeks | Bill my: ❑ Visa ❑ MasterCard ❑ Amex _____(expires)
Card# _____
Signature _____ |

Bill to:

Name _____

Address _____City _____

State/ZIP _____Daytime Phone # _____

Ship to:

Name _____	Book Total	$ _____
Address _____	Applicable Sales Tax	$ _____
City _____	Postage & Handling	$ _____
State/ZIP _____	Total Amount Due	$ _____

This offer subject to change without notice.   Ad # B457 (3/00)

Follow #1 *New York Times* Bestselling Author
NORA ROBERTS
to a land of love and magic in the new Irish trilogy

___JEWELS OF THE SUN   0-515-12677-2/$7.99

Nora Roberts returns to the Emerald Isle and introduces
you to the Gallagher clan, as they struggle to break a
hundred-year spell—and explore the depths of their fiery
hearts...

___TEARS OF THE MOON   0-515-12854-6/$7.99

Return to the Irish village of Ardmore, home of the passionate Gallaghers, where a tale of music and magic fills the air.

And coming soon, the final book in the series...
HEART OF THE SEA

Prices slightly higher in Canada

Payable by Visa, MC or AMEX only ($10.00 min), No cash, checks or COD. Shipping & handling:
US/Can .$2.75 for one book, $1.00 for each add'l book; Int'l $5.00 for one book, $1.00 for each
add'l. Call (800) 788-6262 or (201) 933-9292, fax (201) 896-8569 or mail your orders to:

Penguin Putnam Inc.   Bill my: ❑ Visa ❑ MasterCard ❑ Amex _____ (expires)
P.O. Box 12289, Dept. B   Card# _____
Newark, NJ 07101-5289   Signature _____
Please allow 4-6 weeks for delivery
Foreign and Canadian delivery 6-8 weeks

Bill to:
Name _____
Address _____ City _____
State/ZIP _____ Daytime Phone # _____
Ship to:
Name _____ Book Total $ _____
Address _____ Applicable Sales Tax $ _____
City _____ Postage & Handling $ _____
State/ZIP _____ Total Amount Due $ _____

This offer subject to change without notice.   Ad # B879 (8/00)

A stunning trilogy from #1
New York Times bestselling author

NORA ROBERTS

❑ DARING TO DREAM   0-515-11920-2/$7.50

Margo, Kate, and Laura were brought up like sisters amidst the peer-
less grandeur of Templeton House. But it was Margo, the housekeeper's daughter, whose dreams first took her far away, on a magnificent
journey full of risk and reward.

❑ HOLDING THE DREAM   0-515-12000-6/$7.99

Although Kate lacked Margo's beauty and Laura's elegance, she knew
she had something they would never possess—a shrewd head for
business. But now faced with professional impropriety, Kate is forced
to look deep within herself...

❑ FINDING THE DREAM   0-515-12087-1/$7.99

Margo seemed to have it all—until fate took away the man she
thought she loved...

Prices slightly higher in Canada

Payable by Visa, MC or AMEX only ($10 00 min), No cash, checks or COD Shipping & handling:
US/Can $2 75 for one book, $1.00 for each add'l book; Int'l $5 00 for one book, $1 00 for each
add'l Call (800) 788-6262 or (201) 933-9292, fax (201) 896-8569 or mail your orders to:

Penguin Putnam Inc.	Bill my: ❑ Visa ❑ MasterCard ❑ Amex _____ (expires)
P.O. Box 12289, Dept. B	Card# _____
Newark, NJ 07101-5289	Signature _____
Please allow 4-6 weeks for delivery	
Foreign and Canadian delivery 6-8 weeks	

__Bill to:__

Name _____

Address _____City _____

State/ZIP _____Daytime Phone # _____

__Ship to:__

Name _____Book Total $ _____

Address _____Applicable Sales Tax $ _____

City _____Postage & Handling $ _____

State/ZIP _____Total Amount Due $ _____

This offer subject to change without notice.   Ad # B694 (3/00)

The *New York Times* bestselling series

Nora Roberts

writing as *J. D. Robb*

"A balance of suspense, futuristic police
procedural and steamy romance...truly fine
entertainment." —*Publishers Weekly*

☐ WITNESS IN DEATH   0-425-17363-1/$6 99

☐ LOYALTY IN DEATH   0-425-17140-X/$6 99

☐ CONSPIRACY IN DEATH   0-425-16813-1/$6 99

☐ HOLIDAY IN DEATH   0-425-16371-7/$6 99

☐ VENGEANCE IN DEATH   0-425-16039-4/$6 99

☐ CEREMONY IN DEATH   0-425-15762-8/$6 99

☐ RAPTURE IN DEATH   0-425-15518-8/$7 50

☐ GLORY IN DEATH   0-425-15098-4/$6 99

☐ NAKED IN DEATH   0-425-14829-7/$6 99

☐ IMMORTAL IN DEATH   0-425-15378-9/$6 99

Prices slightly higher in Canada

Payable by Visa, MC or AMEX only ($10.00 min), No cash, checks or COD Shipping & handling:
US/Can $2.75 for one book, $1.00 for each add'l book; Int'l $5 00 for one book, $1.00 for each
add'l. Call (800) 788-6262 or (201) 933-9292, fax (201) 896-8569 or mail your orders to:

Penguin Putnam Inc.   Bill my: ☐ Visa ☐ MasterCard ☐ Amex _____ (expires)
P.O. Box 12289, Dept. B
Newark, NJ 07101-5289   Card# _____
Please allow 4-6 weeks for delivery   Signature _____
Foreign and Canadian delivery 6-8 weeks

Bill to:

Name _____

Address _____ City _____

State/ZIP _____ Daytime Phone # _____

Ship to:

Name _____ Book Total $ _____

Address _____ Applicable Sales Tax $ _____

City _____ Postage & Handling $ _____

State/ZIP _____ Total Amount Due $ _____

This offer subject to change without notice.   **Ad # 564 (8/00)**

PENGUIN PUTNAM INC.
Online

Your Internet gateway to a virtual environment with
hundreds of entertaining and enlightening books
from Penguin Putnam Inc.

*While you're there, get the latest buzz on
the best authors and books around—*

Tom Clancy, Patricia Cornwell, W.E.B. Griffin,
Nora Roberts, William Gibson, Robin Cook,
Brian Jacques, Catherine Coulter, Stephen King,
Jacquelyn Mitchard, and many more!

**Penguin Putnam Online is located at
http://www.penguinputnam.com**

PENGUIN PUTNAM NEWS

Every month you'll get an inside look at our upcom-
ing books and new features on our site. This is an
ongoing effort to provide you with the most
up-to-date information about
our books and authors.

**Subscribe to Penguin Putnam News at
http://www.penguinputnam.com/ClubPPI**